Bread of Angels

Center Point
Large Print

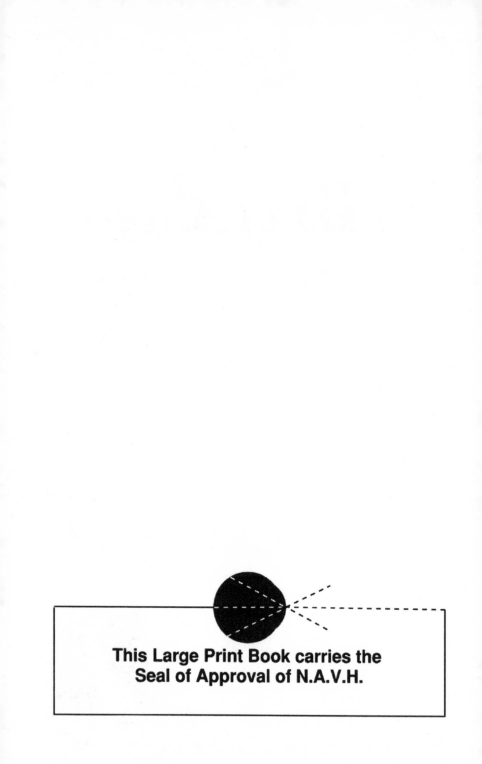

**This Large Print Book carries the
Seal of Approval of N.A.V.H.**

Bread of *Angels*

TESSA AFSHAR

CENTER POINT LARGE PRINT
THORNDIKE, MAINE

This Center Point Large Print edition
is published in the year 2017 by arrangement with
Tyndale House Publishers, Inc.

Bread of Angels is a work of fiction. Where real people,
events, establishments, organizations, or locales appear,
they are used fictitiously. All other elements of the novel
are drawn from the author's imagination.

The text of this Large Print edition is unabridged.
In other aspects, this book may vary
from the original edition.
Printed in the United States of America
on permanent paper.
Set in 16-point Times New Roman type.

ISBN: 978-1-68324-440-0

Library of Congress Cataloging-in-Publication Data

Names: Afshar, Tessa, author.
Title: Bread of angels / Tessa Afshar.
Description: Center Point Large Print edition. | Thorndike, Maine :
    Center Point Large Print, 2017.
Identifiers: LCCN 2017013445 | ISBN 9781683244400
    (hardcover : alk. paper)
Subjects: LCSH: Large type books. | GSAFD: Christian fiction.
Classification: LCC PS3601.F47 B74 2017b | DDC 813/.6—dc23
LC record available at https://lccn.loc.gov/2017013445

Yet he commanded the skies above
and opened the doors of heaven,
and he rained down on them
manna to eat
and gave them the grain of heaven.
Man ate of the bread of the angels.

PSALM 78:23-25

To Beth and Robert Bull,
true friends and beloved companions for life

PROLOGUE

AD 51

I have never served as a soldier, yet I have the strange sense that most of my life I have stared down the blade of a sword, the face of my adversary haunting me. My friend General Varus once told me that Roman soldiers prefer to use the single-edged sword they call the *makhaira* for the killing stroke: having a short blade forces them to come close, so that as your body gives way to the thrust of that unforgiving edge, all you can see is the face of your assassin. You forget the world, you forget the ones you love, you forget hope and lose your fragile grasp on any remnant of a fight lingering in your heart. You see only the visage of your adversary.

I know what it's like to have a *makhaira* at my throat. I know my enemy's face. I know the scent of his breath, the stinging quality of his speech, the poison of his taunts. He has cut me more than once with his short sword. I know his name.

He is called Fear.

He has hounded me from the time he first found me in a meadow, clinging to my father's hand. My enemy has a singular talent for hounding.

Do you remember what you whispered in my

ear that day by the river? When I bent my head to straighten the strap of my shoe, you leaned over and said, "No one shall separate you from the love of God. Not trouble or hardship or danger. Not even the *makhaira*."

I almost broke your nose, I sat up so fast; do you remember?

How did you know? How did you know that I saw the image of Fear more vividly than I did the face of God? That he always seemed more real, more powerful, more immediate than the creator of the sun and the moon? That I could only perceive God from behind the shadow of Fear, that I always felt a little separated from his love?

You have asked me what made me trust God with such alacrity, so ready to jump into that river to die. To leave behind the old, tired self and rise up new.

I think it started with your words. The notion that God's love could overcome the *makhaira*, so that even the thrust of Fear's sword could not rob me of God's healing presence.

Or perhaps I mistake the matter. Perhaps my journey began long before that, when I still lived in Thyatira and believed my future firmly planted in that dear soil. Perhaps I would never have stepped into that river if God had not first stripped me of home and hope. My future had to be destroyed before I would be willing to set foot on the path that led to a new future. A better one than I could ever have thought or imagined.

Do you remember, dear Paul, telling me of your frustration before coming to Philippi, when you sat in Troas, bewildered by the doors God had closed in your face? You were ready to crumple your maps and forget your intentions; your journey had wrecked your careful arrangements more than once. First the Spirit forbade you to enter the province of Asia so that you were forced to abandon the comfort of a good paved road in exchange for the challenges of a narrow dirt track, and then, when you tried to push through into Bithynia, once again he prevented you from following your plans.

So you sat in Troas, twice thwarted, studying your maps and scratching your head, wondering where you were supposed to go next.

If you had gone into the province of Asia as you intended, you would have come upon my old home. But you would not have found me there, for I had left Thyatira long before. It was your vision that brought you to me on that riverbank. Was it only a year ago?

God in his grace drove you to me by the force of his Spirit. How laughable our plans sometimes seem in the light of eternity. How blessed when they are destroyed!

The moon shines too bright this night and I cannot sleep. My head is full of distant memories—shadows and ghosts of what once was. They make me smile and weep. They make me see the hand of God.

I will never send you this letter, which does not even have the courtesy of a proper greeting. But thoughts of you fill my heart, dear Paul, and since you are too far away, I find solace in speaking to you through this epistle.

I lost everything when I was scarcely a woman. I lost everything and found God. But it wasn't until you came into my life and told me the Truth that I found peace.

ONE

Their clothing is violet and purple;
they are all the work of skilled men.
JEREMIAH 10:9

Purple yarn hung from thin trees, swaying in the breeze like odd-shaped fruit; dark-lavender fabric the color of old bruises spread over two rough-hewn stone benches, drying in the sun; a large plum-colored mosaic of geometric designs dominated the otherwise-plain garden. In the shade, a massive vat the size of a diminutive Roman bath sloshed with purple dye so dense it looked black except when a ray of sunlight found its way over the surface, illuminating its true color.

The mistress of this purple kingdom, a young woman in loose, patched clothing, hunched in front of the vat, her forehead damp with perspiration. She had prepared the formula as her father had taught her. It was time to soak the linen. Her father usually conducted this part of the process. His was the genius that had created the dye in the first place; his the skill that turned ordinary yarn into lush, purple beauty. Lydia had never gone through the process of dyeing without his help. Her father was the dye master. She merely acted as his assistant, a role she relished. The thought of dyeing the wool alone made her grit her teeth.

Eumenes was late. He should have arrived over an hour ago.

Lydia wiped the sweat trickling down her temple and stared into the vat. She thought about the unusually large order they had to fill within the next two weeks. There was no time for delay. Every hour counted if they were to make a prompt delivery.

Her stomach churned as she considered their narrow schedule. Most of their local clients suffered from a strange inconsistency. They had no qualms being late in their payments to an honest merchant, but if their merchandise arrived a few days after the promised date, they acted as if the world were ending. Demanding all manner of reparations, they threatened to blight the merchant's truest treasure: his reputation.

When the two orders had arrived, one on top of another, Lydia had objected to her father, demanding that he delay at least one. "It is too much," she had said. "We cannot accomplish it all in such a short time."

He had laughed at her objections. "You despair when we have no orders, imagining that we will

14

grow impoverished and lose our home. When we do receive two perfectly good requests, you worry that it is too much and we will fail to meet expectations. You must make up your mind, Daughter. Which is it to be? Shall we starve or perish of overwork?"

Lydia found that she had no problem dreading either eventuality, which did not help her present situation. Where was her father?

She fetched several of the hefty baskets over-flowing with linen yarn from their workshop, located in the eastern end of the garden. The baskets were heavy—too heavy for a sixteen-year-old girl. Lydia gritted her teeth and half dragged, half carried them, one shuffling step at a time, until they were within easy reach of the dyeing vat.

On the other side of the garden, a three-minute walk from the workshop, lay their modest home with its three rooms, its crooked walls, the leaking ceiling that her father never had time to fix, and the fading furniture that no amount of purple could transform into a semblance of riches. But it was theirs, and she never felt so secure anywhere in the world as when she was nestled within the safety of its walls with her father nearby.

Lydia set the baskets of prepared linen in neat order near the vat, like naked babies ready to be bathed. In truth, she knew what to do. More than once her father had given her permission to complete the task without him. "Your problem is not lack of knowledge," he had said again and again. "It is lack of confidence. You fear you might fail. I trust you will succeed."

She cringed every time he suggested it. "In my ignorance, if I make a mistake and ruin a batch of dye or yarn or a perfectly good length of fabric, who will pay for my error? You know we cannot afford costly mistakes like that."

He never insisted. Her father was too gentle for that. She wondered now if this was some test, this delay. Had he chosen to stay away from home to force her hand and leave her no choice but to embark on the process alone?

She chewed on dry lips. Nausea clawed at her belly as she contemplated the mounds of yarn. Intentional or not, she needed to make a decision. Once she started soaking the linen, there would be no going back. She would have to see the dyeing of the linen through to the end. Stopping at the wrong moment would ruin the batch.

Reaching for a fat wad of yarn, she began to unwind it so that it could be immersed into the liquid properly. Too many dyers filled their vats with an excess of yarn, thinking to save their dye. But that meant the yarn would not soak up enough color and would emerge patchy, without the steadfastness that her father's process produced.

When the linen was ready, she took a deep breath, her outstretched hands shaking as she crouched by the vat, poised to begin the process. An unexpected noise made her grow still. Just outside, along the narrow path that ran adjacent to their land, a man's groan followed by the sound of heavy, shuffling steps broke the silence. Without warning, the door leading to the garden crashed open, hitting the wall with a great noise. Lydia jumped.

Clutching the forgotten linen to her breast, she sprang to her feet. A man she did not recognize burst into the courtyard, half carrying someone slumped against his shoulder, one leg dragging with each step.

She noticed two things before she began to run. First, blood. A great deal of blood clinging to the slumping man so that his hair, face, and leg were covered with it. And second, with dawning horror, she realized that the face so covered in seeping scarlet belonged to none other than her father.

"Oh gods." Her voice emerged as an indistinguishable croak. "Father! What has happened?" The yarn fell unheeded from her nerveless fingers to the stone-paved ground.

Her father roused himself enough to give a weak smile. "It looks worse than it is. This young fellow saved my life."

Lydia spared the man who held her father in a

tight grip a brief glance. She had an impression of light-green eyes and a face that Apollo would be happy to own before she returned her attention to her injured parent.

With trembling fingers, she touched his warm cheek and quelled her desire to snatch him away from the strong, supportive arms of the young Apollo. Carrying her father into the house alone was not a realistic option. She would collapse under the burden of his sinking weight.

"This way. Follow me. We must set him down so that I can see to his wounds," she said. The young man trailed her into the house without comment.

Her father's thin mattress sat on the floor of his chamber, his blankets neatly folded at the bottom. "Settle him on the bed," she said, her voice a thread. "Please," she added, trying to remember manners in the midst of terror.

"It's a small injury, Lydia," Eumenes panted. "Don't worry yourself." The loud groan of pain that escaped his lips as Apollo laid him down on the mattress did little to support his claim.

"What happened?" she asked again, parting his tunic where it lay shredded against his leg. She winced, feeling queasy as she saw the long gash that ran the length of his thigh. The smell of blood, the sight of the wound, the heat of the room made her feel short of breath.

Time seemed to recede, to double in on itself. For a moment she felt the world shift as if she were no longer in this room but in a chamber of dreams, kneeling next to a woman whose face was hidden in shadows. Blood covered everything—the woman's clothing, the sheets— and dripped in fat drops on the stone-gray floor. Lydia took a shivery breath, trying to clear her mind of this strange overlap until her gaze returned to the bedside of her father and her thinking regained its focus.

Eumenes squeezed his eyes shut. Gritting his teeth he said, "Crazy horse."

"A horse did this to you?"

"Not entirely," Apollo said. "I saw what happened. A man was leading a horse by its bridle when the animal began rearing up. Something must have spooked it. The beast pulled away from the hold of its master and continued to balk and rear on its hind legs. Your father was standing in the wrong place at the wrong moment. The horse's hooves knocked him sideways. I happened to be on hand and managed to calm the horse and pull him back."

"He was like Hercules, bringing that monster under control with a touch," her father said.

Apollo grinned. "Your father began to regain his balance. His injuries would have been minor if not for the unfortunate coincidence that he was standing near the top of a hill. His foot slipped at the last moment, and he went over the edge. He cut himself on some jutting rocks and brambles as he rolled down. Most of these injuries are from his fall, not the horse."

TWO

Beloved, do not be surprised at the fiery trial
when it comes upon you to test you, as though
something strange were happening to you.
1 PETER 4:12

"That was no ordinary horse, I tell you,"
Eumenes murmured, his hand clutching his
side. "He attacked me on purpose. I thought
it was the end of me as I gazed into his mean,
black eyes."

Lydia swallowed bile. "Thank the gods you
were spared."

"I won't forget that beast as long as I live. His
coat was an unusual black, glossy with shine
and good grooming. And right here—" Eumenes
pointed to the middle of his forehead—"there
was a white mark that looked like a half moon
with a tiny speck next to it that resembled a star.
It is amazing the silly details you note when you
think you are about to die. The memory of that
white moon and star I shall take to my grave. It
was perfectly proportioned, as if drawn by the
hand of an artist. The beast looked at me with
venom in its gaze and attacked."

Their guest chuckled. "It was just a spooked
horse."

21

"A horse possessed by demons, I tell you. If not for this young man, it would have gone on to trample me to death. I don't know how, but my friend here charmed that animal into calm. One word from him, and the horse stopped its thrashing. I thought I was safe until my foot slipped, and over I went. Even then, my champion would not leave me but clambered down to help carry me all the way home."

Apollo gave a modest smile. "I'd best fetch a physician. Your father will need some stitching for his wound."

"Wait!" Lydia called as he turned away. "What is your name? I can't keep calling you—" she stopped midsentence, realizing that she had been about to call him Apollo to his face. "I mean, I should know your name, since it seems we owe you a great debt."

"Jason. My name is Jason."

Of course his mother would have bestowed the name of a hero upon him, Lydia thought. "With all my heart I thank you, Jason. Now please hurry. I don't want him to bleed to death."

"A mere scratch," her father said.

"And the Nile is a tiny puddle that little girls jump over in their bare feet. Find a good physician, I beg," Lydia said over her shoulder.

"But not expensive," her father said, his voice fading.

"I shall bring you a reasonable—" Jason

22

gave Lydia a furtive glance—"but accomplished physician."

Lydia began to clean her father's wounds with warm water. She shuddered, her whole body shivering uncontrollably. "I might have lost you," she said, shaking her head.

Eumenes patted her hand. "A horse is no match for me."

As she cleaned his dirt-encrusted flesh, she discovered deep bruises already leaving ugly marks on his skin; his left eye was swelling shut, and his right one continued to bleed from a cut in the corner. In spite of the profusion of blood, Lydia realized his claim that his injuries were not fatal was probably accurate. She detected no broken bones, though the physician would have to confirm her suspicions. Relief washed through her, leaving her weak in its wake.

Eumenes's thigh bore the deepest wound, and Lydia suspected that it would require a good number of stitches. She fetched wine sweetened with honey and held his head as he gulped it down thirstily.

"How do you feel?"

"I am as fit as a gladiator."

Lydia snorted. "I see your fall has not interfered with your ability to stretch the truth."

"I stretch no truth when I tell you that you will have to start working on the linen without my

23

help." His voice was strained. "I cannot work for a day or two."

Lydia shrugged, pretending a nonchalance she was far from feeling. "As long as you are there to guide me, I will manage."

He tapped the air above her shoulder. "I knew I could count on you, my brave girl," he said, his voice slurring. His eyelids fell shut and he began to snore softly. She was glad for this respite, for the attentions of the physician were sure to prove painful.

Jason returned with surprising haste, a surgeon in tow. Judging by the man's expensive garment and the gold clasp holding his cloak, Jason's idea of *reasonable* differed substantially from her own. Lydia felt too embarrassed to ask for the rate of his services. He seemed proficient in his craft, which allayed some of her anxiety.

She held on to her father's purple-stained hand through the physician's ministrations. Eumenes tried not to moan as the needle pierced his flesh over and over again.

"A few days and he will return to his old vigor," the physician said when he had finished rubbing salve on Eumenes's wounds. The scent of myrrh mingled with blood made Lydia's head swim.

"He has no broken bones, though he is severely bruised and shaken." The physician wiped his hands on a clean towel.

"His face . . . there was so much blood."

"The lacerations on his face and head are superficial. Let him sleep the rest of this day and through the night. He will need quiet to recover from all his excitement."

"Sleep all day?" Lydia's voice sounded faint. They could not afford to lose a whole day of work. She would have to resume the dyeing process without even her father's oversight.

"I shall return with Jason tomorrow to have another look at him and clean his wounds. We must guard against corruption."

"Tomorrow?" Lydia gulped. Another visit from the sophisticated physician would probably cost a fortune. She felt guilty about her trivial worries when the life of her father had been spared. They would manage the fees somehow, as they always did. She needed to remember this day could have resulted in a tragedy that would have ripped her life apart.

Another realization dawned, knocking all other thoughts out of her head. "With Jason?"

"This delightful fellow." The surgeon clapped Apollo on the shoulder. "He wishes to return and check on your father."

"If you don't mind?" Jason's green eyes crinkled in the corners, a confident smile on his chiseled lips. Lydia doubted any women, young or old, had ever minded a visit from this particular man. No wonder the horse had quieted at his command. It was probably a mare.

25

"Of course not," Lydia said, wanting to kick herself as she felt warmth rise to her cheeks. "I will have to tend to the dyeing. But you must visit with my father whenever you wish. I have not even thanked you properly for coming to his aid. We shall ever be in your debt."

Jason seemed baffled. "Dying? But I thought he had no serious injuries!"

"Oh no! I mean, yes. I was speaking about dyeing linen. Purple dye. That is my father's business. I will have to work on our orders while he recovers."

"You work?"

For the first time, Lydia noticed his toga, which was made of expensive linen and marked him as a Roman citizen. On his middle finger he wore a signet ring made of a great deal of gold and a shiny green stone she did not recognize. Jason was not only handsome and heroic; he was also wealthy. So wealthy that he could not conceive of a woman working in her father's workshop.

She lifted her head and gave him a haughty glance. "Certainly. Don't you?"

He blinked. "Don't you have any brothers?"

"Only child. You?"

"I have two younger sisters. At home."

Lydia gave a sweet smile. "Where else would they be?"

THREE

She seeks wool and flax,
and works with willing hands.
PROVERBS 31:13

Lydia tucked her sleeping father under his woolen blanket, kissed his brow, and walked softly out of his chamber and back into the garden. Settling herself by the vat, she stirred the dye and examined it under the light of the sun to ensure that it was the right hue and consistency.

Like all the dyes her father had developed over the years, this one made no use of the exorbitant sea snail and as a result cost half the price of competing dyes. The purple derived from the precious secretions of sea snails made the color prohibitive except for the wealthiest of patrons, while her father's purple was accessible to many.

Purple-in-One-Vat, Eumenes called this particular dye. They had decided to use this formula for one of the large orders, as it worked faster than his other methods.

Usually Eumenes preferred a more complex process, producing purple through an immersion of the yarn in several baths of varying colors, starting with indigo and ending with a solution made from the roots of the madder plant.

Eumenes had perfected this process to a fine art. No other merchant in Thyatira managed to create Eumenes's vibrant shades of purple, nor make them colorfast without the use of sea snails. Part of his secret was that he used a touch of vermilion to give his purple a deeper hue, closer to scarlet than blue, the color so highly favored by Romans.

For convenience, however, he had also created this rare, simple process of making purple without the use of repeated baths, which made this dye easier to sell to fabric merchants around the empire. One package of dye. One vat of water. A little mordant. Any dye master could make a reasonable success of it. Although it was not their highest grade of purple, the convenience and affordable price made it their most popular product.

It remained a mystery to Lydia why they had never grown rich. Given the undeniable quality of her father's creations, she could not understand how they still managed to struggle from one month to the next, worrying over finances.

There was no denying that her father had little interest in accounts. He kept no track of expenses and purchased what satisfied his artist's heart, not his merchant's head. If he had half the talent for managing money that he had for creating purple, they could have built a sumptuous villa on their land and retired to a life of luxury.

As it was, sumptuous villas were a distant dream, and Lydia could not delay a whole day for her father to recover from his injuries. For the first time in her experience, she would have to work entirely alone.

Grabbing a hefty wad of yarn, she prepared it with careful movements and dropped it into the vat. Perspiration drenched her face as she stirred the dye with a long, wooden rod. She was moving too slowly, she knew. Her father would have finished two wads by now.

When she judged the linen to be ready, she pulled it out of the vat, squeezing the extra dye out before sinking it into a second vat, this one filled with mordant, a substance of her father's creation that made the dye colorfast. The mordant solution was pungent. After years of working with it, Lydia had grown used to the sour, sharp stench. Still, on a hot, breezeless day, even her lungs cringed at the aroma that wafted out of the vat.

Finally came the washing. Lydia threw the freshly dyed yarn in a basket and carried it to the well.

Next to her father's brilliance, the well was their greatest asset. Few businesses boasted a well of their own. To have ready access to water in the dye trade was crucial. To have access to it in one's own backyard was a rare advantage.

Lydia had prepared a water bath earlier. She

29

sank the linen into it now and watched the excess dye seep into the water, turning it violet. Again she wrung out the yarn and carefully hung it from a branch to dry. She would have to replicate this process a number of times until the purple saturated the wool to just the right shade.

Hour after hour she repeated this procedure until her back ached and her thighs began to object every time she bent down. Between immersions she ran back to the house to check on her father. To her relief, he seemed to be sleeping comfortably, his breathing deep and regular.

Not until twilight gave in to the darkness of night did she finally stop. With the aid of a flickering lamp, she examined the piles of linen still remaining. She had been too slow. Mountains of linen yarn lay in their baskets, twisted in knots, needing to be unraveled and prepared.

She would have to start a new batch of dye and mordant in the morning, which would take two or three hours. Only then could the dyeing process start again. She would never be able to finish in time for the promised delivery.

Ominous dreams came to her that night. Confused images of someone writhing in pain, begging for help. Dreams of blood spreading into a lake. And in the end, the old familiar dream of the woman with the sweet smile. Lydia reached out to touch her face, her heart full of longing. To her horror, the smile turned into a grimace of agony. Then the screaming started, a soul-shattering wail that would not stop. Lydia jerked awake, her body shivering in the hot summer air.

FOUR

Why are you cast down, O my soul,
and why are you in turmoil within me?
PSALM 43:5

She knew from experience that she would not be able to sleep again after the dream. Fetching fresh water from the clay jar outside the house, she washed, dressed, and twined her long hair into a braid, which she left to hang down her back. Anticipating her father's hunger, she made bread, her hands kneading flour with practiced strokes, her mind on the work ahead. Before starting her labors, she tiptoed into her father's chamber to find him stirring lightly.

He yawned. "How long have I been sleeping?"

"A few hours. How do you feel?"

Eumenes scratched his cheek. "Better. Is it time for dinner yet?"

Lydia smiled. "The stars are fading. It will be dawn soon. I have brought you hot bread with cheese and olives for your breakfast."

Eumenes rubbed his hands together. "The gods blessed me the day you were born. How goes the dyeing?"

"Everything I have dyed looks purple."

Eumenes laughed. "That sounds promising."

He patted the mattress next to him. "Eat with me. It will be another long day for you. You will need your strength."

He studied her downturned face as she ate quietly. "Anxious?"

She rubbed her aching neck. "It's that I have never done this part of the process before. Now I must manage without help from you."

"You will do a splendid job. In fact, by the time you are finished, you will realize that you do not need your old father at all and put me out to pasture."

Lydia's eyes brimmed with tears. She lowered her lids to hide them from him. "I will disappoint you."

He put a hand under her chin and lifted it. "You know more than most of the dye masters in the famed guilds of Thyatira."

"They must be very ignorant, then."

Eumenes's smile was smug. "They are, compared to you and me. But that must remain our secret. We don't want them to think us boastful."

Lydia gave a weak laugh.

"That's better," her father said. "Listen to me, Lydia. I wouldn't let you get your hands on my dye or my reputation if I did not believe in your ability to accomplish this. I would simply delay the work. But I have no such compunction. When that linen is delivered to the customer, it will have my seal on it. My name. I leave the work in your hands without a shadow of hesitation. I am satisfied that you will do as good a job as I myself would. I have taught you since you were a child, and never was there a more apt pupil, save for myself, of course."

"There is no hope for you. You are definitely veering into boastfulness."

He lifted Lydia's heavy braid for a moment and pulled on it affectionately. "Unfortunately, your talent for dyes is matched by your talent for worry. When I cough and have a little fever, you wonder if I have a wasting disease. I have a tiny scratch—" he indicated the stitches in his leg—"and you conclude I shall surely perish. The very thought of travel is enough to turn you into a trembling mess.

"But, Lydia, in spite of so much fear, you are still the bravest person I know. You press on, press through your anxieties and face the challenges before you. I could not run this workshop without you. I could not manage my travels if I did not have your help. Like a rock, you stay by my side, and no wind of terror overcomes you. You are my valiant, fearful girl."

"Cheap labor, too," she said, her teasing words not managing to hide the catch in her voice.

He tugged on her tunic, straightening the crooked collar with careful hands. His touch was a declaration without words. A declaration of love. Protection. Understanding. A declaration of belonging. "Sometimes you remind me so much of your mother. The same teasing tongue. Like you, she was beautiful. You have her coloring. The amber hair, the turquoise eyes. That is not from my side of the family."

Lydia smiled. "Only you would consider me beautiful. I am plain as yogurt and just about as pale." She played with the darning in her tunic. "I had an odd dream last night. One I have had before. I think it concerned my mother. I can't remember the details. It's a jumble of disconnected memories. I know she was sick. I remember the sound of her screams. Snatches of short images that sometimes come back to me in nightmares. What happened to her, Father?"

Eumenes sucked in a sudden breath and choked on the mouthful of soft cheese he had just put in his mouth. Lydia patted him on the back, trying to calm the coughing fit.

"She died in an accident, as you know," he said when he was able to breathe again.

"When I was a child?"

He nodded. His expression had grown stony and closed.

Lydia pressed. "But how? How did she die?"

"It was an awful tragedy. Lydia, this is not the time to speak of it. You have much to do. And I . . . It distresses me to dredge up that day. This dream. Put it away from your mind."

Remorse made Lydia flinch. Her father was laid

35

low and in pain, and she added to his affliction with her curiosity. She pushed the images lingering from her dream to the back of her mind as she always did. "Forgive me, Father."

Eumenes pulled the blanket up against his chest, looking fragile in its folds. "You did nothing wrong, child. The fault is mine. I cannot bear to think of that day. I prefer to remember her as she was."

FIVE

Establish the work of our hands for us—
yes, establish the work of our hands.
PSALM 90:17, NIV

Lydia gasped as she realized the lateness of the hour; the sun was making flaming streaks in the lightening sky as it rose. She cleared up the meager remains of their breakfast and gave her father a quick kiss on his discolored cheek. "I need to start the new vat of dye."

"I will come and sit with you soon."

Lydia shook her head. "You must remain in your bed until the physician pronounces you fit."

"Speaking of the physician, did you see the size of his gold pin? You'd better try to sell him some purple cloth when he is here. How about that length the moths got into last summer? It seems a fair exchange, given how many holes his needle put into me."

"You stand on your best behavior or he might add a few fresh holes to the ones he gave you yesterday."

At the well, Lydia filled two jars with clear water. As was her habit, she fingered the rough carving on the underside of the old stone wall.

Her fingers found the Greek letter theta, followed by epsilon, and onward, until they spelled *Themistius*. Her mother's father and the original owner of this land. He had carved his name into the stone as a young boy.

Lydia loved touching that wobbly, stone-preserved signature. It felt like touching a part of herself, a rocky tracing that led back into her bloodlines.

Her grandfather had been born to an ancient family whose roots went deep into Thyatira's history. From the time the city had been under Lydian rule, members of her family had lived here, worked here, and raised generations of their children on its enduring soil. After the Greeks took over the land, her family, like other Thyatirans, had mixed with their conquerors, adopted their language and their gods, and become for all intents and purposes Greek. The Romans had inherited a Greek Thyatira, with its subtle and unique lingering touches of the Lydian culture. Many old families like Lydia's had survived the changing of the guard and held on to their traditions.

Her grandfather had been born into a wealthy family that, according to her father, had once owned large parcels of land throughout Thyatira. In spite of good intentions, Themistius had managed, in the course of a wild youth, to squander most of his inheritance. He had held on to this single piece of property by virtue of hard work.

According to family legend, upon the birth of his only child, Lydia's mother, he had been horrified by how little he had left to pass on to his daughter. For the first time in his life, he began to labor with single-minded fortitude in an attempt to save this final legacy, notable only for its well.

On his deathbed, Themistius had gifted the land to his daughter, a small but proud gift, holding within every cubit not only the memory of generations of former ancestors but also his sweat and blisters and fatherly pride.

Like her grandparents, her parents had managed to bring only one child into this world, another daughter. And now it was Lydia's turn to fight for this last piece of her family's inheritance, this tiny patch of land that represented everything good and safe and noble in this world. Home and her father and purple. Lydia was content if the world had nothing else to offer.

By noon Lydia's hands were dyed as purple as the linen, and her face had grown red from exertion. Weariness had already begun to dog her steps, a dark shadow that would not waver.

As it had the day before, the garden door opened without warning, making her jump a second time in two days. She wiped the frown from her face and walked toward her guests, trying to appear welcoming. To her consternation, she found that the physician still carried an aura of great expense, and Jason remained as graceful and charming as her memory insisted. Without thinking, she hid her hands, ugly and stained, in the loose fabric of her tunic.

"How fares my patient?" the physician asked.

"If you will follow me to the house, you will find him recovering. He ate twice already and insists on coming out to help with the work."

"We shall see," the physician said.

Jason fingered a wad of yarn hanging from a branch. "Your work?"

Lydia nodded. "My father is the master. I merely serve as his assistant. This is my first attempt at working alone."

"You seem to have learned his trade well. This purple is deep and rich. And he uses no snails?"

Lydia looked up in surprise. "You have learned much about us since yesterday."

He shrugged. "I find the name of Eumenes is well known. Perhaps I will purchase a few pieces from you. But I think I will wait until I can have a length of fabric dyed and woven by your own delicate hands."

Lydia burst into laughter. Suppressing her squirming vanity, she showed him her purple hands. "Hardly delicate. Everything here, you will find, is purple, including my fingers."

For a moment, Jason seemed taken aback by her abrupt honesty. "It's a lovely shade," he said gallantly.

Lydia snorted. "I am glad you approve."

"Obviously your father has taught you his secrets."

"No dye master passes on all his trade secrets," Lydia said. She breathed a silent sigh of relief as they arrived at her father's door. "My father is waiting for you. I will fetch some wine and leave you to visit in peace."

"It would be more pleasant if you joined us," Jason said.

"Thank you. I must see to the work. With my father indisposed, we are falling behind."

The physician went into Eumenes's chamber while Jason lingered outside. "Why don't you hire a steward? Or another dye master? You might settle for an ordinary laborer, at least, to lighten your responsibilities."

Lydia sensed the censure in his voice. Not every man in Thyatira felt women should play a role in this or any other trade. She crossed her arms. "Because I love working with purple. Besides, I know more than most stewards." She conveniently forgot her own objections to the contrary that very morning. "Please pardon me. I must fetch the wine."

The sound of his laughter surprised a smile out of her. She had expected him to take offense at her forthright admission of skill. Perhaps there was more to him than mere good looks and heroic reactions.

SIX

She dresses herself with strength
and makes her arms strong.
She perceives that her merchandise is profitable.
Her lamp does not go out at night.
PROVERBS 31:17-18

Having no time to dawdle, Lydia delivered the wine and a few almond pastries to her father's door before sneaking out. She had an important appointment with several vats, smelly solutions, and piles of soft linen.

Less than an hour later, she saw Jason walking toward her. Over his arm he held a carefully folded piece of scarlet wool. "Your father sold me this. I couldn't buy a purple handkerchief of this quality for such a price. But he refused a fair payment."

Lydia dried her hands on a towel she kept nearby. "That is a beautiful selection. My father dyed the wool and the weaver finished it last week. But we owe you far more than a piece of fabric. You were gracious to help him in his need. Without your intervention, he might have suffered a graver injury."

Jason waved his hand in the air, as if helping people in need were a daily ritual. "I told you what I really want. I would gladly swap this exquisite length of cloth for a small kerchief dyed and woven by your hands."

Lydia could hold an expert conversation with any man about the process of dyeing purple and to some degree even about weaving. But her life had left little room for assignations and amorous conversations. She went everywhere with her father. If any young men had felt the slightest attraction to her, they had not shown it before the sharp eyes of her parent. She found this flirtation, flowing so smoothly from Jason's tongue, utterly bewildering. Staring at him, speechless, Lydia was half tempted to laugh at the absurdity of his words and half impressed by his shamelessness.

"I see that you need more convincing. Tomorrow I will return to visit your father. And to persuade you of my good intentions."

The physician had the good grace to arrive at that moment, saving Lydia from having to answer. There was no large fold of fabric over *his* arm, she noted with disappointment. *He* would have paid full price. "How fares my father, sir?"

"He is recovering well, as you reported. I have given him permission to join you in the morning. Only for light work, mind. No heavy lifting, or he will tear those beautiful stitches I gave him." He bent to sniff the vat of mordant.

"By Jupiter, that stench is offensive," he said before leaving.

Given that he had smelled her father's urine not an hour past without a wrinkle to his brow, Lydia found his statement unfathomable. She would rather smell purple dye and mordant all day long than be surrounded by bodily emissions.

Which was a good thing, since, in fact, she would have to smell mordant and dye all day and partway into the night for some weeks. Their survival depended on her now.

Lydia worked alone for the next two days. She labored with slow deliberation, vigilant to avoid every possible mistake. Too vigilant. Her ponderous pace made them fall hopelessly behind.

She had stopped sleeping at night, tossing and turning on her mattress, thoughts of her new responsibilities crowding her mind. She felt at war within herself. On the one hand, she delighted in the making of purple as she always had. There was nothing on earth quite so satisfying as kneeling before a vat of dye and trying to decipher its mysteries. On the other hand, the world of purple had suddenly become a place of terror. A battleground of unconquerable proportions. Her father thought her gifted. Capable. But what if he was wrong? In truth, she was quite sure that in his affection for her, he overestimated her ability.

Purple could mean the wreck of every expectation directed her way. It could mean a broken heart, the crashing of every dream, the end of life as they knew it.

In one swift and confusing stroke, purple had become both her beloved and her enemy. Who could sleep through such a divide? Exhaustion tugged at her, making her even slower.

Eumenes came to watch her on the third day, observing her as he leaned on the overstuffed cushions she had fetched for him. "What are you so afraid of, child?" he said after studying her silently for an hour.

Lydia sank against the vat of dye she had prepared while he slept. "I am merely being careful," she said, her voice rising defensively. "We have no time for errors. I must be attentive."

"This is beyond attentiveness. You have seen me do this work a thousand times. Helped me. You know it by heart. And yet you move as if you are a stranger to vats of dye. Why?"

Lydia blinked. "You won't understand."

Eumenes raised an eyebrow. "That never stopped you from talking before."

She clasped her hands together. "I am going to fail," she said with certainty.

"You are *afraid* you are going to fail. That's a different thing."

"You can't comprehend my anguish. You have never feared anything."

"I have never struggled with the spectacular array of worries you contend with, it is true. But this one fear—" he shoved the point of his finger into the air for emphasis—"this, I understand. I had to overcome it myself when I was about your age."

Lydia whirled her head. "I don't believe it."

"It's the truth. I dreaded failing. Fear became like a chain that bound me. Then I realized that I would never achieve anything of worth until I wrestled with this monster in my heart. You know my dyes are different from everyone else's here in Thyatira. Do you think I was born with the formulas already composed?" He shook his head. "By trial and error, I discovered them. I found them in the dark of confusion. I dithered. I wasted time and currency. I failed. But then, in the end, I found my way to places no one else had."

"You failed?" Lydia stared at Eumenes as if seeing him for the first time.

"With striking regularity."

SEVEN

For the righteous falls
seven times and rises again.
PROVERBS 24:16

Her father pulled Lydia sideways until she toppled into his arms. "Child, let me tell you the secret to victory in this hard life. Strive valiantly. Dare to try, knowing that you will make mistakes. You will fall short again and again, because there is no effort without error. In the end, you will either know the triumph of high achievement, or if you fail, you will fail while daring greatly.

"Embrace the knowledge that you will make a mistake sooner or later. Your work will have flaws—some grave, some superficial. Learn to accept this truth, and you will master your art."

Eumenes fetched a couple of balls of linen and began to play with them, juggling them one-handed. "You think failure is the enemy. The thing to dread. It isn't. It's your friend. It's your teacher. It can teach you treasures no measure of victory can. On the way to success, you'd better get well acquainted with its bite."

To her dismay, he threw one of the balls of linen at her, and she had to scramble to catch it midair to prevent it from falling into the vat of dye before being properly untangled first.

"Go on," he said. "Dare greatly. Show me you aren't afraid to fail."

Lydia grasped the yarn to her breast. "But I *am* afraid. What if we lose this customer?"

"Then we will find another."

"What if he speaks ill of your shop because my work is flawed?"

"I will produce fifty who will speak well of it."

"And if all this linen is destroyed?"

"I know where to buy more."

"We don't have any money."

"Then we will make more."

Lydia threw up her hand. "Be practical."

"I didn't become a master at my trade by being practical. I became a master because I dared to face failure. Lydia, you are responsible enough for ten people. You shall never be in danger of growing shiftless and untrustworthy. You have talent, training, and knowledge. You work hard. This one thing holds you back: you would sacrifice greatness at the altar of fear. That road leads only to mediocrity. Believe me. It is a path many choose, and it leads only to disappointment in the end."

Pulling her knees against her chest, Lydia hid her face. "You are an odd man. Most fathers want their children to be a success."

"That's what I am teaching you. True success.

49

Besides, we have nothing to lose. At the rate you have been working, you are too far behind now to ever catch up without a miracle."

A week later, they sat in the workshop with the wooden door open to allow light and the semblance of a breeze into the cramped space. The first order was ready for delivery. They were one day early. Lydia could hardly believe the evidence before her.

"Very good," her father said, examining random pieces of dyed linen. "You did this all by yourself."

"You tricked me, didn't you, when you said you were not well enough to help me?"

"Perhaps a little. I am an old man now, you know. I need a holiday now and again."

Lydia flung a great clump of wool at his head. "I worked my fingers to the bone, you sly, conniving fox."

"You work like a dye master now, Daughter," her father said, pride warming his voice. "Not just an apprentice, tiptoeing around every step, but a true master. I have taught you well."

Lydia put her hands on her hips. "You are just looking for free labor. Now I suppose you will demand that I complete the next order by myself as well."

Eumenes stretched his leg. "I told you to hire a helper. You refused."

She shook her head. "If you looked at the accounts on occasion, you would see that after paying our taxes we have little left for hired help. Rome takes its share very seriously."

"And very deeply. I am sorry I am not a Roman citizen. You would be spared all those taxes."

Lydia fetched a few tools from a shelf and added them to the pile she had been gathering in one corner. "You would look silly wearing a dazzling toga like Jason. I prefer you in your tunic."

"Speaking of that young man, he has visited often these past few days."

Lydia dropped her chin and pretended deep interest in a jar of madder. "He comes to see you."

Eumenes gave a deep sigh. "He comes to see *you*." He leaned forward and picked up her hand. His finger traced a delicate blue vein on her wrist. "You have purple running through your veins. That, you inherit from me. And you love this little piece of land, the crumbling house, the meager workshop, the spacious garden with its well. That, you get from your mother.

"When you marry, be sure you choose someone who loves them alongside you. A man who understands your talent and supports it."

Lydia snorted. "Marry! Who is talking of marriage? Did you hit your head when you fell?"

"You are old enough to speak of these things.

Your mother was your age when she married me."

"Are you ready to start these vats of dye, or do you plan to spin your yarn all day long?"

Eumenes shrugged. "Speaking of dye, I have decided to teach you all my secrets. You know most of them already. Now I will show you those remaining touches that make our dye so unique. Keep these safe, Lydia, for they are your inheritance from me."

Lydia lifted her head. "Father, I should confess. I never did manage to overcome my fear as you wanted. It dogged every step. You said finishing this order on time would require a miracle. I suppose that's what happened. I did not have a sudden spurt of daring confidence."

Eumenes shrugged. "I never expected that my words would change your heart overnight. Words have the power to inspire. But they cannot change a life. You will have to live out this lesson over and over again, push past the fear with one new job after another until my words take root in your heart. In time you will find your fears diminished in force. Fear is a coward. When you resist it, it flees."

"Do you think so?"

"I am sure of it. You are ready, Lydia, to take on the full mantle of my craft."

She felt a thrill that even Jason's green eyes had failed to arouse in her. "Truly? You think me ready? Thank you, Father! I will guard your secrets with my life."

"One day I will be gone. It may be hard for you to prosper here in Thyatira as a woman alone."

"You are not going to be gone. Now let us stop speaking of tales and legends and begin our work, or . . ."

"I know. The doors of Hades will open up and swallow us whole, for we shall run late."

EIGHT

You shall not oppress a hired worker
who is poor and needy.
DEUTERONOMY 24:14

Jason continued to visit Eumenes's workshop.
He was a distraction. He was a joy. He was confusion and happiness in one beautiful, muscle-
bound package. Even Lydia had to admit that
he came for her. He betrayed no shyness in
revealing his interest. His compliments grew
more outrageous by the day, until Lydia sur-
rendered and gave him a piece of purple fabric
that she had woven herself.

"How glorious. To touch what your precious
hands have held and caressed for hours."

Lydia rolled her eyes. "Try to behave, Jason."

"This color is astonishing. Are you sure you
used no snails?"

"Of course."

"What did you use, then?"

"Same as other purple dyers in Thyatira.
Indigo. Madder. A pinch of this. A dash of that."

"Tell me. A pinch of what? I can see that you
love this work. I wish to learn about it for your
sake."

Lydia smiled, flattered. "It will take you a long

time to absorb all the complexities of dye work. I have needed years to learn about each dye; every batch is unique, you see. One must learn proportions and order. It is not a simple formula that we follow. Nature creates its treasures with great variety. One year the indigo is deep; another it's lighter. You have to learn, with your mind and heart, how to shift with every change, how to coax a certain shade out of different dyes."

Jason frowned as if displeased by her answer. "Surely a dye master can learn these things quickly. If he already has the knowledge, he merely has to grasp the subtleties of your father's formulas."

"A dye master?"

Jason grasped her hand in his, his fingers caressing hers with a boldness that made Lydia's heart beat like a Roman drum. "You work too hard," he said. "Look at these hands, almost ruined by hard work. Did you realize that my mother owns several businesses? After my father died, she took charge of his affairs and made them more successful than he ever could have. But she does none of the work herself. She hires capable managers, and they do her bidding."

Lydia sighed. "We cannot afford to hire a steward, Jason."

"Why do you not come to my house and meet my mother? Ask her to guide you. I am certain she would be willing to help."

Lydia heard nothing past the first part of his declaration. "You wish me to meet your mother?"

Jason spread his arms. "Of course. For weeks I have spoken of nothing save Lydia. She is desperate to know the mystery woman who takes me away from home every day."

Lydia could not hide her smile. "I will ask my father."

Jason's home, a palatial, two-story villa, sat on a fertile plain on the outskirts of town, near the Rufus River. A fruit orchard bursting with blossoms was situated on its west side with a flower and herb garden to the east. In the back Lydia could make out the outline of a stable.

A stone-faced slave welcomed them inside with a bow and led them to the rectangular courtyard in the center of the house. Lydia noticed the lack of a cheerful greeting, the absence of a friendly smile, the shadowed eyes, and wondered what manner of household Jason's mother liked to run. A strict one, judging by the slave's precise politeness.

The open courtyard was surrounded by a generous portico that provided a covered walkway for visitors. Interspersed between delicately carved columns, beautiful wall paintings depicted familiar scenes from the lives of the Greek immortals. Lydia wiped wet palms against the fabric of her tunic. In all her travels with her father, she had never seen such a luxurious residence. And they were only in the atrium!

To her bewilderment, Jason did not invite her inside the house but remained with her in the courtyard. Certainly the atrium was more opulent than the whole inside of her own home. But it would have been more cordial if he had asked her within. A house this size would certainly have a formal reception room, a *tablinum* where guests would be received. Lydia had little time to wonder at this odd breach of manners. Jason took her hand and coaxed her to walk along the portico, where in the cool shade of the tiled ceiling, he drew her attention to his favorite paintings.

It became obvious to Lydia, as Jason began laboriously to tell her the tale of each scene, that he assumed her ignorant of Homer and Euripides and Herodotus. Although Lydia did not consider herself a scholar, she had a love for history and the ancient tales of the Greeks and read voraciously whenever she could borrow a copy of an epic poem or a scroll of history. Jason clearly had a great enthusiasm for the stories he told her. His hands whipped about his head as he spoke of the adventures of Hercules, his eyes lighting up with the drama of his tale. If his narrative lacked accuracy, she did not have the heart to correct him, though a few times when he deviated badly from the story, she had to bite the inside of her cheek to keep from laughing out loud.

His mother was late. She kept them waiting for half the length of an hour and arrived with languid steps and without an apology. Like her son, Dione was handsome, with large, round eyes that rarely seemed to blink and a smile that tipped one side of her mouth higher than the other. She received her son's kiss coolly on one cheek and forbore to embrace Lydia, though she did invite their young visitor to sit near her on a marble bench.

"Jason tells me that you help in your father's business."

"Yes, my lady."

"Purple dye, is it?" she asked, her eyes drifting to Lydia's stained fingers.

Lydia tucked her hands behind her. "Yes, my lady."

"You hire no manager or servants?"

"Good stewards are expensive. An expense we cannot afford."

Jason's mother swept the hem of her delicate tunic behind an ankle. "If you managed your business better, you would be able to afford a steward within six months. I could do it in one."

Lydia felt blood rush to her face at the implied criticism. "My father has little time for the accounts. He is truly gifted in his art. It is an absorbing business and leaves no room for account keeping."

Dione snorted delicately. "My husband used the same excuse. I took charge of the accounts and we saw a gratifying improvement. After his death, I multiplied his business many times over." She spread her hands to indicate her luxurious surroundings. "You could do the same for your father. Leave him to his . . . art. Make his life more pleasant by increasing his success."

The marble bench with its feather-stuffed cushion grew uncomfortable. Lydia wriggled where she sat as the silence stretched. Finally she admitted, "I do not know how, mistress."

"Shall I help?"

"I could not impose upon you."

Dione turned to gaze at her son, who stood patiently by her side. "Jason seems besotted. I think a little imposition might be in order."

NINE

No one can serve two masters.
MATTHEW 6:24

"My mother has offered to become your father's partner," Jason said, his cheeks flushed with eagerness.

"His partner?" Lydia's voice emerged in a squeak.

Mistaking her dismay for enthusiasm, Jason plowed through with his exuberant proposal. "She will take care of the accounts and the management of the business while your father continues to create his dyes. It is a perfect arrangement that would benefit everyone. She brings with her enormous advantages. Experience and knowledge, influential friends with greater wealth than what you are accustomed to. And because we are Roman citizens, you will have very few taxes to pay. Your income will increase overnight. You will be able to hire multiple servants to help your father. My mother is already looking for the right steward, one who could manage your father's workshop and lighten his load."

"That is . . ." Lydia stumbled over her words. "That is very kind of your mother, Jason," she said after taking a deep breath, grasping for words that would not insult her young suitor.

"I know. She is exceptionally generous." He squeezed her fingers.

Lydia removed her hand from his hold. "I should warn you, my father has never had a partner. He does not believe in them."

Jason ran a finger through his short hair, setting the golden locks to charming disarray. "How will you afford to hire a manager and servants unless my mother helps you?"

"I would welcome her advice. But I tried to explain to you. We cannot afford to hire a steward."

Jason began to pace, his steps agitated. They were in her garden, where she had started to work on a new batch of dye. Her implements lay in an untouched heap. Jason seemed to have that effect on her. When he arrived, work slowed down or ceased altogether.

"Lydia. I care for you." He knelt on one knee and gazed at her with molten green eyes. "You must know how much I care for you. I want us to have a future together. But my mother would never allow our friendship to grow if you continue to work in your father's business."

"I see."

"I don't believe you do." He curled his hand into a fist. "I am willing to make sacrifices for you. To set aside my own desires and support your work, because I know how precious your craft is to you. Why can you not forfeit a little on my behalf? My mother is willing to help you. She wishes you to succeed."

Lydia tried to speak. Her voice did not cooperate. She cleared her throat. "I . . . I care for you too, Jason. I would sacrifice for your sake as well. Only you must see that it is not my sacrifice to make. The business belongs to my father. It is his decision, not mine. And he would not wish for a partner, no matter how competent."

Jason's smile was like a glimpse of the sun after a month of black clouds and unremitting rain. "Your father adores you. He will do anything to make you happy. Ask him for this favor, and he will give it to you. Promise me, Lydia. Promise you will ask him. So that we can be together always."

"I will try," Lydia said, dazzled. As he took his leave, he looked at her the way a parched man in the desert might look upon a chalice of cool water. It filled her heart to the brim, that one look.

She was quiet over dinner, her thoughts in turmoil. A part of her wanted the whole world to know that Jason—this splendid, valiant man— cared for her. Wanted to be with her always. Was willing to make sacrifices for her happiness. The idea was so bewildering that she wondered if her imagination had led her into the realm of delusions.

When she remembered the condition to Jason's overwhelming proclamation, however, her heart froze with dismay. How could she ask such a sacrifice from her father? It would never work.

She could not deny that there would be many advantages to Dione's proposal. Even without the enticement of Jason's love, Dione offered them financial stability beyond their dreams. No more fear of being destitute. No more struggle to survive. Her father could continue the work he loved without the unyielding demands of his trade. He was growing older. The pace their lives required was becoming too hard for him. Being Dione's partner would offer him more assistance.

Then again, what use was assistance and financial stability if he became unhappy? Eumenes liked to have his own way at work. Surely Dione would wish to exert her opinions on occasion. She would wish to save money where possible, whereas Eumenes desired to create beauty, often regardless of the cost. Their wills would clash. Eumenes would chafe under rules and rations.

Lydia chewed a spoonful of beans without tasting them. And would she be happy? Never to have her hands in a vat of purple again, never to create the dye herself? Was she prepared to give up so much for a pair of bejeweled eyes that looked at her adoringly?

She lifted an empty spoon to her lips, chewing before realizing she held nothing in her mouth. Jason had promised that she could continue to oversee the process. Even as his wife—for that is what he had intimated with his passionate speech—she would be able to direct the dye master and oversee every step. Perhaps that would satisfy her passion. With him by her side, it would surely be more than enough.

"You are quiet tonight," Eumenes observed.

"Am I?"

"Please. If you put anther empty spoon in your mouth and chew, I might choke. What ails you, Daughter?"

Lydia placed her spoon back into the clay bowl. She frowned, trying to string words together that refused to be strung. What if she asked this great favor of her father and he capitulated for her sake and became miserable? How would she bear the burden of his anguish, knowing it to be her fault? And if she did not ask, how could she face Jason's censure and unhappiness? There seemed no way out of her quandary. She could either have a miserable father or an anguished suitor.

She squirmed where she sat on the floor, her body and mind afire with discomfort.

"Come now. Nothing can be so bad. Tell me

your troubles. Did Jason spurn you? Tell me the word and I will beat him to a pulp."

Lydia gave a pale smile. Her father's head reached no higher than Jason's chin, and he was too old to survive a fight with anything bigger than a lamb.

"No one has spurned me. The opposite, in fact."

The air left Eumenes's chest with a hiss. "He has proposed, then."

"Not in so many words."

Eumenes threw his hands in the air. "I begged your mother not to die. I told her I could not raise a daughter on my own. And you see, I was right. This whole room is drowning in your gloom. And why, I ask? The young man has proposed. He has not proposed. It is beyond me."

Lydia began to laugh. "You will be horrified when I tell you," she said, sobering.

TEN

He will turn the hearts of fathers
to their children and the hearts of children
to their fathers.
MALACHI 4:6

The Romans believed that the house of the god of sleep, Somnus, was in a deep valley where twilight ruled. The sun never shone there. No roosters crowed, no dogs barked, no branches rustled in the whispering breeze. Silence and shadows wrapped that slumberous realm in their heavy peace.

Lydia wished with all her strength that she could enter the world of sleep. Enter its forgetful streams and, for a few hours at least, set aside the mighty struggle that divided her heart into two. Instead, she lay on her mattress, agitation making her turn this way and that.

"You can't sleep either," Eumenes whispered from the doorway. In the light of the small lamp burning low in her room, he seemed diminished and fragile.

Lydia sat up. "Dear Father. You must not disturb yourself on my account. We will go on as we have before. We have always been happy together. We need no more than what we have."

66

Eumenes lowered himself at the end of her bed, stretching his legs before him with a heavy sigh. "We cannot go back. We cannot undo the future by returning to the past." He tapped her foot over the thin blanket. "I have decided to go and visit Dione."

"No, Father!"

"I didn't say I will take her offer. But there is no harm in hearing her out, is there? Perhaps I will like her terms."

Lydia shook her head. "You won't like them." She wanted to say more to dissuade him. To warn him not to turn his life upside down for her sake. She opened her mouth and closed it again without saying a word. Something stopped her tongue, turning her mute. A secret relief that the decision was taken from her. More than that—a fledgling joy at the thought of her life with Jason.

She told herself her father was too shrewd to enter into an unwise agreement. He would not give away the business he had built with his bare hands without judicious forethought. His decision would be based on prudence. His affection for her would not sway him into irrational indiscretion.

In any case, Jason's mother would act with scrupulous generosity for Jason's sake if nothing else. Everything would work out well, she told herself.

And she said nothing more.

Her father still sat at the end of her bed, wakeful and vigilant, when she finally slipped into the realm of sleep she so desperately longed to enter.

"You mean to accept Dione's offer after only one visit? Father, that sounds rash." Lydia drew her sweat-drenched scarf from her head and fanned her hot face. They were in the workshop, where her father, true to his promise, had demonstrated the undisclosed mysteries of one of his dyes.

Eumenes sat on a wobbly stool. "Not rash. Decisive. It will be a relief, to tell you the truth. Having someone else take charge of the accounts without needing to scramble to pay exorbitant taxes to Rome will be a vast improvement to my lot in life. You will have your handsome hero, and I will have my dyes to play with. What more is there to concern ourselves about?"

In spite of her father's confident words, Lydia felt uneasy. Beneath Eumenes's cheerful countenance and assuring manner, she sensed a furtive hesitation, as if he were plagued by a reservation he did not wish her to see.

"Why rush into such an important decision?" she asked, her brow furrowed. "Take a month. Take two. I can wait. There is no need to rush into a precipitous concession."

Eumenes scratched his cheek. "There you go

using big words again. I don't know what you just said. But you are wrong and I am right."

"Dear Father," she said, and winding her arms about his neck, she kissed him on his lined forehead. "I am so grateful for your love. Grateful that you would wish to make this sacrifice for me. And perhaps in time we will find that it is a good decision after all and partner with Dione. But for now, please tell me you will wait."

Eumenes smiled and ruffled her hair. "You are the best daughter a man could wish for. How happy I am that you belong to me."

As he left the workshop, his feet silent on the chipped mosaic, Lydia realized that though he had warmed her heart with his words, he had not calmed her fears with a promise.

The next four days passed in a flurry of activity as Eumenes continued to teach Lydia the aspects of each individual dye that he had hitherto kept to himself. He made her practice every step repeatedly until he was certain she had memorized it correctly. Exhaustion became a constant companion. Lydia barely felt its grip as she grew engrossed in Eumenes's teaching, finding his revelations fascinating. She grasped the new concepts quickly, having been exposed to so much of the process already, and with every new instruction, her awe at her father's ability grew. So engrossing did she find their pastime that she hardly noticed Jason's unusual absence four days in a row.

On the fifth day, her father told her to practice on her own while he saw to a few errands in town. They had filled their last order and were in a lull. So Lydia spent the morning and early afternoon working on the most complex of her father's formulas. Already it had become second nature to her.

She had finished making a small batch, admiring its perfect shade and consistency in the sun, when the garden door opened and her father walked in, followed by a reed-thin stranger. Lydia wiped her hands on a rag and stood.

"Lydia, this is Eryx. He is our new dye master."

Lydia stared at the man's thin, sallow face and then back at her father without comprehension. "Our new dye master?"

"Mistress Dione sent him with her compliments."

"Mistress Dione?" Lydia's voice had grown as thin as Master Eryx's arms.

"Is this a new game?" her father asked. "I speak and you repeat my words?"

Lydia expelled the breath she had been holding. "You have signed the contract."

Eumenes looked away. "I told you I would. Now, let me show Eryx our workshop and supplies before introducing him to our treasured well. Then we can all sit to supper." He hesitated for a moment, his voice growing less confident as he asked, "Is there supper?"

She crossed her arms. "You should have asked this morning." *Before you strutted home with a new dye master and a signed contract.*

ELEVEN

Fret not yourself because of evildoers.
PSALM 37:1

The following day, Jason arrived full of good-natured charm and the indisputable attraction that always left Lydia a little breathless. It was as if he were lit from within, bright and glorious like new gold.

"How do you like Eryx? My mother says he is superb."

Lydia shrugged. "He seems to know his dyes."

"And he will soon learn your father's formulas and take over all the hard work for you, leaving you free for me." His mouth tipped up at one corner, making him look less like Apollo and more like his mother.

Lydia made a noncommittal sound. Her father had proclaimed that under no circumstances would Eryx be given the crucial secrets of their dyes. Eumenes was slowly showing him some of the basic procedures for making his purple. These were common among most purple makers. If Eryx learned anything new from her father, it was nothing any other purple dye seller could not teach him.

"As long as we remain partners, Dione can have

half our income, and with my good wishes. But my dyes are my own," Eumenes had said. "You may think me hasty in my decision to welcome her into this workshop. Don't think me naive, as well."

"How long will it be before Eryx is fully trained by your father, do you think?" Jason said, distracting her from her thoughts by reaching for her hand.

"Three months. Less, if he is quick of mind and has some experience." She did not tell him that even after three months, Eryx would not know the full formula to a single dye. Why she kept this decision a secret from Jason she could not explain. *It is my father's decision and his to reveal,* she told herself. But she knew this was only part of the truth.

Her father had once told her that he had never kept a secret from her mother. Their trust in one another was so complete that he could not fathom anything so dire or dark that it might not be shared with his wife. And yet here she was, already refusing to disclose matters pertaining to their business with the man she loved.

It's not that I don't trust Jason, she reasoned with herself. *I will tell him when the time is right.*

Dione might take offense at Eumenes's decision so soon in their partnership. Though there was nothing in their contract that required Lydia's father to share his knowledge with Dione, she might consider his decision objectionable. Lydia tried to convince herself that she had good reason to keep Jason in the dark. Still, the decision to hold the full truth back from him pricked at her like a sharp splinter caught under the skin.

"He is nosy!" Lydia told her father a few weeks later. "No sooner have I started a batch of dye than Eryx leaves his work and stands at my elbow, full of questions."

"I have noticed the same." The creases in Eumenes's forehead deepened. "Yesterday, he asked me if I would allow him to sleep here, in the workshop."

Lydia's head snapped up. "You did not agree, Father? It is bad enough to have him underfoot all day long."

"I did not. He told me a sad story about a sick daughter who needs money for physicians. If he pays no rent for his house and sends her the money, she might find a cure. That is why he wishes to move into the workshop, he claims. I do not believe a word."

"We should tell Dione our suspicions. I think Eryx wants to steal your formulas. She will find you another dye master."

Eumenes's expression grew shuttered. He shook his head. "Not yet. We have no proof."

"Are we to wait until he robs you before we

make a complaint? It would be too late then."

Eumenes grinned. "He won't rob my secrets. I have a plot of my own."

As promised, Dione's patronage drew new customers, most of them sufficiently wealthy to place large orders. Eumenes put several pieces of exquisite purple wool and linen at Dione's disposal, which she wore often during the many banquets and official functions she attended. Inevitably many asked where she had acquired her new garments and came rushing to Eumenes's workshop as fast as their chariots and horses could carry them.

"Who knew it would be so easy? Give a wealthy woman an armful of purple, and you have a long line outside your door, wanting your wares," her father said.

"All this new business is very well." Lydia measured vermilion powder with careful precision before continuing her train of thought. "But how are we going to keep Eryx distracted while we work on the dyes? He is not a stupid man. There is something very crafty about him that makes me uneasy. Let us ask Dione to find us another helper."

"I told you I have a plan." Eumenes pulled a piece of crumbling parchment tucked into his belt. "He will be busy making this while we work on the real dye."

Lydia looked at the parchment. "This is not one of yours, is it? I have never seen it."

"It was the first dye formula I learned as a boy."

"He won't be fooled by that. If you knew it as a boy, he is sure to recognize it."

"I have added enough new steps and ingredients to throw him off."

Lydia studied the parchment more closely. Silently she began to laugh. "Petals of fresh violets? Where is he to find those in such quantity? And sheep urine? Father, that is cruel."

"One of our customers told me of a field covered with violets. Is it my fault it is a twelve-hour journey from here? That ought to keep him out of the way for a full day. Perhaps two, if the weather proves cooperative. And plenty of dye masters use urine as a mordant."

Lydia shook her head. "Not you." She added the cost of the regular ingredients, which every purple dye required. Indigo, plant ash, lime, madder. "It won't be cheap, this ruse of yours."

"He will not need much. The formula as far as the indigo and lime and ash is concerned is the same as the one we use. When that part of the dye is completed, I will give him a small portion to work on independently. I have told him that he will be dyeing wool for a very special customer. It is a small order, but if we satisfy the patron, he may return for more." He shrugged. "Eryx will care nothing whether he is working on a large order or a small one so long as he believes he is learning the formula to one of my dyes."

"What happens when the wool comes out looking inferior?"

"I will tell him he committed an error and set him to work again."

Lydia bit her lip. "I almost pity him."

"I, too." Eumenes's belly shook with laughter, ruining the effect of his compassionate pronouncement, and his daughter joined in ruefully.

He squeezed her shoulder. "One day you will be a great dye master, Lydia. You will run your own workshop. I hope you will be happily married by then, for an unmarried woman in Thyatira will have few opportunities."

"Jason's mother manages many trades with success, and she is a woman."

"Just barely."

"Father!"

"The point is, she is a widow with three children, which grants her freedoms that an unmarried woman cannot have according to Roman law and custom. If we lived in Macedonia, you might be able to manage your own business even without three children and a husband. That is one corner of the empire that allows women a little more freedom. But here, as in most of the Roman Empire, a woman, no matter how skilled or knowledgeable, cannot run a trade."

"Macedonia!" Lydia was sure she looked like she had sucked on an unripe persimmon. "Why would I want to go there? I belong here in Thyatira, with you. We will be partners always, whether I marry or not."

TWELVE

There is one whose rash words are like sword thrusts, but the tongue of the wise brings healing.
PROVERBS 12:18

"Why do you still have your arms drowned in dye up to your elbows?" Jason asked with a scowl. "Isn't Eryx supposed to do this now?"

Lydia wiped her hands with haste. "He needs time to learn." This would be a good moment to tell him the truth, she thought. She could not keep their predicament a secret from him forever. Jason had a right to know. "He . . . he might not be the right man for this work, Jason. We may need to look for someone new."

"What do you mean he is not right?" Lydia had never heard Jason raise his voice before. It was like watching a sunny day turn dark with storms in the span of a breath.

"My mother handpicked Eryx herself so that you could have the right help. Is this an excuse to keep on doing what you want? Is this your way of clinging to this work in spite of how I feel? If you wish to keep on living as you always have, why don't you speak plainly so I don't have to waste my time waiting for you?"

"No, Jason! I am not trying to cling to my

work." She realized that Jason trusted his mother's choice implicitly. He would not accept her intuition about Eryx, nor would he listen to her accusation of the man's dishonesty. She swallowed her desire to tell him the truth. "I am still working because Master Eryx has much to learn," she said. "Whoever is to become our steward must learn my father's methods. Until then, I need to help as before."

The effect of her words was dramatic. In one moment the scowl disappeared and the old, lighthearted Jason reappeared, eyes sparkling, smile peaking with its rakish half tilt. "I see I was unfair. Your father must teach Eryx everything he knows. In the meantime, he still requires your assistance. I cannot find fault with that. It will be impossible to leave your father without good help. As soon as Eryx has been properly trained, you can leave the work to the men."

Lydia frowned. "Except that I would still help with the management, as your mother does with her business concerns?"

"That is what I meant, of course." He sprang to his feet, his movements full of the vigor and grace of a superb athlete. "I have taken too much of your time. For the next few weeks, I will come in the evening, after your work is done. I do not wish to interrupt you. I can be patient for a few weeks until you are free."

He rose, and for a moment as Lydia looked

up to him, he seemed like a giant, a leviathan blocking out the light of the sun.

Certain memories linger in the soul, sharp like the edge of a dagger, aching in spite of the passing of months. The first and only time Dione deigned to visit Lydia at her home was such a memory. Like a brand, the woman's words and manner left their mark.

Dione and Eumenes had been partners for over a month by then. Her man, Eryx, had proved more burden than help. Most of what he did for them was a waste of time, as they kept him busy making fake concoctions, ensuring that he never learned the true process of creating Eumenes's dyes. As a result, his presence brought very little relief to Lydia. She still had to complete the work she had done before his arrival and remained busier than ever, trying to cope with increasingly large and complex orders.

Dione's arrival was unanticipated. She walked into the garden, slave in tow, wafting perfume and displeasure. Lydia, caught in her work clothes, sweat staining her ancient tunic, her hair a tangled mess, her fingertips red from working with madder, stared at Jason's mother, her chin slack with astonishment. If Hera, the mercurial wife of Zeus, had decided to visit her workshop in human form, Lydia would not have been more surprised.

"Mistress Dione!"

Dione wrinkled her nose. "Surely even the gods on Mount Olympus must be offended by this stench. Look at you, child. Never have I seen a girl in such distasteful disarray."

"I beg your pardon. Please come into the house for refreshments, and I will change quickly while you rest."

Dione turned to study the walls of their home at the far side of the garden. "If the inside of your domicile matches its outside, I prefer not to step within. Thank you."

Lydia's eyes flew open. It was one thing to receive insults about her appearance. In fairness, she could not deny the shabby presentation she made, especially in comparison to an elegant woman like Dione, who never seemed to have a single wrinkle in her garments. But no one, not even Jason's mother, had the right to pass harsh judgment on her home.

She straightened her back. "That house has known joy and laughter through many years. It is a home of love, even if it cannot match yours in beauty. I consider it an honor to have lived here all my life."

"You would, child, never having known any better. Tell me, is this how you receive my son when he visits you? If so, I wonder that his attachment has lasted so long. He likes his women well presented."

Lydia flushed. "Jason usually does not arrive until after the evening meal. By then I make certain that I am more presentable."

Dione's cutting remark fingered a concern Lydia had struggled with for weeks. Jason's visits had grown more desultory. He never ate with them. He lingered very little with her and often seemed distracted. His charm and affection had not faded. But Lydia had begun to fear a shallowness to his attachment. In spite of his many hints, he had never asked her father for Lydia's hand, nor approached her directly about his intentions.

Perhaps Dione's words, though humiliating, were a good warning.

Perhaps her drab appearance had caused Jason's ardor to cool. After all, he was accustomed to a world of glittering elegance, abundant prosperity, and cultured women who sparkled like jewels with wit and beauty. Perhaps at the start she had been a novelty in her old tunics and simplicity. Now the novelty was wearing off, and with it the attraction.

Lydia felt close to tears. She blinked them away, unwilling to allow Dione to see how deeply hurt she felt by her words. To Lydia's relief, the woman did not linger long. After a short conversation with Eryx, she left with a swish of her silk skirts. In her wake she left a tiny filament of gold, a stray thread from the embroidery at the edge of her tunic. Spying it in the dirt, Lydia picked it up and stared at the sparkling delicacy now torn from its place of honor at the feet of Dione. Inexplicably, the sight brought fresh tears to her eyes.

After that, Lydia took greater care with her appearance when Jason visited. She wore her best tunics for him and even bought an amphora of perfume to combat the scent of the mordant that lingered on her skin at the end of the day.

If he noticed a difference, he never mentioned it.

THIRTEEN

But now trouble comes to you,
and you are discouraged; it strikes you,
and you are dismayed.
JOB 4:5, NIV

As far as Eryx was concerned, after three months
he knew the formulas to all of Eumenes's dyes.
It had not been easy to convince him that his
knowledge was complete. More than once her
father had sent him home after preparing a fresh
batch of purple. "You have worked hard, Eryx.
Go home to your bed and rest now. I will dye
the linen for you. It will be here tomorrow when
you arrive." Then Eumenes would empty Eryx's
faulty solution at the foot of some unfortunate
tree in the garden and dye the linen in his own
newly prepared vat so it would be ready for the
steward to admire in the morning.

"Why can we not tell Dione that we suspect
him of trying to steal our formulas? He creates
more problems every day," Lydia said one
evening when they were finally left to their own
company.

"Without proof, how can we convince Dione?
It will do nothing but raise her ire. She will think
we are complaining for no reason. Best leave it

alone. We have managed well enough so far."
Eumenes smirked. "Besides, I enjoyed myself
thinking of the man traipsing about the Thyatiran
hillside, looking for rare roots, then staying
awake all night to soak them in clean water and
stirring them in the moonlight."

Lydia shook her head. "You are growing cold-
blooded. He was red as a bowl full of mulberries
when he returned from his search on the hills."

"His cheeks and nose only blistered a little,
and he recovered within the week. No permanent
damage."

Lydia examined a chipped nail. "Mistress
Dione may not be good at choosing stewards,
and she may have a sharp tongue, but I will say
this much for her. She certainly knows how to
draw customers. Our income this month, even
after she subtracted her share, was greater than I
have seen in years."

"Yes. I cannot fault her in that regard."

"How has she managed it? Have you been
studying her accounts? What did we do wrong
before?"

Her father shrugged. "Nothing. We weren't
Roman; that is all. And we did not have powerful
friends."

"Father . . . you have seen the accounts? You
have examined them since Dione took charge of
them?"

Eumenes developed a sudden interest in a

chip at the base of one of the vats. "Yes, yes. Of course I have."

"When?"

"Some time in the recent past."

"How recent? Last week? Two weeks ago? A month?"

"Or perhaps two. What do you want from me? I can't make dye, keep Eryx busy, deal with new customers, keep you from trouble, and examine accounts too. The woman is doing a fair job. You were just admiring her spectacular economy. Let's leave her alone to do what she does best."

Lydia threw her hands in the air. "The mere fact that I admire her pecuniary talents does not mean I think we should trust her blindly."

"You worry needlessly, my daughter. It is the plague that hounds you. What could go wrong? We have our home. We have our purple. We have each other. And now you have Jason, too."

Without warning, the garden gate flew open, smashing against the wall. The force of the blow left a chip in the stone. Lydia barely had time to frown with displeasure when three soldiers stormed inside.

The man who seemed in charge swaggered forward. "Are you Eumenes?" He had blotchy skin and spoke with a strangely hoarse voice, as if someone had once tried to strangle him and had left his thumbprint on the fragile bones of the man's throat.

"I am," Eumenes answered, his mouth open in a good-natured smile. "How can I be of service?"

"You can accompany us to the magistrate's prison, for a start."

"Prison?" Lydia and Eumenes cried at the same time.

"Prison. You are under arrest."

"For what crime?" Eumenes asked, blanching. Lydia, only half-comprehending, felt an unnatural chill that made her whole body tremble.

"Stealing."

"That is ridiculous! My father has never stolen in his life," she cried, growing hot with offense while at the same time turning cold with terror.

Eumenes motioned Lydia to be calm. "What am I supposed to have stolen?"

The soldier shrugged. "The moon, for all I know. Not my business. My business is to fetch you. Clap you in irons. And beat you if necessary." He gave Lydia an appraising look. "Not too hard, if you make it worth my while."

"Why would you beat him at all? He is innocent!" Lydia cried.

"Not when a Roman citizen brings a charge against him, he's not. Are you going to come peaceably, or do I have to put you in chains?"

Eumenes stood, his bearing dignified. "I will come. Lydia, pay the man."

Lydia shook her head in disbelief. She felt caught in one of her nightmares. "Pay the man for arresting you?"

"Pay him for not beating me . . . too hard."

Lydia ran after the soldiers as they bore her father between them. She tried to wheedle, plead, and cajole some answers out of the guards. She knew with complete certainty that her father's arrest was a mistake. By tomorrow or perhaps even sooner he would be out, and they would have a good laugh about his adventures. She needed to discover the source of this scandalous misunderstanding, and within a few hours, everything would be set to right.

The soldiers ignored her.

Finally the one in charge stopped with a growl. "Keep up that haranguing and I will arrest you as well. Understand?"

Swallowing hard, she nodded her head once and followed in silence. Her father was being taken to jail! She could barely comprehend it. Jail represented humiliation. It stood for sickness and despair. Even death. Good men like Eumenes were not supposed to ever face the anguish of a dank cell. Whatever error had occurred, she would not rest until she proved his innocence and cleared his name.

Her father was not brought before the magistrate. Without ceremony, his feet were put in iron chains, and he was thrown into some hole of a prison, which Lydia was not allowed to visit.

"I will go to Mistress Dione, Father." She spoke as loud as she could, hoping he could hear her. His cell was not visible to her from the courtyard. "Do not worry. She has important friends. She will see you are released," she said.

To the jailer, a fat man with dangling jowls and surly eyes, she gave two sestertii. "Treat him kindly and there will be more." He stowed the coins in his purse without a word.

The sooner she rescued her father from this place of nightmares, the better it would be. She ran all the way to Jason and Dione's house. For all the speed that terror lent her feet, it took her over an hour to arrive. At the door, she was met by Dione's slave.

"I need to see Mistress Dione," she panted, bending forward to ease the stitch in her side.

"She is not at home."

"Jason, then!"

"Not at home."

She tried to push the slave out of the way. "You don't understand. It is a matter of great urgency."

"Still not at home." He was a tall man, built with the solid structure of someone accustomed to hard work and heavy lifting. She could not budge him. Calmly, he waited until she stepped back. To her utter befuddlement, the door closed in her face. Lydia banged on the door, screaming. "She will want to hear my news, you fool!"

The door remained as sealed as an Egyptian tomb. Lydia wanted to kick the slave for his obtuse refusal to help. But as she trudged back to the magistrate's prison, an odd image haunted her. The slave's eyes had been full of pity when he had informed her that Dione and Jason were not within. Not indifference. Not cruelty. Not superiority. But an inexplicable pity.

Lydia thought she understood. Dione and Jason had already heard of her father's arrest and chosen not to associate themselves with him any longer. They believed him guilty.

Jason had turned her away without even giving her a hearing.

FOURTEEN

Arrogant foes are attacking me, O God;
ruthless people are trying to kill me.
PSALM 86:14, NIV

"I could not find Dione or Jason," she told her father two hours later, not knowing how to share her suspicions with him. The brusque jailer had allowed the visit after she had paid him another sesterce. At this rate she would run through their ready cash far too quickly. She must conserve their coin for the coming days.

Eumenes, fetched from his cell somewhere in the bowels of the building, now stood before her in the courtyard. From the way he narrowed his eyes in the brightness of the sun, Lydia surmised that he was kept in darkness. His feet remained in rough iron fetters, already rusty from the sweat of another unfortunate prisoner.

She winced when she saw that his ankles were red where the chains rubbed against them. In a day or two, the skin would scrape off. Longer, and . . . She shook her head. His incarceration would last no more than that. He was innocent. Not even Roman justice would condemn a man who had committed no wrong.

Her father touched her wrist gently, drawing

her gaze to his face. "It was Dione who accused me. She has charged me with theft."

Lydia felt the breath leave her chest. Leave her whole body until she turned dizzy. "No," she said, shaking her head wildly. "Where did you hear this? It cannot be true."

"True enough," Eumenes said bitterly. "The jailer told me. Your silver coins loosened his tongue."

"Why would she do such a thing?"

"To secure the workshop for herself."

"Our workshop is insignificant compared to all she owns! It's hardly worth her trouble. You must be mistaken, Father. What can she do with a crumbling workshop without your purple? It is your knowledge that draws customers."

"A knowledge she believes she possesses."

"What? You did not reveal . . . ?"

"Not I. But her man Eryx believes he knows what I know." Eumenes brought his chin down once for emphasis. "She thinks she no longer needs me. It was a ruse from the start. Her desire to be my partner, her wish to help us. All of it was a ploy. She wanted to wrest the workshop from my possession. You thought Eryx was seeking to rob my formulas for himself. I always wondered if he worked under Dione's direction."

"That's why you would not let me complain to her about our suspicions."

"Yes." He lowered his voice to a whisper.

"Did you tell Jason? Did you tell him that we distrusted Eryx?"

Lydia shook her head. "I never told him. Father, this makes little sense. What does Dione gain by her false accusation? She cannot prove you guilty of something you did not do."

"She claims to possess documents that prove my guilt. I don't doubt it. I put my seal to enough scrolls these past three months to fill a valley. By the end, I stopped reading them with too much care. She wore me out with nonsensical details. When she was sure that my attention had strayed, she must have had me put my seal to a scroll that proves some dishonest transaction."

"Even if you were proven guilty through her lies, your property would be forfeit to Rome. What advantage would there be for her in that?" Lydia said through dry lips. Were they truly to lose their home? Their workshop? The land that tied them to generations of her ancestors? It seemed impossible that they should come to such a pass after all their hard work.

"If I had defrauded her, then she could claim part of my property as damages. Our land, our home, our workshop would be divided between her and Rome."

Lydia put a hand to her forehead. She felt as if the world had turned inside out. "I will talk to Jason. He will make her see reason. He will dissuade her from this course."

Eumenes said nothing. She wrapped her arms around her belly. Forced to choose between his mother and Lydia, whom would Jason believe?

Lydia sneaked a sturdy cloak and warm food to the jailer, who, for a few coins, passed them on to his prisoner. Given the jailer's hungry look as he took the bowl from her, she would not have been surprised if only part of the stew and bread were actually delivered into her father's hands.

"He wants to see you," the jailer said upon his return. He held out his hand, like a fathomless pit that swallowed her precious store of coins. Lydia's mouth became a flat line before she laid another silver coin in his palm.

"We have little time, Lydia. Listen to me," Eumenes said. "I want you to go to our house and pack everything valuable you can find. Any coins we have left. Your mother's jewelry. The unsold lengths of purple. All our supply of vermilion. Everything of value that you do not wish to lose. Gather them tonight. You cannot take much, for whatever you take, you must be able to carry in your hands. You must go in the cover of deep night. Be sure no one follows you."

Lydia nodded. "Where do I take everything?"

"Go to Atreus's inn. Remember where that is? We ate supper with him and his wife a few times before her death."

"I remember, Father."

"Good. Ask for a small room. Tell him to give you the chamber he and I used to play in as boys. He will know which I mean. That inn has been in his family for three generations." Eumenes laid the flat of his palm against his temple as if it ached. "He was my playmate when we were children. We often hid in that room. Under the carpet there, you will find a wooden slat that can be moved. There is a generous hole where you can hide our valuables. No one knows about it. Atreus himself may have forgotten. We used to hide our boyhood treasures in there, away from prying eyes. I believe once we put a snake inside that hole."

Lydia's eyes snapped open.

"Don't worry. It won't still be there. I think we put it in his sister's pallet."

"Too bad you didn't save it for Dione's feather bed."

"Yes, well, it would be a very old snake by now." He reached for Lydia's hands. His fingers were burning hot. "Don't fail us. What you take out tonight is all we will be able to save for our future. Your future, Daughter. Forgive me. I fear I have lost your inheritance."

Lydia began to weep. "You have not. The fault is mine. I brought Dione into our lives. I carry this guilt."

Eumenes shook his head. "No, Lydia. The guilt

belongs to that woman. Now hurry. You will not have much time before they come to plunder the house. I want you gone when the soldiers arrive. Who knows what manner of men they may be."

FIFTEEN

They close their hearts to pity;
with their mouths they speak arrogantly.
They have now surrounded our steps;
they set their eyes to cast us to the ground.
PSALM 17:10-11

Lydia worked frantically into the small hours of the night, trying to determine what she should bring and what to leave behind. Everything small and valuable went into her sack. Over her tunic she put on several brand-new purple cloaks. She filled her belt with the precious few pieces of jewelry her mother had left behind: a brooch, two rings, a delicate bracelet, and one belt made of silver chain and turquoise. The costly vermilion, which her father kept in a locked chest in his chamber instead of at the workshop, went into the sack next.

At any moment, soldiers might burst through the door. The thought made her heart race until she could barely breathe. She ignored the feeling of panic and pushed on. Their future depended on her now.

A few more things from the workshop, and she would be ready to leave. She needed to hurry. The moon was hidden behind thick clouds tonight, a perfect shelter for her escape. But a delicate breeze had started to waft, picking up speed by the hour, and she feared she might lose her cloud cover if she lingered for long.

She did not dare carry a lamp into the garden in case she was seen by any spies Dione might have set upon their home. But having walked the path between the workshop and her house countless times through the years, she could have navigated the way blindfolded.

In the workshop, she grabbed the most expensive implements of their trade and stuffed them into her sack. There was one more thing she refused to leave behind. Grabbing an iron chisel, she made her way to the well. Patiently, she worked to loosen the mortar around the ancient stone bearing her grandfather's name. She scraped the mortar with delicate care until a deep groove formed between the stones.

She needed to smash the masonry out of its place using hard blows. To silence the noise, she wrapped the iron in an old rag and began to hit the side of the stone. In the dark she missed and slammed the chisel into the back of her hand, hard. She swallowed the bellow of pain that rose to her lips. Sinking to the ground for a few moments, she waited until the dizziness passed and the pain in her hand subsided to a dull throb. Grinding her teeth, she resumed the work of hitting the rock, until after an hour, it came loose.

She grabbed the stone bearing her grandfather's name, bent to kiss the edge of the well, and whispered, "Goodbye, home. I will never forget you."

Her feet were nimble and fast as she clambered to a cracked marble bench and climbed over the wall of their garden at the opposite end from the garden door before making her way to Atreus's inn. As she walked league upon league, she wept bitter tears, tears of rage and sorrow and a grief that would not be assuaged. Still she walked on, furtively looking behind to ensure no one followed.

She hid behind a clump of dense bushes outside the inn until the sun rose. Then, schooling her features into a calm she did not feel, she marched to the door and knocked.

Atreus himself opened the door. "Good morning, Master Atreus," she said, her voice polite. "My father sends his greetings. He has been arrested. The charges are false. But he fears he shall find no justice at the hands of Rome. He asked that you give me a room for the sake of your friendship. He told me to ask for the room you used to play in as boys."

As she stepped over the threshold, Atreus's gentle hand on her shoulder, she felt as if she had left behind everything she knew.

Eumenes was brought before the magistrate the next afternoon. He spoke only once to Lydia as they marched inside the governor's fortress.

"Is it done?"

Lydia kept her words cryptic in case the soldiers had sharp ears. "Yes, Father. I made sure no one followed. He gave me the room you requested. Everything is as you directed."

Eumenes nodded. His skin shone with sweat. In spite of the thick cloak that covered him, he shivered as if he would never be warm again. Lydia worried that he might have caught a chill in the dank atmosphere of his subterranean prison.

The magistrate was a man of sizable girth with small, delicate hands that would have fit better on the wrists of a willowy matron. Lydia recognized him. He was one of Dione's friends who had placed an order with her father. His cloak, fastened on his shoulders with fine gold pins, was made of rich purple, she noticed. Her eyes narrowed as she recognized her father's work. The cloak was fashioned from one of the fabrics they had placed at Dione's disposal.

The magistrate was Dione's man. To add insult to injury, she had bribed him with their own merchandise, though no doubt the fabric had come accompanied by a heavy purse of coins.

Within moments he confirmed Lydia's suspicions.

"This is a serious charge," he said without preamble. "Theft against a Roman citizen, a respected patroness of our city." He looked over a scroll that he held open with those narrow-boned, white hands.

Lydia's heart sank. She knew words could not sway corruption. Nor could reason or compassion. Corruption answered to one master only. Money. More money than she had to give. Still, she could not sit and watch her father be charged for a crime he had not committed.

"My lord, I beg, please allow me to speak. I am this man's daughter. He is a respected member of the guild. You can confer with any dye master in Thyatira and they will vouch for him. Many will bear witness to his honesty, I am certain."

"And yet this—" the magistrate shook the scroll—"will bear witness to his dishonesty. Your father's seal against the word of his friends. Whom do you think I should believe?"

"The truth!"

"The truth is that an honored Roman widow put her trust in him and became his partner in good faith. He thought to take advantage of a helpless woman, not realizing that she was more clever than he."

"That last part, at least, is true," Eumenes said under his breath.

The magistrate pointed a finger at Lydia. "You are the daughter of a thief. By his actions your father has destroyed your life as much as his own. Your honor is shattered. Your life is destroyed. In a moment I will pronounce a formal sentence upon your father, but let him know that his worst punishment is *your* fate.

"No man will marry you now. No one will want you. You will have no children, no friends, no home. You will be considered an outcast."

Eumenes staggered where he stood, as if kicked in the chest.

The magistrate stared at him with bloodshot, swollen eyes. "I see you begin to understand my meaning. You have ruined more than your own life. Hear now your sentence. Under any other circumstance, you would be condemned to hard labor for the rest of your life. Mistress Dione, however, has asked that we show you mercy. It is a mark of her impeccable character that in spite of your nefarious behavior, she shows you no malice.

"Instead of what you deserve, you will receive a more charitable sentence. You will be stripped of your property, part of which will be given to your victim as reparations. Because she has asked for clemency on your behalf, we waive the sentence of hard labor in a mine and settle for a flogging. Thirty lashes. Let it be a lesson to you should you be tempted to dishonesty again.

"You will be free to leave after your scourging, but you may not return to your former workshop or residence. All you once owned is now forfeit."

"Thirty lashes!" Lydia thought she had cried out, but only a croak emerged from her lips. A younger man could die from such a brutal flogging. How could someone of her father's age survive such violence?

The soldier who had arrested Eumenes walked over to take charge of him. He leaned over and whispered into her ear. "Don't worry, girl. I'll be soft on him. No bones broken. Just a few bloody scars. Give him a month and he will be good as new."

There was no time to prepare for this latest horror. Immediately after his audience with the magistrate, Eumenes was taken into the courtyard to receive his beating.

Lydia followed, her mind a whirl of confusion. Their world had shattered in a matter of days—of hours—and it was as if her soul could not catch up with this terrible heartache. She had never felt so alone. There was no man or god to help her or her father. They had been abandoned by all.

SIXTEEN

If you pour yourself out for the hungry
and satisfy the desire of the afflicted,
then shall your light rise in the darkness
and your gloom be as the noonday.
ISAIAH 58:10

Lydia had never seen a man scourged. The sight of the *flagrum* clutched in the soldier's fist made her gasp.

This was no ordinary whip. It was short, made of three thick leather strips. Toward the end of each strip, small pieces of metal had been embedded into the leather, using a series of knots. Lead, she thought. The lead pieces had sharp edges, and as her eyes fastened upon them in helpless horror, she noticed some were encrusted not just with rust but with dried blood and gore. Another poor victim's flesh, never cleaned off before the next flogging.

Eumenes's tunic was torn off his back and his hands were tied to a post in the magistrate's courtyard. The soldier who had promised Lydia not to beat him too hard stepped forward, flexing his right hand around the handle of the *flagrum*. He winked at Lydia before raising his arm in an arc and lowering it with a violent motion.

The leather whistled as it flew through the air.

Her father screamed. Lydia swallowed convulsively. Three faint red lines appeared on his skin. Another lash, followed by another. Scream upon scream until Eumenes's voice grew hoarse. By the fifteenth lash he began to bleed profusely, his entire back and buttocks torn into quivering ribbons of flesh.

Still the whip came down, rose, came down. Lydia turned her back and vomited on the stone-paved ground. The sound of her father's suffering, of the *flagrum* flying, smashing, tearing, and then flying through the air again followed her even as she bent over, sick and shivering with horror.

She forced herself to take deep breaths. Her father needed her to remain strong and capable. Soon the flogging would end. She needed to pull herself together and arrange for a cart. Then a physician.

Frantically, she looked about the courtyard. A young boy who ran errands for the soldiers sat against a wall, eating raisins. Lydia motioned him over. Giving him a few copper coins, she said, "Fetch me a cart and driver. Any cart will do. Do you understand? Do it quickly, and there will be more coins waiting for you upon your return."

Twilight had fallen when the endless scourging ceased. The soldier who had beaten Eumenes rubbed his neck and shoulders as if they were sore from his hard work. She wanted to spit on his face. She wanted to tear his flesh the way he had torn her father's. Instead, she strained to appear calm.

He noticed her waiting and motioned for a couple of his men to cut her father down. "See? Told you it wouldn't be too bad," he said with a grin that revealed yellow teeth with brown edges.

Lydia nodded. "My thanks." She forced the words out of her frozen mouth. She could not afford to make an enemy of him. Falling to her knees next to her father, she touched his arm. He moaned softly. They had dropped him, belly down, and his face was turned toward her. She saw that he sweated profusely and his skin had turned an odd gray color, like wood ash left over after a hot fire.

"Thirsty," he croaked.

Lydia rushed to the soldier. "Please. Do you have any water?"

He nodded to a large clay jar sitting on the far side of the yard. Lydia raced and found to her relief that someone had left a dipping cup next to the jar. She filled it with water. It was warm from the sun. With her finger she brushed over the top to get rid of a few drowned bugs. Longingly, she thought of the cool, fresh water in their well. No. Not *their* well anymore.

She quashed the thought and hastened back to her father, thinking now only to alleviate his suffering. He groaned as she moved his face softly off the dirt, high enough to be able to take the water into his mouth. Most of it spilled, but he managed to take in a few swallows. She persisted, giving him more.

He began to shiver, shaking violently. At first she thought it was the beating. Then she recognized the telltale signs.

Not now, she thought in despair as he lost consciousness, his arms and legs jerking in haphazard motions. She found the strip of hardened leather she always carried tucked in her belt for such occasions and pressed it firmly into his mouth, holding his tongue under to make certain he would not bite down and injure himself or choke as he fought his old nemesis.

The attack did not last long. They never did. It was over within moments. Afterward, he lay unconscious, twice tormented, once with a Roman whip and again by his old sickness.

The boy arrived with a farmer and his cart in tow. Straw filled part of the cart, the only measure of real kindness they had found in the course of this day. A bit of softness to cushion Eumenes's body as he lay on his stomach, his blood congealing in agonizing stripes that pulled on his wounds and drew the flies. Lydia could not even cover him with his cloak. The wool, though soft, scraped his tortured body and made him cry out in pain.

They were still a good distance from the inn when Lydia told the farmer to check his donkey's hoof. The animal jolted the cart too much, she said. The old man rolled his eyes, but the sight of her coin made him compliant, and pulling over to the side of the road, he bent to his donkey.

Just then another man in a smaller cart stopped to inquire if he could lend assistance. A cloak covered his face, which in any case would not have been recognizable in the falling night. He lingered for a few moments as Lydia dismounted the cart to direct the farmer's examination, then departed as if he had grown tired of waiting.

After several moments of heated discussion, the farmer told Lydia that nothing appeared wrong with the donkey, and with a final grumble, he returned to his seat on his wobbly cart. By the time he dropped her off at the open market, the night had grown pitch black.

Scratching his thin hair, the farmer poked through the straw in his cart, looking for a missing man. He knew that he had taken on two passengers. But only one had alighted. How a man as sick as the beaten criminal could have jumped out of the cart and made his way anywhere was beyond him. He shrugged his shoulder and tucked his coins more securely into his belt.

With careful stealth, Lydia rushed back to Master Atreus's inn, walking through circuitous alleys and dark paths to ensure no one followed.

None did. But in the more likely event that Dione would make inquiries later, the trail would lead her to none other than an old farmer who had dropped off his lone passenger at the market. Eumenes had simply vanished.

"How is he?" she asked Master Atreus as soon as she arrived.

"In your chamber, resting," Atreus said. "Poor man."

"Thank you for your help," Lydia said, her face a frozen mask.

"When my wife died, your father came to my aid. Grief had muddled my brain, I think. I could hardly run the inn and cared little if I lost it. With his own money, Eumenes hired a manager to run the place until I regained my senses. If not for him, I would have lost my inn as well as my beloved wife. He held me when I wept and sat with me through many a long night. No man was a better friend to me in all my life. You are safe here for as long as you need. I will give you what help I can."

"I did not realize."

"Your father is not the kind of man to flaunt his good deeds."

It was a full day before Eumenes recovered enough to string a few words together. "How did you know I would be flogged yesterday?" he asked, his voice weak.

"I did not know." Lydia stopped braiding her hair.

"Then why have Atreus wait outside the prison gates?"

"We did not know what fate awaited you, but we thought it best that Master Atreus be at hand, though out of sight, when you came before the magistrate."

"You thought I would be sold into slavery and planned to kidnap me from whatever transport they put me on!"

Lydia shrugged, not bothering to deny him. He knew her too well. "As I said, we did not know what sentence the magistrate would hand down. We tried to be prepared."

"A more addle-brained idea is hard to imagine. They would have arrested you and Atreus if you had attempted such foolishness. That would have served me well, seeing you both in prison for my sake."

Lydia made a calming gesture. "It all came to nothing in the end."

"Why the second cart?"

"Because I did not want Dione to find out where we are staying, both to protect Master Atreus from her venom and to shield you from further harassment. She will hound you for your purple once she discovers you have made a fool of her."

"How did you do it? I was only half-conscious during that wretched ride."

"I told the farmer to drop us at the market, and then concocted an excuse for our cart to pull over on the way there. When the farmer was busy with his donkey, I motioned for Master Atreus to catch up with us. It was the work of a moment to place you in his cart instead."

"Perhaps you should stop working for me. Your talents are wasted making purple. You should work for the emperor as one of his spies."

Lydia's smile was bitter. "I think Mistress Dione has proven you wrong. She had me fooled for months on end. I never considered her kind or generous. But it didn't occur to me that she was a thief."

SEVENTEEN

My complaint today is still a bitter one,
and I try hard not to groan aloud.
JOB 23:2, NLT

Atreus managed to find a physician who knew how to keep secrets as well as treat illnesses. Lydia thought him a conscientious and knowledgeable man, less ostentatious than the physician Jason had brought to their home and positively economical in comparison.

As they waited for Eumenes to regain his strength, she wrote letters to a few of her father's closest associates, asking for aid. They could not hide in Atreus's inn forever. They needed to think of a more permanent solution. Most of Eumenes's colleagues did not even answer. A few sent brief letters of regret.

One man, a Jew named Avraham, agreed to meet with her in the market after sunset. He stood behind the cover of a high wall, his face half-enveloped in the corner of his cloak.

"Some believe the magistrate's allegation that your father tried to defraud Mistress Dione," he said. "For myself, I know Eumenes is innocent." He rubbed his jaw as if it ached. "I have known him long enough to be certain of his honesty."

"My father would never rob anyone," Lydia said, her voice hot with indignation. "I am surprised his friends are so quick to condemn him."

"Dione is a powerful resident of this city. It is hard to doubt her word, especially accompanied by a document that bears your father's seal." He stared at his feet, dirty from the dust of the road. "I have tasted of her greed firsthand. She robbed a cousin of mine with her tricks. He was like a brother to me, yet I was helpless to come to his aid. He had to leave Thyatira after Dione finished with him. He has never returned." Avraham readjusted his cloak to ensure his face remained covered.

"You should be aware of one thing: Dione has warned every man in our trade not to assist Eumenes in any way. So even those who wish to help your father find their hands tied."

He cleared his throat. "I am sorry, but I cannot openly lend your father aid as he deserves. She is a Roman and I am a Jew. She could crush me with one word. A small bribe and my business would be wrecked."

"I understand."

Avraham pulled out a purse. "This is not much. I owe more than this to your father, who helped me when my trade was on the verge of bankruptcy. Because of his generosity, I recovered. Take this.

May it be of some service. And may the Lord be with you."

Lydia took the purse and thanked the man. She thought over his words. It seemed not only had they lost their reputation, their workshop, and their home, but they had lost their country as well. There was no place for them in Thyatira any longer. If Dione were standing before her, she would have spit in her face.

In spite of Lydia's best efforts, Eumenes developed a fever. The physician said his wounds showed signs of corruption. He treated the lacerations with aloe and packed them with soft lamb's ear leaves. Eumenes did not complain, though Lydia knew his pain was grave.

"Has no one come to see me?" he asked on the fourth day of his recovery.

"I have not told anyone where you are. I thought it best to remain hidden for now. When Dione finds out that the purple she stole from you is a sham, she is liable to grow somewhat indignant."

He gave a pale smile. "I wish I could see the look on her face when she first makes that discovery. Every single one of Eryx's formulas is useless. She won't see a single copper coin from my purple. She has a strong arm, I bet."

"A strong arm?"

"When she gets mad, she throws things. Far.

A priceless amphora full of perfume. Her silver chalice. A small slave. A strong arm."

"She will certainly throw a fit."

Eumenes stifled a groan. The physician had given Lydia a costly potion to help alleviate his pain. She poured a little of the mixture in his wine, then waited until he fell asleep before she withdrew.

Lydia had not told Eumenes the details of her visit with Avraham, dreading that the ill news might affect his precarious hold on health. He needed to recover his strength before they could speak of their future.

Every day, while he slept, she returned to Dione's house, hoping to speak to Jason.

Her initial anger toward Jason had simmered to a deep ache. She thought she understood his reaction. It was natural that he should believe the word of a beloved mother. Either Eumenes was a thief or Dione was. There was no other option. Of course Jason had to accept his mother's claims.

With the passing of days, Lydia hoped that his feelings for her would prove more powerful than his indignation. Even if he believed Eumenes a thief, in time, he must wish to hear from Lydia, if only to accuse her of wounding him.

But the gates of his home remained closed to her. She trudged back to the inn day after day, taking precautions to ensure she was not followed.

Jason wanted no part of her. Unless she convinced him of her innocence, she would lose him as well as her home. If he believed her, however, he might be able to convince Dione to allow Eumenes to practice his trade in his home city once again. Perhaps, for the sake of her son, she would be content with owning their land, if not Eumenes's knowledge.

That afternoon, Lydia altered her usual course. Recalling Jason's love for horses, she circumvented the villa and headed to the stables instead. She recognized a groom who had once accompanied Jason on one of his visits to her home. The young man was trying to control an excited horse. The animal, his glistening black pelt shining even in the shade, rose on graceful hind legs, jerking his head back in a bid for freedom from the groom's hard hold.

"Behave, Drakon," the groom shouted.

"Have you seen Jason?" Lydia asked, stepping forward.

"Mind you don't get too close, mistress! This is a monster more than a horse, with the temper of Medusa." After several minutes, the fire in the horse's temper finally seemed to run its course, and he stood still, his nostrils blowing great puffs of air as he recovered from his exertions.

The groom wiped his sweating neck with a thick forearm. "None but Master Jason can

117

handle this animal. In his hands, the horse melts. One word from the master, and he will charge and attack like a legion of soldiers. Another word, and he becomes as docile as a lamb. Without the master here, the horse is not safe."

Just then, Drakon turned his head so that Lydia could see his face fully for the first time. The memory of her father's words rang with sudden clarity in her mind:

"He attacked me on purpose. . . . And right here—" Eumenes had pointed to the middle of his forehead—*"there was a white mark that looked like a half moon with a tiny speck next to it that resembled a star. . . . It was perfectly proportioned, as if drawn by the hand of an artist. . . .*

"If not for this young man, it would have gone on to trample me to death. I don't know how, but my friend here charmed that animal into calm. One word from him, and the horse stopped its thrashing."

This was the horse her father had described, this Drakon. Black and unusually shiny, with a perfectly proportioned white half moon and star in the middle of his forehead.

Her throat grew parched until she could barely swallow. The beating of the blood in her ears drowned every sound in the stables. She thought furiously of the events that had brought Jason into their lives, and she understood with a sickening clarity what had truly transpired five months before.

Jason had not happened upon her father in his moment of need; he had not saved him. On the contrary, Jason had been the source of Eumenes's accident. He had intentionally set his monster of a horse on her father. His rescue and further care had all been a ruse. A pretense.

So the plot against Eumenes had begun long before Dione's offer of partnership. How far back did their treachery go? How deep did it plunge?

Jason was not an innocent victim of his mother's manipulation. He was a willing tool of it, a poisonous dagger thrust into their lives in the pursuit of more wealth.

Mother and son must have heard of Eumenes's talent, seen a sample of his incomparable work, and decided they wanted it for themselves. And they had come up with their wicked ploy. So simple. So effective. She was the perfect fool, falling into his plans without a moment's resistance.

Perhaps he had first seen her in the market. Or spied on her as she left the house on some innocent errand. He had taken the measure of her, no doubt, and known how remarkably easy it would be to manipulate and deceive her.

She was just a step to grind his boot on, on the way to grasping the mysteries of Eumenes's purple.

Jason had never cared for her. Never loved her. Every declaration, every tender moment had been a sham, a greedy ploy to rob her of her inheritance.

Lydia could not breathe. To be deceived by Dione hurt. But to be betrayed by Jason—Jason, whom she had trusted and loved—that was enough to wither a soul.

They had lost everything because she had seen a pair of brilliant green eyes and believed their false promises.

Shame descended on her then—stifling, burning shame, gagging her like a murderer's choke hold.

EIGHTEEN

How long will you torment me
and break me in pieces with words?
These ten times you have cast reproach upon me;
are you not ashamed to wrong me?
JOB 19:2-3

Blindly, Lydia ran, desperate to be anywhere but in that place where *he* ruled like a king. For days, she had haunted Dione's home, frantic to find Jason and seek his help. Now, when she was determined to avoid him, she ran straight into his filthy, treacherous arms.

"Lydia! Where have you been? I have searched everywhere for you."

To her astonishment, he gazed at her with a perfect imitation of love, the old expression that used to melt her from the inside transforming his features into a mask of caring. Everything in her rose up in a bitter storm of fury. Words burned on her tongue, tripping to leave a trail of accusation.

Caution interfered.

If he played the lover, he had a reason. She needed to understand his motives before revealing that she had discovered his true nature.

She tried to look neutral. "Have you? That is strange. I have come to your house day after day, seeking you. They never allowed me entry."

"That stupid slave. I will tend to him. He did not tell me." He pulled on Lydia's arm. "Come. We need to speak. There is a small cottage here where we can have some privacy."

The cottage must have belonged to a steward or head groom. A woman, probably his wife, was bent over a fire, cooking something that smelled of onions and garlic and fried pork. Lydia's stomach turned. Jason waved the woman out, and without a word of objection or a single question, she scooted outside.

Why had Lydia never noticed how his servants acted around him? Not with affection or loyalty, but with an unquestioning fear that hinted at his treatment of them. She had assumed it was Dione's rough tongue that held them in check. Now she saw they acted the same around Jason.

"Where are you staying?" he asked without preamble.

"With my father."

The good-natured mask cracked a little. "And where is he?"

"Not at home, since we no longer own our house."

He made a waving motion with his hand. "All that is forgiven. I have spoken to my mother. Master Eumenes may return. I have told her how I feel about you, and she has changed her mind about his continued punishment. He made a mistake. I believe he has learned his lesson."

Lydia crossed her arms. "Why would you want him to return?"

"As I said, my feelings toward you have not changed."

"That is true."

The green eyes narrowed, became acute. "I don't understand your attitude, Lydia. Your father stole from my mother. I should think you would be grateful for my clemency."

"I think you will find it was the other way around. We were the ones robbed."

He made a sound of frustration in his throat. "It matters not what Eumenes has convinced you to believe." He took her hand. She felt as if she were being caressed by a snake. It took her whole strength not to snatch her fingers away.

"What matters is that I want you back."

"Do you?"

"Why should we get caught in our parents' quarrel? I know you will not abandon your father. So let him return to the business he loves. And you alongside him. We will resume where we were forced to leave off."

Lydia withdrew her hand. She had heard all she needed to hear. "How is Eryx faring?"

Jason looked at her sharply. "He manages well enough."

"Not if he is using the formulas my father gave him."

The color left Jason's face. "Perhaps you should explain what you mean."

Lydia's smile was cold. "Or perhaps you should start by explaining a few things to me. Tell me about Drakon. Tell me about the horse you have trained to attack and withdraw. Tell me about the day you met my father and slithered your way into our lives. Tell me about your insistence that Eryx work for us, while he snooped his way around every batch of dye we made. Tell me about my father's thirty lashes, or the fact that our home no longer belongs to us. Perhaps *you* should explain."

Jason raised a brow. "Comprehension has dawned at last, has it? Thank the gods. I thought I would choke if I had to pretend to be enamored of you one more day."

Lydia swallowed bile. "Do not fret. You are no longer required to play the lover around me. There is still one thing I don't understand. Why did you keep insisting that I stop working? It could have made no difference to you."

Jason shrugged. "We knew Eryx could manage to sneak his way around one of you. The two of you together, however, would be more difficult to mislead."

Lydia nodded, pretending that his crushing words had no effect on her. "I thank you for speaking truth at long last." She turned her back, intending to leave. He grabbed her arm and pulled her back, his touch hard enough to hurt.

"Let me go," she said, her voice low.

"Not until I have what I want."

"And what is that?"

"The formula for the purple. Tell me where your father is. If he gives us what we ask, we will take care of you both. He can still practice his craft so long as it is not in Thyatira. You can leave in peace. My mother is even willing to give you a heavy purse to start you on your journey."

Lydia laughed. She was shocked by the bitter sound that emerged from her throat. That was not Lydia's laugh. It was not the laugh of a sixteen-year-old girl who believed the world, in spite of its many sorrows, was still a good place. A place where happiness could knock on your door and come in to stay. This new laugh belonged to someone older and harder.

"If you think I believe any promise that comes out of your mouth, you must be mad."

Jason dragged her against his chest. His arms clasped her with bruising force. "You will tell me what I ask. In peace or with blows, I care not."

Once, when Lydia was younger, a man had taken to following her. She had found his unwanted attention alarming. Something about his manner had made his admiration feel threatening. When her father found out Lydia's dilemma, he gave her a useful private tutorial on men and their anatomy. It was a lesson she had never had to use. Now it came to her like a sunburst, his words and the hours that he had made her practice just the right defensive move.

She pulled her knee back. Then with all her strength brought it up and struck.

Jason's hands went slack. He doubled over, his face turning a puce color. Apparently there was more than one way of making purple, she thought with a smirk.

At first, a strange sound emitted from his throat, no louder than a whisper, but more intense, filled with agony. Lydia stepped away, and he fell to his knees. He managed to take a breath finally, and as he let it out, emptying his lungs of pain, a whistling howl left his twisted mouth.

The woman who had occupied the cottage earlier burst back inside, her eyes wide. She took in the scene: Jason on his knees, purple in the face, his hands clutching his groin, words failing him; Lydia rubbing bruised arms. The woman bit her lip. But as she left, Lydia saw her shoulders shaking with wicked mirth, and she joined in, laughing and crying all the way back to their chamber in Master Atreus's inn.

NINETEEN

I came naked from my mother's womb,
and I will be naked when I leave.
The LORD gave me what I had,
and the LORD has taken it away.
JOB 1:21, NLT

"You went to see Jason?" Her father's face, bright with fever and pain, filled with understanding as he waited for her to speak. Her heart overflowed with thankfulness as she studied that visage. Here was a good man, a kind man, honest and clean. Jason and Dione could not take that from her. They could not rob her of all the years of affection and protection that Eumenes had bestowed on her. The gift of his love would be hers to keep forever.

"How did you know?"

"I thought you would want to meet him. To plead our cause. I take it from your expression it did not go well. Did he refuse to believe you?"

Lydia dropped her eyes as she confessed the truth. "It is worse than that." Word after bitter word, she forced herself to tell of her discovery. "So you see," she said in the end, "you have been cursed with a fool for a daughter."

Eumenes squeezed her fingers. "I fear it is

worse even than that. You have been cursed with a fool for a father, for I believed him too. I confess I did not think him worthy of you, though I never said so. I told myself that if your heart longed for him, I should do what I could to win him for you.

"When I went to see Dione that first time, she told me that she would forbid him from coming to you again unless I became her partner. She said our station in life was beneath her son. At least as her partner, I could improve my lot in society."

Lydia choked. "That is why you agreed to become her partner?"

"I kept you too busy to notice. Jason stopped coming after that. I saw her threat was genuine, and I believed Jason too weak to resist her demands. I never dreamed he was a willing partner in a terrible scheme. Though I believed him too dependent on his mother, I never thought him dishonest. That is why I sealed the contract. You see, child? They misled both of us."

Lydia started to shake with sobs. "I feel so ashamed. He has left me utterly humiliated."

"No, Lydia! The shame is all his, my beautiful girl. His, the offense. His, the guilt."

"For my sake, you lost your home. Your future." She did not add that his reputation and friendships were lost to him as well. Eumenes knew, of course. He had lived in Thyatira all his life. He understood how his imprisonment and conviction would affect his place in society.

"It was my own decision, Lydia. If you blame yourself for this, then all my sacrifices will have been in vain. I want you to know joy. Start afresh. Find a new life. Prove the magistrate's predictions of your future wrong. Create the purple I have taught you, and make it even better."

"We will do it together, Father. Leave Thyatira and start over."

Eumenes's smile was sad. "Do you remember that old Roman general from Philippi, Varus? The one who wanted to buy you from me?"

"As a favor to you, he said, because I was too much to handle for any father and would require the discipline of a highly trained military man to take me in hand."

Her father laughed. "You were ten, and he already had the measure of you."

Lydia slumped against the wall. "You should have sold me. You would have avoided the conundrum in which we now find ourselves."

"It's not too late. If you continue to speak like that, I could still sell you. But that was not why I brought up the subject of the old general. Philippi has a strong dyers' guild, you know. And as I have mentioned before, Macedonia is more accepting of women in business."

"Jason's mother has no problem conducting her trade here in Thyatira," Lydia said bitterly.

"Dione is a widow. She has always worked in conjunction with either her husband or her son. Besides, she never participates in the business. Instead, she hides behind crooked managers like Eryx who do her bidding without question. In Philippi, you could have a greater measure of freedom. We could start again there and ask the general for help."

Lydia shrugged. "I will follow you anywhere. You are my home now. As long as we are together, we have all we need."

A part of her truly believed that. With her father beside her, they would recover from this deep wound that Jason and Dione had dealt them. But another part of her, deeper and older, plunged into fear. What would happen to them? How could they start in a new country? What would they do when their money ran out? How would they survive? If she was so foolish as to trust a man like Jason, how could she survive in a world filled with dishonest men who would plunder your soul for a tarnished copper coin?

The next morning when she awoke, she found her father already sitting up in bed, drinking warm milk that Atreus must have brought him.

"Happy birthday!" Eumenes said with a grin.

"What?" She winced as she massaged her neck. Her bones creaked from tossing and turning too much.

"It's your birthday today, you dolt. You are seventeen."

"Oh. I had forgotten." She pulled a hand through sleep-tangled hair.

"I had not. I dispatched Atreus to pick up a special gift for you. I made arrangements before I knew I would be arrested. But I did not have a chance to retrieve it from the man who sold it to me. Fortunately, or we might have lost it in the scramble of our move." He lifted up several scrolls tied with a leather strip. She noticed that his hands were not steady.

"I bought you a book! Now when you can't sleep, instead of twisting and turning in your bed and thinking dark thoughts, you can read."

Lydia came up on her knees. "Where did you find a book? That must have cost you a fortune."

"Not so much as all that. I know a Roman nobleman whose daughter is getting married. His funds are smaller than his consequence. That is not a fact that he wishes to publicize. He gave me this book out of his personal collection in exchange for a piece of purple linen."

"That's a terrible transaction. The linen was worth more." In spite of the chiding words, Lydia felt flooded with warmth.

Eumenes grinned, undeterred by his daughter's censure. "It's a copy of Homer's *Odyssey*." He leaned forward to untie the leather strip around the first scroll and unfurled it a little for Lydia to see. The top of the parchment was yellowed with age. Greek characters, painstakingly written by the hand of some nameless scribe, ran in fascinating order across the page.

Lydia knew how to read and write, thanks to her father; through the years, she had read several epic poems and histories and plays borrowed from wealthy colleagues and patrons. But she had never owned her own book. Her fingers caressed the pliable surface.

"It tells the story of a man named Odysseus, who was away from home for twenty years, having adventures," Eumenes said. "He did manage to return home eventually. And when he did, he felt it wise to conceal his identity at first. After two decades, he did not know what awaited him at home. Was his wife still faithful? Had his enemies taken over his land? So he dressed himself as a beggar. His disguise was so effective that no one recognized him. Not even his wife or son."

"You can't really blame them after so many years."

"Ah, but even after the passing of decades, there was one thing about Odysseus that had not changed. He had a distinctive scar.

"When Odysseus was a boy, he went hunting with his uncles. During the hunt, a wild boar attacked him, and its tusk ripped a big piece of flesh right above his knee. A horrific wound that almost killed him. He survived the attack, but the boar left its mark on him. That scar is what gave Odysseus away when he went home so many years later. His childhood nurse happened to see the mark and recognized him because of it.

"I tell you this because like Odysseus, you bear a scar from a boar."

Lydia frowned in confusion. "I do?"

"No one can see it. Your scar is here." Eumenes placed his hand on his chest. "Deep in your heart, where it is hidden from view. Still, you cannot disguise it. You cannot wipe it away. Those closest to you see it and recognize it. It still hurts." He reached for her hand and held it. "I do not know how to heal it."

"Father . . ." Lydia shook her head. "I don't understand."

"Months ago, you asked me about your mother. Remember? You asked how she died. I did not tell you then. It is time that I speak of that day."

TWENTY

For the enemy has pursued my soul;
he has crushed my life to the ground;
he has made me sit in darkness
like those long dead.
PSALM 143:3

"All your life, I have tried to keep you safe. To protect you from harm." Eumenes's voice shook. "It is an impossible task, I have discovered, keeping your loved ones shielded from suffering. Pain has a way of finding you, no matter where you hide. It found you when you were still very young. And it ushered an unbearable weight of fear into your heart."

"When my mother died?"

Her father nodded. "We were traveling to visit your mother's cousin at the time, a week's journey from Thyatira." He sucked in a shuddering breath. "We were a close family, the three of us. You were your mother's joy, and mine. To lose her would have been bad enough, but to lose her in such a savage manner!" He shook his head.

Lydia turned pale. Images of her recurring dream rose up clearer than ever. Her mother screaming in anguish, blood everywhere, a growing crimson lake on her clothes, her face, her hair.

Eumenes squeezed his eyes shut. Tears turned his lashes into a sticky web. "On the third day of our journey, we came to a field of lilies. They were her weakness, flowers. She insisted on leaving the carriage to walk through the field. The road we traveled on was riddled with holes the size of a giant's head, and the caravan was moving as slowly as a wounded turtle. So we left you in the caravan with an acquaintance and disembarked to stroll, cutting our way into the field, still keeping up with the caravan. I was several steps ahead of her. Neither of us saw the boar until it was too late."

"The boar?" Lydia had a flash of memory. One she had never seen before. Next to her mother's collapsed form lay a pile of quivering flesh, spilling out of her, still half-attached. Her bowels. Lydia pressed the back of her hand against her mouth.

"I watched in horror as that beast charged her. I tried to pull her behind me, to become a shield against that enraged animal. It was no use. The boar moved much faster than I did.

"The men in our company rushed at it with sticks and spears. I only had my bare hands, though I tried to help. By then the beast had done its worst. As we carried your mother's mangled body into the carriage, you ran from the woman

135

who was trying to protect you from that sight. Your horror was so deep, you could not make a sound. Your mother was still conscious, you see, but her injuries were grievous."

"She was screaming, 'Help me, help me!'" Lydia remembered, doubling over. It was with a child's eyes that she saw, a child's heart that she felt.

"Gods, Lydia. How I prayed you had been spared that sight." Eumenes clutched at the sheets. "We took her to the nearest inn. There was no hope of making it to her kinsman's house. How she survived the journey I cannot say. For three days she lingered in this world. Three days of anguish, her screams battering my mind, until I thought I might go mad. The physician could not help. His potions were useless.

"We forbade you from coming to her. Still, several times you managed to slip in and see her, though of course by then we had covered her under a pile of sheets and blankets so that only her face remained visible.

"She burned with fever. Her wounds turned putrid until her flesh grew black. I loved her more than my own life, but by the end, I begged Hades to come and take her. Surely his realm would be more merciful than what she suffered."

Lydia wept, racking sobs that hurt her throat. She wept for her father, for her mother, and for the little girl who had witnessed too much. She wept until she ran out of tears, spent from the torrent of ancient pain.

Eumenes ran a shaking hand over his stubble-coarsened cheeks. "The boar dealt your mother an incurable wound. But you received your own wound from that wild animal.

"A child so young should feel safe in this world. We had done everything to make our journey well guarded. We hired an expensive caravan and took every precaution. Still, the worst came to pass. Our world fell apart. I think your little soul learned that at any given moment, your dreams can be ripped from your hands, and the ground under your feet can cave in and leave you spiraling into an abyss of pain for which there is no cure.

"Now fear has made a home in you. You worry about everything. The boar marked you like Odysseus's boar marked him. But it has not won. Though you suffer the pain of that scar, you prevail.

"Because in spite of so much fear, Lydia, you are still the bravest person I know. You press on, press through your anxieties and face the challenges before you. Like a rock, you stay by my side, and no wind of terror overcomes you."

Lydia shook her head in denial.

"It is true," her father insisted. "You must believe me. Because the worst has come to pass again. You have been betrayed. You have lost your home. You have lost everything that brought you security. And I am afraid—" Eumenes patted her on the head, his touch gentle as a whisper—"I am very much afraid, my precious daughter, that your suffering is not yet done."

Her father's wounds improved and began to scab over, though he remained weak and unable to travel. Left without the distraction of nursing him and the busyness of work, she found herself at the mercy of her thoughts.

The conversations were the worst part—conversations Lydia succumbed to in her own mind. What she said to Jason and Dione in her imagination: words to vindicate herself; searing pronouncements of their guilt. Words of revenge, where with cruel precision she explained their violation and condemned them with such persuasion that they repented. In her thoughts they always repented. And she won. She found vindication.

Then the cycle began again, and the arguments started once more. She could not sleep. Her mind would not rest.

"Betrayal works like leaven," her father told her one late evening.

"Leaven?"

Eumenes shifted on the mattress, which he rarely left these days. "It gives rise to bigger things so that by the time it has done its damage, it isn't merely the act of betrayal from which you need healing. It infests the mind with resentment and bitterness. And those are much harder blights to overcome than mere betrayal.

"Have a care, my Lydia. Jason and Dione have stolen the land that came to you from your ancestors. It is a small thing to lose, though it seems so grave to you now. One day you will find another land. Another home. Another place to set down your roots."

Lydia snorted, wordlessly denying his reassurance. As if any place in the world could replace the land her forefathers had bequeathed her. As if any other corner of the earth could be home.

"There are much worse things you could lose. Don't allow Jason to take your joy—your peace—or he will have truly robbed you. For such things, there is no replacement."

TWENTY-ONE

The LORD watches over the sojourners;
he upholds the widow and the fatherless.
PSALM 146:9

Philippi would have to wait. Eumenes's health grew worse. The chill he had contracted while in prison settled in his lungs. His body, weakened by shock and the blood loss brought on by flogging, hadn't the strength to fight illness as well.

"Inflammation of the lungs," the physician pronounced and doused her father in infusions of fenugreek and willow.

All the fenugreek in the world was not enough to save him. Eumenes's breathing grew labored.

"You can't die!" Lydia said to him. "You can't leave me all alone. What would Mother say? Pull yourself together."

"I fear Charon awaits to ferry me across the river Styx and into Hades."

"Well, tell him to find another passenger," Lydia wailed. "We are going to Philippi. The river Styx and its ferryman will have to wait."

Eumenes laughed weakly. The laughter turned into an ugly cough. "My beautiful daughter, how I shall miss you. Never forget how much I love you. How proud I am of you."

"Please, Father. I can't lose you, too! I have nothing left."

Eumenes took a broken breath. "Remember that even Pandora's box, with all its host of plagues and mischief for humanity, held one good thing."

"Hope."

"Hope." Eumenes gave a faint nod. "There is never so much sorrow in a life that it should become devoid of hope. Hope may grow fragile as a thread of silk; it may get stuck inside the box of your misfortunes. But it is there. Don't misplace your hope, my sweet child, not even when all of Pandora's monsters chase you. You must hold on to that treasure after I am gone."

"What shall I do without you?"

"Go to Philippi. Live your dream."

Death, Lydia learned, could not be reasoned with. Could not be delayed. Could not be cheated. It took whom it wished. No man or woman was a match for its power.

Death was the enemy she was helpless to overcome.

One day, even Dione and Jason would be caught in its snares, all their schemes turned to impotent dust. First, though, it beckoned to her father. And Eumenes went, powerless as all mankind against its inexorable call.

In seven short days he was gone, and no force in the world of men could bring him back.

Weeping, Atreus quoted Euripides over the body of his friend:

> After his mighty labors he has rest.
> His choicest prize eternal peace
> within the homes of blessedness.

Lydia was not sure she believed in any kind of peace, eternal or otherwise. If there had ever been any gods on Mount Olympus, they had either vanished, too disgusted with humans to bear with them longer, or lost all ability to care. Yet she had to believe that if indeed there were homes of blessedness somewhere, her father had made his way there.

Grief. Betrayal. Shame. Fear. Grief. Betrayal. Shame. Fear. Grief. Betrayal. Shame. . . .

The unrelenting monsters in her box. The waves that pounded relentlessly against the shores of her mind in an endless cycle until Lydia almost collapsed.

Atreus, like a gentle battering ram, started to bang on her door one afternoon. She had not left her chamber since her father's funeral.

She ignored him at first, hoping he would grow tired and leave in time. She had no patience for his compassion. To her annoyance, he would not go away. The banging continued until she thought her head might burst. Lydia opened the door a crack and looked out cautiously.

"Do you want to read your father's letter or are you still too busy wallowing in self-pity?"

"What?"

"Eumenes left you a letter. Some instruction. Do you want it?"

"Yes. Yes, of course." She felt ravenous for any word from him, some faint trace of him lingering in the world.

"Come below and have something to eat and drink. I may consider giving it to you then." Atreus turned on his heel and tramped down the shallow stairs.

Lydia forced food and weak wine down her throat as Atreus watched. Only when he was satisfied that she had eaten enough did he give her the scroll. She spread the parchment open with shaking hands and frowned with disappointment.

"This is not my father's hand."

"No. It's mine. He dictated it to me one day when you had left on an errand. He did not have the strength to hold a stylus by then."

Lydia gulped and nodded. There was no greeting. Just an abrupt start:

I told you not to lose hope. I said you should go to Philippi and live. If Atreus is giving you this letter, it means you have not listened to me. Now stop being stubborn and arrange for passage to Philippi.

Atreus tells me that he will not charge us for our room. This leaves you sufficient silver to purchase a place on a reliable boat and still have enough funds to start a modest workshop of your own when you arrive in Philippi. You will be the most magnificent dyer of purple they have ever seen!

You will find I have written a letter to General Varus. He always did admire my dye. I have assured him you know all my secrets. He will buy a few pieces from you and introduce you to his friends. And perhaps, if he feels generous, he may set you up in your own workshop. A humble life, but good.

Roman law requires that you have a man as your guardian until you wed, and I have named Atreus as such. He promises not to interfere in your affairs unless you need his help. As an unmarried woman, you will not have the opportunities open to a widow. But with your rare skills, you shall prevail. Carve a place for yourself in this world. Do not be afraid. I know you will endure. You will overcome every obstacle in your path.

Remember the lesson of the farmer. I will always love you.

"What does he mean about the farmer?" Atreus asked when she rolled up the scroll and held it against her chest. "He said you would understand."

"The farmer." Lydia smiled faintly and caressed the scroll, holding on to its solidity. "Yes. I understand."

On a cool day the previous spring, her father had taken Lydia into the hills outside Thyatira. The wind had blown chill that day, she remembered. It was before Jason and Dione had appeared in their lives, and she had been feeling carefree, having just finished a profitable order.

Her father had thrown his cloak over her when she had shivered in the cold. It had been such a casual gesture, one of a thousand like it, imbued with unbounded affection. Now Lydia would give anything to have those hands shield her against the cold again.

"What do you see?" he had asked her.

She had grinned. "Are we testing my eyesight?"

"No. This is a heart test," he said cryptically.

"I see several very splendid villas."

He shrugged. "They did not used to be here. This whole area was made of farmland and orchards. Then as Thyatira grew and became crowded, the wealthy merchants decided to move their homes out of the city. They came here because in late spring, the blossoms would bloom, and later in the summer and fall there would be fruit and harvest. Red, gold, and green covered the hills, transforming them into the Elysian Fields. It was a stunning sight. They came, drawn to the beauty of the valley.

"The farmers were happy to sell their land for good profit. A handful lingered on, clinging to their old way of life." He pointed to a small piece of land surrounded by three luxurious villas. "Do you see that one?"

A pitiful parcel of land, brown and barren, sat in the middle of the villas. In the western corner a modest farmhouse, with one wall crumbling and another poorly repaired, straddled the land. "That's not very pretty," Lydia had said with the disdain of the young.

"No. It isn't, not in early spring. This is planting season, when they plow the land, turn it over, and make it ready for the next harvest. The land is plain and ugly now."

Her father then pointed to the dilapidated farmhouse. "I know the man who lives there. He must be ninety years old by now. Born in that house and raised to the work of farming, he continues to do what he knows. Plant wheat and barley. Some of our bread comes from that farm."

"That must be convenient for the residents in the villas," Lydia had said, wondering why her father thought this land presented a test for her heart.

Eumenes had shaken his head. "They despise that little farm."

"Why?" she had asked, astonished.

"Because in the winter and early spring it is barren and unsightly. Worse. Right about now, the old man starts to apply fertilizer to the soil, and it stinks! That's what the owners of the villas have to bear with. The stench of manure and the unsightly appearance of the bare ground."

"But you can't have a harvest without fertilizer and plain dirt!"

Her father had looked at her the way he sometimes did, with unblinking eyes that seemed to delve into her deepest heart. "Life is like this valley, Lydia. You can be like the owners of the villa, wanting only the beautiful end result. The good things of life: its fruitful seasons, its rich harvest. Or you can be like the farmer, bearing with the stinky seasons in order to produce a harvest."

Lydia pressed her father's letter against her lips. She was in the barren season now. The one whose stench made your eyes water. And from beyond the grave her father was prodding her for a decision. Which did she propose to be? The farmer or the owner of the villa?

Lydia gritted her teeth. "I will be a farmer."

TWENTY-TWO

From the fruit of their lips people are
filled with good things, and the work of
their hands brings them reward.
PROVERBS 12:14, NIV

Thyatira lay on a main highway linking two
river valleys. But there were no harbors in the
beautiful Hermus valley. To go to Philippi, she
had to find her way to Troas and, from there,
purchase passage on a ship to Neapolis, the
closest harbor town to her destination.

This was no simple voyage. A woman alone,
without servants, without the protection of a
father or husband or brother, traveling long
distances, presented a vulnerable target for any
vagabond, not to mention the ordinary evils of
travel such as sickness and drowning. Atreus
had recommended the owner of a particular
caravan—"somewhat honest and not entirely
reprobate"—which was not high praise but
apparently the best Lydia could expect. She
traipsed all the way to the market in search of the
man but found that he was away on business for
the week.

She breathed a sigh of relief. She knew she
could not take advantage of Atreus's friendship

and hospitality forever. Still, the thought of delaying her inevitable journey felt more like a reprieve than an inconvenience.

She was lost in dire thoughts of bandits and murderers as she trudged back to the inn, her head full of dread as she considered the many things that could go wrong, when a plaintive voice drew her back to the land of living.

"Help me, mistress, for the sake of mercy."

Years later, as she relived that moment over again and again, she could not explain what made her stop. Beggars were a common sight in Thyatira, so common that one barely took note of their plight. They were like the trees growing in the plains, like the wilting flowers of the wilderness. They melted into the background of consciousness.

But the voice, the words, something in the beggar's tone, an odd discrepancy in her manner, drew Lydia. She was a young woman about the same age as Lydia, with wide eyes the color of rich honey. In spite of the dirt and the bug bites, Lydia thought her face pleasant. A wave of pity filled her. The girl's clothes were not the typical rags of a beggar; though faded from overuse and covered with filth, Lydia could see that once they had been of good quality.

The honey-colored eyes, too large for the emaciated face, stared at Lydia with an odd expression. Humble and yet defiant, as if the world had not managed to shatter the spirit that had been brought so low by circumstances.

This could be her fate, Lydia thought, if she were unable to make her way in Philippi. Her resources were limited. A year from now, she could be the one lying in the dust of the road and begging strangers for a loaf of bread or a shred of mercy.

"What is your name?" Lydia asked, unable to walk away.

"Rebekah, mistress."

"That is a strange name."

"It is Jewish."

Lydia nodded. A sizable community of Jews lived in Thyatira. Her father's colleague Avraham was one such. "I once visited Jerusalem when I was younger. I remember it well."

The girl's visage came to life. "You have been to Jerusalem, mistress? Did you visit the Temple? The outer court where Gentiles are allowed to visit?"

"I only passed by it and never entered. The walls had crenellations on top and were made of yellowish stone, which turned golden in the light of sunset. Have you ever been there?"

Rebekah shook her head. "My father went every year. But I was never allowed to accompany him."

Lydia, who had accompanied her father every-where, thought this a strange response. "How is it that Thyatira has treated you so ill, Rebekah?"

" 'What region of the earth is not full of our calamities?' I cannot blame Thyatira for my sorrows, mistress."

Lydia's eyes widened. "I have never known a beggar who could quote Virgil and with such pure accent. You sound more like a scholar than a beggar. Can you read and write, then?"

"Yes."

Lydia tipped her head down. "Are you hungry?" The words left her mouth before she had an opportunity to think them through.

"Starved."

"Come. I will feed you. Today, at least, you shall eat well."

Master Atreus raised a thick, gray brow as he saw Lydia's guest. She shrugged. "This is Rebekah. She can quote Virgil."

Master Atreus's other eyebrow rose to join the first. He shook his head and turned away. "Keep your door open in case she decides to rob you. That way, I can come faster when you scream."

Rebekah turned red and dropped her head. "The Lord forbids us from stealing. I would never do that."

"She is Jewish," Lydia said to Atreus in clarification. The thick eyebrows lowered this time and he gave a short nod.

"Don't mind him," Lydia said. "He is only

151

jealous. He can't quote a single word of Virgil. He is good with Euripides, though."

Lydia offered the girl a seat on the couch. She gave a quick shake of her head. "I am filthy, mistress. Best I sit on the floor."

Her manners were not those of a street urchin, Lydia noticed. She fetched the bowl of lentils and onions left over from noon, found the loaf of bread she had not eaten, added olive oil to a chipped plate, and placed the meager offering before the girl. The food was cold, the bread stale. It seemed to matter little to Rebekah, who stared at the dishes, her eyes welling up.

She said a quick Hebrew prayer before taking a bite from the bread. Her eyes drifted closed. Lydia, whose cooking skills left something to be desired, gave an amused smile. She had finally found a truly appreciative consumer of her culinary talents. All it required, apparently, was starvation.

When she was finished, her strange guest stacked her bowl and plate neatly, as if they were made of glass rather than chipped pottery. "I can wash these if you wish," she said.

Lydia waved a hand in the air. "I will take them to the courtyard later."

Rebekah rose to her feet. "May the Lord bless you for your generosity," she said as she turned.

Lydia realized she intended to leave. "Wait!"

The girl turned back. An unspoken question

stamped the lines of her face. A question Lydia could not answer. Why had she asked the girl to wait? Curiosity? Pity? Compassion? She did not know what urged her. Only that she could not allow the girl to return to the streets of Thyatira without a measure of help.

She took a deep breath. "Would you like to stay here tonight? Just for tonight. This is not my home. I cannot offer you a more permanent shelter."

Rebekah grew utterly still. "Thank you, mistress," she whispered. Then she said, her voice thin and quivery, "Are you certain? I smell bad."

She did. The rank odor of someone who had gone without a proper wash for long days and even weeks. Lydia realized that she was shamed by her own condition. More than physical discomfort, her state of uncleanness was a humiliation to her soul.

"Do you want to take a bath?" she asked. Who was saying these things through her lips? She had not intended to speak those words. And yet, no sooner had they emerged from her mouth than she was searching for a few bronze quadrantes. "Take these. You can go to the public baths. They are still open. Return here when you are finished."

Rebekah sat frozen, the coins in her hand. "You will grow weary of it," she said.

"Of what?"

"Of me thanking and blessing you for your kindness."

"Probably. Don't take too long. Atreus likes to go to bed early."

At the door the girl hesitated. "Was that your supper? Did I eat your food? I am sorry I was such a glutton and left nothing."

Lydia shook her head. "Anyone who can eat my cooking with such obvious enjoyment is welcome to it." She sat on the couch and stretched aching feet. "I have little appetite and only cooked to keep Atreus happy. You did me a favor eating the food before it started to grow strange things." She rubbed her back, which had grown sore from her long walk. "One more thing. My name is Lydia. Not mistress."

"Yes, mistress."

Lydia half expected the girl not to return. She would probably think of better things to do with coins than take a bath. But she came back after an hour. Without layers of dirt marring her skin, Lydia saw that she was remarkably lovely. A narrow nose, shapely lips, arched brows over eyes that were as deep as woods in autumn.

She frowned as the light of the lamp illuminated the girl's tunic. "Your garments are soaked!" Lydia said.

"I washed them. Now everything is clean." Her

smile glowed, though her teeth chattered. She opened her hand. "There was a little money left after I paid for the bath. I bought you this. It is sweetened with honey." In her spotless palm she held a rounded loaf of bread.

Unexpectedly, Lydia felt her throat clog with tears. She took the bread, still warm from the baker's, and held it as if it were a delicate treasure. It was no different from a thousand honey loaves sold in Thyatira every day. She thought of Rebekah—homeless, hungry, friendless Rebekah—who had bought the bread and, instead of saving it for herself, offered it to another.

Lydia bit into the rough wheat and found it sweeter than anything she had ever tasted. For the first time since her father's death, she enjoyed the taste of food. "Thank you," she said.

The girl slept on the floor that night, a blanket for her mattress, folded over to cover her against the night cold. Lydia would have offered her Eumenes's old pallet, but she suspected that a Jew would find it unclean. Her father had died on that pallet. What Lydia held as precious, his last resting place in the world of the living, Rebekah would find repugnant.

Wet clothes were a different matter, however. "Get rid of those soaking things. You can wear my old tunic for the night. I don't need another person dying of an inflammation of the lung."

"Another person?"

"There is a plague of it in this place. Or at least, my father died from it, and that is plague enough for me."

In the morning, by the time Lydia opened sleepy eyes, Rebekah had already risen, changed into her own clothes, now dry, ground flour with the hand mill, made dough, and prepared sufficient fresh bread to feed Atreus as well. She must have moved as silently as a breeze. Lydia had heard nothing.

"Master Atreus said to call him when you awoke; he said he would bring the cheese and olives for the morning meal."

"When did you see him?"

"I went to fetch fresh water from the well so you could wash when you awoke. He was downstairs, ready to interrogate me with a hundred questions. I gave him a piece of warm bread, and that seemed to assuage his curiosity."

Lydia smiled. "You better call him then, before he breaks the door down in search of his breakfast. The woman who cooks at the inn does not arrive until it is time to prepare the noonday meal."

Atreus dropped off cheese and olives before picking up a thick loaf of bread and hurrying out again. "Large party arriving today. No time to loiter," he said through a full mouth. He

156

stopped halfway down the steps, turned, and yelled, "Good bread," before disappearing from view.

Rebekah laughed. "He likes his food, I think."

Lydia, replete and reasonably rested from a few hours of unbroken sleep, studied her unusual guest. "How came a young woman like you to be cast out on the streets of the city? Did you lose your father?"

"My father lives."

"Is he in prison?"

"No. He has a successful trade in bronze. With the garrison always full of soldiers, the demand for bronze is high."

Lydia leaned forward. "I don't understand. Your father is alive. He enjoys success. Then how came you to such a pass?" Lydia, whose own father had been a lion of protection, laying down everything he had for the sake of her contentment, could not fathom the discrepancy in the girl's story. Fathers meant safety. Shelter. Stability.

Rebekah's face turned into a wooden mask. "He asked me to leave his house and never return. He said I was no longer his daughter."

"He disowned you?"

"Yes, mistress."

Lydia could not conceive of a circumstance that would prompt her own father to cast her out of his house and heart. What had the girl done? How horrible must her crime have been? What secrets did those innocent eyes, looking at her like great bruises, hold? What monstrous violence hid in their depths?

Lydia stiffened. She wondered if Atreus could arrive fast enough if she screamed, and as subtly as she could, she increased her distance from the girl.

TWENTY-THREE

I will rejoice and be glad in your steadfast love,
because you have seen my affliction;
you have known the distress of my soul,
and you have not delivered me
into the hand of the enemy.
PSALM 31:7-8

As if reading her thoughts, Rebekah said, "Do you want me to leave?"

Something about her expression made Lydia go still. A touch of despair, of helpless anger. Of anguish. Lydia had seen that look before, on her father's face, when he had been wrongly accused and convicted. "Not yet," she said. "Tell me what you did."

"I refused to marry the man my father chose for me."

Lydia blinked. "Perhaps you'd better tell me the whole story. Start from the beginning. How did you come to be so learned?"

Rebekah sat down slowly and tucked her legs to one side with neat precision. "When my younger brother was of an age to be tutored, my father hired the best scholar in the province of Asia. Benjamin rarely sat still, and his tutor, a young man more at home with scrolls than children, could not manage him. So my father sent me into the schoolroom to be Benjamin's keeper while he learned. My poor brother had little liking for books. He wanted to be a soldier. He found the hours of instruction a torment and could not wait to be released at the end of the day.

"I, on the other hand, soaked up the scholar's instruction like a parched land. I was not supposed to be learning anything. My father wished nothing but that I keep Benjamin in hand. Instead, I learned Greek and Latin. I read Homer and Virgil and Herodotus. I discovered a world full of wisdom and beauty.

"The scholar—a Jew, as tradition demanded—instructed my brother on the Scriptures as well as on philosophy and literature. I had never heard anything like what he taught. He expounded upon the Lord like a poet who knows the mystery of words. He breathed life into the Law. It was like being dead and coming alive. I had heard of the Lord since birth, attended synagogue, learned my prayers. But I had never known the majesty of God.

"The tutor, noting my thirst and potential, spent more time with me than with Benjamin. Not knowing my father well, he boasted to him one day of my accomplishments. He told him that he had never known a quicker mind. I would have warned him if I had known of his intention."

"Warned him of what?" Lydia asked, puzzled.

"Educating girls is a waste of time to my father. Worse. A dangerous undertaking, for filling a woman's mind with knowledge will likely corrupt an already-inferior soul."

Lydia grimaced. "Inferior soul?"

"My father has little respect for our sex. Every morning, in his prayers, he thanks God that he was not born a woman. Women, as far as he is concerned, only serve one useful purpose: to breed male children.

"He was furious that I had received so much instruction. Imagine the offense! His son had barely learned to read and write while his daughter proved an adept scholar."

"He was not proud of you?"

"He whipped me until I could not leave my bed for a week. My brother's tutor was dismissed, of course, and a new man hired. I was ordered to keep my distance from the schoolroom after that."

Lydia winced. "I am sorry."

"The chamber where my brother studied had a curious construction. Above it lay a cramped room where few liked to go, for it tended to become stuffy in summer and freezing in winter. It had one advantage: sound carried from my brother's room with absolute clarity. No one had paid mind to this oddity. Few spent enough time in the room to even notice it.

"I asked my mother if I could complete some

161

of my tasks there. Sewing, weaving, darning. You never saw such an industrious girl. I came out of that room with armfuls of work finished. Of course, in the background of my very feminine labors was the nasal droning of the new scholar. Thus, I continued to learn. The years passed in peace, and I knew contentment though I had little freedom."

A trickle of admiration welled up in Lydia for the girl. She had not only survived in that oppressive environment; she had managed to find a way to prosper. "Were you discovered?"

Rebekah twisted her fingers until they turned white. "No one ever knew about the education I secretly received. My life changed by different means. Father had a friend, Elihu, who visited our home sometimes and brought his wife when he came. Elihu had amassed a fortune but had no children.

"His wife, Bayla, spent her time with my mother and me when she visited. We would not dream of mixing company with the men. I did not know her well, for unless pressed, Bayla rarely spoke a word. There was something about her that reminded me of a terrorized animal. Her eyes darted about as if in a haze of dread, and she jumped at every sound. Bayla had a lot of accidents."

"Accidents?" Lydia asked, confused.

"Accidents. She always had bruises because she

fell or knocked into things. Once, the bruise on her arm was shaped like four fingers. I asked if she had fallen into someone's hand by accident."

"Her husband beat her?"

"Severely. Elihu was a cruel man."

Caught up in Rebekah's story, Lydia found herself holding her breath. Half an hour before, she had wondered if her guest had committed an unspeakable crime. Now she sat spellbound as if at the feet of Aesop himself, hearing one of his remarkable fables. She thought of Jason, who in spite of his youth and charm had proven also to be a cruel man.

"Was Elihu young and handsome?"

"No. He was old and ugly. A tormenter without mercy. I did not know then that my future was inexorably entwined with his wife's. I pitied her lot in life, not understanding that the same fate awaited me.

"Last year, Bayla died. I think she simply lost her hold on hope and slipped away. As our great king David put it, 'her life was spent with sorrow.'

"When she died, no one seemed to even notice that she was no longer in this world. No one mourned her. Missed her. Elihu cast about, searching for a new wife. A new chance to have sons."

"Oh no," Lydia muttered.

Rebekah nodded. "Why his eye fell upon me, I

cannot say. But my father had drawn the marriage contracts before he even spoke to me."

Lydia expelled her breath. "Did he not know how Elihu had treated his wife?"

"He knew. It did not matter. The marriage would bring many advantages to our house. My mother agreed as she always did."

Silence filled the room. Lydia wondered how a young woman might survive the brutality of such a coldhearted father along with the disinterest of such a weak mother.

"I begged and pleaded," Rebekah said into the silence. "I reasoned. It made no difference. My father would not be moved. In the end, I simply refused to give my consent. He had me locked in my workroom without food, thinking to break me. Of course he did not know the secret comfort I received in that chamber.

"That week, my brother's tutor was teaching him the Psalms. I lay weak with hunger while the Word of God washed over me. It gave me courage and held me together when I thought I might fall apart. The Lord became my food. He became my comfort. His Word became my prayer.

"I remember one morning after a sleepless night, I cried out in my heart: *My enemy is too great for me, Lord. I cannot bear the weight of this affliction.* At that very moment, as if in answer to my silent prayer, my brother's tutor cited a psalm of David, his voice rising into my room as clear as an angel's song: 'I will rejoice and be glad in your steadfast love, because you have seen my affliction; you have known the distress of my soul, and you have not delivered me into the hand of the enemy.'

"I knew that day that the Lord heard my cry; he cared for my distress. I knew that he would deliver me. In life or in death, I would taste of his freedom.

"The next day, my father resorted to flogging me. I told him it made little difference, for if I agreed to marry Elihu, then my new husband would flog me every day. I should have held my tongue, I suppose."

Lydia thought of the courage it had taken to stand up to such a man and found herself looking at Rebekah with respect instead of pity. Eumenes would have held this girl in high esteem, she thought, for facing so much fear without giving in to it. "That's when he threw you out?" she asked, her voice gentle.

Rebekah nodded. "Elihu became furious when he discovered that I was unwilling to marry him. My father said I had shamed him before his friends and cast me out of the house, proclaiming me a stranger to him."

"How did you eat?"

"For the first few weeks, I lingered near our home. I knew where they kept the trash pile before emptying it in the dumps outside the city, and the servants would sneak food for me in there. I thought the sight of me might soften my father's heart. He did not waver. After three weeks he threatened to have me arrested and thrown into prison if I refused to move away from our old neighborhood. It was no empty threat, for the very sight of me was an embarrassment to my family. So I moved."

Lydia shook her head. "I don't understand how you have survived."

Rebekah smiled. There was no hint of bitterness in that smile. No resentment. It held a world of peace. "The Lord has cared for me. He has held me in the palm of his hand."

TWENTY-FOUR

A friend loves at all times,
and a brother is born for adversity.
PROVERBS 17:17

"Did he hold you in the palm of his hand when your father tried to force you to marry a brutal man? Or when he renounced you and threw you out of his home? I mean no disrespect, Rebekah, but if this is an example of what your god's palm looks like, I would rather be under his foot."

Astonishingly, Rebekah laughed. "He does not always keep us *from* danger, but he preserves us *in* danger. I have known hardship, but my heart has felt secure in his steadfast love."

Lydia gave a slow nod. "I think I know what you mean. My father was like that. He could not always protect me from harm. But even as disaster visited our family, I knew I was safe as long as I had his love."

"Your father told you he loved you?"

"Often."

"I cannot imagine my father saying such a thing to me. I think his jaw might break if he attempted it."

By tacit agreement, Rebekah spent the next night at Atreus's house. And the next.

"You might as well stay this whole week. I can do nothing to arrange for my trip until the caravan owner returns," Lydia said.

As they spent their hours together, Lydia found herself divulging her own story to her guest. She held nothing back, not even the shame of her unrequited feelings for Jason.

"God has preserved us both from very evil men," Rebekah said.

"I don't feel very preserved," Lydia said, though she felt a profound relief at the simple acceptance in Rebekah's words. She had not judged Lydia's folly.

"We have both lost our homes and our families. We are both cast adrift from all we knew," Rebekah said. " 'Better times perhaps await us who are now wretched.' "

"Virgil again. Shouldn't you be quoting the poets and philosophers of your people?"

Rebekah smiled. " 'Fear not, for you will not be ashamed; be not confounded, for you will not be disgraced; for you will forget the shame of your youth.' The prophet Isaiah."

The prophet's words carried a weight that even Virgil's prose lacked, Lydia had to admit. They contained a promise that pierced her heart like a sharpened arrow, for shame and disgrace were her constant companions since her final encounter with Jason. Would there come a day when she could be free of their piercing bondage?

"But isn't that a promise for your people only?" she asked.

Rebekah's face went very still. "I think," she said after a long silence, "it is a promise for all who seek the Lord."

At the end of the week, Lydia returned to the market in search of the caravan owner. This time she did not go alone. Rebekah followed along, like a faithful servant who had been with her since childhood. Her presence brought a comfort that steadied Lydia's wavering world.

But it also brought a thorn.

Every day, she felt a deepening attachment to the girl. It seemed to her as though Fortune had thrust a true friend into her life at a time when all her attachments had been robbed or lost. Before Rebekah, Lydia had been drowning in an ocean of dark isolation, pounded by the utter loneliness of her life.

Her father had bid her to start afresh. To make a new life. How was a woman alone to accomplish such a thing? She could be swallowed by the dragon teeth of a thousand misfortunes before she even arrived in Philippi. Fear consumed her like a raging fire when she thought of it.

Rebekah had nothing worldly to give. No fortune, no useful connections, no stability of her own. Yet she offered a treasure greater than all this. She offered loyalty and friendship. She brought with her a deep well of wisdom that could anchor a flailing soul to something deep and secure. Something she called *the Lord,* but Lydia thought it was Rebekah herself.

Her pace slackened as Lydia realized that every step toward the market brought her one step closer to losing Rebekah.

Worse. She was condemning Rebekah to an unimaginable life of misery. What would become of her when Lydia left? Thrown back into the streets of Thyatira, how long would she last?

They were both silent, wrestling with worries that seemed to have no remedy. When they found the owner of the caravan, Lydia asked when the next group of travelers would leave.

"In a week," said the man, his cheeks puffed with a mouthful of dates. "I will bring you as far as Troas. From there, you must arrange for your own ship to Neapolis, though I can give you the names of a few good captains and trustworthy vessels."

"How much will that cost?" Lydia asked.

A fortune, she thought when she heard the sum. She added the numbers in her head: the price of the caravan to Troas plus the journey on the boat. And then she doubled it. The cost for two passengers instead of one. She had kept a careful tally of her remaining coins and valuables. She knew to the last copper coin how much she had. If she sold everything except for the valuable tools of her trade, she would be able to pay the passage for two.

But then she would arrive in Philippi with nothing. Nothing to help her start a small workshop.

"I will purchase two places on your caravan," she said.

When Rebekah found out what Lydia had done, her eyes grew round, not with wondrous joy but with horror. "No, mistress! You cannot make such a sacrifice. You cannot hazard your future for my sake."

"I can if I wish," Lydia said, her jaw set at a mulish angle. In truth, she had felt more at peace since she had made the decision than she had for many weeks. She had been her father's caretaker for much of her life. With him gone, she felt adrift and uncertain. Rebekah not only offered her friendship; she also provided her with a purpose. Another person to look after. Another life to protect.

"Mistress Lydia, how could I live with myself if your future were destroyed because of me?"

"You underestimate yourself. I need your help. I cannot run a workshop alone. I will teach you my trade, and you shall be my apprentice. You are intelligent enough to help me in a hundred ways."

"You cannot eat intelligence," Rebekah said tartly. "Believe me. I should know."

Lydia cracked a rare smile. "You can with me."

Atreus, upon hearing her decision that evening, called her rash and told her she had lost her senses. "How will you afford the expenses of a new workshop with so little money left?"

"You helped me because my father helped you," Lydia said. "Now it is my turn to help another."

"You should claim to be a widow," Atreus advised as the day of their departure drew near. "Even the shadow of a dead husband provides some protection, as well as greater freedom once you arrive in Philippi. Not many doors will open to an unmarried young woman. Whoever heard of a young girl in trade? It cannot be done. Not even if I write you a letter of introduction as your guardian. No one would trust anything you produce. At least an imaginary dead husband would provide you with a measure of respectability."

Lydia noticed Rebekah's expression. "Their god does not allow lying," she told Atreus.

"This hardly counts as a lie!" Atreus protested. "It harms no one and helps two unprotected women."

Rebekah rubbed her arms. "What happens when the people of Philippi find out that Lydia made a false claim? If she can lie about being married, she can lie about the quality of her purple, or the worth of her merchandise. Small lies can cause as much damage as great ones."

Lydia could see the sense in both arguments. "It would be almost impossible to set up a workshop as an unmarried woman. No one would care how honest I was. They simply would ignore my merchandise."

"The Lord will make a way for you. He will open doors you could not carve with your own strength or craftiness."

Lydia exhaled a deep breath. "Just as he made a way for you when I first saw you, homeless and hungry?"

Rebekah grinned. "Exactly like that. For he sent you to me, and look at me now, bound for Philippi and a new life. My family disowned me, and yet I have been given a friend who is closer than a sister."

If Lydia gave in to Rebekah's urging, it was not because she trusted in her god, she told herself. She had been as betrayed by the gods as by Dione and Jason. Whether Rebekah's Lord proved superior to her own pantheon of deities remained to be seen. She had little trust to offer the god of the Jews. She chose not to lie, in the end, because she knew deceit of any kind would torment her friend. Their lives were now irrevocably tied together. If Lydia lied, Rebekah would perforce have to lie as well. To protect Rebekah, Lydia told the truth, though she worried that it would cost her all hope of success.

TWENTY-FIVE

For you bless the righteous, O LORD;
you cover him with favor as with a shield.
PSALM 5:12

Lydia knew next to nothing about the Aegean Sea and worried that since it was autumn, they might get caught in stormy weather. To her relief, two different ship captains assured them that unlike in the Mediterranean, the winds attacked the Aegean Sea most fiercely in the summer months, and they had already missed the worst of the storms.

They purchased passage on a peacock-blue grain ship made of old oak. She and Rebekah joined about twenty other passengers and numberless sacks of wheat on board. The captain of the ship, a Greek man with long, leathery cheeks and guarded eyes, greeted them as they came on board.

"Traveling alone?" he asked.

Lydia nodded, her shoulders tensing.

His gaze moved from Lydia to Rebekah. "I have two daughters your age. Sit over there, and stay out of trouble." He pointed to a shaded corner of the ship, almost hidden by large sacks of grain.

The girls scrambled to obey. Less than an hour later, before the ship had a chance to move, one of the sailors found them. He was a large man with an expansive naked chest that glistened with sweat.

"Look what I found!" he cried with glee, his mouth breaking into a big grin.

The captain seemed to appear out of thin air. "Leave them alone," he roared. "And tell the others the same." His dark brows drew together like a thundercloud. The sailor strutted off. After that, no one bothered them.

"I told you the Lord would provide," Rebekah chirped with glee.

As predicted, the trade winds remained calm, and by nightfall, they were anchored off the mountainous island of Samothrace, where they had their dinner and slept for a few hours. In the morning, they pulled up anchor and returned to the Aegean.

The wind carried with it the taste of brine and the smell of fish and kelp. Lydia's skin grew damp with sea spray and turned golden in the autumn sunlight. By early afternoon they arrived in Neapolis.

Their feet were finally touching Macedonian soil. Now that the threat of drowning and molestation by sailors had passed, Lydia had to face the fact that she had arrived at a strange city with barely any money in her pockets.

She and Rebekah, alongside a few other passengers from their ship, strolled past the cisterns of Neapolis and made their way to Philippi. They traveled on the wide, paved road called the Egnatian Way, which took them directly to their destination. The road into Philippi was uphill all the way, and Lydia found herself panting after an hour. Before nightfall, they could see the walls of the city twinkling like gold in the fading light. A large gate stood in the middle; it hung wide open.

Philippi was larger than Thyatira and far more sophisticated. Lydia and Rebekah, gaping with wonder, found an affordable inn where they could stay, thanks to their ship captain's recommendation.

They spent several days making themselves familiar with Philippi, walking through the open market—which the Philippians called the *agora* in the manner of Rome—gazing at the magnificent buildings of the forum, and asking local merchants about life in the affluent city. It was a privileged world, exempt from Roman taxes because the town residents had been given Roman citizenship as well as rights. They clung to Latin as their official language, though most spoke enough Greek to accommodate visitors.

"Latin!" Lydia said with a moan. She had a tolerable grasp of the language, though nothing like Rebekah's pure, scholarly knowledge. Greek was the language she felt at home with, the one she had learned from birth. She would have to improve her Latin if she wanted to find acceptance in Philippi.

The city was governed by two men, both of whom hailed from the hallowed courts of Rome itself. They bore the dignified title of *praetor*, the common address of *magistrate* not being good enough for the refined Philippians. If you could not reside in Rome, then you might as well live in Philippi.

For almost a hundred years, the city had retained its military heritage, situated as it was strategically on a great highway. But it had other unique qualities.

"Money should have its own temple here," Rebekah said. "The people seem to worship it most diligently."

Lydia agreed. Merchants sold every imaginable commodity, as well as what seemed beyond the realm of ordinary human ingenuity. Gold, pearls, silk, fresh fruits, spices from the farthest corners of the world, slaves. There was little you could not obtain in Philippi if you had the means. And the people liked their purple, Lydia noted with satisfaction.

Rebekah said, wide-eyed, "Have you noticed, some buildings have glass in their windows? Glass! The one thing that seems scarce in this part of the empire is people of Jewish heritage. And you can forget about a synagogue."

Her tone was lighthearted as she said the words, but Lydia noticed the drooping shoulders. She was not the only one struggling with loss. Rebekah had her own share of grief to contend with. One day at a time, they would help each other persevere, Lydia determined.

For all its grandeur, the city had its limitations. Once, when ambling through the agora, examining the impressive merchandise, they came across a public latrine. It was large and well maintained. But when the girls tried to step over the threshold, a woman barred their way with an outstretched forearm. "Men only," she said with a sneer.

When they had walked a little way, Rebekah whispered, "What are women supposed to do?"

"Hold it until they get home." The girls looked at one another and quickened their steps.

On the morning of their fourth day in the city, the young women went to the enormous public baths, washed themselves until their skin shone red from vigorous scrubbing, put fragrant oil on their hair, donned their best clothes, and, thus groomed and prepared, presented themselves before the old Roman general.

Manius Antonius Varus received them after he had read the letter from Eumenes. He was a balding man of late middle age who had maintained the physical fitness of his early training in spite of many years of retirement.

"So your father is dead. I am sorry to hear it. He was an exceptional craftsman, and more importantly, a good man."

"Thank you, master." Lydia felt the threat of tears at the mention of her father and stared at the marble floor for a moment. Taking a grip on the brewing emotional storm, she forced herself to go on in an even tone. "In his last hours, he thought of you and asked me to deliver this gift into your hands." Lydia gave him the stunning length of purple linen her father had chosen for the general.

"Ah. Like a poem." Varus unfolded the fabric and caressed it with appreciative fingers. "Your father's letter mentions that you are his equal in every way when it comes to creating purple."

"He taught me everything he knew."

"And yet you are a mere girl, not even married." Varus threw up both his hands. "Your guardian a world away in Thyatira. Bring me what you have, and I will find you generous buyers for the sake of Eumenes. But it would be madness to set you up in a shop. I cannot do it."

Lydia blinked. It took her a moment to realize she had been dismissed. "But, General Varus—"

The general held up a finger, forestalling her words. "It is impossible. You would only fail. Whoever heard of an unmarried girl in trade, on her own?" He pulled open a purse and extracted a few denarii. "In appreciation for your gift. And there will be more if you can bring me purple like this. Just none for a workshop. Put that idea out of your head, my girl. It is foolhardy. I blame your father for encouraging you in this reckless venture. No one in Philippi would accept you."

Lydia clutched the coins, trying to quiet the clamor in her heart. With her small nest egg poured into travel expenses, she had counted on the general's help for the workshop. She did not know how to proceed now. No workshop meant she could not produce purple. What was she supposed to sell him if she had no dye?

The young women walked out of Varus's sprawling villa in silence, each struggling with her own dark thoughts. They had walked almost a full league when a running youth hailed them, panting in his effort to catch up. "Mistress! Mistress!"

The young women stopped, puzzled.

"Lady Aemilia bids that you return to the villa. She wishes to have a word with you."

"Lady Aemilia?" Lydia asked, confused. The general, as far as she knew, had no wife.

"The general's mother. She lives with him."

Lydia nodded, and they followed the young man back to the house. Likely the old lady had seen the linen she had brought Varus and wanted a length for herself. Too bad Lydia could not provide her any. She had sold most of her stores of purple to pay for their passage to Philippi and had no means of creating more.

If Varus was approaching old age, his mother, Aemilia, had crossed that bridge long before and entered an ancient realm few lived to see. She had more wrinkles on her face than hair on her head. Yet she looked at Lydia with a sharp, birdlike intelligence. Leaning to pick up a round, white fruit from the gold plate before her, she gestured for the women to sit.

As she bit into her fruit, Lydia realized with some astonishment that the old woman was biting a peeled onion as if it were an apple. Aemilia lifted the onion, juices dripping down her hand. "Always loved them. Garlic, too. When I was younger, my husband forbade me from eating them. They made me stink, he said. Now I am old and rich, and a widow, and I can do whatever I wish. I still have my own teeth, which is a fair accomplishment at my age. So I eat what I please."

Lydia nodded, unsure how to respond.

The lady crooked a finger, signaling Lydia to bend closer. She fingered Lydia's tunic with hands drenched in onion juice.

"Is this your work?" she said.

"Yes, my lady."

"Your own? Not your father's?"

"My own."

She nodded. "It is excellent." She turned to look

out her window into the courtyard. "My spies told me of your visit to my son. I went to see him after you left. He showed me your father's letter and the linen you brought him. Exquisite work, that piece."

Lydia bowed her head in thanks.

"My son is a fool."

"Mistress?"

"He is a good man. But his vision is limited. When he looks at you, all he sees is a young woman. And that's the end. Do you know what I see?"

Lydia shook her head. "No, mistress."

"I see potential. You want a workshop?"

"It's my most cherished dream."

"They say young Caligula has promised to appoint his favorite horse, Incitatus, as a consul when he becomes emperor. I have met the Roman consuls; believe me when I say the horse would be an improvement. I think if a horse can be a consul in Rome, then a young girl should be able to own a shop in Philippi."

Lydia would have laughed out loud, except she suspected it would be an act of treason.

"What are your terms? I do not have a lot of time to waste, in case you failed to observe the significance of these wrinkles. I am not looking for long-term investments, you understand?"

Lydia's mouth hung open for a moment. "What *are* you looking for, mistress?"

The general's mother laughed. It was a sur-
prisingly youthful sound. "I am looking for a
little diversion, and I suspect you shall provide
it. I will enjoy proving my son wrong. He is too
puffed up with his own importance, as are most
of the successful men in this city. In this whole
empire, from what I have seen. I find it annoying.
It will do Varus good to recognize his fallibility
upon occasion, particularly in regard to women.
Here is our bargain, then: you will succeed.
Understand? Failure is not part of my plans."

Lydia would have gulped, except her throat had
grown too parched to produce any spittle. "I will
not fail you."

"Mind, I want my money back within the year."
Aemilia bit into her onion again with strong,
healthy teeth, splattering onion juice everywhere, including on Lydia. "And a lifetime of
purple goods at half the price in your store." She
shrugged. "But then, look at me. How long am I
likely to live? So that should hardly be a deterrent
to our bargain."

Lydia straightened the corner of her shawl.
"Two pieces per annum at half price. The gods
have given you the gift of long life, my lady. You
will likely outlive me and Zeus himself. I will be
bankrupt within six months if I set no limit on
this bargain."

Aemilia slapped her knee and laughed. "I accept
your terms. You may call me patroness."

TWENTY-SIX

Better a small serving of vegetables with love
than a fattened calf with hatred.
PROVERBS 15:17, NIV

The shop was not much larger than a vegetable cart. No tidy shelves, no smooth counters, no colorful mosaics brightened its stark outlines. But it belonged to Lydia. And for the past seven months it had been gaining more attention and drawing new customers every day. At night, she and Rebekah would bar the door with the fat crack running down the middle, roll out their beds, and sleep on the floor. They ate bread and water, with wild herbs when they could find them, for the first three months after starting their venture so that they could afford the materials they needed for making Eumenes's purple dye. After that, the shop paid enough to allow for a few eggs, olives, beans, and upon occasion even a fish.

They sold only wool, dyed in purple, mostly in the form of yarn that women could weave at home. Between them, Rebekah and Lydia had started weaving lengths of fabric, which disappeared from the shop almost as soon as they produced them.

They could not afford other merchandise yet. But with careful management, Lydia hoped to expand to linen fabrics by the following year, when she had finished paying off her debt to Aemilia.

The workshop consumed all of her hours and most of her thoughts. Days would go by when Lydia would not once think of Jason. When she did, the familiar shame and bitterness rose to the surface, choking her. Time could hide the scars. It did nothing to heal them, however. They remained caustic and bleeding, hidden under mountains of work and the passing of hours, still wielding power.

Lydia ground her teeth, banishing Jason from her mind. Brushing a length of dark purple until it shone, she hung it from the wall, arranging its folds artfully. Rebekah had left early in the morning to purchase more bushels of wool. Soon they would have to stay up all night to weave in order to keep up with the demand for their goods.

A man strolled into the shop. He was in his middle years, with a generous belly covered by the folds of a plain toga. Lydia noted the creamy quality of the wool, its uniform weft and warp, which lent the garment a delicate sheen. His short-sleeved tunic was made of soft, rich linen. Running a hand over the fabric she had just hung on the wall, he examined it with the expert movements of one familiar with textiles. Lydia noticed that the skin of his fingers was smooth and white, with a faint trace of blue near the tips.

She smiled.

In spite of the modesty of her shop, she must have made enough impact on the market to rouse the interest of her competition. He had come to appraise her work for himself.

"Did your father make this?" he asked. "Or your husband?"

"I made them. And this?" She pointed to his purple-edged cloak. "Did you make that?"

He smiled, his eyes crinkling. "Was I that obvious?"

Lydia shrugged. "Clearly you know your textiles. Your clothes are elegant; your hands are too soft to have done any labor. Not for years. You don't do the work yourself. But you still love it." She pointed at the tips of his fingers with her chin. "You still dally with the dyeing process, enough to get your skin stained."

He laughed. "Clever. Of course I already knew that. Never seen purple so fine. What is your accent?"

Lydia skirted the question. "You Romans and your Latin. It's not civilized to make a language so difficult. I will have an accent until the day I die."

"You must admit it is a beautiful language. Living in Philippi is like living in a little piece of Rome. And you did not answer my question."

Lydia sat on the corner of a vat. "Next you will be asking me how I make my purple. My name is Lydia."

"I am Gaius Antiochus Rufus. Everyone knows my shop. You should come and visit me one day. In fact, you should come and work for me. I will pay you an outrageous salary, Mistress Lydia of Nowhere. You won't have to stay in this hovel. You will wear silks and linens and eat lamb and goose every day."

Antiochus. The middle name he had inherited from his family sounded Greek, though his cognomen, Rufus, was a common Latin name. The toga he wore marked him as a Roman citizen, like all the residents of Philippi whose roots went back several generations. So he hailed from Greek heritage originally, though he had mixed enough with Rome to earn himself a Latin name. "Thank you, Rufus. I like being my own mistress, even if my dominion is not as vast as yours."

Rufus did not answer. A strange look passed over his face. Lydia noticed his muscles stiffening, as if an unseen hand had transformed his flesh into wood. He groaned. Without warning, his eyes rolled to the back of his head, and he dropped to the floor, a dead weight. A small twitch shook his arm. Then another.

Lydia gasped. She ran to the door and closed it, taking time to drop the bar down to prevent anyone else from coming in. She saw a trickle of bloody saliva at the corner of the man's lip where he had bitten his tongue. Looking around frantically, she noticed a skinny piece of wood on the pile they kept in a corner for burning. She rubbed it with furious haste, using the edge of her tunic until most of the rough bark and dirt came off. Opening his mouth, she carefully grasped his tongue and placed the wood over it to keep it trapped, so he wouldn't swallow it once the jerking started in earnest.

Less than a moment later, his arms and legs began to spasm. Hips, knees, elbows, even his waist bent and straightened in a mad rush of uncontrolled movement and bizarre angles.

Kneeling by his side, she held the stick steady so that he wouldn't bite his tongue again. To her relief, the attack did not last long. The jerking slowed down and finally came to a stop. His body relaxed, though he remained unconscious for half the length of an hour. Lydia removed the stick from the man's mouth and, wetting a rag with water, began to wipe his face.

As she expected, he was confused when he opened his eyes. "Where am I?" he mumbled.

"You are in my shop. I am Lydia. I sell purple. Do you remember coming here?"

He groaned and ran a hand over his eyes. "No. I feel . . . strange." He looked around. "Did I . . . ?"

"Have a seizure? Yes."

Even in his state of confusion he seemed horrified at the thought. Romans considered the disease an ill omen. To a Roman citizen, there would be few things more humiliating than falling about, foaming at the mouth before strangers.

"Don't worry," she said, her voice gentle. "No one saw you. Only me. I locked the door when you first collapsed."

His cheeks looked more lined after the attack and had turned paler than his white toga. She fetched a cup of water and helped him sit up, which was no easy task given his girth. He leaned against the wall and drank thirstily.

Lydia allowed him to rest awhile, covering him with an additional cloak. "You look better," she said when she heard him stirring.

He grimaced. "I remember nothing."

"You lost consciousness. I closed the door to protect you from prying eyes. Your mouth may be a little sore. I had to place a stick there to prevent you from choking or injuring your tongue. The seizure did not last long."

"How did you know what to do? Another woman would have run, shrieking."

"It's only the . . . what do you Romans call it? *Morbus caducus.* The falling sickness. Hippocrates taught that it was merely a physical disorder due to natural causes. No demons involved, unlike what some Romans claim."

Rufus took another sip of water. "For one so young, you seem very knowledgeable. Are you a physician as well as a dyer of purple?"

"My father suffered from the disease. I took care of him many times."

He grimaced. "It doesn't happen to me often. Sometimes I forget I have it." He turned his head toward the wall. "It was decent of you to close the door."

Lydia straightened his tunic, which had grown tangled against his leg. "Let your mind be at ease, Rufus. What happened here remains between us. No one will hear of it from me."

A spark of new life entered his eyes. "I have an idea. I will send my handsome son here tomorrow. He will charm you into working for me. He charms everybody."

A trickle of the ice from Lydia's heart seeped into her voice. "You will find I am immune to the charms of handsome sons."

TWENTY-SEVEN

Remember not the former things,
nor consider the things of old.
Behold, I am doing a new thing;
now it springs forth, do you not perceive it?
I will make a way in the wilderness
and rivers in the desert.
ISAIAH 43:18-19

To Lydia's aggravation, Rufus did send his son over to the shop the following day. The man's annoying presence was mitigated by the fact that he arrived bearing a basket the size of a Phoenician ship, filled with foods she hadn't tasted in long months. Or ever. Walnuts and almonds, jars of olive oil, fresh cheese, pomegranates, raisins, quince. And best of all, roasted lamb and goose.

While Lydia and Rebekah drooled over the contents of the basket, Rufus's son, Antiochus, pored over their merchandise. Every now and again, as he touched some yarn or a piece of dyed wool, Lydia caught a flash of raw hunger in his eyes. He was a few years older than Lydia, twenty or twenty-one at most. Under the carelessness of his comments, she sensed a lurking intensity that was too old for his years.

"Where do you process your dye? And your wool? Where do you wash it? Dye it? Dry it? There is no space in this chicken coop." He walked restlessly from one wall to another, fingering merchandise as if the feel of purple comforted him.

"For some things we go to the river. For others—" Lydia pointed to the back of the shop— "there's a courtyard back there."

He opened the back door and examined the space she indicated. "My bath is bigger than that. I can't imagine how you manage. You should work for us. We will give you everything you need to create magnificent things."

"I have everything I need here."

"You have no room to grow here. You will remain negligible, barely making ends meet for the rest of your life. If you don't go broke first."

Lydia frowned. "Your father said you were charming. I see he exaggerated."

Antiochus laughed. "I can be charming if I choose." He bent over her basket and grabbed a handful of almonds, crushing the shells with his fingers and discarding them unheeded on the floor.

Popping an almond into his mouth, he said, "I understand my father made a fool of himself yesterday."

Lydia stiffened. "He was ill, if that's what

you mean. And the basket was unnecessary. But please let him know I am grateful."

He studied her for a moment. "You did my father a good turn. Now let me repay your kindness. Let me show you Philippi. And introduce you to some important people. People who can be useful to your trade. If you really want to succeed in this city, you need more than talent. You need connections. And you need to get into the dyers' guild. You won't be able to do that without help."

"Why would you want to help me, a stranger to you and to Philippi?"

He shrugged. "As I said, you did my father a good turn."

Lydia pressed her lips together. "Your father told you to do it."

"He may have. What of it? Do you want my help or not?"

Lydia knew the offer could prove invaluable to her business. But she wished Rufus himself had offered to accompany her. Antiochus made her uncomfortable. Then again, any young man would. "Can Rebekah come?"

Antiochus turned to observe the silent girl for a moment. "Whatever suits you. Tomorrow then. I will come in the morning."

"We will have to close the shop if we both go with him," Rebekah said after he left, as she swept the floor clean of almond shells. "What exactly happened with Rufus? You said he was ill and you let him rest here awhile. But he is acting as if you saved his life."

Lydia waved a hand. "He makes too much of my help. I closed the door to preserve his dignity. Men don't like to be sick in public. I think he feels he owes me a debt for that. In any case, he is a pleasant old man. Perhaps he can help us."

Antiochus arrived in the afternoon without an apology for his lateness. Lydia had donned her best clothes—a dark-purple tunic that showed off the superior dye produced in her workshop, covered lightly by a thin cloak. She had given her second-best tunic and new shawl to Rebekah. They had risen early and dressed one another's hair in loops and braids and curls. They could not hide their youth, but at least they looked respectable.

"Where are we going?" Lydia asked as she tried to keep up with Antiochus's brisk steps.

"My father's workshop. You might as well start there. The other shops are not far. We are bound to run into one or two members of the dyers' guild while we are there."

Rufus's shop was located on a long street near the city walls, only a stone's throw from the Egnatian Way. There were iron grates on the windows of the ground floor, and the facade of the building looked like it was made of marble. At the main entrance there were two Doric columns with a stucco of Minerva, patron goddess of art, stretching between them.

Lydia gulped. For a moment her desire to establish herself as a successful seller of purple seemed like nothing but the rash dreams of youth. How had she ever believed she could compete with grand establishments such as this? Workshops with long histories and powerful connections. There was no room for her in Philippi. She wondered if that was the reason Antiochus had brought her here. To teach her humility. To show her the futility of her desires.

Antiochus must have read her thoughts. "Can't compete with all this, can you?" he asked, his eyes narrowed and shining.

"I am not trying to start a rivalry. I merely want to make my own purple."

"You waste your time. Before the year is up, you will be out of business."

Lydia pressed her lips together and refused to answer. To her relief, Rufus arrived to welcome them with a smile. He showed her about the shop with its built-in marble counters and rows of shelves full of beautiful textiles—yarns in every imaginable shade of purple, scarlet cushions, cloaks lined with fur, tiles stained in shades of lavender and periwinkle and magenta, clothes decorated with gold and silver. His manner lacked Antiochus's disparagement. He acted like an amicable host, happy to have their company.

"What do you think?" he asked Lydia like a boy hungry for affirmation.

"It's the most impressive shop I have ever seen."

"Now will you come and work for me?"

For a moment, Lydia was tempted. Truly tempted to give up her dream of building her own workshop. Tempted to enter into Rufus's employment instead. How much easier life would be if she walked away from those cherished longings. If she stopped saving and worrying. Here, she would have a simple life. She would oversee other workers. Her hands would stop feeling rough and calloused. No more dark circles under her eyes from sleepless nights.

An image of her father's face floated to the forefront of her mind. The wild hair that he often forgot to comb, the thick brows shot through with white, the mischievous grin that goaded her to laughter, the arms that held her like an anchor, securing her in the midst of every storm.

He had labored and struggled for years to create the best purple. He had fought to keep that formula from falling into other hands. Lydia had to try to succeed, not only for her own sake. She had robbed him of his dream with her stupidity. She would not rob him again in order to live a life of ease.

"Thank you, Master Rufus. I will work for myself."

He wagged a thick finger at her. "I like you. You have spine, Lydia of Nowhere. And you know how to keep a confidence. A rare quality, I have found.

"Come. Let me introduce you to some of my friends. They will raise their eyebrows at you and make snide remarks about the fact that you are a slip of a girl with no husband or father behind you. Do not allow them to shake you. You must win them over if you wish to succeed in Philippi. You will need these new associations. I will open the door. It is up to you to walk through. Earn their respect. Make them forget your unusual circumstances. Mind you don't put me out of business now."

They both laughed. But under the jest, Lydia sensed that Rufus really believed she could succeed. Succeed enough to be a threat to him. Rufus's belief settled in her veins like a warm spray of hope.

On her way out, he bent his lips to her so only she could hear. "I have come to a conclusion about you. You hail from Thyatira. They are famed for their production of purple."

Lydia forced herself to smile. In Thyatira she was known as the daughter of a thief. As unjust as the accusation may be, it still had the power to rob her of this fragile new start. "Perhaps I am."

"No shame in that. It is no Philippi and it certainly is not Rome. But it is not so bad that you need to hide the fact under a bushel."

If she could buy a bushel big enough to hide her past, she certainly would. She hoped Dione and Jason's vile lies would not chase her all the way into Macedonia.

TWENTY-EIGHT

Yet he commanded the skies above
and opened the doors of heaven,
and he rained down on them manna to eat
and gave them the grain of heaven.
Man ate of the bread of the angels.
PSALM 78:23-25

Eleven months after the workshop opened, Aemilia walked in to inspect the fruits of her investment. Leaning heavily on a cane, jewels adorning her sparse hair and sagging throat, she arrived with her harried slave in tow. "It's not very large, is it?" she said, wrinkling her already-wrinkled brow.

"No, Patroness." Aemilia's judicious investment had been stretched to its limits. A larger space would have been impossible.

"Varus would not be impressed with this shop."

"The size of my workshop may not thrill him. But its purple shall."

"You could at least install a marble shelf somewhere."

Lydia stared at her shoes. There was neither money nor space for a single marble tile, let alone a whole shelf.

The old lady sniffed. "I received your final

payment this morning. You may have no marble in your shop, but you have discharged your debt to me. And a month early, too. I do admire a woman who keeps her word."

"Thank you, Patroness."

"You still need a bigger shop."

"With marble shelving."

"Precisely. Then I can bring Varus and enjoy myself at his expense."

"I will try my best to oblige you, Patroness."

"Well, don't take too long about it. At my age, when my mind wanders, it doesn't come back."

Lydia tapped her forehead with the flat of her palm. "We still cannot manage to pay the membership dues for the guild. If we were part of the dyers' guild, I would be able to buy our wool for a better price. As it is, I pay more than the other dyers but have to sell my merchandise at the same rate as they, or lose my customers."

With a restless motion, she came to her feet and paced to the open door. Gray clouds had not broken all day. "What an unsolvable conundrum! If I want to save money, I need to become part of the guild. But I cannot afford to become part of the guild unless I save more money. It's been a year, and we have made no breakthroughs. We are floundering, Rebekah. I don't know how to overcome this obstacle."

"You paid off your loan to Aemilia and put a

smile on her face when you added a beautiful wool tunic to her payment. You have established your own workshop, and, though modest, it creates the best purple in this city. We have a roof over our heads. Food in our bellies. I would not call that floundering."

Lydia shrugged. "We barely survive. After I pay taxes to Rome, taxes which my colleagues do not have to pay thanks to the privileges of citizenship, there is little left. The guild membership would improve our circumstances. We cannot grow without it."

"Have I told you about manna?"

Lydia turned to her friend. "No. Why? Can he solve our problems?"

"Manna is not a person." Rebekah stretched her feet to make herself more comfortable as she prepared madder roots for a new batch of dye.

"I have told you how my people were once enslaved in Egypt. After four hundred years of captivity, their lives grew unbearable. The Lord could not abide their suffering any longer, and he sent them a prophet named Moses who would lead them out of Egypt."

"I remember this story. The ten plagues in Egypt; the hard-hearted pharaoh who refused to free them; the death of the firstborn sons. And that dramatic rescue, when God parted the sea for his people. The Hebrews passed safely to the other side, while Pharaoh's army was crushed under the waves."

Rebekah nodded. "After they escaped, they remained in the wilderness for forty years, living like nomads, cultivating no fields of their own. They had some cattle, which they had brought from Egypt. But they had no wheat, no barley. Nothing for their daily bread. Nothing to fill their stomachs. They started to fear starvation. They even complained that slavery in Egypt was better than this uncertain life in the wilderness."

"What happened?" Lydia asked, drawn into Rebekah's story in spite of the strain of worry that tugged at her thoughts. For over a year, Rebekah had spoken to her of her God. Lydia found him both fascinating and incomprehensible.

"God had not brought his people all the way out of Egypt to starve them in the wilderness. He had other plans for their lives. So he sent them manna."

"What is *manna?*"

"I don't know the precise answer to that question. I can tell you what our Scriptures say. Every morning, the campsite of the Israelites would be wet with dew. When the dew evaporated, in its place a substance as fine as frost, white like coriander seed, blanketed the ground. This was heaven's food, sent to them by God every day."

"What did it taste like?"

"I have never tasted it myself; the Lord stopped

sending manna when Israel conquered the Promised Land. We are told that it tasted like honey wafers.

"In the mornings, families were supposed to gather as much as they needed for one day. No more, for the following morning, God promised to provide the necessary measure for that day.

"Some people did not trust this promise and gathered more for later. To their disgust, they found that the additional manna turned putrid, crawling with maggots."

Lydia scrunched her nose. "Maggots infested the manna within one day?"

"Only the food of those who did not follow God's directions."

"So this food—this manna—would not last more than a few hours before going bad?"

"Yes and no. Once a week, on the Sabbath, which is our day of rest, God commanded the people to do no work. Not even to collect manna. On those days, the manna lasted an extra day, and they could eat their fill from what they had gathered the morning before."

Lydia returned to her stool and started to work on the pile of madder alongside her friend. "I see where this story is headed. God wanted the people to trust him for their daily needs. Trust him to provide for them not just once but continuously."

"You have understood the heart of the matter."

"You want me to wait on God's manna? For the workshop?"

"Sometimes, in the wilderness of life, that is your greatest act of faith. Trusting that God will provide for each day. One of our poets by the name of Asaph called manna the 'bread of angels.' Can you imagine? He said, 'Man ate of the bread of the angels.' "

"Is that what angels eat? Manna?"

"I don't know if the angels eat anything. They are not flesh and bone like us but creatures of fire and spirit who come into the presence of the Lord freely. I think Asaph was speaking not of physical manna but of what it represents. Perhaps what fills the angels' hunger is trust. Trust in God's faithfulness. In his provision. In his goodness. Perhaps an angel's longings can be assuaged only when he places all his confidence in God.

"Do we not have this in common with the angels? Do we not suffer a hunger that can only be alleviated with faith? In a way, we have to learn to eat the bread of angels. Every day, trust God to give us our sufficiency for that day. Not just with food, you understand? But with everything. Your business. Your future. Your heart."

Lydia dropped a madder root unheeded back on the pile. "Bread of angels for my heart," she whispered.

"If you want, we can pray and ask for it."

"You pray. I will listen."

Rebekah waved a hand. "You have listened to me pray for over a year. It's time you learned to do your own praying."

"But I don't know how! I don't know Scripture by the scroll-full, as you do."

"You don't have to pray like me. Pray like yourself. God will be happy to hear from you after all these years."

Lydia grimaced. "I'm not even one of his people. I don't belong to him. He will probably ignore me."

Rebekah leaned forward. "There were many outside the lineage of Abraham who, in the end, came to belong to our Lord. Rahab. Ruth. Naaman. All of them Gentiles like you. Consider, Lydia, what might happen if you trust him with your prayers. With your heart. He might give you the bread of angels."

TWENTY-NINE

You do not know what a day may bring.
PROVERBS 27:1

"You have been in Philippi for over a year and a half. Still not joining the guild, Lydia?" Rufus asked as they walked slowly through the forum.

Lydia forced her fluttering hands to still. "Not yet, Rufus. Perhaps next year."

Rufus cleared his throat. "If it is a matter of money, I could lend you what you need. Cover your dues for the year until you can repay me."

Lydia gave a small shake of her head. Accepting such a loan would change their relationship. It would place her too much in Rufus's debt. And what if she could not pay him back in a timely fashion? She would have to repay him with merchandise she could ill afford to give up. They were barely surviving, she and Rebekah, on what they made now. It was too great a hazard. "I thank you, my friend. But I will wait. The time is not right. That is all."

"I understand. I wish you would consider me a true friend and come to me when you need help."

Lydia gave an impish grin. "I offer you the same."

Rather than laughing as she expected, Rufus nodded, his expression grave. "I will remember that, young woman. You have already proven yourself. My reputation once rested in your hand, and you preserved it."

Although Philippi was not a large city, it boasted more dazzling public buildings than a sprawling municipality. As a Roman colony with more than its fair share of wealthy, retired soldiers in addition to prosperous goldsmiths and the income of the rich mines nearby, Philippi had a lot of money floating about and many bored, affluent residents willing to spend it.

The elegant theater in town, nestled at the foot of a hill, provided the most popular entertainment. Lydia and Rebekah could not afford to attend a play, but upon occasion, when their busy schedules allowed, they would climb the hill behind the theater and watch the actors perform from a distance.

Rebekah, whose love for poetry combined with her extraordinary memory enabled her to learn most of the lines, would speak them later in perfect Latin and Greek. Some of the plays were too lewd for Lydia's tastes, and Rebekah refused to attend them. Still, there were sufficient performances suitable to the two friends' liking that they were able to enjoy a large variety of productions. From Plautus's comedies to Seneca's tragedies, each act held its own mesmerizing charm.

Sitting on a gray slab of rock, surrounded by clumps of bushes while the voices of actors reverberated throughout the hillside, was like entering another world, where Lydia's puny problems paled in comparison to the great tales of the age. It was her favorite escape. When the problems of life grew too overwhelming, she would pack a hunk of bread and cheese and drag Rebekah off to the theater.

They never guessed that this simple pastime would change their lives.

One evening, as she and Rebekah were getting ready to close the shop and prepare new merchandise for the following day, they heard a commotion outside the store. Because their neighborhood was not safe after dark, they tended to bar the door by sunset. This night they had lagged behind. Before Lydia could close and bar the door, a man stumbled into the shop.

He staggered one way, then the other, and finally managed to steady himself. "Ladies," he said, with a regal bow of his head. "I beg your pardon for this unssseemly intruuusion. I believe . . . I am quite lost. I mean that both prrrracticly and . . . metaphysically. But prrhaps at this moment, the practical is of greater importance." His voice, slurred as it was, did not lose its rich, deep resonance.

Spellbinding, Lydia had thought the first time she had heard it at the theater. She elbowed Rebekah in the ribs. "That's Leonidas! The actor."

"At your ssservice," the actor said with a bow. His knees wobbled, and he lost his balance and fell on his face.

Lydia and Rebekah exchanged a glance before running to help him. "Here! Sit on this pile and lean against the wall," Lydia said.

"Most kind. I believe I ammm about to be sick. Violently. You . . . might wish to get out of the way."

Just in time, Rebekah managed to grab a basin and stick it under his chin. Lydia didn't know whether to laugh or groan with vexation. On such a busy night, they did not have time to waste on an inebriated actor, regardless of his genius on stage.

"Most abominable imposition," Leonidas murmured after he had finished heaving. He accepted a handkerchief and wiped his mouth, though it took him three tries to find the right location on his face.

"Where is this?" He seemed to have a difficult time focusing, and his gaze had a tendency to land somewhere between the two women.

"You are in my shop." Lydia named the street. At the blank look on Leonidas's face, she named the larger street that intersected with theirs. Still no recognition. "You are in Philippi," she said at last.

"Oh, that is reassuring. I know where that is. Now, could you point me in the direction of home?"

"Where is your house?" Rebekah asked, and when he responded, she sighed. "Clear on the other side of town."

Lydia exhaled a long breath. She could not throw the man out in his muddled state. "I don't think you ought to try it, Leonidas. I fear since you are . . . unwell, it would not be safe for you to wander alone. You might be robbed . . . or worse. Were you accompanied by friends? Are they nearby? We could try to find them."

"I had some companions earlier in the evening. None that you would call friends unless you were exceedingly unfastidious. But I lost those several hours ago."

"Then perhaps you should consider staying here this evening, as our guest. I cannot in good conscience send you out on your own."

"That is the most charming offer I have received all day. All year, even. Just point me to a bed, and I shall take my leave of you."

Lydia made up her own bed for the man in the farthest corner of the shop, which was, in fact, not very far. After sending him to his bed, she sat at the new loom, weaving for several hours while Rebekah spun wool.

"You will have to share your bed with me tonight," Lydia told her friend, before giving in to a huge yawn.

"It matters little. I could sleep on a hedgehog, I'm so tired. I can't believe the great Leonidas is sleeping in your blankets."

"Passed out, more like."

"Perhaps we could sell the bedding at a special price. 'Here slept the famed actor. You too can lay your head where he drooled.'"

The sound of laughter filled the shop. Within moments, it was replaced by the sleep-softened breaths of two exhausted women mingled with the loud snores of their unexpected guest.

THIRTY

Commit your actions to the LORD,
and your plans will succeed.
PROVERBS 16:3, NLT

The sun was at its zenith when Leonidas finally awoke. He groaned for long moments before managing to open his eyes. "Have I died?" he asked.

"I hope not," Lydia said. "It would be hard to explain a corpse in my bed." She handed him a cup of hot water sweetened with honey, along with a piece of bread.

The actor took a sip of the water and made a face. "O goddess, why do you try to poison me? Have I wronged you in some unforgivable way?"

"I am no goddess. My name is Lydia. I am a dyer of purple. And I thought I was helping you."

"Here is my advice to you, Lydia, dyer of purple. Never hand a man water first thing in the morning unless it is for shaving. Is that the sun I see beyond the door?"

"You recognize it, do you?"

"The moon and stars are by far my favorite companions, I will not deny. Did I spend the night in your glorious company, my goddess?"

Lydia snorted. "Not exactly. You slept here. Rebekah and I slept there."

"Then I am even more unfortunate than I thought. But it returns to me now. You gave me your sweet hospitality last night when I was lost and unwell. How rare to find goodness on this earth, and to have it flow from the hands of one so dazzling. That glorious hair like a river of flowing amber, and those are surely not eyes but jewels—Persian turquoise set with stars.

"What are you doing working with dye? Such a face should be seen and admired by all men. Why don't you join me on the stage? We are not so narrow-minded as in ages past. Women can enter the noble profession of acting now. You will be as bright as Juno."

Lydia looked at the dissipated, handsome face for a moment. "You should never write your own lines."

He dissolved into laughter. It was perhaps the first genuine sound that had come out of his mouth. "Perhaps not," he acknowledged. As he rose, he gazed about him for the first time. He seemed dazed at the sight of a length of fabric that Lydia had just hung on the wall.

"Did you make this?"

Lydia nodded.

"I take back everything I said about you working with dye. You belong on Mount Olympus. What are you doing working in this little hole in the middle of nowhere? Not even Rufus's shop with all its splendor has anything so fine to offer. And how much, pray tell, do you want for this?"

Lydia told him. "A bargain," he said. Immediately, he pulled out his purse and counted out the money. "And here is a little extra for your trouble last night." He folded the fabric and held it close to his chest as if he could not bear to part from it. At the door, he turned around. "You and your friend come to the theater tonight. I will have them save the best seats for you, O Lydia, my goddess of purple." And he was gone as abruptly as when he dropped in, though he staggered less on the way out.

Rebekah grinned. "Your kind heart certainly paid off. He bought the most expensive piece in the whole shop and didn't even try to barter."

Lydia stared at the money resting in her hand for an arrested moment. "That's not all. The extra coin he gave for our trouble last night? The sum is the exact fee we need for joining the dyers' guild."

Rebekah's mouth dropped open. "Bread of angels!" Her pronouncement burst into the room, loud with wonder.

For a moment the women stood transfixed, unable to utter another word. Lydia hugged the coins to her chest. When she finally spoke, her voice shook with joy. "Praise God in his heaven.

Our wait is over." The gift of coins, so carelessly given by the actor, could change their lives. She began to dance around the shop, pulling Rebekah behind her by the hand.

Out of breath and flushed with excitement, she came to a stop and counted the coins again. "And to think, if we didn't like going to the theater, we would never have recognized him or offered to keep him here last night."

"The Lord mediates his provision by curious means. When you least expect it. Where you least expect it. Leonidas in our workshop! Who could dream of such a thing?"

"You know, I've been praying for six months. Why didn't God send Leonidas when I first made my request? Why make me wait so long?"

"Because you were learning to put your trust in the Lord. Six months is not such a long time to pray. In any case, I think this is the day to give praise, not make complaint about his timing. He did reward your long wait with the best seats to a proper theater performance."

Lydia laughed, the sound carefree and full of joy. She was nineteen, she owned her own store, and she was about to become a member of the dyers' guild in Philippi.

THIRTY-ONE

The LORD works out everything
to its proper end.
PROVERBS 16:4, NIV

"You must move from this dismal place,"
Leonidas pronounced in his official actor voice
as he wiped his brow with a piece of linen. "It
smells of month-old refuse out in your street, a
vile assault to any sensible nose. Do you know
I have to drink three cups of undiluted wine
merely to bolster my courage in order to visit this
workshop?"

"You have to drink three cups of undiluted
wine merely to get out of bed," Lydia said.
"Besides, I always make it up to you when you
come."

Leonidas had become more than a good
customer and friend; he had grown into an
irreplaceable asset. Within days of his visit,
many of his friends started traipsing to the shop,
making generous purchases. Their ranks included
actors and philosophers and writers. Men who
cared nothing about whether Lydia was a maid or
married. They broke social rules every day and
did so with relish. Her pool of customers grew to
include a more sophisticated body of patrons.

"It won't do. You must move. And I know the perfect location," Leonidas said.

Lydia sat on an upturned basket. "Enlighten me."

"I have a friend. Filthy rich, with an abundance of rental property in Philippi. One of his shops has just become vacant. Used to be occupied by an olive-oil seller. Died in his sleep last week, poor fellow, leaving no one to manage the business. It's bigger than this hole you call a shop, and in a better part of town."

"Which means I cannot afford it."

"You can. It will cost you a few pieces of purple. My friend adores the cloak I bought from you. I told him you would make a matching pair for him and his mistress if he gave you his shop at a lower rent."

Lydia straightened. "Does it have a marble shelf?"

"Two."

The new store proved a vast improvement to Lydia's previous accommodations, with two marble shelves as Leonidas had promised and a silver-colored wall sconce. They purchased a wider loom now that they had more room and were able to produce better lengths of fabric.

The shop brought them an additional gift. The middle-aged woman who had worked for the olive-oil seller stopped by one day to see if they had found a shawl she had left behind. The new loom stopped her in her tracks.

"Do you know how to weave?" Lydia asked, noticing the woman's admiring gaze.

"My father was a weaver. I learned as a child."

"Have you found new work since your master died?"

She shook her head. "If you don't want to work in a mine, jobs are scarce."

Lydia gestured to the loom. "Show me what you can do."

Two hours later, she hired the woman. This left Rebekah and her free to oversee the dye production. Within a month they had increased their merchandise twofold.

Aemilia brought the general to the new store. She gazed about, her small eyes sparkling. "This is an improvement," she said. "What do you think, Varus? Is it not a lovely store?" She ran her fingers over a piece of scarlet linen. Lydia hoped they weren't stained with onion juice.

"It's on the small side," the general said.

"Small, but of exceptional quality. Have you ever seen such purple at these reasonable prices? And can you imagine? It's all managed and created by women. I am shocked to my depths. What will women attempt next? Apply for political office?" The old lady stared at her son, her eyes wide with innocence.

The general made a strangled sound in his

throat. Roman women could not hold public office. They were not even allowed to vote. Words must have failed him. Lydia knew the feeling. Words often failed her when she was around Aemilia. "Would you like to see a few pieces, General?"

Before he could respond, Aemilia spoke. "I would like to give a feast. A very lavish one, Manius," she said, calling her son by his given name as only a family member could. "For my birthday."

"Your birthday is not for another nine months, Mother."

"How do you know? Were you there when I came into the world? I want a feast for my birthday, and I want it now. I might not live until the actual day decides to dawn."

The general tapped his hand on a marble counter. "Fine. Have a feast."

"I would like to invite a lot of people. The two praetors and their wives, for a start. A few of your military friends. No vulgar people, mind. Tribunes and generals and the like. The consul, the legates. The owners of the gold mines. I suppose you should include those dreadful wives of theirs. I shall have a full list for you by this evening."

Varus raised a brow. "I see. In other words, you want every person of rank and influence in Philippi."

"Quite so, my dear Manius. It's so reassuring to have an understanding son. Oh, and don't forget these two," she said, pointing a crooked finger at Lydia and Rebekah.

Varus put his chin in his hands. "I see."

"And I shall need a new tunic. This lovely crimson will do."

Lydia winced. The old lady had picked the most expensive piece of cloth in the whole store. After giving away free cloaks to the landlord of her new store, and adding a linen tunic for Leonidas in thanks for his assistance, she could ill afford a half-price item of such value. Considering what Aemilia had done for her, however, Lydia could deny her nothing. "I will wrap it for you at once."

"Charge the full price, child. My son is paying for it. It is my birthday present."

Varus looked toward the heavens in resignation.

On the way out, the old lady stopped. "Wear something appropriate for the occasion, Lydia. None of your old, fraying tunics. Make yourself a new garment worthy of the crowd I am gathering. And for pity's sake, do something with your hair. For such a handsome woman, you have an odd lack of appropriate vanity."

Lydia dithered, as wordless as the general had become. Aemilia added in a whisper only she could hear, "When you come to the feast, stop in my chambers first. You and the Jewess. You cannot come to such an evening bare of jewels. I will loan you a few pieces."

Lydia's head snapped up. "Jewels?"

"I said we shall make you a success, didn't I? This tiny shop, pleasant as it seems, is only a start. Wait until I am finished with you."

"Has it occurred to you that perhaps God has sent Aemilia to help us?" Rebekah asked when the general and his mother had left.

"I think Aemilia is under the impression that she *is* a god."

Rebekah smiled. "But God knows better. And he can use her in ways we cannot imagine. King Solomon said, 'The Lord works out everything to its proper end.' Aemilia thinks her plans rule the world. In the meantime, God is using those plans for his own ends in your life, Lydia."

THIRTY-TWO

For every beast of the forest is mine,
the cattle on a thousand hills.
I know all the birds of the hills,
and all that moves in the field is mine.
PSALM 50:10-11

Lydia stood next to Aemilia, her palms perspiring, her scalp tender from the ministrations of the servant Aemilia had sent to tend to her hair.

"Smile, my girl," the old lady said. "People are going to think I am torturing you."

"You *are* torturing me. Why did you make me come to this feast? I feel like a buzzard in the midst of a flock of swans."

"Idiot child. You are the swan. Prettier than all the women here and more talented than the men. If they stare at you, it is because they are dazzled."

"They are dazzled by the size of this blue jewel you fastened to my shoulder. A pigeon's egg would blush in shame next to it."

Aemilia laughed. "My husband's taste. He had as much understanding of elegance as a turtle. But he did have a fair understanding of expense."

Antiochus, who had arrived in the company of

his father, Rufus, approached them. "I hear your new shop is an improvement."

"Thank you," Lydia said, her voice stiff. Antiochus had a talent for making pleasant compliments sound like insults.

"Of course you could fit ten of them in my father's workshop. I told you to set aside your foolish pride and join us. You will never grow to be of any consequence if you remain on your own. A woman," he sniffed.

"That's precisely what I said." Aemilia slapped Antiochus on the arm harder than the young man expected, judging by the astonished look on his face and the way his body lurched to one side. "Here is a young man of some sense, Lydia. You ought to listen to his advice."

She gave the young man another jovial slap on the arm. This time her aim improved and when he lurched, he spilled half his wine on his toes. "On the other hand, Antiochus, perhaps Lydia might find many new patrons this evening. Who can predict such things? Perhaps she may even be able to move to more substantial accommodations in time. I myself shall support her in that endeavor. After all, look at my beautiful tunic. Where else could I find such perfection? Not in your father's shop. As spacious and stately as it may be."

Antiochus gave a cold smile. "Support her all you want. If you live that long."

Lydia clamped down on a gasp. She had always known Antiochus had an acidic tongue. But foisting it on a respected woman like Aemilia took some nerve.

The old lady did not seem shocked. "I intend to make a point of it," she said with a sweet smile. "Now, you may wish to find a slave to help you clean your feet. You really ought to be more careful with your wine."

Lydia and Rebekah had made a habit of sneaking out of the shop whenever they could for a walk to clear their heads. If they had time, they would leave the city for a longer stroll, enjoying the ravishing countryside around Philippi.

Their overnight explosion of business after Aemilia's feast had prevented any such outings for far too long. Lydia, noticing her friend's pale features, put a stop to their demanding pace one afternoon and insisted they leave work for a few hours.

"I am glad you suggested we come away for the afternoon," Rebekah said, surveying the gently sloping field that sat in the shadow of Mount Orbelos.

"I have been working you too hard." Lydia gave her friend's hand a squeeze. Rebekah looked wan. Her beautiful skin had grown sallow and thin.

Rebekah shook her head in negation. "It's only

for a season. Life won't always be this over-whelming." She picked up a round stone from the ground and twirled it between red fingers. "We've never come this way before. What a peaceful spot."

"It looks that way now, but ninety years ago, a savage battle was fought right here. Roman turned against Roman. Brother against brother. Thousands died on this field. Rufus told me about it." Lydia took deep breaths of the crisp spring air as they strolled through the wild grass.

"Which battle?"

"The one that changed the course of Rome's history." Lydia bent down to run her fingers over a clump of lamb's ear. "These fields once glistened red with the blood of young men. You couldn't run without tripping over their bodies, mangled with wounds received from swords and arrows."

"The battle Mark Antony and Octavian's forces fought against Brutus and Cassius after the senators murdered Julius Caesar?"

Lydia nodded. "History was forged here, right on this unremarkable spot. Mark Antony and Octavian were Caesar's men; they wanted to preserve what he had built and to maintain his values. Of course, they also wanted his power. The two senators wanted a republic instead. Their armies met here; Mark Antony and Octavian won the war, which is why Rome now has emperors."

"If these fields could only speak."

"There is an amusing anecdote about the poet Horace from that battle." Lydia shielded her eyes from the sun. "Wasn't he the one who said, 'Live bravely and present a brave front to adversity'?"

"Did he fight here?"

"On the losing side. When Brutus killed himself, Horace realized he could not escape defeat. He threw away his shield and ran for his life. No poems. No brave front. Just ran as fast as his skinny, poetic legs allowed."

Rebekah laughed. "Sometimes courage means running away from a fight." She settled herself on a lumpy gray rock and adjusted her sandal. "Do you smell something strange?"

"Something burning. Yes." Lydia scanned the field. From the corner of her eye, she saw a streak of light in the distance. "There!" She pointed before it disappeared behind a clump of bushes. A shiver of apprehension ran through Lydia. The women grew quiet.

In the silence, they heard a terrible sound, like the shrieking of a tormented child. "What is that?" Rebekah asked in dread.

They saw the strange streak of light again. This time it was closer, and they could make out its source. A rabbit, on fire as it ran, screaming with anguish. Lydia gasped with horror. The animal was too far away. They could not reach it. They could not help. It would die, eventually. But it would suffer the torments of hell until it did.

Quietly, Rebekah bent over and retched.

Lydia stood frozen, unable to get the animal's unearthly shrieks out of her mind. "How could such a thing happen? Do you think it walked too close to a camper's fire?"

Rebekah shook her head. "There was an arrow protruding from its side. Did you not see it?"

"An arrow? Perhaps someone tried to kill it. Put it out of its misery. I would do the same myself, if I could."

"Perhaps." Rebekah pointed east. "It came from that direction. From behind that crop of bushes. Let's go and see."

"Rebekah, I think that area is covered with marshes. It might be dangerous."

"We'll be careful." Rebekah started to run without waiting to see if Lydia would follow.

Lydia set off in pursuit, barely able to keep up. Her stomach turned into a large knot. "I don't have a good feeling about this," she said, panting.

"Hush," Rebekah whispered. "We are close."

"Close to what?"

Rebekah came to a halt before a long wall of tall bushes. Turning, she motioned Lydia to follow in silence.

Carefully, they picked their way around the outcropping of stones and thick bushes that prevented them from seeing farther. The ground was growing more marshy with every step. Lydia feared they would go too far and find themselves sucked to the bottom of a pit. But something drove her friend onward. They looked for stones and dry patches to step on, avoiding the mud when possible.

Mark Antony brought a whole army through here, Lydia reminded herself. He found stretches of land wide and dry enough to safely bring thousands of soldiers through the marsh without losing any men to its deep pits. She and Rebekah could manage.

She had barely finished that thought when her foot sank ankle-deep into mud.

THIRTY-THREE

The blessing of the LORD makes rich,
and he adds no sorrow with it.
PROVERBS 10:22

The thick, oozing soil sucked her sandal right off her foot, swallowed the leather whole, and to her consternation she realized that the shoe could not be retrieved. This was ridiculous! She opened her mouth to demand Rebekah stop her mad pursuit of shadows when her friend came to a dead stop. Lydia stretched around her friend's shoulders and saw that just beyond the bushes stood a man. He had a pile of arrows next to his foot and held a bow in his hand.

Antiochus! Rebekah lifted her arm to hail the man. Just in time, Lydia clapped a hand over her friend's mouth to prevent her from speaking and pulled her to her knees so they could not be seen.

Antiochus grabbed an arrow. Lydia saw that it was very slim and delicate, not sturdy enough to kill even a rabbit. The short tip was black with pitch. He dipped the arrow into the fire he had burning nearby until it flared into flame. "Come now," he whispered. "Don't play coy. Show yourself."

A moment later, a fat gray rabbit came into

view, its whiskers shivering. In a flash, Antiochus released the fiery arrow. It landed in the rabbit's leg. The fire sparked against the gray fur and caught. The creature sat for a moment, dizzy with pain from the wound in its leg. It wasn't deep enough to kill it. But it must have hurt. Then the flame caught and grew, spreading against the long fur. The rabbit began to emit the same tormented scream they had heard before.

Antiochus laughed. He laughed with delight as if he had heard a good joke.

Rebekah struggled against Lydia's hand, which had never released its hold over her mouth. Lydia tightened her hold and dragged Rebekah farther back so they could not be detected.

"Why didn't you let me stop him?" Rebekah wailed when Lydia finally let her go. "I need to go back. He's not hunting for food. He is just tormenting them. He will keep on doing that if someone doesn't interfere."

"He's not safe; can't you see that?" Lydia hissed. "He would have harmed us if he saw us there, Rebekah."

"But we need to help those poor creatures!"

"No! We must keep this to ourselves. He can never know we witnessed it. He would destroy us if he knew that we saw this. That we saw this part of him."

"We will tell his father, then."

"Antiochus would deny it. Whom do you think

Rufus would believe? My word, or the testimony of his own son?"

"He must know Antiochus is no angel."

"But that is a far cry from knowing that his son is a monster. He will not believe me because he will not wish to believe me. Do not think that because he likes me, he will place me above his only son! I am too insignificant to make an enemy of Antiochus."

"We could tell Demetrius, Rufus's manager. He is a good man, and clever. He would believe us."

"What can he do? A mere slave? We cannot be impetuous in our response. Think it through, Rebekah. We will not win if we choose to wage this battle. This is one of those times when, like Horace, we have to run the other way."

Lydia took a deep breath and held it. They had worked so hard to make a place for themselves in Philippi. To lose all they had achieved and once again face unjust accusations, to clash wills against another powerful enemy, was more than she could bear. Antiochus would loose all the dark forces of his nature against her. That was not a battle she wanted to fight.

Rebekah's legs folded up as if her strength had left her, and she sat down hard. "I fear he will grow worse if he is not stopped now. Grow more monstrous with the passing of the years. I will abide by what you say, Lydia. But I pray we will not regret this decision one day."

"My mother is dying." The general slumped against his chair, his sagging cheeks glistening with tears.

"I have faced men wielding spears taller than I am. Faced soldiers coming at me with death in their war cries. Faced defeat in battle when all seemed lost. But never have I felt so bereft of hope as at this moment. I always knew she would die, even though she seemed immortal. Still, I cannot imagine my life without her. She is a vexing woman. A stubborn pain of a woman. And the greatest joy I ever had."

"Oh, General! This world will be a darker place without the spark that lights Mistress Aemilia's eyes." Lydia, who had been summoned to the general's villa in the middle of the night, sank on the stool facing him.

His jowls shook as he wept, whimpering like a boy instead of a seasoned soldier of middle years. "Half the people in this city think her demented. The other half judge her too old to mourn. They are mistaken. When she is gone, it will be as you said. My light will dim."

Lydia reached for his hand. "When my father died, I thought I could not go on. He was my home."

"How did you carry on?"

"At first, for his sake only, I went through the motions of living. I could not bear the thought of his disappointment if I gave up. So I put one foot in front of the other. In time life began to taste good again. Not one day passes that I do not miss him. But I live, and I take pleasure in the life I have."

The general wiped his face and took a deep breath. "She has asked for you."

"She probably wishes to remind me that I owe her another piece of purple cloth at half price and that she will not allow death to cheat her of her rights."

The general laughed as she had hoped he would. He brought her to Aemilia's bedside, where she knelt to say farewell.

Aemilia, breaths labored, cracked her eyes open. "You took your time."

Lydia, who still had a stitch in her side from running all the way to the villa, bowed her head. "I beg your pardon."

"Listen, both of you. Lydia, I want Manius to adopt you."

"What?" the general and Lydia cried at the same time, their voices cracking on the same note.

"Dear Mother! You must know how impossible this request is."

She waved a weak hand in the air. "Manius already has an heir. The son of his father's brother. I wish the boy no harm, though he is a bore. For Lydia, I only ask this, Manius. Adopt her so she can become a citizen of Rome." The labored breathing grew worse, and she became silent and gray. They waited.

Finding strength from some deep, unconquered cistern, Aemilia went on. "How can she achieve true success while paying exorbitant taxes to Rome? Adopt her, for my sake, my son. Leave her no money or property. She will not need it. She has a good mind and a rare talent, which will serve her better than all the property in the empire. Merely lend her your name, and the strength of Rome."

Lydia's jaw grew slack. Upon occasion, a wealthy man like Varus, who had no natural heir, would adopt a young man to inherit his estate after his death. But no one adopted a woman. It was unheard of. If Varus accepted this unusual responsibility, he would give more than the rights of citizenship to Lydia. He would give her a man's name and position to back her own.

Already she had achieved something unthinkable for an unmarried woman. With Aemilia's help, she had established herself in trade with a modicum of success. More than this, however, would be impossible. She could go no further. Not without a man's name. She held her breath, wondering what Varus's decision would be. He must think his mother's request exceedingly ill-considered. His agreement might earn him the censure of all of Philippi. Even a deathbed wish would not press a man so far against his convictions.

Varus took Aemilia's hand. "I promise, Mother. It shall be done as you say."

Lydia's breath caught.

"I wish he had been this malleable when I was in good health." The old lady laughed, the sound a thread.

Lydia reached for her champion's fragile hand. "You think of me at this hour? In your suffering, you remember me?" Her voice broke.

"Well, you are certainly more pleasant to think about than dying. And one more thing. I leave you the hideous pin with the great blue stone. I shall laugh in the land of Hades every time I see you wearing it."

Rebekah's words rang in Lydia's ears. *The Lord works out everything to its proper end.* "*Carissima domina.* Dear lady. May God give you safe passage. And thank you from my heart."

THIRTY-FOUR

You are my God, and I will praise you;
you are my God, and I will exalt you.
PSALM 118:28, NIV

Aemilia's funeral was stately enough for an emperor. Lydia was one of the few who wept genuine tears at her loss. She noticed Antiochus's absence among the many who had come to pay their respects.

There was a rumor that Antiochus had disgraced himself with a very young girl. Money had been exchanged and the rumor stifled. No official charges were brought against him, but a cloud hung over him nonetheless. Lydia wondered if his absence was due to this disgrace or was a public statement of his dislike for Aemilia, even in death.

At home, she kicked off her sandals and leaned into the hearth where they cooked their meals. A banked fire lent some warmth to the chilled autumnal air.

Rebekah sat near her and gently began to undo the tight braids and loops of hair that made Lydia's scalp itch and ache. Lydia sighed with relief as her friend combed through her loosened hair, her movements gentle.

"I've been thinking," she said.

"Should I worry?"

"Thinking about God. When my father died, I had no one left. Then you came to me, like an anchor, a sister of my own, a gift I did not deserve. It is easy to overlook the many times we were given help. Heaven's help. I am done overlooking the work of his hand. The gifts of his kindness.

"More than coincidence, more than the generosity of men or the mercurial attentions of the empty gods of Greece, we have received the interventions of a holy God. And now I find myself a citizen of Rome. For your sake, I think, my Rebekah, in order to bless you, God has blessed me."

Rebekah smiled. "I think he has blessed you for your own sake, dear friend. For the sake of the plans he has for you."

"I know nothing about such plans or why he would bother to have them. I only know this. Your God is my God.

"After the funeral, General Varus told me about a single-edged sword the Romans call the *makhaira*. It has a short blade and is used in close combat, so close that the victim can see only the face of his killer. The general said grief is like an enemy holding a *makhaira* at your throat. All you see is the face of grief, as the rest of the world fades.

"I think I know what he means. All my life I have contended with a *makhaira*-wielding enemy of my own. Fear. I cannot see the Lord as clearly as you do. I cannot draw near to him because of it. But, Rebekah, he is real. And I am his."

Rebekah held on to Lydia's hand for a moment. Her eyes filled with moisture. "I, too, have an enemy who wields a *makhaira*."

"You, Rebekah?"

Her friend closed her eyes. "It is loneliness. I have you, sister and friend. But I long for something else. It is as if there is a hole in my heart that nothing can ever fill. Not intellectual pursuits. Not friendship. Not work. Not even the Lord. It is as if I miss some great piece of myself."

"I think the whole world could say the same."

A month after the funeral, General Varus adopted Lydia in a private ceremony. After eating a simple meal together, Lydia returned home. She fetched a large bundle from a shelf, where she had placed it in preparation for this day.

"I unearthed this earlier," she told Rebekah. Unwrapping folds of soft wool, she picked up a gray, battered-looking stone, the stone she had taken from the well of her old home. The one bearing her grandfather's name. Themistius. Her fingers touched the crooked letters reverently. She kissed the rough masonry, her lips warm against its cold surface. The only link other than her blood that bound her to generations past. To bones buried in the soil of Thyatira.

With great care, she wrapped the stone back in the wool. "I will have the mason etch my father's name here, under my grandfather's name. We will use this as the cornerstone of our shop," she told Rebekah.

"Our shop?"

"The one we will build together. You and I and God. I think God likes purple too."

THIRTY-FIVE

The wisest of women builds her house,
but folly with her own hands tears it down.
PROVERBS 14:1

Purple dominated the spacious chamber: purple curtains, purple cushions with a golden fringe, delicate purple and blue mosaics on the floor, depicting a calm sea. The woman who ruled this purple kingdom bent over a length of purple fabric under the light pouring through the narrow window.

Chloris skidded into the room, coming to a breathless stop before Lydia. "You have a visitor. Lady Appollonia is here."

Lydia sighed. "What did we say about you moving at a decorous speed?"

"That I should do it?"

"Yes, you should." Lydia folded the fabric with care and began to walk toward the reception room.

"Not that way," Chloris said. She hooked her thumb behind her and pointed. "That way. She is waiting in the *vestibulum*."

Lydia took a slow breath and held it for a moment. She reminded herself that Chloris was very young and new to the household. "You left my guest in the entrance hall?"

Chloris bit her nail. "I shouldn't do that?"

Lydia pulled the slave's finger out of her mouth. "Or that."

Lydia had known Chloris's father for many years and had given him odd jobs whenever she could. Though a hard worker, Belos had the brains of a mouse when it came to managing money and had landed himself deep in debt the previous year. The threat of prison had closed in upon him like an iron jaw about to swallow him. He had no assets left to sell save for his beautiful daughter.

Ten days earlier, Lydia had spent a fortune in cash to retrieve the child from the slave trader before she was officially put on the block. Now she had a juvenile to oversee and a great deal of unwanted trouble besides. Still, she could not deny a burgeoning fondness for the girl. Awkward, sweet, honest, and altogether charming, she had managed to worm her way into Lydia's affections. Perhaps her childless state had begun to play tricks on her mind, and her womb was clutching at any available straw, including Chloris.

"I apologize for this rude welcome," she said as she greeted Appollonia. "Chloris has only been here a few days. She isn't properly trained yet."

Appollonia was dressed in the somber colors of a new widow. Over her simple tunic she had wrapped a drab, black shawl, customary attire for mourning women. Her normally impeccable hair was flat on one side and sticking out in wisps on the other. The shapeless shawl covered most of her curvaceous figure, making her appear like a lost, ailing magpie.

Appollonia's husband, Dryton, had died five weeks before, leaving three children under the age of seven and a young widow. Her eyes filled with tears when she saw Lydia, and without warning, she threw herself into her hostess's arms. The force of her unexpected embrace rocked Lydia.

They weren't close—acquaintances more than friends—so the emotional outburst came as a surprise. Dryton had been a colleague of Lydia's, another seller of purple in Philippi, and they had belonged to the guild together.

Lydia regained her footing and wrapped her arm around the young widow. "Come. Let us go to my dining room. We will recline at our leisure and have a light lunch together."

Before long, the two women were ensconced on Lydia's comfortable couches, platters of enticing food before them. A salad of green leaves fragrant with mint and coriander, fresh cheese, and soft-boiled quail eggs in a pine-nut sauce served with warm bread, followed by perfectly roasted fish. But even the appetizing food at Lydia's table with its exquisite aromas did not seem to tempt the grieving widow. She only played with her food, putting a small piece of mint or a single pine nut in her mouth now and again.

"You know Dryton left me everything in his will?"

Confused by the woman's obvious distress, Lydia said, "That seems a good thing."

"It frightens me half to death. I don't know how to run his business," Appollonia said, trying to control her tears. "I fear he would be very disappointed in me."

"You will learn, in time."

She shook her head. "I think not. I will only ruin his beloved workshop. He has left me his business, six slaves, a small orchard, a wagon, and a dovecote. A dovecote! What am I to do with those wretched birds? And if I can't even manage a bunch of noisy doves, how will I deal with a thriving business?"

Lydia bit the inside of her lip. "I am sure you will find a good buyer for the doves. They are very popular."

"Speaking of buyers, I have one for the dye business. I think perhaps I should sell. What do you think? Dryton always spoke highly of you, Lydia. In truth, I fear I was jealous of you. You were only one step lower than a goddess in my husband's eyes."

Lydia's eyes widened. She waved a hand, denying the widow's exaggerated assertion. "He trusted me as a colleague. That is all, Appollonia."

"Which is why I thought I should ask your opinion. The offer comes from Antiochus, the son of Rufus."

Lydia felt every muscle clench. Choosing her words carefully, she said, "Do you think Dryton would have approved?"

Appollonia shook her head vigorously and wiped away fresh tears. "He would never sell. That business was like a beloved son to him. But what else can I do?"

"Hire a manager. Dryton ran everything himself. You don't have to."

"Antiochus says managers will only rob me blind."

"How much has he offered you, may I ask?"

Appollonia named a figure. "That's outrageous!" Lydia cried. "I have not examined your husband's accounts, obviously, but just looking at his shop and its inventory, and judging by his reputation as a man of sound business, I would say his trade is worth four times what Antiochus is offering you. Five, if your husband had additional merchandise stored in a warehouse, which is common practice for those of us engaged in the textile trade. Antiochus is the dishonest one, trying to take advantage of a young widow."

"But, Lydia," Appollonia said, brows drawn together. "Everyone loves Antiochus. Just last year the city honored him with a marble plaque, naming him an outstanding citizen and a benefactor of Philippi."

"Of course they did. He has bribed more officials than there are fish in the Aegean Sea. He throws lavish feasts and invites everyone who might do him a favor. He gives away wheat and oil and wine for imperial feast days. All this he gives not because he is a generous man with a good heart but because he wishes to increase his influence and build his personal empire. He cares nothing for honesty.

"Do not be fooled by a marble plaque, Appollonia. Antiochus's offer is an outrage. Do not let your inheritance go lightly."

The widow seemed to wilt against the back of the couch. "Well, if he is as bad as you say, perhaps I should not trust him." Her eyes grew large. "How about you? Do you want to buy my husband's business?"

Lydia sighed. "I regret I cannot. I do not have sufficient free cash available at the moment."

"Then where am I to turn?"

"As I said, what your business needs is a trustworthy manager."

"Where am I to encounter such a paragon?"

"They are not easy to find, I grant you." Lydia chewed on her lip. She knew her next words might help a friend, but they might also place her in harm's way. Taking a deep breath, she took the leap. "Antiochus has an excellent steward."

THIRTY-SIX

For he crushes me with a tempest
and multiplies my wounds without cause;
he will not let me get my breath,
but fills me with bitterness.
JOB 9:17-18

Appollonia frowned in confusion. "Antiochus?"

Lydia nodded. "When Antiochus's father, Rufus, was in charge of the workshop years ago, he purchased a slave named Demetrius and trained him in the business. Demetrius was an educated man, and clever. He learned the trade quickly.

"I know him well and have crossed paths with him many times through the years. I can recommend him as a virtuous and capable man. He told me once that he liked working for Rufus, but when the business passed to his son, life changed. Shady deals, cut corners, cruel treatment of his workers. Demetrius chafes under Antiochus's rule, but as a slave, he is helpless to change anything."

"That is sad, though many slaves suffer a similar fate. In any case, it does not solve my problem. If Demetrius belongs to Antiochus, he cannot help me."

"That is the point. He does not belong to Antiochus."

The sound of hurried steps interrupted her explanation. At first Lydia thought Chloris had returned to clear the table and determined to deliver another lecture to the girl about maintaining a graceful gait. But to her astonishment, the rapid footsteps belonged to Rebekah.

Rebekah did not interrupt personal meetings without good reason.

Her friend bent her head in apology. "Forgive my intrusion, Lydia. Antiochus is here. He insists on seeing you and refuses to leave until he does."

Appollonia sprang to her feet. "Oh, gods, how did he find out I would come to you? How did he know I would seek your advice about selling the business? Do you think he has spies in my household?" A delicate hand surged to trembling lips. "Or worse. He has the power to practice sorcery."

Lydia grasped her guest's chilled fingers and gently pulled her back to the couch. "Calm yourself. His only magical power is to fool people into thinking that he is a good man. His visit here pertains to another matter." She gave Rebekah an intent look. "Keep Chloris out of the way. Make sure she doesn't stumble into his path by accident."

"She is well hidden."

"Where have you put Antiochus?"

"He is downstairs in the courtyard. Refused to wait for you in the shop. I suspect the only reason he agreed to linger below stairs is that he hopes to pick up a few trade secrets from the backroom workshops."

Lydia's mouth turned into a flat line. She took the time to smooth down her pale-green tunic, straightening the gold pins that held her mantle on her shoulders, adjusting every fold to perfection. "I better go to him before he takes it into his head to come looking for me." She turned to her guest. "Appollonia, it is best you stay here until Antiochus leaves. Rebekah will remain with you. She is my dearest friend and excellent company. You will be safe with her."

Lydia walked down the narrow stone staircase that led to the courtyard. Her townhouse, a large, elaborate building not far from the city walls, also housed her shop, which sold purple dye as well as purple cloth and yarn of every imaginable variety. In addition, she offered a selection of luxurious men's and women's clothing that had become the latest fashion. The weaving and dyeing workshops, along with the store, took up the whole of the lower floor, while her living quarters occupied the upper level.

She and Rebekah had come far since the days they lived and worked in a rented workshop no bigger than a vegetable cart. The building she had erected on the foundation of her ancient family stone would have made her father proud. It had taken ten years of constant work and sacrifice. But she had built an edifice that rivaled the grandest shops in Rome itself.

The house was built around a courtyard—what the Romans called an atrium—with marble floors and an elegant, carved fountain in the middle. This last extravagance was a necessity more than an opulent decoration; the atrium contained a rectangular hole in the roof in order to allow both light and air circulation throughout the house. The fountain served to catch rainwater, which in Philippi could at times be abundant.

As suspected, Lydia did not find Antiochus waiting politely in the courtyard. He would be in the dye workshop, no doubt. There were a dozen sellers of purple in Philippi who belonged to the dyers' guild. Each shop had its own specialty. Few carried the true purple, derived from sea snails at great expense and affordable only to the wealthiest of clients.

Lydia's dye was still the best of the lot. Thirty-two years had passed since Eumenes had invented the initial formulas. Lydia had managed, by dint of experimentation and teeth-gritting nerve, to improve on a few of her father's formulas. No one in the city matched them in quality or steadfastness. Antiochus had never outgrown his jealousy, nor his desire to get his hands on her purple.

She pasted a smile on her face. "I thought I would find you here," she said as she walked into the workshop.

Antiochus was bent at the waist, smelling the contents of a vat. Lydia was not worried that he would unearth her secrets. Better men than he had tried to discover her procedure without success, and Antiochus, in spite of his appetite for winning, was not talented with dyes.

At the sound of her voice he swiveled around in haste, not noticing that the corner of his cloak sloshed into the vat behind him. "Afraid I will discover your precious formula?" Though in his middle years now, he dressed his hair like a young man, using too much oil and perfume. She could smell him from the other side of the chamber, which was not easy, given the pungent aroma of some of the materials they used.

"You are welcome to explore my vats all you wish." She pointed to the edge of his cloak. "But you might want to take that out first. Or throw the whole lot in to get the color even. No charge. Consider it a professional courtesy."

Antiochus sucked in wet, pink lips, and hastily pulled his cloak out. She grabbed a rag from a nearby bench and handed it to him.

He dabbed at the wool, his movements jerky and uneven. "As it happens, I am here to conduct business. But it has nothing to do with your dye."

Lydia sat on a bench, pulling the feminine

folds of her tunic modestly around her. "What business?"

Crumpling the rag Lydia had given him, he threw it on the floor before turning to face her. "I want the slave. The one you took from under my nose."

She raised an eyebrow. "Chloris? You speak as if I stole her. As I recall, I purchased her according to all the proper requirements of Roman law."

"You knew I wanted her; her father must have informed you. And you sneaked your way in before the public auction just to take her from me."

"Oh, Antiochus! What a thought. It so happens I don't like public auctions."

"You go to public auctions all the time!"

"Not for slaves. Those I find repugnant."

"Why did you pay twice what she was worth if not to ensure that I would not get her?"

Lydia's eyes turned into round balls. "Did I overpay by that much? What a fool. I must take more care the next time I go shopping."

Antiochus approached Lydia, his steps as soundless as a stalking wolf's. The smell of his sweat warred with heavy perfume. "Do you really want to make an enemy of me, Lydia?" His voice had grown soft. "You will find me a much better friend, I assure you."

Lydia hid her hands in the folds of her dress.

She forced herself to smile. "I have taken a liking to the girl and I aim to keep her. Perhaps in a year I will tire of her and you can have her then. She might cost you a lot less money if you wait awhile."

"In a year she will be too old."

Lydia could feel the blood rushing to her face. "She is only ten."

"As I said, too old."

"Then change your tastes," she said, her voice like iron.

Antiochus gritted his teeth until the bones in his jaw stood out. "I will give you seven days, starting today, to change your mind." With jerky motions, he pulled off his cloak and threw it at Lydia's feet. "You can keep this. It's ruined," he said, enunciating each word with deliberation. "This is not the first thing I have destroyed. You will find I have a talent for that."

"I know," she whispered.

"Remember. Seven days."

He walked out, his steps measured. Somehow he had managed to fold his animosity and hide it under a perfectly calm exterior before he greeted the world outside. Bile rose up in Lydia's throat. She was not fooled. She knew his rage percolated just beneath the surface, poised to strike with deadly aim.

THIRTY-SEVEN

Anxiety in a man's heart weighs him down,
but a good word makes him glad.
PROVERBS 12:25

Lydia rested her forehead against a shaking palm. An oppressive weight pressed against her chest so that she could only breathe in shallow huffs.

Fear.

Unreasoning, gnawing, hungry fear. Next to it, Antiochus looked like a tame squirrel. She resisted its rising hold as she had learned to do since childhood. She would do the right thing even if fear swallowed her up. She would persevere through it as she always had. But oh, why did she have to be so enslaved by its power?

"How did you fare?" Rebekah's soft voice came from the door.

Lydia tried to repress the quaking in her voice. "He seems displeased with me. He believes I took Chloris with the intention of depriving him."

Rebekah smiled. "Well, to be fair, that is exactly what you did."

"Maybe so. But it was ungenerous of him to reach that conclusion. He is determined to make me his chief enemy. He did give me seven days to change my mind. Merciful, by his standards."

Rebekah was not fooled by Lydia's light tone. She wrapped her arms around her friend and held her for a moment of pure, fortifying love. "We will find a way. With God's help."

"Well, he had better send us his assistance soon. I have stepped on a hungry lion's tail, and he is roaring in my ear. How is Chloris?"

"Subdued as always when there is mention of Antiochus."

"Thank goodness her father spoke to me before the auction."

Antiochus had offered Belos enough for the girl to clear the father's debts and end his financial woes. Belos, pathetic parent that he was, did have enough heart not to want Chloris in the clutches of a man like Antiochus. At least he had not been fooled by Antiochus's charm like most of the rest of Philippi. Instead, Belos got drunk on cheap wine he could not afford and sold Chloris to a slave trader. Then he ran all the way to Lydia's house, blubbering with tears, begging her to buy the girl.

"Why didn't you come to me from the start?" Lydia had said. "I could have relieved your debts and moved the girl into the safety of my home quietly. Now I have to contend with a slave trader's greed as well as with Antiochus."

"Forgive me, mistress! I was too scared to approach you. I thought you would berate me and tell me to take care of my own problems. But now that the child is sold, I can't bear to leave her unprotected. You have a kind heart. I beg you to help her."

Lydia had managed to buy Chloris at an inflated price before she was placed on public auction. The last thing she wanted was a bidding match with Antiochus. Such an affront to his pride he would never forgive. Besides, she was not sure she could have won. Antiochus had three generations of money to throw around.

"Appollonia is still waiting," Rebekah reminded Lydia.

"Graces help me. I forgot about her."

"She tells me that you spoke to her of Demetrius. You do not intend to take Demetrius from Antiochus also? Not after Chloris?"

Lydia pulled down the neck of her tunic and tried to take a deep breath. "It's a good solution. Appollonia is out of her head with grief. She needs a skilled steward to protect her; anyone could cheat her while she is in this state of mind."

Rebekah snorted. "Anyone could cheat her in any state of mind. She understands nothing about managing a business. But can't you come up with another solution?"

"What would you have me do? Run the business for her? I barely have time to care for my own workshops. She needs a manager who will not take advantage of her naiveté. You know as well as I there is no man better suited to the job than Demetrius. And I would like to do him a good turn. He has been a gracious friend to us through the years. Just last month he helped me make a profitable trade. At Antiochus's expense, I might add. And it wasn't the first time he has proved of benefit to me."

"If Antiochus finds out what you are planning, he will stop at nothing short of ruining you."

Lydia pressed the bridge of her nose. "He will smash his honorary plaque over my head and dye his new cloak with my blood. But let us not concern ourselves with such dismal thoughts."

Rebekah bent to retrieve the man's cloak from the ground. She frowned at its stained corner. "What's this? Was he trying to sneak out a sample of our dye?"

"He's not that clever. He could drink the whole vat of dye and urinate purple for a week and still not figure out my father's formula. The stain on his cloak is a mere accident. And a reminder to me that he is good at destroying things."

"You must hold what I am about to tell you in strictest confidence, Appollonia. Antiochus can never know that you have received this information from me."

Appollonia nodded, her eyes wide.

"Just before Rufus died last year, he secretly sent for a magistrate. Rufus had a legal certificate of manumission drawn for Demetrius and gave him his freedom. But he made Demetrius promise that he would work for Antiochus one additional year to help put the affairs of the workshop in good order before leaving."

"Wait. I thought Demetrius belonged to Antiochus."

Lydia shook her head. "No. Rufus is the one who bought him. He never gave him to Antiochus legally. Demetrius continued to work at the workshop when Rufus's health prevented him from overseeing the workshop personally and he all but retired. Rufus knew Demetrius was a far better manager than his own son and allowed the arrangement to go on.

"But as he lay dying, his conscience smote him. Demetrius had served him faithfully for two decades. In some ways he was closer to Rufus than his only son. The old man felt he owed him a better legacy than a lifetime of servitude to Antiochus. So he gave Demetrius his freedom, with the proviso I spoke of. According to the law, Demetrius is no longer a slave.

"More to the point, twelve months have passed since that day. This very week, Demetrius will be free of his promise. He will be able to work where he chooses.

"The news of his manumission will come as a great shock to Antiochus. His father never told him what he had done. As far as Antiochus is concerned, he has inherited ownership of

Demetrius along with everything else from his father. He does not know that in a matter of hours Demetrius will walk away. Indeed, the man is already legally free to do so."

"Free to manage a different workshop in Philippi?"

"Precisely."

Appollonia pulled her drab shawl tighter about her shoulders. "Antiochus will not like this."

"He will not. If you choose this path, you will no doubt have a few battles before you. But you will have Demetrius to help you. I doubt Antiochus will dare to come directly against you. Demetrius is privy to many of his business secrets. He will not want to rile him."

Appollonia shook her head. "How do you know all this?"

"I was there."

Appollonia's eyes widened. "You were *there?* The night Rufus gave Demetrius his freedom?"

Lydia shrugged. "Rufus sent for me."

"Why would he do that?"

"We were friends. I think he wished to have company, on such a night."

"But why did he choose *you?* Philippi is full of influential men who counted themselves his friends. Why did he call on you?"

"I once did him a small service. He trusted me after that, in a way prosperous men trust few people. We enjoyed a rare friendship based on

259

respect and mutual admiration. He helped open many doors for me when I first came to Philippi."

"No wonder Dryton admired you so much." Appollonia twisted the edge of her shawl until her fingers turned white. "I would be a fool not to take this opportunity. Tell Demetrius to come and see me the moment he is free of his promise. The job of steward to Dryton's trade is his if he wants it."

She rose to take her leave. There was color in her cheeks now and a determined gleam in her tear-soaked eyes. At the door, she turned. "I doubt your service to Rufus was as insignificant as you say. I know what your help has meant to me."

Lydia slumped on the couch after her guest departed. She could not believe it was only the first day of the week, at least according to the Jewish calendar. She seemed to have gathered enough troubles for a month. Six more days until the Sabbath. Six more days before she and Rebekah could go to the river and have a quiet day of rest and prayer.

Lydia knew it was a sorrow to Rebekah that there were too few Jews in Philippi to establish a synagogue. But for the past few years, the two of them, along with the other Jews and God-fearers in the area, had made a habit of gathering at the river on the Sabbath to pray and worship God. It was a welcome respite and time of refreshment for Lydia as she learned more about the God she had chosen to follow.

With a deep breath, she forced her mind back to the matter at hand. Crafting a letter with carefully chosen words, she sealed the papyrus with her ring and called her servant, Epaphroditus. A capable and intelligent man, he had worked at the shop for several years and had proven himself worthy of her trust. She handed him the freshly written scroll.

"For Demetrius. Give it into his own hands, and no other."

THIRTY-EIGHT

The slave does not remain
in the house forever.
JOHN 8:35

"Are you free at last, my friend?" Lydia asked
Demetrius. Two days had passed since he had
fulfilled his promise to Rufus and walked away
from Antiochus's workshop, a man at liberty
according to both Roman law and the gentler
whispers of moral responsibility. He had come
to see her in the cover of night in an attempt to
hide their association from Antiochus.

"Hard as it is to believe after so many years,
I am a freedman." Demetrius rubbed his hands
together.

"Cause for celebration." She handed him a
goblet of wine. "From the sun-drenched hills of
Italy, where you and I have never been. You will
find it mellow and sweet, fitting for this joyous
occasion."

"And here comes Chloris with our supper,"
Rebekah said. For once, the girl walked at a
decorous pace, looking like a princess in her new
pink tunic and gold beads. Lydia dismissed her
with a smile and told her she could retire for the
evening.

Demetrius leaned forward and whispered, "Is she the girl Antiochus fumed about for days? But she is only a child!"

"She is that. But she is also ravishing, a combination he can't seem to resist." Lydia took a sip of her wine. "Tell us, how did Antiochus take the news? Did he lose consciousness when you told him you were leaving?"

Demetrius smirked. "If only he had done me that favor. But no, he remained upright for two full hours, and would not allow me to sit either. At first, he accused me of forging the documents of manumission. Threatened to throw me into jail. When I pointed out both his father's and the magistrate's seals, he grew quiet."

"A pleasant change," Lydia said.

"It did not last, sadly. He said he would ruin me wherever I went. Expose me as a false and conniving steward, so no one would hire me in Philippi or anywhere else in the Roman Empire. I had already spoken to Appollonia by then, for which I thank you. I told him that I had a new employer who trusted my loyalty.

"He changed tack then, and offered me a plump salary if I stayed on as his manager."

"What did you say?" Rebekah asked.

"I thanked him for his generosity and told him that the honor of working for him for these many years was enough to last me a lifetime."

Lydia put an olive in her mouth. "Did he let you go, then?"

"No. There followed more threats. Shouting. Bribes. In the end, I rose up and left whilst he was in the midst of another tirade."

"And how do you like Appollonia?" Rebekah said.

Demetrius hid his face in his goblet for a long moment as he drank. When he raised his head, Lydia noted that his cheeks had turned red. "She is very beautiful."

"She is very inexperienced. Antiochus will come against her; you know that," Lydia warned.

The good-natured cast of Demetrius's face turned hard. "He best watch his step, or he will have to contend with me. I will not stand aside and allow him to harm her. Not even for the sake of Rufus's memory."

Lydia nodded, satisfied. "That is all I needed to hear. Now dig into this lamb while it's still hot."

Demetrius grinned. "The next supper is on me. Appollonia is paying me a fair salary, as well as a percentage of the proceeds of every sale. Was that your idea, perchance?"

Lydia shrugged. "It might have been. Given the fact that she will have to depend on you entirely for the running of the workshop, I thought it a fair arrangement."

"One I much appreciate. I will be a wealthy

man come next year. And she will be a wealthier woman. If ever you need a favor, Lydia, I am your man." He chewed on a delicate pastry. "How is old General Varus? Is he still among the living?"

"Yes, God be praised. He has inherited his mother's talent for long life, and I appreciate it more with every passing day. Life is much easier with his name behind me. It took him a decade, if not two, to finally accept my involvement in business. He now smiles when he sees me and no longer lectures me about the evils a maiden faces in the world of trade."

"I imagine the trunkfuls of tasteful purple goods you have sent him over the years have worn down his objections. Still, I am your servant, Lydia. If ever the general's name proves insufficient and you need help in any matter, call on me."

"I think our friend is very taken with the young widow," Rebekah said after their guest had left.

"Demetrius? You jest. He is past all that nonsense."

"He is a handful of years older than you, and you are only forty-two! Not exactly an old woman, for all that you act as one sometimes."

"Thank you."

"My point is that over the years, I have seen men fawning at your feet, sick with love, desperate for your attention, and you don't even notice. If Demetrius is falling in love with Appollonia, you would be the last person in Macedonia to realize it."

Lydia scratched her head. "I don't think I am as hopeless as that."

"Name one man who would have declared his love for you if you had given him the slightest opportunity. Just one name will suffice."

Lydia cleared her throat, unable to think of the requisite name. "In any case, if you are right, I pity the man. Appollonia still mourns for her husband. And Demetrius does not strike me as the man to draw her attention. Her head is full of romantic notions and athletic, handsome men."

"That is a pity, for he is just the man for her. Protective, loyal, caring, kind, intelligent."

"And the gawkiest man I ever met."

"Gawky men can make marvelous husbands."

Lydia threw her hands in the air. "I found her an honest manager. Husbands are beyond my aptitude."

THIRTY-NINE

Those who sow in tears
shall reap with shouts of joy!
PSALM 126:5

Lydia was sorting through a sample of glass beads newly arrived from Cyprus when Rebekah settled herself on the stool before her. "These are pretty," she said, rolling a few beads in her palm.

"They will make lovely buttons for the new Greek tunics. And I am considering designing a matching belt, using the same beads." The Greek-style tunic, the *chiton*, had grown in popularity in recent years. During the cold winter months, especially, its longer sleeves provided additional warmth, while the buttons or pins at the shoulders and arms lent the garment an added sense of distinction.

"Every woman who buys a *chiton* will want to buy its matching belt. Two sales in place of one."

Lydia grinned. "That's what I thought."

"I almost forgot. This letter came for you today. From Judea."

Lydia broke the seal and quickly read through the contents. She clapped her hands. "It is from Elianna and Ethan."

"Your friends in Jerusalem?"

Lydia nodded. "I only met them once, and that was thirty years ago. Yet in a strange way, God has knit our hearts together most dearly."

"You never told me how you met."

"My father was trying to expand his business at the time. We traveled all the way to Judea to find new buyers for his dye, which he had perfected not long before. I was eleven at the time and probably a great nuisance to him. But he would not be parted from me, and in truth, I would not be parted from him, so off I went to Judea."

"I wish I had met your father. He is everything my own father was not."

Lydia pressed her friend's hand. "I, too, wish you had met him. He would have loved you."

Rebekah smiled. "It is odd that you have been to Jerusalem, and I, a Jew, have never visited. Your friends were merchants there?"

Lydia nodded. "Ethan's parents invited us to their home to discuss my father's dye, and Elianna joined us. It was an unusual meeting, what with an eleven-year-old and a woman participating in the business discussion. The land of your forefathers is not nearly so open-minded toward women as we are in Macedonia."

"It must have been a successful gathering. Thirty years later, and still they buy their dye from you."

"They were not convinced at first. My father's purple was a risk to the merchants of Judea. They did not know him; nor could they accept his word that the color would last. I gave Elianna a piece of purple cloth I had dyed myself. In truth, it was no more than a shameless attempt to convince her to purchase my father's wares.

"Months later, Ethan's father, Master Ezer, placed a small order with us. Our first from Judea. But Ezer could not sell it. No one would take a chance with an expensive dye from an unknown merchant. Not until Elianna created a collection of fabrics, all in various shades of purple. It became an instant success in Jerusalem, and they could not keep enough of my father's purple on their shelves. Other sellers of cloth did not wish to be left behind, and the orders started to come in.

"Later, Elianna wrote a short letter to thank me and to say that my simple gift had been the inspiration of an idea that had saved her father's workshop from ruin and helped her family in a difficult time. I still remember every line. I felt so important."

"Is that when you started to love this work? You don't do it for your father's memory alone. It's like purple runs in your veins."

Lydia leaned back against a wall. "Long before that letter, I loved purple. I love its dark secrecy, its murky appearance in the vats, more black than blue. I love that I can create something that no one else can equal. I love that I can change color and shade and hue with a wave of my hand and turn something ordinary into something unforgettable. I even love the acrid smell of the mordants.

"No, that letter did not make me love this work, though it made me appreciate the value of it more. I think I was created for this. I think God made me to do this work."

Rebekah poked her in the side. "God might have a few other plans for you besides dreaming up shades of purple and building a successful shop. Now tell me, what made you keep in touch with Elianna all these years?"

"Elianna grew sick for a long time and stopped her work. I never knew the details. But upon occasion, she would write me a letter to ask how I fared. After my father died and we came to Philippi, I could not afford to send a letter to the house next door, never mind all the way to Judea! Some years passed, and I thought I had lost her. Then I wrote her a letter, and to my surprise, she began to correspond again.

"She gave our name to her friend Viriato, and the orders from Judea started coming in again. Though she knew my father was dead, she trusted me to make a good dye and run the business well. She had done as much for her own father's workshop and understood my challenges as an unmarried woman. In every letter, Elianna encouraged me. From her I learned wisdom and perseverance. I learned women could achieve their dreams as well as men.

"Imagine my surprise and joy when I heard that she had married Ethan after many years of waiting and that, together with Viriato, they run her father's old workshop again."

"You are surrounded by Jewish friends. You see? This is God's way of drawing you even closer to himself."

Lydia laughed. "You may well be right, for they write to tell me that they will be coming to Philippi in a few weeks, all three of them."

FORTY

For the thing that I fear comes upon me,
and what I dread befalls me.
I am not at ease, nor am I quiet;
I have no rest, but trouble comes.
JOB 3:25-26

Lydia tossed the blankets to the foot of the bed and climbed out. Was there ever a mistress so fickle as sleep? The room had grown chilly with the evening air; she wrapped herself in the soft wool of her shawl and ambled over to the narrow window. The moon was full, a large ball of light in a sky on fire with stars. Below her, the world rested in stillness, dozing dreamily through the night watches. Inside her, a tempest gathered. No moon-bright light was luminous enough to penetrate the darkness of fear that threatened to engulf her.

The problem was that she had taken on the responsibility for her own safety as well as the protection of those she loved. She had hired herself for a God-sized job, and she knew she would fail. This world was redolent with danger and pain. Even if Antiochus did not breathe threats and menace down her neck, another peril would take his place. Sickness, accidents, financial disasters, death. Suffering knocked on the human door in endless shapes, bearing boundless faces.

Did Lydia really think she could be wise enough, strong enough, astute enough to shield herself from pain? Insulate her loved ones from disaster? Of course not! She *knew* she was not qualified for such an impossible task. Knew one day she would fail.

Rebekah often reminded her that she needed to discharge herself from the job of being everyone's protector. "Leave that work to the only one qualified for it, Lydia. Entrust the Lord with your security. With your future."

Lydia knew Rebekah was right. But how could she teach her heart to change its ways? How could she teach it to trust the Lord's mercy above the world's sorrows?

She leaned her forehead against the cool stones framing the window. *Lord God, release me from this need. Release me from being the guardian of everyone's safety.*

Barefoot and silent as a cat, she wandered out of her chamber and stopped briefly in the next *cubiculum*, where Rebekah slept. Her breaths came steady and deep. Nothing short of an earthquake would wake her up once she fell asleep. Lydia envied her friend's talent for easy, uninterrupted slumber.

Affection rolled over her like an immense

wave as she studied Rebekah. Faithful to the bone. Brilliant as a Greek philosopher. Wise. Unflappable. What a gift God had sent her the day she found Rebekah, bruised and half-broken, starving on a side street in Thyatira. No one had recognized her worth then, abandoned and alone, thrown out like refuse. God alone had recognized the precious jewel, covered by grime and besmirched by the abandonment of those who should have loved her. He had known her value and had used Lydia to rescue her.

She closed the thick curtain over the window, both to keep out the cold and to allow Rebekah a few extra moments of rest in the morning. She had worked long hours that day, helping to complete a large shipment of purple linen, and had not crawled into bed until long past midnight.

Lydia lingered in the chamber and said a short prayer of thanks for her precious friend.

Next, she went to check on Chloris, whose pallet had been set up in a small antechamber attached to Rebekah's bedroom, away from the other servants and household slaves. The girl seemed restless. Lydia knelt by the side of her mattress and placed a soothing hand on her forehead. The soft skin, damp with moisture, burned like a kitchen fire.

Fetching a lamp, Lydia looked at the girl more carefully. She had pushed away her covers and lay restless and shivering, her old tunic twisted about her body like a rope. Every few moments, she moaned as if in pain. Heat emanated from every part of her; she burned like a tiny, lightless sun.

Lydia swallowed.

Though loath to interrupt Rebekah's hard-won rest, she raced to fetch her friend.

"Do you think it's serious?" she asked when Rebekah had examined the child.

Pulling her cloak tighter around her shoulders, Rebekah nodded. "I haven't been able to rouse her. I think we should fetch a physician right away."

"I will send Epaphroditus," Lydia said, already running toward the stairs. "Agnodice is in town, thank the Lord. I saw her yesterday when I went to the agora. She will know what to do."

Agnodice was the only female physician in Philippi, and highly skilled in the healing arts. Her expertise was so widely acknowledged that wealthy residents of other cities in Macedonia often asked for her services. Years before, when they were both young and struggling to establish themselves in their respective professions, the two women had formed a firm if unlikely friendship. Agnodice was a woman of strong opinions. To disagree with her on any matter was to be wrong. But she seemed to tolerate Lydia's notions, even when they were not in absolute accord with her own.

The physician arrived in rumpled clothing, with red, swollen eyes, her large medical bag clutched in the bosom of her latest servant, a tousle-haired boy of twelve.

"Who's dying?" she said. "Someone better. I had finally fallen asleep for the first time in two days when your servant roused me."

"Forgive the intrusion, Agnodice. The child is only ten, and she is burning with fever. We can't rouse her." Lydia led the way to Chloris's room.

The physician sighed. "Well, let's have a look."

Calm, expert fingers began their examination of Chloris. "Bring me more light," she barked. "I need to know if she has a rash."

Chloris mumbled in her feverish dreams, but she did not awaken. Most of her words were too slurred to understand. Upon occasion she would mutter a phrase or word that the rest of them could make sense of.

"Did she just say Antiochus?" the physician asked, a thread of amusement running through her voice. "That's enough to bring on a fever to any pretty young girl." She sat back and washed her hands in a bowl of water held by her assistant. "She has no rash."

"Is that good?" Rebekah said, her voice tight with anxiety.

"That is good. Now we wash her with cool water and pour herbs down her throat and hope she will keep them down."

"Is she in danger?" Lydia entwined her fingers together until they turned bone white. She could not bear the thought of Chloris being taken by fever. She had only just been rescued from the clutches of Antiochus.

Agnodice gazed up for a moment before returning her attention to her patient. "I will not lie to you or give you false comfort. You might wish to pray to your god. Who knows? If he exists, he may show pity for her youth and beauty." Her tone made it clear that she did not hold out much hope in any god's intervention. "In the meantime, I will do what I can with my own remedies."

Years ago, Agnodice had confessed to Lydia that she had lost her faith in the gods. "In my youth I worshiped Asclepius and his daughters like a good little physician. I honored his snake-entwined staff in every aspect of my practice." She had taken a long swallow of her wine before going on. "I saw no mercy. No cure. No healing. No matter the size of the offering, the length of the prayer, the depth of the faith. Asclepius, bless his cold heart, never did care. So I turned to my own herbs and created better remedies." She had finished the dregs of her wine. "Those work, upon occasion. No, Lydia. I am done with gods."

"The Lord is not the same as other gods, Agnodice. His love is unfailing."

"Yet as many Jews perish through painful, incurable diseases as do people of other nations. So either this god of yours is powerless like the rest, or he doesn't care about his people. You keep your god, merchant. I'll hold on to my herbs."

Lydia had leaned forward. "Will your herbs comfort you when you have no peace? Will they counsel you when you struggle through the quagmires of life? Will they be your companion when you are lonely and afraid?"

For a short moment, Agnodice had looked bleak. "No one can give you those things, Lydia. Now pour me more wine and keep your mouth shut about the goodness of your god."

Over the years, Agnodice and Rebekah and Lydia had had many more discussions about the Lord. But none had been as raw or revealing as the first. At least now the physician did not argue against prayer and sometimes actually asked for it, claiming that it cost her nothing and did no harm, even if it did no good.

"When will you know if she will recover?" Rebekah asked, bringing Lydia back to the present.

"When the fever breaks and she awakens. I make no promises, mind."

A passage Rebekah had once quoted from Scripture came to Lydia. *"The thing that I fear comes upon me, and what I dread befalls me."*

Chloris lay burning and unconscious, caught in the dreams of her fever, and Lydia could do little to help. How well she understood Job's anguished words.

"Then we will pray that God will break her fever." Rebekah caressed Chloris's flushed face. "We will pray that he will guide your hands, Agnodice, and bless your medicines with his healing."

Lydia nodded her assent. But beneath her willingness to seek God's help ran a river raging with helpless dread.

When the light of the moon had grown wan and distant, Agnodice called for Lydia and Rebekah. Abandoning their intercession, they ran to Chloris's bedside. Lydia did not have to ask why the physician had hailed them. The girl's breathing came shallow and fast, her chest rising and sinking in its battle to retain air. Every few moments, she would skip a breath, as if her lungs no longer bore the strength to move. Lydia had the eerie feeling that the child's soul was already moving away from its fragile shell toward whatever lay beyond.

Lydia swallowed convulsively. She had seen this strange respiration once before. Hours before her father had died, he had started to breathe like this, hollow breaths too tired to hold on to life.

"She is dying," Agnodice said in a drained

voice, as if she had read Lydia's mind. "I can do no more. Say your good-byes."

Lydia sank to her knees. She had feared the worst. And it was coming to pass.

FORTY-ONE

Its teeth are lions' teeth,
and it has the fangs of a lioness.
JOEL 1:6

Rebekah never ceased praying. Time passed, the moments lazy and sluggish, while Lydia squatted next to Chloris and counted the girl's breaths. *One, two, three, skip; one, two, three, four, skip; one, two, skip, skip.* By some inexplicable miracle, Chloris held on to her feeble grip on life, hour after hour.

"She should be dead by now," Agnodice said, placing a warm poultice on the girl's chest. She had long since given up trying to dribble her medicines down her patient's uncooperative throat. "I don't know what keeps her alive."

"God," Rebekah cried, "save this child from the hand of death."

Who can overcome death? Who can save any of us from its immutable clutch? Lydia buried her face in her hands. Had she not watched her own dear father succumb to its savage hold? Now it clamped its teeth on Chloris, and no one could change that. Even God stood back and allowed the great enemy to have its way.

She went back to her counting. *One, two, three, four, five, six.* She arrived at twenty-three before she realized there had been no skips. No breaths lost. Had her attention wavered? She started to count again and arrived at fifty. And then one hundred.

"I think she is breathing better," she said, holding her own breath as Agnodice bent over to examine Chloris. The physician threw a startled glance in Rebekah's direction.

"I don't know how, but her breathing is much improved."

"Will she live?"

"An hour ago I would have said impossible. But now?" She flung her hands in the air. "Ask her." She pointed her thumb in Rebekah's direction. "Where my medicines and poultices have failed, her prayers seem to be succeeding."

Rebekah raised her arms aloft. "Thanks be to the God of heaven and earth!"

Daybreak brought golden sunshine and a sky empty of clouds. As if unable to resist that blue, luminous expanse, Chloris awoke, weak and confused, her voice a croak, her head full of pain. But she awoke. And her fever broke. Agnodice, after another careful examination, assured them that she would live, though she could not explain the girl's recovery.

"I would like to take the credit, but I don't deal in the realm of miracles. I can at least tell you that it is not the Roman fever; it won't return to plague her." She washed her hands in a basin swimming with scented petals. "Give her broth and cooked pears today. Mix wine with water and honey, and add this bag of herbs. It should help keep the fever at bay." She began to pack her bag. "I will come tomorrow to see her. Now I am going to bed. Try not to wake me. If you have another emergency, send for her," she said, pointing her chin at Rebekah.

Dizzy with relief, Lydia clasped Agnodice in her arms. "God bless you," she said with feeling.

"You should ask him to bless *you*. I am going to send you a bill so big, you will have to shear a whole flock of sheep and dye the wool into the colors of the rainbow to pay for it."

By the following morning, Chloris had recovered so much that keeping her still and in her bed as Agnodice had commanded became a Herculean task. Rebekah looked ashen from nursing her two nights in a row, and Lydia, fearful that her friend might fall victim to the fever next, sent her to bed.

"If you stop fidgeting, I will read you a marvelous story. It is called *The Odyssey*," she told the girl.

"What's it about?"

"About a man who wandered from home for twenty years. A man with a very distinctive scar."

It had been a long time since Lydia had thought about Odysseus's scar. Many years had passed since she had been a fragile child. Her life had changed beyond recognition since then. She lived in a different country, spoke a different language, had different friends. She had lost everything she once held dear and had found, to her amazement, that the Lord had brought new attachments and provided her with a different home, no less precious than her first.

She had succeeded in a competitive business without the partnership of a man. She had earned respect and influence among her colleagues. She thought of her many accomplishments by the world's standards. Her shop, which she had started from nothing, had grown to be much more lucrative than her father's business had ever been. She had been awarded Roman citizenship, garnered influence in Philippi and beyond.

And yet not a single one of these realities had managed to disguise that old wound or the throbbing scar it left behind. Not all the purple in the world could hide it. Not all the years in the fabric of time could bury it. In a field of beautiful lilies, a wild boar had stolen her mother and robbed Lydia of security. Its scar would never be healed, she thought.

Every day, when she opened her eyes, fear chased her through each wakeful hour. Now, with Antiochus's threats hanging over her, that old enemy had grown sharper than ever.

FORTY-TWO

The enemy said, "I will pursue, I will overtake,
I will divide the spoil, my desire shall have
its fill of them. I will draw my sword;
my hand shall destroy them."
EXODUS 15:9

"We need you below stairs," Rebekah said as Lydia emerged from Chloris's cubicle.

Lydia winced, reading trouble in her friend's expression. "What now?"

"There is a problem with the indigo."

The particular purple they were currently working on began with indigo, a dark-blue dye extracted from the leaves of a species of plant that grew in the faraway Tamil country. Other plants, harvested closer to Philippi, could produce indigo. But Lydia considered this species superior to the rest. Using their own ancient techniques, the indigo producers of Tamil processed the leaves into a paste.

Lydia purchased indigo paste from a merchant who brought the dye by caravan all the way from Tamil, navigating through tough terrain much of the way and relying on established trade routes for only part of his complicated journey. She had found the merchant to be a reliable man, one she had counted on throughout the years. Never before had she encountered a complication with one of his deliveries.

"What problem?" Lydia began to walk rapidly below stairs, Rebekah in her wake.

"The color is wrong. We have tried several batches. But none of them work."

Lydia began to run toward the workshop. They had a large order of fabric due in Corinth in two weeks. There was no time for problems with the dye. There was no margin for a crisis of any kind.

The dye master stood when Lydia came into the chamber. One glance and Lydia knew the gravity of their problem. Instead of the opaque, almost-black color you would expect from indigo, the liquid in the vat was a weak blue.

"Start another batch," Lydia said. She watched every stage like an eagle, trying to catch a mistake. There were no mistakes. The indigo was faulty.

Pale with tension, Lydia knelt over the vat holding the indigo paste and examined it closely. She detected nothing wrong at first, until she sniffed the paste. Hit by a pungent smell, she drew her head back. "What is that smell?"

The dye master shook his head. "I don't know, mistress."

Lydia smoothed some on her palm. A mild tingling turned into a small fire. Hastily she washed her skin and dried it on a fresh towel.

Bunching the towel into a ball, she said, "I have never had a problem with this dye. Rebekah, when this batch was delivered, did we conduct a test before making payment?"

"Yes. As we always do. We detected nothing unusual."

For hours, Lydia and Rebekah and the dye master worked on the indigo. First they soaked the paste in water. Then they tried a solution of wine and water. By the time midnight arrived, they had made no progress, and they were exhausted.

A loud banging on the front door caused the three to pause.

"Excellent. New trouble. I was growing weary of this one," Lydia said before heading for the courtyard. Epaphroditus, who slept in the shop, had already opened the door when she arrived.

"Antiochus! I might have known." Lydia turned around and headed back to the workshop. "Come back tomorrow. I might be able to dredge up some patience for you then."

"Whassa matter? Bad day?"

Lydia stopped midstep. She took a deep breath and turned. "Have you been drinking?"

"Celebrating." He weaved where he stood.

"I don't have time for this. Go home."

"Don't you want to know what I was celebrating?"

"No!"

Antiochus grinned. There was a great stain on his toga, which had become twisted on his shoulder. He pointed a finger at Lydia and turned it round in a circle. "The beginning of your demise."

"I don't know what you mean. Now get out. I am busy."

"Having trouble with your indigo?"

Lydia turned cold. She walked up to the man, her nostrils flaring. "Did you ruin my indigo? What is that stench that clings to the paste? What have you done?"

Two large hands flew into the air, looking like fat scales. "What am I, one of the gods? How would I ruin your indigo? If you are struck down by calamity, don't blame me. I have just come to enjoy your anguish."

"Get out," Lydia said through gritted teeth.

Antiochus bowed, almost toppling over his feet. He began to laugh uproariously. "Day seven, Lydia. Day seven is here. And you have not given me what I wanted. So I am giving you what you don't want. Consider it a first payment." He ran a hand through his tangled hair. "Or you could always give me the girl and we stop here."

"You can't have her."

"Then enjoy your ruined dye. I may not know your formula for your pristine purple, but I do know you can't make it without good quality indigo."

Rebekah came to stand by her friend, placing a protective hand on Lydia's shoulder. "You have delivered your message, Antiochus. Leave now."

Lydia slumped when the door was barred. "You heard?"

Rebekah nodded, her visage grave. "I don't understand. Did he sneak into the workshop? I am certain the dye was fine upon delivery. It must have been tampered with while under our roof. Has he planted one of his spies in our midst?"

"Or bribed one of our own people." She leaned against a column. "We can no longer even feel safe in our own home. As long as we remain blind to the source of this mischief, we cannot protect ourselves against another incident."

"Let us consider one thing at a time. First, we need to contend with the damage he has already wrought. The indigo is ruined beyond repair?"

Lydia nodded. "We did everything I could think of. This shipment of purple cloth to Corinth cannot get there on time unless I can secure a large amount of indigo within the next two days. Where am I to find so much indigo at a decent price? I will have to pay full market value for it, which will reduce our profits to practically nothing. We were counting on that money, Rebekah.

"And if we wait on a new shipment of indigo, it will delay the delivery of the fabric by weeks. Our clients will never place another order with us again. Not with so many other merchants vying to win their favor. They are among my best customers, and they expect a reliable transaction." She rubbed her forehead. "It's like the week from the bowels of hell. Will it never come to an end?"

Rebekah squeezed her arm. "Chloris lives. Appollonia perseveres. Demetrius can look forward to a contented and prosperous future. And Antiochus has not won yet."

"Are you never afraid, Rebekah?"

"Of course I am. But then I remember the bread of angels. God will send us his provision for this trouble. Tomorrow is the Sabbath. We will go to the river and pray."

FORTY-THREE

The Spirit of the Sovereign LORD is on me,
 because the LORD has anointed me
 to proclaim good news to the poor.
He has sent me to bind up the brokenhearted,
 to proclaim freedom for the captives
and release from darkness for the prisoners.
ISAIAH 61:1, NIV

Dawn invaded the night all too soon. But it came bringing with it the gift of a day of prayer. Still bleary-eyed from too little rest, Lydia donned her clothes in haste and stopped at the workshop one final time to check for any breakthroughs with the indigo. There had been none.

"Shall we leave?" Rebekah asked, already wrapped in her cloak. A drowsy Chloris stood curved against her, sucking on the pad of her thumb.

Lydia raised an inquiring eyebrow.

"She claims she will explode if we force her to stay in bed another day. It will be good for her to enjoy some fresh air."

The air was crisp and dry as they walked, and with every step, sleep lost the last vestiges of its hold on the weary women. Green ruled in this part of Philippi: thick, verdant bushes, gurgling

291

water the color of jade, and a few trees with delicate leaves and crooked trunks.

Over the final bend of the road, before they arrived at the place of prayer, Lydia could see a group of women already gathered by the water. She had managed to walk ahead of the others and stopped for a moment to study the scene. Five or six women sat together. There was not a single man among them. The two Jewish families who resided in Philippi and often joined them on the Sabbath were away visiting family.

"We shall be a small group today," she told Rebekah. "Just women."

Her friend smiled. "It will be a quiet day."

The river Gangites was not wide here, flowing with a soft murmur that soothed Lydia. She settled herself on a blanket near the water, and Rebekah and Chloris joined her.

They began the morning with prayer. Lydia found it hard to focus. Her heart was weighed down with the indigo problem and the bigger challenge of Antiochus's threats. She worried for Chloris's safety. If Antiochus had managed to get his hands on her dye, then clearly he had found a way into her household. What if he managed to snatch the girl by the same means?

Upon occasion, one of the women would stand and quote a passage from the Jewish Scriptures. Lydia tried to quiet her racing mind by focusing on the words of the Law. They had no scrolls to read from and depended entirely on the treasury of their memories. Most of them quoted short passages, sometimes a mere line or two. Then Rebekah, her dark hair covered modestly with a blue veil, stood up. Her voice was soft and pleasant, like music from a stringed instrument; her Greek would not have shamed a scholar. She quoted from the prophet Isaiah:

> The Spirit of the Sovereign LORD is on me,
>   because the LORD has anointed me
>   to proclaim good news to the poor.
> He has sent me to bind up the brokenhearted,
>   to proclaim freedom for the captives
>   and release from darkness for the
>   prisoners—

Lydia sat up. She needed good news. If there was someone in this world who could release her from the darkness of fear and the prison of danger, she wished they would show up.

Rebekah continued her proclamation:

> to proclaim the year of the LORD's favor
>   and the day of vengeance of our God,
> to comfort all who mourn,
>   and provide for those who grieve in
>   Zion—
> to bestow on them a crown of beauty
>   instead of ashes,

the oil of joy
   instead of mourning,
and a garment of praise
   instead of a spirit of despair.
They will be called oaks of righteousness,
   a planting of the LORD
   for the display of his splendor.

They will rebuild the ancient ruins
   and restore the places long devastated.

Lydia listened with care, deeply moved by the promises Rebekah quoted. "Who is the man the prophet speaks of, Rebekah? Who is the one who binds up the brokenhearted and comforts all who mourn?"

"This passage foreshadows the Messiah, the Promised One of Israel who will set us free from our captivity and lead Israel back into the paths of righteousness."

"Sisters," a man's deep voice interjected. "Allow me to interrupt."

Lydia nearly toppled over with shock, startled by the interruption. In the shadow of a clump of trees a few cubits away sat five strangers. She had not noticed them approach or sit, too caught up in her thoughts. "Who are you?" she asked.

A short, wiry man with unruly hair came to his feet. He had a kind smile that contrasted with the sharp intelligence of his gaze. She noticed an air of intensity about him, like a storm held back. "My name is Paul, and I am from Tarsus. These are my friends. Here is Silas, a true follower of God, and that young lion next to him is called Timothy. Near me sits my friend Luke, who is a physician. And this handsome fellow is a Roman architect and engineer, Marcus Cornelius Marcius."

Lydia saw a blur of faces. Turning back to the man who called himself Paul, she said, "I am Lydia, a seller of purple. And this is my friend Rebekah."

"Forgive our intrusion," Paul said. "We are visitors to your city. We wished to join the prayers for the Sabbath and heard the faithful gather here. When we arrived, you were already in prayer. We did not wish to encroach. May we join you?"

Lydia glanced at her companions for approval. "This is a place where we worship the Lord. You are most welcome."

The men came forward and settled closer. Paul addressed Rebekah when he had sat down. "How well you spoke the words of the prophet! Better than a scribe in the Temple. Not a single mistake in that long oration. I should know, for I was trained as a Pharisee in Jerusalem under the honored teacher Gamaliel, and I come from a long line of Pharisees."

"A Pharisee, you say?" Rebekah took a step

forward. "We are not often honored by men of your distinction in Philippi."

Paul waved a hand. "I am not here as a teacher of the Law. My friends and I have traveled a long way that we may impart glorious news to you on this fine Sabbath, for I know the man about whom the words of the prophet were written. You might even say that I have met him.

"His name is Jesus, and he is the Messiah."

FORTY-FOUR

All we like sheep have gone astray;
we have turned—every one—to his own way;
and the LORD has laid on him
the iniquity of us all.
ISAIAH 53:6

Lydia was intrigued. Here was a Jewish teacher of the Law, traveling with a Roman and a Greek. To the best of her recollection, Pharisees did not keep company with Gentiles, whom they considered "unclean." More provocative still was this man's willingness to sit with a group of women and hold discourse. That in itself was an extraordinary breach of Jewish custom. She concluded that this was no ordinary company of men. Smoothing her amethyst-colored tunic, she addressed them.

"Master Paul, I am not a Jew, but I am what you Hebrews call a God-fearer. I notice that some members of your party are not Jews either, and yet I assume they believe in this Messiah, or they would not be here. Please, sir, tell us about this man. Tell us about this Jesus."

Paul slapped his thigh and stood. "I hoped you would ask, for he is the fulfillment of the very Scripture that Rebekah quoted earlier. There are many prophecies about the Messiah in the Bible. Is that not so, Rebekah?"

"Yes, master." Her tone was cautious.

Paul nodded. "Some are hundreds of years old. Others, thousands. They foreshadow the coming of a savior."

Lydia tucked a stray curl behind her ear. "A savior for the Jewish people."

"Ah." Paul's thick brows shot up. "I am glad you raised that point. The forefather of the Jewish people is a man called Abraham. His name means 'the father of nations.' In fact, he could not father any children. God made him a promise that in spite of his advanced age, he would indeed have a son. And that through his descendants, every nation on earth would be blessed.

"The Jews are the children of God's promise, the seed of Abraham. It is from us that his salvation comes. But from the start of our history, the Lord intended to bless all the nations through us. Greek, Roman, Persian. It is of no consequence. This gift is for everyone."

Lydia leaned forward. "So I don't have to be born Jewish to have salvation?"

"You do not." Paul clapped and smiled. Then the smile vanished and his expression grew grave. "But you have a greater problem than that of your birth. One far more influential on your destiny than your mere heritage."

"What is that?"

"The problem of sin. None of us are free of it. We are born enslaved to sin, bound to its temptations and twists. It bends us from the inside out, even the best of us."

Lydia felt spellbound. "How, then, can one be set free?"

"Not by one's own efforts, I can promise you." Paul pulled on his beard. "The Pharisees make a minute study of the Law of God. They break it apart, tear it into small compartments, and create hundreds of rules in order to ensure the Law is upheld properly. Follow these statutes, and you can be righteous, they claim. Do not break these regulations, and you can avoid sin. But it is a useless practice."

Rebekah gasped. Silas covered a smile with his hand.

Paul continued. "How can a man rule his heart? Tell his heart not to hate or bear resentment or feel jealousy? How can a man demand that his whole soul love God and force his mind into perfect obedience? I tried for years, and still I could not perform even one little command from Solomon. To trust in God with all my heart and lean not on my own understanding. Every chance I had, I 'leaned.' And I don't think I am alone in this struggle. All humanity shares in it."

Lydia could not argue with that. She was a great leaner herself.

She noticed Rebekah shifting her cloak and sinking deeper into its folds. "I have always understood that to be the reason we offer sacrifices. The blood of the sacrifice covers our sins, washes them clean as if they never existed."

Luke smiled. "She is clever, isn't she?"

"Yes, indeed." Marcus nodded. "I had to learn all this like a child, from the beginning. She is two steps ahead of you, Paul."

"Let us see if I can catch up." He nodded at Rebekah. "You are right indeed. And yet, how long after offering each sacrifice do we remain pure? Clean of every moral offense? We would have to traipse over to the Temple by the hour with an unblemished sacrifice to keep up with our transgressions. The world population of cattle, pigeons, and turtledoves would soon dwindle and disappear from the earth."

A faint chuckle escaped Rebekah's lips. She swallowed the sound, forcing her mouth into a flat line. She was not one to be bent by the force of a good argument, Lydia knew.

"Our God is a good Father, brimming with compassion and mercy. He is patient with us in the midst of our failures, slow to anger, desiring to reason with us in spite of our wandering ways." Paul looked into the distance. "But God is also holy. Who can come into his presence?"

"The one who is holy," Rebekah said.

"The one who is holy." Paul nodded. "Unblemished holiness is required of us. We can't be *almost* pure. Close to spotless, with only a bit of tarnish here and there. What is required is *perfect* holiness."

"Well then, who can be saved?" Rebekah rubbed her forehead. "You are making this into an impossible task. I thought you said you came bearing good news. So far you have succeeded only in making me despair."

Lydia winced. If even Rebekah felt discouraged, then there was no hope for her.

Paul grinned. "Allow me to make amends. God always intended to save us from this snare. To make us residents of his kingdom, children of his heart. His love for us knows no boundaries.

"God gave us countless promises in his Word, foreshadowing his coming salvation. Remember the Passover lamb?"

"I know this story," Lydia said. "It was the final plague that God unleashed on Egypt, worse than any that came before. The destroyer took the life of every firstborn male in Egypt. Except for the firstborns of Israel. It passed over their homes because each household had sacrificed an unblemished lamb and painted their doorframes with its blood," she said. "But what has this lamb to do with your Messiah?"

Paul raised both hands in a gesture of appeal. "We are like Egypt in the time of the plagues. We have hard hearts and blind eyes. A destroyer is loosed in our midst. It can sneak into our homes and steal our very lives, our joy, our hope, our future. Death itself has the last word over us, and we cannot overcome it."

Lydia felt something flare in her heart, something hot and angry and afraid all at once. "That is truth."

"Like Egypt, we need an unblemished lamb, don't you see? A lamb whose blood would force the destruction of sin and death to pass over us."

"A lamb better than the ones we sacrifice on feast days?" Rebekah frowned.

"Precisely. A perfect lamb, from God. One imbued with the Spirit of the Lord, empowered to bind up the brokenhearted and to release prisoners from their captivity. Who is not a prisoner in this world? Who does not need to be set free?"

Lydia pulled up her knees against her chest and listened with her whole heart. She knew what it was like to be a prisoner in need of freedom.

"Iron bars are not the only dungeons that constrain us. Greater chains bind us. In this life sorrow hounds us, and we cannot escape its sharpened talons. Our souls grow thin with weariness and despair. Grief turns joy into ashes. We are betrayed by those we love. Shamed by those who hurt us and, worse, shamed by our own actions. Guilt eats us like a monstrous beast we cannot fight. And we grow enslaved, held captive by fear.

"Grief. Betrayal. Shame. Guilt. Fear. We are slaves to such dark masters. Jesus came to set us free. Free from sin and death."

Lydia's eyes snapped open wide. She clenched her hands, and still they shook. She opened her mouth to ask a question. No sound emerged.

She bent her head a fraction and straightened the strap of her shoe. Then she heard Paul whisper, only for her ears, "No one shall separate you from the love of God. Not trouble or hardship or danger. Not even the *makhaira*."

FORTY-FIVE

But he was pierced for our transgressions;
he was crushed for our iniquities;
upon him was the chastisement
that brought us peace,
and with his wounds we are healed.
ISAIAH 53:5

Paul could not have known. No one could have known, for she had told no one except Rebekah. The two of them sometimes still joked about the *makhaira* at their throats. She continued to see the face of fear more clearly than that of God.

And those words. *Grief. Betrayal. Shame. Guilt. Fear.* They had been the continuous incantation of her heart when her father died, the emotions that had ensnared and almost broken her.

She supposed she had never truly outrun them. They lay buried somewhere deep inside and raised their ravenous heads when circumstances unearthed them from the place she had tried to entomb them. They rose, living still, to torment her. She was as impotent against them now as when they first took root in her soul.

But God knew. Had always known the power

they still held over her. And he had revealed his knowledge through Paul.

Only the revelation had not come accompanied by a hammer of condemnation. God had not said, *You are unclean. Unacceptable. Unlovable. I know your heart, and I reject you. I know your darkest secrets, and I despise you.* Instead, God had sent an invitation to freedom. He had whispered to her his desire to set her free.

A part of her resisted such a simple promise. Surely God would not forgive *her* so easily? Wipe away her guilt for ruining her father's life and bringing disgrace upon them with her selfishness? All for the sake of a handsome face and empty promises. She cringed as she remembered.

"He can set us free?" she asked, finally breaking her silence. "This Messiah, this Jesus, can set us free from the bondage you spoke of?" Silence fell on the small gathering. Lydia realized that she had spoken aloud, interrupting an ongoing conversation. She felt herself turn red.

Paul looked at her, his gaze sharp as a sword. "There is nothing in the world so damaged that it cannot be repaired by the hand of Almighty God," he said as if he could read into her soul. "The answer is yes—Jesus can set you free from every chain that binds you. He is the only one who can."

"Then let us go to him at once," she said,

gathering her cloak and coming to her feet. "Where does he live?"

"I dearly wish to grant your request, Lydia. But Jesus has returned to the Father. You can receive the Holy Spirit, who will impart to you the Lord's presence. To see Jesus face-to-face, however, you will have to wait either for his return or for your time to be united with him in death."

Lydia frowned. "What?"

"He has been crucified," Rebekah said.

"No!" Lydia sank back to the ground. Why had God raised her hopes if the man was dead?

Paul raised a hand. "We offer sacrifices to acknowledge our sins, do we not? We offer them with the hope that the blood of the sacrifice will wash us clean."

Lydia straightened. "He had to be sacrificed for our sins?"

Paul exhaled. "Crucified for our sake. Laid in a tomb, dead. And then on the third day, he rose from the grave. He rose with a new body that will never perish. A new body that allowed him to eat and speak and embrace and walk through closed doors and appear and disappear at will. Hundreds saw him and live to bear testimony, for he remained on earth forty days before returning to his Father.

"He reigns over a new kingdom. A kingdom more of heaven than of this earth. Everyone clamors to be a citizen of Rome. Is it not so? Think of the many advantages that belonging to the greatest empire in the world may offer a man. But Rome cannot take your tears away. It cannot restore your life. It cannot take away your sorrow or crying or pain. It cannot overcome death. These things you shall only find in the kingdom of Jesus.

"This is why he has the power to give us a garment of praise instead of a spirit of despair. It is why in him we can rebuild the ancient ruins of our lives and restore the places in our hearts that have long remained devastated by our histories. That is what the prophet Isaiah foretold."

Thunderstruck, Lydia listened. *There is nothing in the world so damaged that it cannot be repaired by the hand of Almighty God,* Paul had said. And this Jesus was the key to that repair, the doorway to such restoration.

Rebekah had many questions. Lydia understood her friend's reservations. Even understood her cynicism. For years she had studied the Jewish Scripture. Knew great tomes of it by heart and could argue its sense with a Pharisee's expertise. She needed her proof when presented with a man who claimed to be the Son of God.

It was different for Lydia. She knew—knew bone deep—that despite her unanswered questions, she had found the one answer that mattered. This Messiah was the one she had waited for.

The Lord had opened her heart to this knowledge. She knew Paul's testimony to be the truth. Her feet wobbled as she stood. "Master Paul, what do I have to do to enter into the Lord's Kingdom?"

Paul laughed, a hearty sound rising out of his chest that reminded Lydia of the gurgling noise of a clean brook. "There is a river here. I can baptize you this very moment. You can join the family of God. *My* family."

Lydia stepped forward. "I am ready."

Paul asked her a thousand questions. Did she repent? Did she believe? Did she receive? Did she renounce evil? Yes! With a resounding, unquestioning, hopeful, tear-filled certainty, she answered yes to each question.

He blessed her and pressed her into the river, purple clothes and all, her head dipping under the water, hair entangled and wet, spread in a hundred directions by the currents. Her breath held, impeded by the river. Her old self was being washed, cleansed, dying even—dying to the past, dying to death, dying to self—and rising up to take a breath like no other in her life. A breath pure and free of guilt. Washed of shame. She felt as if she was newly born.

Then Paul, Silas, Timothy, Luke, and Marcus laid hands on her head and began to pray, words she did not catch, sounds she did not understand, some speaking in languages utterly unknown to her. Their prayers had a strange power. Where she had always been empty, she began to be filled with an inexplicable contentment.

Tears fell, blinding her. Her nose ran. Her wet hair clung to her face and head in haphazard clumps. She cared nothing for these things. Her soul lived! The Holy Spirit, the men called him, this new presence within her. He took away the loneliness and grief. She felt changed by this visitation, this infilling. Altered forever. She would have fallen over if they had not held her up in their strong arms.

When it was over, Lydia stood, shaking, her legs weak, her body spent. For the first time in her life, she was utterly at peace.

"You are the first," Paul said, "in this whole realm. The first to believe. The first to be baptized."

Lydia laughed. She turned to the gathering of women. Rebekah stared with wide eyes, her mouth slightly open. Chloris looked like a gazelle, an expression of awe transforming her young face from beauty to something transcendent. Other women from her household took in the scene in silence. She saw that many were affected by what they had witnessed, weeping in silence.

She was their mistress, their patroness. By

virtue of her position, she held over them a world of unspoken power. Her decision to follow the Christ obligated them to do the same. Where she went, they must follow. Her God would have to be theirs. Yet Lydia knew that this decision needed to be an inward one, true to one's heart. Not one made for the sake of obligation or as a mark of respect toward their mistress.

She cleared her throat. "Sisters," she began. "Those of you who belong to my household: know that I will not demand this faith of you, nor will I hold it against you if you choose not to follow me. Let this decision come from your heart, not from my urging. I invite you to join me in this blessing, freely. Beloved, let Jesus rule in your hearts, for he is life."

Rebekah came to stand by her. "You have been touched by God," she said. "I see it in your face. He has changed you."

Lydia's smile shone. "You still have to contend with your objections. I understand."

Rebekah shook her head. "I suspect God will never answer all my questions. Perhaps it is a matter of faith more than understanding." She went to Paul. "Master, I wish to be baptized."

She emerged from the water without the shattered expression Lydia had borne. God's touch on Rebekah was more understated. A subtle shifting in her soul that lacked the dramatic experience Lydia had had, yet no less real because of it. Rebekah went into the water brimming with questions and came out with peace.

Chloris followed, and then the rest. The waters were stirred by the women's steps of faith, salted by their tears, washed by their newness.

FORTY-SIX

Oh that my vexation were weighed,
and all my calamity laid in the balances!
For then it would be heavier
than the sand of the sea.
JOB 6:2-3

By the time Paul performed the last baptism, the sun had dipped low in the sky and the afternoon had grown old.

Lydia observed the fading light with bewilderment. Her mind had not registered the passing of the hours. "Master Paul, will you and your companions consider staying at my home as my guests? For as long as you remain in Philippi, my home is at your disposal."

Paul inclined his head. "You are most gracious, Mistress Lydia, and honor us by your invitation. But our message is not welcomed by all, as it has been here today. We bring with us Good News and trouble, both. I would not burden your household with any unrest which our presence might arouse."

The thought of this man dragging the strife of the world into her already-troubled home gave Lydia a moment of pause. One thing she knew with certainty was that he would also bring with him the peace of God. She was surprised to find no anxiety in her heart as she contemplated the possible problems that might visit her through her guests. Besides, had she not learned through the bitterness of her father's unjust arrest and subsequent death that she should not turn her back on those in distress merely to save herself a bit of inconvenience?

She bowed her head. "It's of no consequence. If you agree that I am a true believer in the Lord, come and stay at my home. My servants will make you comfortable and provide you with bedding in the courtyard. The women sleep above stairs and will not burden you."

Paul turned to Silas and Luke for a silent exchange. "It would be no burden to us to share your company and an honor to tell you more about our Lord Jesus. My companions and I would be pleased to accept your invitation."

After their long day, everyone had generated a great appetite. Rebekah arranged for food to be sent to the men in the courtyard. Among the more conservative members of Roman society, women did not partake of meals with men during a formal feast, and while this was far from a formal affair, Lydia did not wish to intrude upon her guests.

To her delight, Paul sent one of the servants to ask her and Rebekah to join them for the evening meal. "We belong to one family now," he said.

"Let us eat together as brothers and sisters."

As they ate in the *triclinium*, leaning comfortably on couches, Paul and Silas spoke of the Lord to them. Lydia found herself sitting across from Marcus Marcius. He had the bearing of a soldier rather than an architect. His dark eyes were surrounded by laugh lines that looked like faint sunbursts; his hair, cropped close to his scalp in the Roman fashion, seemed almost black except for a hint of gray at the temples. She noticed his hands, which were unusually clean but scarred from fingertip to wrist; his right palm bore a large, sun-shaped cicatrix.

He was a handsome man, which put her on her guard. Since Jason, she found good looks in men an offense. But something in the cast of Marcius's face and the lines around his eyes caused her to wonder about him. Something about the man tugged at the walls she had erected around her heart. She forced her attention to Silas, who was telling the story of a blind man whom Jesus had healed.

During a lull in the conversation, Marcius leaned toward her. "My thanks for your hospitality, Lydia. It has been weeks since I have partaken of such a delicious meal."

She felt her heart pick up its tempo, and she tried without success to quench its enthusiasm. "I have a good cook," she said. "You met her at the river this morning." Lydia held out a plate of fish to him. "Try her roasted tuna with mint sauce. Her specialty."

He laid the warm piece of bread he had just dipped in olive oil on his plate and reached for the roasted tuna. Her gaze lingered on the scarred hands. The man was a curiosity. A cultured Roman, judging by his speech and manner and patrician cognomen. And yet he bore the scars of a servant.

"How is it that you, a Roman born and bred, came to follow the Lord, Marcus Marcius?" she asked, unable to swallow the question—unable to resist the intrigue of him.

"Please. If I am to have the honor of remaining in your home, call me by my praenomen. Call me Marcus."

"Marcus, then."

"I began to follow the Lord when I was a slave."

Lydia blinked. "A slave?" She had never heard of a Roman of his class being sold into slavery. "You were a slave?"

"For three years." Marcus closed his hands into fists. The whole room had grown silent.

The Greek physician, Luke, reached over to clasp him on his shoulder with long, reassuring fingers. "Not many men would have survived what you went through, my friend. Fewer still would emerge with a whole heart."

"That, I owe to God and his faithful servant Jacob."

Lydia was beginning to understand the attraction of that angular face. It was stamped not only with a superficial beauty but also with pain. He was acquainted with deepest sorrow. And something even more compelling. It was as if Marcus had discovered secrets men seldom unearthed and had entered depths heaven revealed to a select few. He was nothing like Jason, Lydia realized. Jason had been all surface, the shallows pretending to hide fathoms that weren't there. This man knew depths she could only guess at.

"Will you tell us your story, Marcus?" she asked, holding her breath.

He looked at her, his dark eyes narrowed. She turned the color of the beets in the salad under that careful scrutiny. She had no right to ask him such a question. No right to delve into his past. She was about to apologize and take back her request when he smiled at her. His smile was warm and understanding, as if he recognized that her request went beyond a meager curiosity. As if he understood the root of her question better than she did. He nodded once, and without fanfare began his story.

"I was born in Rome to a patrician family long on pride and short on coin," he said. "Our fortunes had dwindled over the decades so that by the time I was a young man, we lived in the crumbling ruins of a once-grand villa with little land left for farming and no more treasures to sell. My mother, Atia, had rough hands for want of a servant. I remember her washing our laundry herself, something a patrician woman is never supposed to do.

"As an only son, I knew what was expected of me. The army beckoned. For the sake of the glory of Rome and in order to restore the fortunes of my family, I had to join the thousands who fought to secure Rome's ever-expanding borders. I had no interest in the army and even less in warfare. From the time I can remember, I had a passion for building. Houses, bridges, libraries, aqueducts. It mattered not. The intricacies of design and structure drew me like the irresistible song of the sirens. My hope was that once I joined my division, I might be assigned to work with the engineers who often served in the Roman army.

"When I turned sixteen, I boarded ship in the harbor of Misenum at the northern end of the Bay of Naples. Our galley was a long, narrow trireme, not large but fast. With two hundred men on board, including the oarsmen, we were jammed tight, sleeping on deck wherever we could find space to sit. We were headed first for Baetica in the Iberian Peninsula, where we were to deliver fifty men, and from there to pick up provisions and make our way to Britannia, where I was assigned to serve.

"We never made it as far as Baetica. The wind was against us from the start of our journey. It took us seven days on the Mediterranean Sea traveling westward to cover the distance that should have taken two. On the seventh day, we came across a small merchant ship. It was packed with wheat and passengers, destined for Rome. Though many years have passed since that fateful afternoon, I remember the lines of that dainty ship, smaller than our trireme, and slow. Merchant ships use sails only. They have no room for oars and oarsmen."

Lydia smiled. "I can picture it exactly. It was on such a ship that Rebekah and I made our way to Philippi."

"Then you can understand our concern when we detected the second ship. It took us some time to recognize it for what it was. Pirates had not disturbed those waters for over fifty years. And yet here was an Illyrian quadrireme, sleek and fast, eating up the wind, heading for the merchant vessel.

"Our commander did not hesitate. He ordered the captain to engage the pirates. What choice had we? We could not leave the merchant vessel defenseless."

Lydia set her napkin aside, her appetite forgotten. "Had I been a passenger, I would have welcomed your help most fervently. I cannot imagine being pursued by pirates, though I assume engaging them could have been no easy feat either."

"We were Roman, two hundred strong and ready for battle. None of us conceived of defeat. I thought they would turn and run when they saw us. Why risk engaging a fully armed Roman warship? I did not know the pirate captain then. He was Illyrian by birth, the son and grandson of generations of bold marauders. Far from running, he turned and rammed straight into us.

"I had never been in a war, never even seen a skirmish. That day I saw a glimpse of hell in the chaos that ensued. Many died with the initial impact. The Illyrians boarded our galley within moments, undeterred by our arrows and spears. We fought with our swords and fists and whatever else we could lay hands on. Ill prepared for an engagement that came too fast, we did our best to overcome the pirates. Our best proved insufficient. We lost the battle. Many of my comrades died. Young like me and unseasoned for war, they were easy prey in the hands of rough men.

"The Illyrians executed most of our experienced officers and captured thirty-seven of us as slaves. Pirates make better money through slavery than the seizure of goods."

Lydia was not the only one who gasped. Sounds of shock filled the chamber. Marcus spread his arms.

"In the course of one hour, I went from being a proud Roman patrician to an Illyrian slave. Worse yet: they did not intend to auction me at some distant port, where perhaps I might find a way back home. For me, they had another plan.

"Though we had lost the battle, we had inflicted a good deal of damage. Many pirates and the slaves who served them had died at our hands, their bodies floating in the warm waters of the Mediterranean Sea. The pirate ship needed new oarsmen. That became my assignment."

Wrapping her arms around her stomach, Lydia leaned back. She could not imagine a worse fate.

FORTY-SEVEN

Blessed is the one who perseveres under trial
because, having stood the test, that person
will receive the crown of life that the Lord has
promised to those who love him.
JAMES 1:12, NIV

"I found out the fundamental rule of rowing within the first hour of my new life. Rowing is pain. It exerts a brutal punishment upon every muscle you have. From the moment you pull on that long oar, battling the weight of water, every part of your body screams with agony. For protracted periods of time, you find no respite. Your only reality is the oar in your hand, the sound of the drum in your ear, and the sight of the man next to you, pulling in tandem, pulling to live.

"They chained me to a man of middle years with a beard that reached his chest and a stench that could make you gag. Soon I would smell the same. But that first day, I did not know it. I felt superior to everyone. I was a Roman, after all.

"For the first few hours, my oar mate said nothing. I stumbled with the oar, trying to learn the rhythm, trying to avoid the added punishment of the oar master's whip. Then, as night fell, the ship dropped anchor, and we could finally rest. I collapsed forward, half-insensate from pain and exhaustion. 'Drink this,' a kind voice said in my ear, and my oar mate held a chipped wooden cup to my chapped lips and forced water into my mouth. 'I am Jacob,' he said. 'Jacob Ben Samuel. I have served on this ship for four years. I have survived, and so shall you, young Roman.' "

"Jacob?" Rebekah asked.

"Yes." Marcus's lips softened for a moment. "He was one of your people. I told him that I was not serving any filthy pirates for four years.

"Jacob Ben Samuel laughed softly and passed me a piece of bread. 'Eat, then. You will need your strength if you are to walk out of here on your own feet.'

"My fingers were a mass of blisters by the next morning. The blisters burst and turned into new blisters. I still carry the scars on my hands. Our days began with pain and ended with pain.

"Pride is a powerful force. It shapes your view of the world, of yourself. For all its power, I found that it breaks easily and leaves behind nothing. By the end of the first month, my pride had crumbled. Courage, hope, confidence disintegrated in its wake. There is no greater shame for a Roman than to be reduced to slavery. Not only defeated but captured, shackled.

"I gave in. I tried to wrap my chains about

my own throat. Death by suicide was the only honorable option left to me.

"Jacob saved me." Marcus looked at his scars. "He was the kindest man I have ever met. Day by day, he gave me a reason to live.

"At first he taught me the simple lessons of rowing. How to hold the oar. How to protect my back, my elbow, my shoulder from injury. Our Illyrian masters switched our positions from one side of the boat to the other, but they kept us chained to the same partners. So Jacob and I spent more hours together than most brothers.

"There were days when we were pushed beyond what our bodies could endure, beyond weariness, so that every shred of strength left us. In those moments Jacob would whisper in my ear, 'One more pull. One more pull. Don't give in, boy. One more.' And it was his voice, the warm concern in it, the sheer civility of it in the midst of unthinkable brutality, that pushed me to persevere. Jacob taught me resilience. He taught me that my mind could be stronger than my body.

"With the brashness of youth buoyed by Roman pride, I had boasted to Jacob that first day that I would not serve a pirate ship for four years. I would not have served for four months if he had not cared for me. They would have dragged my beaten body out of the hull of that quadrireme. As it was, I remained enslaved for three full years.

Jacob began to speak to me of God when the first month had ended.

"For three years, I heard of this God. How he had inclined his ear to the misery of the slaves in Egypt and sent them help. God, Jacob said, carried my tears in his bottle and would one day give me beauty for the ashes of my life. Like you, Lydia, I became a God-fearer. Driven day after day, past agony, past exhaustion, past the voice that whispered this thing could not be done, I pulled on the oar and gave my bitterness to Jacob's God.

"My friend saved my body from death on that ship, but he saved my soul from worse."

Lydia had never been enslaved, captive to brutal masters. But she had come close to giving in. She understood how Marcus felt about Jacob, for she felt the same about Rebekah. It was her kindness, her counsel, her love of God that had helped Lydia hold on through the harshest years.

"How came you to be liberated from those wretched pirates?" she asked Marcus.

FORTY-EIGHT

Jesus said, "Father, forgive them, for they
don't know what they are doing."
LUKE 23:34, NLT

"One morning we came across a ship. I recognized it immediately. It was a Roman warship, a trireme, much like the one I had served on when I was captured. Something in me rebelled. I could not aid in the enslavement of other men like me. I could not participate, even unwillingly, in the killing of my countrymen.

"There were other Romans who served as slaves on our vessel. I cried for their help. I encouraged them to revolt. The impending battle had forced the Illyrians on deck, leaving only one man below with us. As I screamed for rebellion, the oar master came at me with his whip, dagger drawn, intending to silence me. He miscalculated in one regard. Three years of pulling oars makes you strong. I was no longer a puny boy, easily overcome. In a moment, I had wrapped his bruising whip around my hand and pulled him helplessly to the ground. His dagger ground into my hand." Marcus showed his palm, where the sun-shaped scar twinkled white in the firelight. "I knew how to keep my head in the midst of pain. Within moments, I held his keys in one hand, his dagger in the other."

Folding his palm into a fist, Marcus grinned. "Not a great price for escape. We freed ourselves from our chains and joined the fray on the side of Rome. The Illyrians were winning until we arrived. Our help turned the tide of the battle, and the Romans gained the upper hand. Not only did they overcome the Illyrians, but they also earned a rich prize from the holds of the pirate ship and returned to great glory at home. The shame of my slavery was washed by that triumph and the part I played in it.

"The commander of the Roman vessel, Lucius Antias, knew he owed his life and victory to our intervention. When he discovered my role in the battle, he offered to give me any reward I wished. At the time, Jacob was still a slave by Rome's reckoning. He would be placed on the auction block in Rome. As my reward, I asked for his freedom. Within days, Jacob had his certificate of manumission. He returned to his home in Caesarea a free man, though he took part of my heart with him. He will always remain my dearest friend.

"Upon my arrival in Rome, I discovered that both my parents were dead. When he heard of my loss, Antias, who had listened to my story and learned of my dreams as we traveled together, insisted on giving me part of his share of the prize money for capturing the Illyrian ship. 'I will still be a richer man than I was before I met you,' he told me. 'Not to mention less dead than I would have been if you had not led the slaves into a revolt against the slave traders.'

"The money he gave me was sufficient to see me through the years of training as an architect and engineer. It paid for my education, my books, my equipment, my lodgings, and my food for the years that I studied. To him I owe a debt I can never repay, though I have tried many times.

"When my training was complete, I decided not to remain in Rome but to travel throughout the empire in order to find the most interesting jobs. Wherever I went, on the Sabbath, I sought a synagogue, if one could be found. I continued to worship the God of Abraham, though in my heart, I longed for more. Where was this Messiah we were promised? Where the power of the prophets of old? Where did Gentiles like me fit in?

"When traveling in Ephesus last year, I developed a cough I could not shake. Luke happened to be visiting Ephesus at the same time, and the members of the synagogue introduced him to me.

"He healed my cough and told me of the Christ. As I recall, he had an iron clamp down my throat when he said, 'You should live a long and healthy life, given the strength of your body. But would you not rather have eternal life, Marcius?'

"I have a great respect for iron clamps, particularly if they are occupying my throat. So I said I would."

Everyone laughed. The architect could hold the attention of a bored three-year-old with his storytelling. He had led a fascinating life, Lydia thought. But beyond that, he had come away with a heart made stouter by loss and tragedy. That he had survived was a testimony to his strength. Yet there was more to him than a man who had survived an experience that would have killed others. The brutal existence on that ship had failed to twist him. Lesser men would have left bitter, filled with hatred. Marcus, she sensed, was a man at peace, unmolested by the storms of rage.

"That is an impressive scar," Lydia said, pointing to his hand. "But the tale behind it is even more impressive."

"I follow a scarred Redeemer. Somehow I think our scars become holy in the shadow of his. And his plans are made perfect in the demolition of our own devices. This is not the life I once thought I would live. But it has proven better than any life I might have chosen."

A scarred Redeemer, Lydia thought, and she was put in mind of her own scarred heart. Could the scars borne by Jesus transform her own scars? The ones she bore from the death of her mother, from Jason's betrayal and the loss of her father, from the theft of her home? Could such monsters that pursued her dreams and shaped her waking moments with their darkness actually become holy?

"What of the Illyrians? Do you despise them? Do you not wish to revenge yourself upon them?" she said.

Marcus shrugged a shoulder. "I have forgiven my cruel masters."

"Forgiven them?" Lydia spit out the words as if they tasted bitter on her tongue.

"While he hung on the cross, caught in the agony of such a death, Jesus found the strength to speak a handful of words. Shall I tell you my favorite? He said, 'Father, forgive them, for they don't know what they are doing.' He said this about his tormenters and murderers. Roman and Jew. It did not matter to him. He spoke forgiveness over them, although they betrayed him and robbed him of life itself.

"I say the same words when I am tempted to hate. Those poor Illyrians. Hell has a hold on their souls, and they are barely out of it, though they live on this earth. I will leave them safely in the hands of Jesus. Unforgiveness would only chain my heart to them. And I am a free man now."

After Lydia bid her guests a good night, she retired for the evening. In the quiet of her chamber, she relived the moment of her baptism and asked herself if she had committed an error.

Had she rushed into this new faith? Was this Jesus to be trusted?

Peace chased away doubt at the thought of his name. She thought of Marcus's expression as he said, *"I am a free man now."* He had meant it. He lived in freedom because of Christ.

Could she be free of Dione and Jason? Of the boar? Of Antiochus? Of fear itself?

The thought of Antiochus reminded her of the ruined indigo. Rebekah had said that God would send them his aid. He had sent Paul and his friends. They knew nothing about indigo, however. Perhaps her soul needed help more than her dye.

She pushed her blanket aside and tiptoed past sleeping servants and down the stairs, avoiding her guests who slumbered in the atrium as she made her way into the workshop where the indigo was kept. Sinking to her knees, she stared into the ruined paste, trying to devise some way out of her dilemma.

Worse yet, she needed to discover the identity of the person who had destroyed the dye. There could be no true safety under her roof until she determined the means by which Antiochus had gained access to her home.

FORTY-NINE

He said, "It is finished," and he bowed
his head and gave up his spirit.
JOHN 19:30

The morning had turned cool. Early autumn had taken a hard, unseasonal turn toward winter. Lydia came out of the workshop, feeling pale and drawn. Earlier, when she had taken a moment to comb her hair before a polished mirror, she had noted dark shadows like soot smudging her eyes.

"The peace of God to you, Lydia."

Her head snapped up. "Master Paul! I did not see you."

Paul waved a reassuring hand. "Trouble?"

Was her turmoil written on her face, clear as the Latin alphabet? Was she so easy to read? She wondered if she should dump her worries upon the poor man. For all his generosity of spirit, he remained a relative stranger to her. He gazed at her with a steady calm, giving the impression that he could carry the weight of many a burden without breaking. His inviting tranquility loosened her tongue.

"Our supply of indigo was ruined. I have ordered a new shipment, which won't arrive for a week. Perhaps two. Too late for us to finish this order in a timely manner. Even if we work day and night, we will not complete it in time."

Paul sat on a marble bench and invited Lydia to sit on its twin near him. "Marcus told you one of the sayings of Christ while he hung on the cross. Do you want to hear another?"

Lydia nodded.

"He said, 'It is finished.' He was speaking of his work on earth. Of his victory over darkness. Of his conquest over death and evil. 'It is finished.'

"I find such comfort in that pronouncement. In the reality that the work of the Messiah is accomplished. Fulfilled. Completed. And therefore, all the works that my soul needs—its redemption and restoration and forgiveness, its renewal and re-creation and salvation—all this is now accomplished. The most important work in the world has been completed.

"I sometimes fancy that the completed work of the cross casts its shadow on other parts of my life too. Because Christ has finished the most crucial work on earth and in heaven, something of that completion covers all the unfinished parts of my life. What remains undone in me, through me, finds a resting place in Jesus' finished work."

Lydia's shoulders slumped. "I do not think my indigo will find a resting place in Jesus, Master Paul. It is ruined. I am not finished with *my* work. I am late. Forgive me. But commerce makes a person practical. It is very well to speak of the cross's shadow. Still, that shadow will be no good when my angry customer demands to know why his order has not arrived at his doorstep on the expected day."

Paul bent and looked into Lydia's shadowed eyes. "You are deeply burdened by this?"

She leaned her head back and closed her eyes for a moment. "A business is built or destroyed on the back of its reputation. Even small failures can leave a significant mark."

"I understand your conundrum. It is very real," he said. "But when Jesus says, 'It is finished,' dear Lydia, you can rest in the absolute authority that flows from those words. They are more real even than your indigo." Paul gave a smile. "Fetch me this ruined dye."

"The indigo?"

"Bring it to me, if you please."

Lydia scratched her head. Then, turning, she called, "Epaphroditus, help the dye master fetch a vat of indigo, if you please." The vat was heavy, requiring two men to bring it into the courtyard, half-bent under its weight. "We purchase our indigo as a prepared paste," she explained. "The seller extracts the dye from the leaves of indigo plants, and this is how it comes to us."

Paul took a squinting look at its contents and nodded. He leaned forward and extended a hand over the vat. His lips moved in silent prayer for a few moments. "I think you should try using it again," he said, straightening his back.

Lydia exhaled the way a dragon might breathe. "We have tried many times, Master Paul. It is no use. A rubbish dump is too good for this muck."

"Will you not try one more time?"

"For your sake then." In moments, the dye master had set up the necessary vats with Epaphroditus's help and bathed a small clump of wool inside the dye. It emerged a royal blue. Lydia, who had slouched against the wall, arms crossed, shot to her feet. "It is impossible. Do it again. Use more wool this time."

With every trial the wool emerged the perfect shade, a royal blue, the prerequisite first step to Lydia's purple. "I do not understand. Use another sample of paste," she said, her voice urgent.

Paul adjusted a pillow against the wall, making himself comfortable, chewing on mint leaves he had plucked from a large pot nearby. Silas and Marcus had joined them, and hearing the explanation from Paul, observed the frenetic activity with wide smiles.

"I never grow weary of days like this," Marcus said. "Not all the glory in Rome compares to it."

After one hour of trials, Lydia finally had to believe the evidence before her eyes. "How can this be?" she asked. "I tested the indigo from every single vat. They were all ruined. Not even a string of yarn emerged the right color. And now look at them!"

In her excitement, she had pushed the dye master aside and soaked the wool in the vat with her own fingers, forgetting to utilize the long staff they used for the job. Her hands were blue up to the wrists. She raked them through her hair, pushing aside an annoying clump that fell on her cheeks.

Pulling on his beard, Paul came to his feet and peeked inside one of the vats. "I believe we call it a miracle. The Lord sometimes moves in mysteries we cannot comprehend."

Lydia froze, arrested by Paul's words. "God healed my indigo. This is what you meant when you said Christ's work is more real than my indigo?"

"Yes and no. This time, the Lord chose to give you a miracle. By virtue of his intervention, you will finish your work on time. God has the power to work supernaturally in our midst.

"I don't want you to think this will be his response to every one of your problems, however. They don't call them miracles because they are common."

Silas grinned. "Well, they are more common when Paul is around. Or Peter and John."

"My point is that the work of Christ casts its shadow on your life whether you receive a miracle or not. He may give you forbearance instead of a miracle. Or peace in the midst of turmoil. He may give you wisdom when you have no more answers. Or he may hold your hand as only the Christ can and impart courage to steady your shaking knees. His work is finished. You see? That fulfillment will cast its shadow on all your unfinished work.

"You can give up your anxiety about being late. Because the Lord has completed the greater work, you can settle into peace, for his work will brace and empower your small tasks. They seem of such importance to you that their weight becomes a great burden, bearing you down. But when you are pressed, Lydia, and filled with fear, remember him whispering, 'It is finished,' and it will cut your challenges down to size. He will empower you to finish what you must."

Lydia twisted blue hands, trying to make sense of Paul's teaching. She opened her mouth to speak when Chloris galloped into the courtyard, her skirts held high to give her knees room to pump freely. "He is here! Here at the door!" Her chest rose and fell in a fast rhythm that owed more to terror than to her race.

"Who is here?" Lydia asked, though she already knew the answer.

"That man. Antiochus. I was sitting by the window above stairs when I saw a carriage draw up. He is headed inside this very moment. Oh, what shall I do?"

FIFTY

Eye for eye, tooth for tooth,
hand for hand, foot for foot, burn for burn,
wound for wound, stripe for stripe.
EXODUS 21:24-25

The sound of feet clattering against the stone steps outside interrupted all conversation. Lydia grabbed Chloris by the arm and shoved her into one of the workshops.

"Not a word. Not a sound. And bar the door after me," she hissed before shutting it.

Paul, Silas, and Marcus stared at the unfolding drama, refraining from asking any questions. "I will explain later," she whispered. "Pray for me."

Rebekah arrived in the courtyard. "Antiochus is here!" Lydia nodded, signaling her knowledge. "What is he up to now?" Rebekah hissed. There was no time to answer. Antiochus bounded in, face red, his hair oily with sweat.

"You've gone too far this time, Lydia."

Lydia raised a warning finger. "I do not recall inviting you to my home. And lower your voice. You disturb my guests."

Antiochus spared a glance for Paul and his friends. "They might as well know what manner of woman offers them hospitality. A slithering

337

water snake of a woman. This is the last time I allow you to interfere in my affairs."

"If you are here to talk about Chloris again—"

"I am here to talk about my slave, Demetrius."

Lydia wondered if he had discovered the part she had played in convincing Appollonia to hire Demetrius. She wiped her face clean of expression. "What about your slave?"

Antiochus slapped his hand so hard on the marble bench, the sprig of mint Paul had set there bounced. Marcus took a step forward, his eyes narrowed. Lydia gave him a reassuring smile. He took no action but remained close, his expression alert, like one of the emperor's Praetorian Guard, ready to swoop if Antiochus took a wrong step. Lydia felt a loosening of the knot in her belly. She had not felt so protected since the passing of her father.

"If you cannot behave like a civilized man," she said to Antiochus, "I must ask you to leave this house. I have no knowledge of any slave that belongs to you." That was no lie, for Demetrius had been declared free.

"You know full well the part you played in this outrage. There is no use denying it. I have it from the mouth of the magistrate. You were there a year ago, as my father lay dying, out of his mind with disease and fever. You were there, goading this treachery."

The magistrate! She had not considered that

the man would reveal her identity to Antiochus. Lydia's shoulders drooped. Fear, like lava, heated her veins. "Your father swore me to secrecy. What would you have me do? Break my oath?"

"You should have fetched me that night. What man in his right mind would give away a valuable slave like Demetrius? You must have seen that the old man had lost his sanity. The illness had robbed him of his senses, and he never had much to begin with." He pointed a forefinger toward her. "Look at the company he kept! You had no right to encourage him in his madness."

Lydia stretched out a placating hand. "Antiochus, your father was weak but in his right mind. You can ask the magistrate. He would not have sealed the documents if he suspected Rufus incapable of thinking straight. You know very well that many wealthy men give faithful slaves their freedom in appreciation for their years of service. There was genuine affection between Demetrius and your father. Rufus wished to repay the man for his loyalty and kindness throughout the years."

"You lie! Why did he keep all this a secret from me? Not a whisper, not a single warning. Why would he do that unless he was demented? And you encouraged this lunacy. Instead of stopping it, you smiled and squeezed his hand and admired his good decision. The magistrate told me."

"I did not suggest the deed, Antiochus. Rufus

came up with the idea. I cannot deny that I agreed with his arrangement and, yes, I told him so.

"But you misunderstand. Your father did not tell you because he knew you would not accept his wishes. He wanted to die with peace between you, not an unpleasant quarrel that would make his last days bitter.

"He thought of you, of your welfare, till the end. He made Demetrius promise that he would continue working as your steward for a full year and put the affairs of the workshop in good order before leaving. He arranged all this so that you would be handed a strong, healthy trade. I am certain Demetrius kept that promise and served you most faithfully until the final hour."

"One year? What is one year to me? Do you know how much it will cost me to replace that slave?"

"I am sorry for your loss. But you cannot blame me for your father's decision. He asked me to attend him that night as a friend, and I could not deny his final wish. This much is true. I could not even serve as a legal witness; the magistrate said as a woman, my testimony would bear no weight."

"Rufus was sick! If you were his true friend, you would have dissuaded him from this madness. And as he is dead, I cannot contend with him. But you, Lydia, had better watch your back. From this moment on, I will hound you until you are nothing but a ruin and your workshop is cinders on the ground. I will take Chloris from you, and I will crumple her like a sheet of papyrus. I will make you watch while your own insignificant workshop collapses at your feet."

He noticed the vat of indigo sitting in the courtyard for the first time. "You will be ruined as completely as this indigo paste." He smirked. His eye caught the mountain of yarn, dyed dark blue.

"What is this? You bought new paste already? Must have cost you a fortune. After paying so much for Chloris, I wonder you can afford it."

Lydia's dye master, unaware of the layers of tension, waded into the conversation. "Oh no, Master Antiochus. This is not fresh paste. It's the old one. The ruined batch. The mistress's God restored it. Master Paul prayed for it, and it is as good as any batch of indigo I ever worked with."

"What?" Antiochus turned sharply to Paul and Silas and Marcus. "What nonsense is this?"

"None that concerns you," Lydia said. Her throat felt raw.

Antiochus laughed. "Gods now, is it?"

The dye master shook his head. "Not gods. God. These men are Jews, and they teach there is only one true God reigning on earth. It is the power of their God that has wrought this miracle."

"Is that so?" Antiochus turned to Lydia. "Let's

see how many miracles your guests have up their sleeves in the days to come. You will need them."

Lydia slouched in wordless dread as Antiochus stormed out. She collapsed on the bench, shaking. Rebekah knelt before her friend and took her icy hand in her own. "At least he knows nothing about the part you played on behalf of Appollonia."

Lydia nodded. "Rebekah, remember the rabbits?"

"I remember."

FIFTY-ONE

Get rid of all bitterness, rage, anger, harsh words,
and slander, as well as all types of evil behavior.
Instead, be kind to each other, tenderhearted,
forgiving one another, just as God
through Christ has forgiven you.
EPHESIANS 4:31-32, NLT

"Not a pleasant man, is he?" Paul said. "He is after Chloris?"

Lydia nodded. "I bought her so he could not get his hands on her. She is only ten, Master Paul! The law would grant him the right to do whatever he wished if he owned her. I was once a girl her age, and I cannot imagine the harm such a violation could do."

"You did right." He patted her hand. "I think I understand the matter with Demetrius as well. You have been carrying heavy burdens indeed."

Lydia became aware of Epaphroditus leaning against a column, his face bloodless. She saw that he trembled like a tiny leaf in the midst of hail. He came forward and fell to his knees. Lydia blinked. "What is it, Epaphroditus?"

"Forgive me, mistress!"

She frowned. "Forgive you for what, man? Rise up and speak. There is nothing to fear here."

"I have wronged you." Epaphroditus kept his gaze glued to Lydia's sandals and took a gulping breath. "It was I who spoiled the dye. My hand poured in the poison that ruined it."

Lydia sprang to her feet. She felt heat rise to her cheeks. She had believed him to be her trusted servant! For years, she had placed her confidence in him.

"You betrayed me, Epaphroditus?" Her voice emerged like a bark, hard and sharp. "Tell me what possessed you! Was I ever unkind to you? Unjust? Ungenerous?" She was turning to a rabid dog, every word a bite.

Paul, who had spent several hours the evening before speaking to the man, raised a calming hand. "It is good that you have confessed, Epaphroditus. Tell us what happened."

Epaphroditus wiped a trembling hand across his eyes. "I had no choice. Antiochus threatened me. He said he would expose me if I did not obey him. Gave me that foul concoction to add to the paste."

"Expose you for what?" Lydia crossed her arms across her chest.

"He is my cousin, you see. My mother and his father were brother and sister . . ."

Lydia raised a brow. "That is a misfortune, and I pity you for it. But it is not a crime to be exposed."

"Let the man speak," Paul said with a frown.

Lydia swallowed her rage, rattled by Paul's displeasure.

"We grew up together, Antiochus and I, though we lived in very different worlds. My father was a gambler. Before I turned twelve, he had lost everything we had. If not for Rufus's kindness, we would have starved. One night, when Antiochus and I were scarcely more than boys, he sneaked a jug of wine from their cellar into our home, and we drank ourselves full until our heads were muddled.

"Antiochus had the notion of riffling through my father's personal belongings. My father had a rough side to him. He drank too much, and as soon as he laid his hands on a few denarii, he gambled it away. Invariably he lost what little he had, which put him in a foul temper. I avoided him as much as I could.

"I tried to dissuade Antiochus, terrified that my father would discover our meddling. He would not listen. I feared a sound beating. I received far worse.

"Antiochus unearthed a gold ring that belonged to Rufus. 'My father's ring!' he cried. 'We thought it lost. Your thieving father took it.'

"Imagine my shame. My terror. If my father had landed in prison, we would have been ruined. I begged Antiochus to keep my father's theft a secret. He felt sorry for me and promised not to mention it to anyone.

"Last week he came here, bearing that ring. He threatened to expose my father to the world if I would not undertake his demand. What was I to do? Can you imagine being branded the son of a thief? Can you imagine what such a life would entail, without honor, without a shred of respect from those who were once your friends?"

Lydia's breath hitched. "I can. Yes."

"My father is feeble and old now. If Antiochus brings this accusation against him, they will imprison him without regard for his white hairs. It would kill him and ruin me. It has been shameful enough growing up under the shadow of my father's degenerate ways. But if it became known that he is a thief as well as a wastrel, there would be no future for me in Philippi. Who would trust the son of a man low enough to rob his own family?"

"What you mean to say is that you harmed me in order to protect yourself." Lydia shook her head. With sudden clarity, she remembered the letter she had entrusted to him. The letter that told Demetrius to meet with Appollonia for a favorable employment opportunity. "What else did you do besides ruining the paste? Did you tell Antiochus about Demetrius? Did you read my letter and betray its contents to your cousin?"

"No, mistress! Never. If I ruined the dye, it was because I was pressed. I had no wish to add to my crime."

Lydia studied the man's trembling lips, his stooping shoulders, the clasped fingers. She believed him. But it was not enough. "I would have kept you with me had you told me the truth about your father. As it is, I want no false servant in my house. You can pack your things and leave."

Epaphroditus's eyes welled up. "You are just to revile me, mistress. I have wronged you."

Marcus, who had remained silent through most of this exchange, spoke up. "Epaphroditus, why did you confess? No one would have known your guilt if you had not spoken of it."

Epaphroditus turned to Lydia. "I have seen the power of your God." He pointed to the vat of indigo. "Seen his care for your welfare. I do not wish to insult him. He is mightier by far than Antiochus. Let my cousin do what he will. I will take my punishment. Before your God, I repent. I am sorry that my conduct caused you so great an anxiety.

"Mistress, you have always shown me charity. I ask for no mercy, for I do not deserve it." He turned to leave.

Paul stepped forward. "It is too soon to speak of forgiveness. But I ask a favor of you, Lydia. Allow Epaphroditus to remain here until you have had time to think the matter through. You can always cast him out at your leisure. The man has confessed. Everything is in the light now.

And I think he will not easily be persuaded to betray you again."

Lydia bit her lip. Before Antiochus had arrived like an outbreak of pestilence, before Epaphroditus had confessed to his perfidy, she had been basking in the sheer goodness of God. Basking in the realization that he had been moved by her plight. The ordinary troubles of a merchant's life had not seemed too mundane to him. He had wrought a miracle for Lydia's sake, as if her heart mattered more than the laws that governed heaven and earth.

This was the same God who had declared words of forgiveness while nailed wrist and ankle to a wooden beam. No one had confessed their wrong to him. Repented for their betrayal. Still, he had offered mercy where none was deserved.

She was no Jesus! She could not offer her forgiveness. Epaphroditus had shattered her trust. She could offer a grain of tolerance, perhaps. "Epaphroditus!"

The man stopped. Turned. Waited.

"You may remain while I take time to consider. None here will divulge your secret, though your cousin's tongue is worse than an adder's bite, and will likely not be still."

"Thank you, mistress."

"Epaphroditus!" This time it was Paul's voice that called out.

"Yes, master?"

Paul pulled out a purse of money. "Will you look after this for us? We are about to go to the agora before we head to the river. I would not wish to lose it to a pickpocket in the crowds. I know it will be safe in your hands. It is all the money we have for our journey."

At this mark of absolute trust, Epaphroditus's face crumpled. He took the purse and grabbed Paul's hand. Bending his head low, he kissed the sun-browned fingers, his tears drenching Paul's skin. "Will your God accept me, master? In spite of my sin?"

Paul clapped him on the back. "With a smile of welcome."

Lydia covered her mouth with a hand. *"Can you imagine being branded the son of a thief?"* he had asked. As she grappled with bitterness, it occurred to her that if anyone ought to understand his heartache, it was she.

FIFTY-TWO

For if you forgive other people
when they sin against you, your
heavenly Father will also forgive you.
MATTHEW 6:14, NIV

"My companions and I are bound for the agora to preach the gospel and then to the river," Paul announced. "We will return this evening to instruct the new believers. Invite more people if you wish, Lydia."

"I will send for a few friends," she said. "Dinner will be waiting for you."

He patted his belly. "My thanks. Your cook is a gift from God."

Chloris, who had sneaked back into the court-yard after Antiochus's departure, sidled close to Lydia. She clasped the child to her side in a comforting gesture.

"You will be in our prayers," Paul said as he wrapped his cloak more closely about his shoulders.

"Perhaps I should remain here," Marcus said. "In the event Antiochus decides to return." Lydia felt a flare of heat in her cheeks.

Paul looked from one to the other. "Good thought," was all he said.

It was late morning when the men left for the agora. Lydia, now in possession of miraculously perfect indigo paste, set to catching up on a job too long delayed. Before she could be truly galvanized into action, however, Marcus pointed to her head, where earlier in the morning she had run her indigo-stained fingers. "You might want to wash that out before it settles permanently. I am not certain the world is prepared for blue hair."

Lydia clapped her hand to the side of her head with a gasp before running above stairs to try to undo the damage. It took her half an hour, and what with Rebekah and Chloris dissolving into gales of laughter, they proved of no assistance. She had to get rid of the dye by herself. Why did the man have to see her like that? She looked old and wilted with sleeplessness, and now, her hair was blue.

Finally she returned to the workshop, pretending a dignity she did not feel. Marcus gave her a welcoming smile. He proved his wisdom by making no comment, and she proved hers by diving into work.

These days, Lydia limited herself to overseeing the process, allowing others to do the manual labor. She still personally prepared the secret additions to the dye in order to prevent outsiders from duplicating her father's formula. Other than Rebekah, no one knew certain steps in the making of her purple. The common parts shared by most sellers of purple, she left to her well-trained dye master and servants.

Marcus listened with rapt attention as she spoke to the dye master. She liked his quiet demeanor. He was not a man who needed to draw attention to himself.

"Where do you live when you do not travel with Paul?" she asked him. Something about the Roman made her want to know everything about him. She felt disconcerted by her own curiosity but could not seem to stem the tide of it.

"This is my first time accompanying Paul and his companions. Not an experience I shall soon forget. I keep a house in Ephesus. Nothing so grand as your residence here, but it is my own design, and comfortable, though I am seldom there. My work draws me to different parts of the empire. If not for a faithful servant, the house would by now be filled with dust and rodents."

"Do you enjoy traveling?"

Marcus looked away. "I used to enjoy it more. As I grow older, I long for home." He shrugged. "A more settled life. In truth, I do not need to travel so much. I can find enough work close to home to provide a comfortable existence. The jobs abroad once seemed more interesting. That is all." He rubbed his jaw.

Epaphroditus walked through the far side of the courtyard, going into the shop to help with customers, a job he handled with reliable expertise. She caught Marcus staring after him.

"You think I should forgive him," she said.

"What I think is of little importance. It is what God thinks that matters."

"I already know what he thinks."

"Forgiveness is not a matter of how we feel. But a continued relationship is. There, you must choose."

He pulled a hand through his short hair. "Have you ever studied a great oak? One branch will bend to the east while another bends to the west. They grow in opposite directions, never touching. Never uniting. And yet they are warmed by the same sun. Fed by the same roots.

"Sometimes God's people are like those branches. They are separated from one another for reasons only the heart comprehends. And yet the light of the Son illuminates both; his presence feeds both.

"God asks you to forgive Epaphroditus. That is not a matter of choice. Only a matter of time and obedience. He leaves it up to you, once you forgive him, whether you trust him to remain here and work for you. It would do neither of you any good if you keep him and yet continuously judge him a deceiver. No man can last under such a bitter weight. Best you let him go if his actions have shattered your trust beyond repair.

"I ask you one question, however, before you

make your decision. Is it Epaphroditus's betrayal you feel so keenly, or has he pressed upon a wound already there? Is he paying one price for his sin and a second for an earlier betrayal in your life?"

Lydia's head jerked back. Turning red, she remembered Jason—Jason, who, in the guise of love and affection, had torn the heart out of her with his duplicity. Was Epaphroditus paying for Jason and Dione's wrongs? She had determined that no one would ever play false with her again.

Epaphroditus was no Jason; nor did he bear any resemblance to Dione's artful cunning. Even she had to admit as much. His hand had been forced by Antiochus's manipulation. Still, she tasted bitter bile at the mere thought of forgiving him. Was her response too harsh? Did he merit a mercy she could not find in herself to give?

Marcus did not press his point, another quality Lydia liked about him. He knew when to let a matter lie.

When the dye was at a stage that no longer needed Lydia's oversight, Marcus suggested that they take a short walk outside. Unused to the dyeing process, he probably was in dire need of fresh air, she realized.

"Luke says you are a gifted architect and engineer," she said as they left the atrium. "If one wants to build a palace or a grand villa, you are the man of the hour, according to him."

Marcus gave a noncommittal smile. "I designed several public buildings in Rome and Ephesus, which are still standing." They were just outside her house now, and he came to a stop. "Speaking of buildings, there was something I noticed about yours. Do you mind if I have a closer look?"

Lydia shrugged. "By all means."

They walked near the western wall of her shop. Unlike the facade, which was made of valuable marble, the side walls had been constructed from cheaper brick. Lydia saw the cracks in the brick before Marcus pointed them out. He ran his fingers over them and examined the base of the building with experienced eyes.

Lydia blanched. "I had not noticed that. Is there a problem with the foundation? That would be a tremendous expense, I suppose."

Marcus shook his head. "You need not be concerned with your foundation. That is why I wished to examine it more closely. Fortunately, this is a superficial problem. The cracks would have started some time ago. Over the years, water from rainfall and dew has crept inside the bricks. They have expanded due to the moisture. Do you notice how long this wall is? Because of its length, as the bricks expand, they have nowhere to go. So they crack."

"That is a relief! What can be done about the bricks?"

Marcus placed his thumb into an especially

wide crack. "You need a good mason. He can fill in the cracks with ease."

"But won't new cracks develop over time?"

"Indeed they will."

"Is there a permanent solution? It seems futile to keep paying a mason to repair a wall that will simply break down again."

Marcus nodded. "Send me your mason, and I will instruct him. If he is an experienced man, he will need no more than three days to complete the job. For my part, I will charge you nothing. Consider it a gift for your hospitality."

Lydia was taken aback not by his generosity so much as by her own response to it. It astounded her to find how much she enjoyed the care of a capable man in the ordinary things of day-to-day living.

FIFTY-THREE

So we do not lose heart. Though our
outer self is wasting away, our inner self is being
renewed day by day. For this light momentary
affliction is preparing for us an eternal weight
of glory beyond all comparison.
2 CORINTHIANS 4:16-17

During the day, her guests would make their way into the agora to share the Good News with any who might listen. They always had entertaining stories upon their return.

"Damalis followed us again," Luke said one evening, sounding frustrated. "She makes such a ruckus, that girl, no one can hear a word we are trying to say."

"Damalis?" Lydia frowned. "Is she not Trachalio and Gaius's slave? The girl famed for her ability to tell the future?"

"The very one," Paul said, pulling on his beard. "She has a spirit. Of divination, I think. Poor soul."

"Not so poor," Lydia said. "She earns her masters a tidy sum by divining the fortune of her many patrons. They say she is never wrong."

Paul's lip curled. "She may not be wrong. She is certainly wronged. Twice enslaved—once by the laws of Rome and again by the cosmic powers over this present darkness."

"How is she a nuisance to you?"

"The girl has taken to following us," Luke explained. "She creates havoc with her screaming and shouting, disrupting any chance we might have at holding a meaningful discussion. 'Servants of the Most High God,' she yells, and that is the end of our day."

"At least she is not lying," Lydia said.

"She's not helping, either," Paul interjected.

For two weeks, Lydia's life took on a new routine. In the evenings, the household would gather together to eat supper and listen to Paul and Silas as they taught them the mysteries of God's Word. Slowly, their fledgling faith grew deeper roots and became strong, thanks to the instruction they received.

In the mornings, everyone in the household returned to their regular duties. Marcus elected to remain with Lydia and Rebekah more and more often. He offered his help where needed, though at times he would find a quiet spot and work on drawings and plans, his mind occupied with the challenges of some aqueduct he was designing.

He seemed unflappable to Lydia. A deep, calm sea whose mystery she could not solve. After three years of being under the whip of slave traders, he had come away without any bitterness.

358

When she knew him better, she asked him about his time on that ship. "Why do you seem so healed?"

He laughed. "It started with the lesson of the tree, I suppose."

"What tree?"

"Upon occasion, when the wind picked up and the sails carried us forward unaided, our masters allowed us on deck for an hour or two of fresh sea air. The Illyrian captain owned a strange table, which he kept there for his charts and tools. The top of that table was made from one solid piece of wood, the round cross-section of a massive tree.

"Jacob showed me the table once. Each ring signified a year in the tree's life, he told me. I found this astounding, for there must have been hundreds of rings. That tree had lived in a faraway forest for centuries before a woodsman's ax had cut it down to make furniture for an illiterate pirate.

"Some rings were thinner, darker; others were fat and light. Those rings, Jacob said, spoke of harsh years and easy ones. The years of desperate struggle that stunted the tree and the years where it grew without obstacle. Flaws and blemishes pointed to the brutal years the tree had endured. But this tree survived. Survived those years, though it recorded every one within itself. It became what the struggle and the ease made of it.

"Jacob told me that I was like that tree. My mind had absorbed every struggle, every agony, every harsh word spoken against me; every fear, every indignity I had ever suffered had left its mark on me.

"But in another way, I was also different from the tree. Unlike the tree, I did not have to become the sum total of my history. I could learn to become the opposite of what failure and terror would make of my life.

"Jacob taught me that I need not become bitter and raging. I could choose to be a kind man. A man who brings good into the world. I could become like the pirates who treated me like an animal. I could become heartless, empty of compassion, bent on my personal ambitions and greed. Or I could let God teach me how to be human.

"Jacob, whom I had once considered beneath me because of his lineage—Jacob the slave, the Jew, the not-Roman—Jacob taught me how to be a man.

"In the merciless brutality of that Illyrian galley, I began to learn the lesson of the tree."

Marcus helped Lydia fold a length of new fabric. "Now may I ask you a question?"

"Of course."

"Did you pray? Before we came? Did you pray for God's help?"

Lydia nodded slowly. "We started praying on

the first day of the Jewish week. It was the day Antiochus began to threaten me. That same day, I told Appollonia to hire Demetrius."

"That was when Paul had his vision. We set sail for Philippi hours later."

"What vision?"

"We were stuck in Troas. Twice the Spirit had turned us away from where we had intended to go. We had no plan to come to Philippi, or anywhere near Macedonia. We sat in Troas, wondering where to go next and why God seemed to block our path.

"That evening, Paul had a vision while the rest of us slept. A strange man stood in the middle of our chamber. Paul thought at first that perhaps he had eaten some bad cheese, and this might be a momentary hallucination. But the man remained, unmoving as a Greek statue and just as pale. He was tall and broad in the shoulders, Paul said, with cropped golden hair and a clean-shaven chin.

" 'Come,' he cried. 'Come over to Macedonia and help us!'

"A few hours later, we boarded ship, and God led our steps here. To you. I think we were sent to Philippi, at least in part, because of your prayers."

FIFTY-FOUR

For we do not wrestle against flesh and blood,
but against the rulers, against the authorities,
against the cosmic powers over this present
darkness, against the spiritual forces
of evil in the heavenly places.
EPHESIANS 6:12

Lydia had to meet a business associate at the agora and accompanied the men there. As soon as they arrived, Damalis, who had been engaged in an intense conversation with a young man, left her client abruptly and began to follow the men. Paul and Silas exchanged an exasperated look. Damalis began to shout. She had a deep voice, loud enough to be heard from the stage at the theater. "These men are servants of the Most High God!" she bellowed.

"We know," Silas said, gritting his teeth.

Everyone turned to stare their way, making Lydia squirm. Paul motioned his companions along.

The girl followed, undeterred by the quickness of their steps. "They have come to tell you how to be saved!"

"I am worn out by her noise," Paul said.

Throwing his cloak at Timothy, he turned to face the slave girl.

She pointed at him, her fingernail filed to a sharpened end, like the tip of a spear aimed at his heart, Lydia thought. She felt a chill go through her. Through the girl's small pupils, something dark and malevolent stared at Paul. "Servant of the Most High God!" she shouted.

"What are you doing?" Luke asked, a desperate edge creeping into his voice.

"Setting her free from her misery. And us from ours."

Luke clasped his shoulder. "Consider, Paul. Consider what you do." Lydia looked from one to the other, sensing an unspoken danger.

"I have considered," Paul said. "Silas, come and help. Pray while I get rid of that filth."

Damalis herself was hardly more than a child, her face fresh and youthful beneath the thick coat of cosmetics she had applied. But her eyes were ancient, Lydia thought as she studied the girl. In those eyes she sensed fear and a hideous hatred. She took a hasty step back, running into the steadying arms of Marcus. "What is happening?" she whispered.

"Paul is evicting the demon," Marcus said, his voice grave.

"I command you in the name of Jesus Christ to come out of her." Paul's tone was measured, lacking fanfare.

The girl staggered and blinked as if coming to herself after a long sleep. She placed a hand to her head. "Is it gone?"

"Yes, child. And good riddance to that rubbish. Jesus has set you free."

"Gone? Am I really free?"

"What do you mean she is free?" a man yelled, striding forward. He wore a large gold ring on one hand and a bigger one on the other. "What have you done?" he demanded of Paul.

"Here comes the storm," Lydia said, cringing.

Paul shrugged. "She was troubled by a demon."

"Troubled! That was no trouble! That was income, you foreign imbecile. Great piles of it." He turned to the girl. "He is a fraud, and knows nothing. Come. Tell me my future."

Damalis frowned. She pulled on a loop of hair. "I cannot, master."

Her master's face turned the color of grapes. "Trachalio!" he yelped. "Where are you hiding, partner? Come and see what has become of our poor Damalis."

If there had been commotion when Damalis had followed them with her loud proclamations, now there was a genuine horde. Shoving and thrusting, the crowds gathered close, sensing entertainment.

Marcus shook his head. "There goes our hope for a quiet afternoon."

A sweating man, bald except for a halo of dark

hair, dug his way into their circle. "What's the ruckus? What are you screaming about, Gaius?"

"These men—" he pointed at Paul and Silas—"have ruined our Damalis."

"What's that you say? Ruined?"

"She has lost the demon and can no longer predict the future."

"Impossible." The man named Trachalio caressed Damalis on the cheek. "Come now, little mouse. Show us your demon. Tell my future. Better yet—" he glared at Paul—"tell his. Tell him the manner of his death. Don't miss the gory details. That will cheer up your master Gaius."

Damalis bit her lip. "I cannot, Master Trachalio. The demon is gone. My head does not hurt. My stomach is not churning. I don't feel it ripping inside me."

Trachalio roared. "Put it back!" he demanded, raising a fist at Paul. "Put the demon back immediately."

Paul pulled on his beard. "I cannot."

"If you can take them out, you can put them in," Gaius said.

"It does not work that way. Besides, even if I could, I would not subject the girl to that misery again."

The crowd exploded with disapproval, threatening voices intertwining to make a rumbling noise.

"Such an uproar in the midst of our usually

civil city," said a familiar voice. "What have we here?" Antiochus asked, his voice a pleased drawl.

Lydia drew in a sharp breath. They did not need Antiochus in the midst of this volatile company.

"Antiochus! Just the man to help us," Gaius said, striding forward. "You will not believe our misfortune. These foreigners have by some nefarious means cast out Damalis's demon. You know from personal experience how accurately she could tell your future. With the demon gone, she is useless."

Antiochus thrust his chest out. "What do you mean? Who has power to be rid of demons?"

"These men do. By some trickery or other, they have cast a spell on Damalis. Or squeezed the demon out of her. I know not. But our great investment is gone! Our hopes for great wealth are shattered."

"These men? They are guests of Lydia."

Everyone turned to stare at Lydia. "They are indeed my guests. But—"

Trachalio scratched his white pate. "That's awkward."

"Lydia should know better than to entertain such ruffians in her home," Antiochus said. "I would almost say she is responsible. They certainly should pay for this damage, which has not only harmed Trachalio and Gaius but should be seen as an unacceptable insult to all the good people of Philippi. Who are they to abuse our ways?"

"My thoughts exactly." Trachalio loosened the neck of his tunic. "Either they restore Damalis to her former self, or they repay us."

"Repay with the skin of their backs," Antiochus said, his eyes shining with an odd light.

FIFTY-FIVE

Yet I am confident I will
see the LORD's goodness while I am
here in the land of the living.
Wait patiently for the LORD.
Be brave and courageous.
Yes, wait patiently for the LORD.
PSALM 27:13-14, NLT

"Come, men and women of Philippi," Antiochus shouted. "Let us drag them to the authorities and give them a taste of Roman justice."

Several men grabbed Paul and Silas roughly and dragged them along. Lydia tried to intervene, but no one listened to her. Rage seemed to welter in the air. The crowd was tainted by it. They screamed insults at Paul and Silas as they marched them deeper into the agora. Finally they arrived at the forum, where heavily armed Roman guards were stationed, a centurion in charge.

"What's this?" The centurion stepped forward, his cloak flapping crimson behind him.

Antiochus stepped forward. "These men— these Jews—are causing a riot in our midst. We demand to see the praetor."

This, at least, was an improvement, Lydia thought. She would make her case with the praetor and convince him to set her guests free.

The centurion, who had been about to bite into a fat pancake covered in fig paste, groaned and set the pancake aside. He tilted his head toward one of the soldiers. "Fetch the praetor. Tell him we have trouble."

The praetor, a man born and raised in Rome, carried himself like a prince. His immaculate toga swayed about him in the wind, while his hair, drenched with aromatic oil, remained undisturbed even when a blustery gust arose. "What commotion is this?"

Gaius struck Paul on the shoulder, causing him to stagger. Before Paul could open his mouth, Gaius yelled, "We want justice. The whole city is in an uproar because of these two men. You can see for yourself, we almost have a riot on our hands, and all on the account of these Jews."

The praetor glanced at Silas, then Paul. "What are they guilty of?"

"They are teaching customs that are illegal for us Romans to practice," Trachalio said.

"Rabble-rousing traitors," Antiochus added. "They preach some god who performs miracles. A god above all other gods. It's against Roman decency."

Lydia stepped forward. "They are honored guests at my home. This is a misunderstanding."

"Misunderstanding, nothing," Gaius howled. "They have harmed our Damalis. She can't divine the future anymore. They used a terrible magic, and now she is useless."

The mob swelled in the force of its anger. "Punish them! Punish them!"

The praetor held up a hand. "Calm yourselves, people of Philippi." He motioned to the centurion. "Get them stripped."

"What are you doing?" Lydia cried, horrified. "Please listen to me. They are my guests."

"I am sorry for that. But unless we give this crowd what it wants, it will not settle. Can you not sense their taste for violence? Your guests should not have meddled with the slave girl."

Paul struggled against those holding him. "Wait. Men of Philippi, hear me!" The centurion slammed an elbow into his mouth. Paul fell to his knees.

Through a haze, Lydia heard Silas shout, "Wait, brothers. What my friend was—" He went no further, as he too received a brutal blow.

Lydia ran to the praetor. "Please! You must stop this. You are making a mistake."

The Roman shook his head. "Can't stop now. Do you want a real riot? I will give them a beating to cool tempers and dispatch them for a night in our jail. By dawn, when the crowd has calmed, I will set them free."

Lydia staggered back and stood shuddering, powerless to help her friends.

In a matter of moments, Paul's tunic was

stripped from his struggling body. The noise of the crowd had grown to such a crescendo that his attempts at speech were drowned by its cacophony. The centurion, thick wooden rod in hand, delivered his first strike. Paul's whole body shook. Before he had time to take a breath, the rod pummeled his back again. He screamed.

Lydia cried out, shaking with horror. It was her father's fate all over again. Marcus pulled her into his arms, cradling her face against his chest to protect her from seeing the worst.

"They are strong," he whispered into Lydia's ear. "They will recover."

The strikes did not slow. Lydia could hear the sound of the rod striking flesh and the groans of her dear friends as they struggled through a hurricane of pain. She wondered if they would ever walk again.

When the flogging finally stopped, Paul and Silas fell on their faces. Lydia's vision was blurred with tears. Through a veil of consternation, she saw a small figure bend toward Paul for a short moment.

Damalis.

Her eyes were streaming, her face streaked with dark kohl and smudged cosmetics. "Thank you," she said. Someone grabbed her arm and pulled her away.

Paul smiled.

"What do you have to smile about, you troublesome rat?" Antiochus asked before delivering a vicious kick to his side.

Paul grunted. He spit a thin rivulet of blood where he had bit his lip. His smile widened. "I am smiling because it was worth it."

Antiochus pulled his leg back to deliver another kick. Lydia shoved a fist in her mouth to keep from crying out. The centurion pushed Antiochus aside. "He's had enough. He's bound for prison now."

Paul and Silas were hauled to their feet. Battered they might be, but they had both survived their brutal treatment.

Lydia and Marcus, along with Luke and Timothy, followed their friends as they were marched to prison. Lydia was crying openly, thinking of her father, remembering his fate and convinced that the same awaited her guests.

The prison was a stone building at the base of a hill. To get there, they had to navigate a set of steep stairs. The jailer, a short man with muscular arms, came out to meet them. "Good day, Centurion. What do you have for me today?"

"These men caused a riot in the agora."

Antiochus, who had walked ahead of the soldiers to the prison, added, "They are slippery, these two. No doubt they will try to escape."

"Make sure they don't get away," the centurion barked at the jailer. "And no visitors, understand? Or you'll have to answer to me and my men."

"No, Centurion. They will not be escaping my jail, and that's a promise. I will put them in the inner dungeon. Not even a cricket can find its way out of there."

Lydia watched them vanish through the narrow doors of the prison and down a set of narrow steps. She felt as if her past were conspiring to choke her. The memory of her father, sick after a short stay in prison, beaten and broken in body, rose up like a specter to haunt her. *Not Paul and Silas, Lord!*

Before Marcus could catch her, she sank on the cracked stone of the pavement in front of the prison.

"I warned you not to make an enemy of me," Antiochus hissed. "This is just the beginning."

FIFTY-SIX

And we know that God causes
everything to work together for the good
of those who love God and are called
according to his purpose for them.
ROMANS 8:28, NLT

Marcus convinced Lydia to return home. "The praetor promised to set them free come sunrise. They will be home in a few hours. Luke will care for their wounds, and you will feed them one of your delectable meals. By tomorrow night, all this will be a memory."

Since the jailer refused to allow visitors, Lydia saw no benefit in lingering. Marcus, Luke, and Timothy began to pray for their friends as soon as they arrived home. Lydia and Rebekah joined them, though Lydia felt numb, weary to her marrow, and unable to dredge up hope.

"How could you offer a miracle for my indigo and not intercede on behalf of these men, Jesus? They are yours! Your soldiers. Why would you abandon them?" Lydia railed, angry at God for what seemed like an incomprehensible betrayal.

Marcus watched her, his eyes heavy with worry.

At about midnight, the earth shook. That was the only word for it. It trembled under them and grumbled with a savage noise. Lydia and Rebekah cried out. As if unsatisfied with the first tremor, finding it too insignificant, the ground shook again. The very walls moved. They could hear a crack shattering one of the massive stones on the floor of the courtyard.

The earth grew still, and peace reigned for a few moments. "Earthquake," Marcus said, his voice steady.

No sooner had the word left his mouth than there was another tremor, the worst yet. The foundations of the house heaved beneath them. Lydia toppled sideways and rammed into young Timothy. He was so muscle-bound that he probably did not even feel it.

Finally the world quieted down.

"When we prayed, *Lord, move,* we did not quite have that in mind," Luke said with a lopsided smile.

The quake had erased all traces of sleep, and the small company stayed awake through the night, interceding on behalf of their friends.

An hour after dawn, Paul and Silas arrived at Lydia's house, moving gingerly but grinning as if they had been at an all-night feast instead of in a rat-infested jail.

Lydia rushed forward to welcome them, kissing Paul's hands first, then Silas's. "We were so desperately worried."

"Well, she was," Luke said, laughing. "I knew

you would be fine. I will take care of your wounds as soon as you have eaten something."

"We are quite full, thank you. Our jailer, Valerius, already fed us a hearty meal. And he had our wounds cleansed too, though I would be grateful for one of your curative salves, Luke."

"Your jailer, Valerius, fed you?" Marcus said. "You are friends, are you?"

"Valerius is as a son to me," Paul said, laughing. "Give me a bath and a change of clothes, and I will tell you all about our adventures."

Lydia stared, confounded. How different this seemed from her father's experience. Like Eumenes, these men had received a violent and unjust beating, more demeaning even than what had happened to her father, for theirs had been a public flogging. And yet, in spite of their dreadful trial, they stood on their own two feet and bantered. She shook her head, impatient to hear their tale, wondering how they managed to seem joyful.

"You saw us delivered to prison, I believe," Paul began. "We were taken to the inner dungeon, where the jailer clamped our feet in the stocks. A stifling, nearly complete darkness fell, filled with the moans of our fellow prisoners and a stench that hit you like a punch. The reek surpassed anything your imagination could have thought possible. The smell of wounds turned putrid, vomit, and human excrement mingled with the odor of unwashed bodies. I was thinking what a place of misery we had landed ourselves in when Silas said, 'Thank God it is not too hot. It's quite comfortable, overall.' "

Everyone laughed.

" 'You'll be wanting to sing songs of praise next,' I said. And this fellow God chained me to proclaimed it an excellent idea and mourned the fact that he had not thought of it himself."

Lydia's mouth fell open. "What did you do then?"

Paul shrugged. "We sang songs of praise and prayed. That dank, malodorous place became quite cheerful. Then the earthquake hit. Did you feel it here?"

"Hard to miss," Timothy said. "Mistress Lydia fell on top of me."

Lydia colored. Marcus slapped Timothy playfully on the arm. "Try to behave, pup."

Silas nodded. "I tumbled around quite a bit myself. When the heaving of the world stopped, we found that everyone's chains were broken and the doors had flown open. We were free to walk out if we wanted."

"The other prisoners were either too weak to move or too scared," Paul took up the story again. "Silas and I remained for the jailer's sake. We figured Antiochus's wrath would have no end if we escaped in spite of his warning.

"Then I saw a sight that froze my blood.

Valerius, our jailer, convinced his prisoners had flown, was gripping his naked sword. It pointed at his belly."

"For a Roman, dereliction of duty carries a sentence of death," Marcus said. "Killed by his own hands, at least the jailer would leave his family a measure of honor. They would not be stripped of their home or inheritance."

"Exactly." Paul nodded. "I shouted to him, 'Stop! Don't kill yourself! We are all here!' The jailer turned, a look of astonishment on his face. Still holding the sword, its sharp end keeping perilously close company with his innards.

"Finally I convinced him to put the sword down and come and see us for himself. He was astounded to find that we had not escaped, and fell down trembling before us.

" 'Why did you not escape, you and your friend?' he asked. 'The doors were open, your fetters loose.'

" 'My God will release us from this place in his own time. We did not wish to see you come to harm for the sake of our liberty,' I told him.

"Valerius invited us to his own home, which was not far from the prison. We had hardly entered into his domicile when Valerius cried as if the words were bursting from him, 'I have seen the fearsome power of your God in the earthquake that broke your chains. I saw, also, his mercy through you. Sirs, what must I do to be saved?' "

Paul took a deep breath. For a moment his eyes drifted shut. "Every stripe, every agonizing stroke of that wooden rod had paved the way for this moment. What a bargain! What an economical exchange to pay with our own blood for the life of a man. Had we not landed in prison, we would never have come to know him. Nor would Valerius have seen a glimpse of God in that earthquake.

"For those who love God, all things work together for good. Even a beating becomes an instrument of salvation in the hands of the living God. Valerius and his whole family were baptized only a few hours ago. The Kingdom of God is growing."

Luke, Marcus, and Timothy cheered aloud, thrilled with the news of Valerius's newfound faith.

Lydia swallowed hard. She had accused God of abandoning his children. All the while, he had been unfurling his plan, purchasing the life of a whole family.

FIFTY-SEVEN

Surely there is a future,
and your hope will not be cut off.
PROVERBS 23:18

"I am afraid we had a little fun at the praetor's expense," Silas said later, when most of the household had gone to bed, leaving Lydia and Rebekah to keep their visitors company. "He sent his sergeants to set us free early this morning. But we refused to leave the prison without an apology." He gave a toothy smile.

"We had to clear our reputation, after all," Paul said.

"How did you do that?" Lydia asked, confused.

"We explained that we were Roman citizens. We had been beaten hastily and without a lawful trial."

"What?" Lydia cried. "You are citizens? But why did you not say so at the forum?"

"I believe I was too busy entertaining an elbow in my mouth. We were never given an opportunity to speak. Never asked to give our side of the story. You can be sure I told the praetor what I thought of what passes for justice in his city."

Lydia thought of the pompous Roman facing the sharp end of Paul's tongue and sputtered. "What did he say?"

"He swallowed convulsively a few times and apologized for himself and on behalf of all Philippi."

Paul pulled on his beard. "We would not be a burden to you, Lydia. Though we have done our best to clear our name, it seems the people of Philippi have taken a dislike to our ways. We will leave you in peace so that your business will suffer no damage by our presence."

Lydia stared at Paul for a moment before coming to a weighty decision. One that might change her life.

The decision to allow her new friends to remain in her home required no thought, though it presented a hazard.

The determination to trust them with her past, though, was another matter. No one in Philippi, save for Rebekah, knew her father's story. It was maintaining the secret that kept her safe, that protected her from ruination.

But here, in this company, where prison seemed a blessed place, a place of salvation and praise, she felt protected, even with her secrets.

"Master Paul," she said, her voice trembling. "My father was Eumenes of Thyatira. Once, he too was beaten for an unjust charge. He was imprisoned because of it. Unlike you, he crumbled under the weight of his sufferings. Death took him from me.

"You may stay in my home as long as you wish. I am honored to have you for a guest. No prison, no whip mark, will lower you in my sight."

A heavy silence fell in the room as each person digested the significance of Lydia's revelation.

Marcus reached over and held her hand for a moment. "I am a man who once served as a slave and bore the brunt of many careless whips. How sorry I am to hear of your father's suffering. He will find no judgment in our midst." To a man, they all smiled and nodded their agreement. Lydia felt tears trickling into her mouth. They carried with them the balled-up, pushed-down bitterness and fear of years. By accepting her so simply, these men had set her free of a shame that was never hers to carry.

Marcus lifted a cup of wine and took a small sip. "I did not know you were Roman citizens," he said to Paul and Silas, giving Lydia a chance to recover.

Paul shrugged. "It didn't seem to matter. Should I speak of God or my status in this world? My citizenship is in heaven."

Later, when Lydia had had a chance to catch up on sleep and felt more rested, Marcus found her sitting on a marble bench in the courtyard.

He sat beside her and played with the fringe on the cushion. "It seems you have had your own horrors to contend with."

Lydia gave him a quick look. "I suppose I have."

"Before I knew Jesus, I met a Persian priest who told me the legend of the patient stone. According to the Persians, there is a magical stone that has the ability to wash away the unbearable pain of your sorrows.

"If your heart is shattered and you have run out of fortitude, if the pain of your world has grown past forbearance, the patient stone can save you. All you have to do is hold it in the palm of your hand and tell your story to the stone. If your sorrow is genuine and profound, the stone will break in two. Upon breaking, it will shed one drop of blood. And with that breaking and bleeding, it will wash away the burden of your sorrow. The memory will remain, but its weight will be gone, taken into the stone by its death.

"I remember after hearing that story how I longed to possess such a stone. To hold it and be set free from my sorrows. The miracle is that I did find it. In Jesus.

"The suffering of the human soul is grave and brutal enough to break even the hardest stone. Enough to make a rock bleed. And every heart needs a patient stone. So God gave us one. Not a legend. But a real flesh-and-blood Savior who breaks and bleeds for the things that have shattered us.

"This hope is the anchor of our soul, firm and secure. Against all the adversity that blows like a storm from our past and our future, he holds us fast."

Lydia exhaled. An anchor for her soul.

Marcus held out his hand. In his palm lay a cross, carved exquisitely out of shimmering black stone. "I made this for you. As a reminder for those hard days that assail all of us. A reminder that you have your very own patient stone."

Slowly, Lydia took it from him. It was the most beautiful gift she had ever received.

Marcus joined Lydia the next morning, as if working alongside her were his normal habit. She found herself enjoying his company too much to object. Midmorning, Rebekah came looking for him. "Master Marcus, will you please come and look at the lintel over the shop? There seems to be a crack in it."

"The lintel? The marble one with the flowers?" Lydia asked. "That mason we hired told me it would still be here in a hundred years, and I am certain we are a few years shy of that."

"Let me have a look," Marcus said.

Together they walked into the street and stood gazing up at the marble. "That's a crack, I can confirm with professional certainty," Marcus said. "Don't worry. I won't charge you for that diagnosis."

"How is that possible?" Lydia took a few steps closer, squinting to see if she could determine the source of the damage.

Marcus joined her. "I will have to go up and have a closer look before I can determine the cause."

Lydia fetched a block and set it directly under the lintel. Marcus watched with a frown as she climbed on top. "Have a care, Lydia. It's probably not safe to stand directly underneath the marble until we determine what is wrong with it."

"I shall not take long." Lydia could see no more clearly from the top of the block than she had standing on the sidewalk. She was about to climb down when a creaking noise, the sound of stone groaning, emanated from above her head.

"Watch out!" Marcus cried. The lintel toppled down, straight toward her. Lydia cried out. Her legs seemed frozen. She saw the heavy stone crashing down and yet felt helpless to move.

One strong arm wrapped about her middle. She felt herself lifted off the block, flying through the air, and landing safely several steps away. The marble crashed where moments ago she had been standing. It shattered into five large pieces. Each one was heavy enough to have crushed her.

For a moment no one spoke.

Marcus's arm remained wrapped about her.

Lydia, trembling now with horror, leaned back into Marcus's chest. He had picked her up with one arm and sailed her through the air like a child's toy.

"You saved my life," she said.

"It's the oars. I have never completely lost the strength or agility they gave me. Are you well?"

"Better than my lintel."

He pulled her back against him, his hold tightening for a moment. She realized that she was not the only one trembling. The terror of the experience must have addled her mind, for she felt no desire to leave that encircling embrace.

Rebekah ran to her side, her face the color of bleached wool. "Lydia! I thought you would be killed."

"I thought the same."

Marcus cleared his throat before stepping away. "It seems we were all in agreement. Thank God we were wrong."

The patrons within the shop, drawn by the noise of the falling masonry, came outside to investigate. "I am sorry for the disturbance," Rebekah spoke, her face a study of calm. "If you accompany me, I will see that you receive some delicious pastry, which our cook just pulled out of the oven." Warm pastry proved more beguiling than a few pieces of broken marble, and everyone made their way back inside.

Marcus squatted to examine the broken pieces

of carved stone from every angle. His face was grim when he stood. "Someone loosened that lintel on purpose. I can see the chisel marks. That is most likely how the crack appeared in the first place."

Lydia shook her head. "This must be the work of Antiochus. Is he reduced to damaging my store now? I will merely have the marble replaced. He could have killed someone by accident, that fool."

Marcus rubbed his neck. "He grows careless in his desire to harm you. We must stop this madness."

He scrambled up the stairs that led to the roof, taking them two at a time. A while later he returned, a white powder marking his fingertips. "I found this at the edge of the roof. It is dust from the marble. Whoever the man was, he loosened the lintel so that it could fall at any moment, from a strong wind or by the mere passing of time."

Lydia looked around. "Could he still be close?"

"If he is, then he is well hidden by now. I saw no sign of him."

Lydia covered her mouth. "Epaphroditus."

Marcus cast a sharp gaze her way. "Loosening the marble would have required hours of labor, and Epaphroditus would have been missed if he were absent for such a long period."

"He could have done it while everyone slept."

"Too loud. The noise would have disturbed

more than one sleeper. It could not have been Epaphroditus."

Lydia nodded. Whoever had damaged the lintel was not a member of her household. Which left a thousand other nameless men as potential culprits.

FIFTY-EIGHT

A man of many companions
may come to ruin, but there is a friend who
sticks closer than a brother.
PROVERBS 18:24

They had finished eating supper in the dining room when Paul approached Lydia. "We have made a decision. Silas and I will remain with you another day. But then we will depart from Philippi."

Lydia gasped. "So soon?"

"After what happened in the agora, it is best we leave the city until tempers cool. And besides, we must share the message of Christ with other cities. Don't worry. We will not leave you abandoned. Though we take Timothy with us, Luke will remain here along with Marcus."

Lydia sank onto the couch. "I shall be sad to see you go."

"We leave a piece of our hearts here in Philippi with you. Silas and I were reminiscing over our journey. Did you know that we had first planned to travel to Asia Minor? We would probably have stopped at Thyatira if we had gone that way. But the Holy Spirit prevented us from entering that area. Instead, he led us all the way here, to northern Greece, where you, Lydia of Thyatira, resided." He smiled.

"Are you aware what a treasure you are? I suspect you do not know your own worth, your importance to the Kingdom of God. In truth, most of us don't fully comprehend the significant place we occupy in God's plans. But let me tell you what I see in you. As I told you before, you are the first follower of Jesus in this part of the world. But more than that, your home has become Philippi's first church. Here many shall seek and find the Light of the World.

"The Lord has given you a mighty talent for your trade in purple. He has opened doors of great success for you. Though he has given you his blessings because he loves you, I believe he has also elevated you because he knew your success would one day pave the way for his Kingdom."

Paul drew a small scroll from his belt. "This is a gift for you. It is a copy of the words of the prophet Isaiah in Greek. I hope it will help to strengthen your faith."

Lydia took the scroll and cradled it. "I cannot imagine a more precious gift."

"We hope to return one day, if God wills. When possible, I will write you and let you know where I am staying. In the meantime, we have one more evening together."

"Shall I invite our friends for the evening meal tomorrow?"

"I hoped you would offer your hospitality once more, as you have done since we arrived. Include Valerius and his family, I pray. He told me he has several comrades who wish to hear our message. We shall celebrate the Lord's Supper with you and exhort you one final time before we depart."

With care, Lydia set her scroll upon the table, fighting tears. Then she remembered Paul was not taking all his companions with him. "Thank you for remaining with us, Luke. And you, Marcus." Try as she might, Lydia could not keep the heat from rising to her face as she addressed the Roman. What had happened to her brain? Other women her age had grandchildren. And here she blushed like a schoolgirl, drooling over her guest.

"It is our pleasure, I assure you," Luke said. Marcus's smile was noncommittal.

"Will you be returning to the school of medicine tomorrow, Luke?" she asked. The Greek had fallen into the habit of visiting the school regularly, studying with other physicians and collecting new remedies. He had met Agnodice several times and held her in high regard for her professional achievements.

"I plan to go early."

"If you see my friend Agnodice, will you invite

her for supper tomorrow? I doubt she'll come once she hears we aim to speak of God. But I never give up on her."

"I would not give up on her either. Brilliant mind, accompanied by a tongue that terrorizes me."

Lydia laughed. "You do know her. Meanwhile, I will send a servant to invite Valerius and his family, as well as Leonidas. I wonder if General Varus will consent to join us. I would like you to meet him, though he rarely leaves his villa anymore. The city will be honoring him with a plaque in a few days, thanking him for his generosity to Philippi. He is sure to come for that. A great crowd is bound to gather, and he will not want to miss such an occasion."

Chloris ran into the room, which seemed her habitual mode of transport. The child appeared constitutionally incapable of a decorous walk. "I have good news for you, mistress," she said in her high voice.

Lydia frowned. "What news, Chloris?"

"Your friends are here," she said, clapping her hands as she swayed on the balls of her feet.

"Which friends are those?"

"These ones," a voice said from the door. "We are a week early! Just call us your personal nightmare from Jerusalem."

Lydia froze as she looked at the owner of that voice. Thirty years had passed since they had been under the same roof together. Lydia was no longer a child, and her friend was long past girlhood. But she would have recognized Elianna anywhere. The spiral curls, barely touched by white, the stunning face, the smile that could illuminate a palace.

"Elianna!" she cried, and ran as fast as Chloris ever had into her friend's arms. They shrieked like children and clung together for long moments.

"And Ethan," she said, noticing the new lines around his unusual eyes with their mosaic of colors and the abundant white shot through his hair that only made him seem more distinguished. "Welcome, my friend."

Beyond them, she looked for Viriato. In some ways, she remembered him best, for he was a man you did not easily forget. As wide as a doorframe and as muscular as a gladiator, he bore a thick scar that ran from under one eye and disappeared into his beard.

"Viriato! You have not even aged a day."

He scratched his cheek. "With a face like this, I could not afford to. I see you have simplified your vocabulary. I have understood everything you said so far."

Lydia laughed. "If you want someone with a large vocabulary, you must meet my friend Rebekah." Rebekah glided forward with her usual quiet grace. Viriato blinked twice and just stared. Everyone laughed, including Viriato.

"And here are my other honored guests, Paul and Silas. And next to them Luke, Marcus Cornelius Marcius, and Timothy."

Ethan took a hesitant step forward. "Paul? Paul of Tarsus? I recognize you!"

Paul grew still. "I do not remember meeting you."

Ethan waved a hand. "I heard you speak at Antioch once. About the Christ. It was inspired. There was too much shouting afterward, or I would have introduced myself."

Paul tilted his head. "Are you followers of the Way?"

"We are!" Ethan rose on tiptoes in his excitement. "I am astounded by the goodness of God. That we should find you here, in Lydia's house of all places, is beyond belief! Shall we have the honor of hearing you teach?"

"It is my sincere hope, though we intend to leave Philippi in two days."

Lydia's gaze swiveled from Paul to Ethan and landed on Elianna. "You are disciples of the Christ?"

"We are indeed. But, Lydia, is this true of you, also?"

Lydia grinned. "God brought Master Paul all the way to Philippi to tell me the Good News! At least that is what I tell him."

Elianna covered her cheeks with her hands. "I have seen enough of God's hand at work to cease being surprised by his plans. And yet he still astounds me."

"And you? How came you to follow Jesus, Elianna?"

"Remember how I wrote to tell you that I was sick for many years? The Lord healed me with one touch."

Lydia shook her head. "I see that we have much to speak of. I hope you plan to stay for many days."

"We would not wish to inconvenience you."

"What inconvenience? I shall put you all to work."

Viriato rolled his eyes. "Sounds familiar."

Paul turned to Ethan. "What news of Jerusalem?"

Ethan shook his head. "Matters with Rome grow hot and shall come to a head soon, I fear. Jerusalem has no future. Our Lord predicted its destruction, and we are concerned that such a day may not tarry long. As to the church, you will have heard the persecutions we have suffered.

"We travel now partly to ascertain if we can move our workshop to a different part of the world. As much as we shall miss our home, we have two daughters and grandchildren to consider. My oldest granddaughter will soon be pestering us for a husband. What future can she expect in our nation? What would it benefit our family if we leave them a great inheritance, only to have it razed to the ground by war and famine?"

Lydia thought of Elianna as grandmother to a child almost grown. Her friend was only seven years her senior! Lydia wondered if she had missed out on the best of life by never marrying. Missed out on being a wife and a mother. Purple had its joys. But it was not the equal of a family.

Then she thought of Rebekah and smiled. She did have a family, though it did not look like Elianna's.

Chloris pulled on her tunic to grab her attention. "Mistress, your friend is very pretty for such an old lady."

"Glory to God, Chloris. Please refrain from telling her so."

FIFTY-NINE

The heart is deceitful above all things,
and desperately sick; who can understand it?
JEREMIAH 17:9

The next morning, her guests from Jerusalem
left to meet with a landowner in order to confer
over property that might serve as a workshop.
Lydia found herself serving patrons in the shop
since they were shorthanded. One of her servants
had fallen ill with a severe chill, and the rest
were kept busy with the large company she
now housed from different parts of the empire.
She loved the noise, the conversations, even the
disarray of their presence. These were not empty
acquaintances. Each one had become a part of
her family, bound by ties of blood shed for them
on a cross far away.

She had remained awake with Elianna and
Rebekah, speaking late into the night, swapping
life stories. They had each waded through
tempests of hardship. Seasons of poverty. They
had struggled with shame and come away bearing
its scars. Elianna was perhaps the most healed,
having left the past truly behind. Lydia thought
it was her age, not in natural years but in God.
She had walked with Jesus the longest, and it

had left its mark on her, a deep reliance on his faithfulness that nothing could shake.

Now, after too few hours of sleep, Lydia waited on customers with heavy-lidded torpor, barely awake. Her heart picked up its tempo when Antiochus walked in, another man in tow. She spared a short glance for his companion and, not recognizing him, returned her gaze to Antiochus.

Sleepiness fled. His presence always dragged in trouble behind it. "How may I help you, Antiochus?"

"I ran into an old friend of yours and, spurred by kindness, brought him here to see you." He pointed to the man standing next to him.

Lydia stared at the toga-clad man blankly. He had thinning blond hair, showing a red scalp burned too often by the sun. His flesh, a little on the corpulent side, was soft and sagged under his chin. His eyes almost disappeared into the folds of skin above and below them. In the tiny slits left, she saw their color. Green.

Lydia staggered. She recognized the eyes. Beneath the added flesh, beneath the wrinkles and sags, this was Jason, the man she had once loved.

"We ran into each other at a tavern," Antiochus said, drinking up the moment of her recognition. "He told me he was from Thyatira. The mention of that city nudged my memory. I recalled that once, many years ago, my father told me he believed you were a native of Thyatira before you came to Philippi. So I asked him if he knew you. Lydia with hair the color of dark wheat and turquoise eyes, with veins that bleed purple.

"Imagine my delight when he told me that he knew you well. You and your father. Eumenes, was it?"

"Greetings, Lydia," Jason said.

The world rocked. She had lived through an earthquake only days before, and the ground had not shaken so much as it did now. Her tongue seemed stuck to the roof of her mouth. She felt like a sixteen-year-old girl again, bereft and without help.

An arm bumped against her side. She turned to find Marcus smiling down at her. She felt another presence to her other side, and to her astonishment discovered Epaphroditus, his face devoid of color and wet with perspiration. But he did not budge and stood beside her like a stone column.

"Hail, Antiochus!" Marcus said in cheerful tones. "What brings you to the competition? Are the prices better here than at your shop? The quality certainly beats anything you produce."

A few customers tittered. Antiochus turned a dark shade of crimson. "I have no business with you, Roman."

"That's uncivil. I have business with you. Epaphroditus here tells me that you know of an excellent stonemason." Marcus pointed outside. "Lydia's lintel smashed to the ground the other day; did you notice? Her mason had promised it would last a century. As an engineer, I found a few oddities to the accident."

Antiochus shrugged. "Shoddy work. She probably didn't pay well."

"The thing is, according to Epaphroditus, your man can put marble up and he can bring it down with the same ease. Whichever direction you want it to go, he is your man. Now that is a mason I would like to speak to in person."

Antiochus, aware of the sharp ears that listened to this conversation, threw his cousin a filthy look. "I wouldn't trust anything he has to say."

Epaphroditus stepped forward. Lydia could feel him shaking. "Hadn't you better leave, Antiochus? You and your friend?"

"Yes, leave." Marcus crossed his arms. "Unless you want to share the name of your mason with everyone here."

Antiochus shoved the tip of his finger into his cousin's chest. "You will regret this betrayal. I hope your bag is packed. You are not long for Philippi. As for you—" he nodded toward Lydia—"you have not heard the last of me. Or your old friend Jason."

"Must we leave so soon?" Jason said. "I was just starting to enjoy myself."

Lydia forced herself to smile. "Jason, you

should tell your new friend Antiochus who you think kicks hardest: me or Drakon. Personally, I would bet on me."

Her old nemesis turned puce. She remembered his tendency toward that color when he was in distress. It made her smirk. "Shall I show you the way out? It's through the door. That rectangular thing that leads outside."

Jason glared at her. "We will meet later. You can count on it." Lydia felt the promise land with the power of a gladiator's blow.

After her unwanted visitors departed, Marcus grinned at the silent customers who had stopped pretending to look at the merchandise and were openly ogling the exchange. "The entertainment was free. The purple is not. But it is the best value you can find for your money anywhere in the empire. Please enjoy at your leisure."

He bowed like an actor and, anchoring one hand on Lydia's shoulder and the other on Epaphroditus, guided them out. "Rebekah," he called. "Would you mind the shop? We need to discuss something."

Lydia was too shaken to protest. Marcus ushered them to a corner of the courtyard and watched as Lydia sank onto a bench. She hoped she had made a convincing pretense of serenity while speaking to Antiochus. Inside, she was a mangled mess. She had started to shiver and could not stop. Marcus laid his cloak around her shoulders. It smelled of eucalyptus and mint. The warmth of his body still lingered in the wool, and she huddled inside the folds, finally starting to come unfrozen.

"You came to my aid," she said to Epaphroditus. "Do you really know the mason Antiochus hired to destroy my lintel?"

He dropped his head. "We knew him from the time we were boys. A lot of mischief, that one. He is in Antiochus's pocket."

"Antiochus won't appreciate your coming to my defense. He will avenge himself on you for certain."

Epaphroditus wiped the sweat from the back of his neck. "I would rather be an outcast in this world than cast out of the Kingdom of God. Guilt is a terrible companion at night. I've had enough of it; let my cousin do what he will."

"I think with the threat of exposure, Antiochus will think twice before endangering your life again," Marcus said. "I will search for this mason. I may be able to press him into a confession. Epaphroditus has done you a great service by divulging his name."

"I thank you for your assistance, Epaphroditus."

"Mistress." He bowed and returned to the shop to help Rebekah.

"Who was that man, may I ask?" Marcus adjusted the pin on his tunic. "Jason?"

"He and his mother accused my father of

theft. It was a false charge. But they bribed the authorities and my father was declared guilty."

"So that is the secret Antiochus wishes to reveal."

"It would be enough to ruin my reputation as a merchant. In the eyes of Roman society, the daughter of a thief might as well be a thief." She huddled deeper into Marcus's cloak. "Once I believed myself in love with him."

Marcus's eyes widened. "With Jason?"

"I have better taste in textiles."

Marcus started to laugh. " 'The heart is deceitful above all things, and desperately sick; who can understand it?' " he quoted. "Textiles are a little easier to discern than men." He reached over to caress Lydia's cheek with a fleeting touch. "I could not help overhearing your comment about a kick. I must confess that I burn with curiosity."

Lydia stared at the ceiling. In halting tones, she told him the story of Jason and Dione, culminating with the infamous kick. Marcus's laughter rang so loud, several people drifted into the courtyard to discover the source of his hilarity.

The laughter washed over her like healing balm from heaven. Far from judging her, far from thinking her tainted and stupid, Marcus seemed to admire her.

Not since her father had been alive had she entrusted all her secrets to a man. Marcus had entered that hidden world, which was filled with her flaws and shortcomings, and come away still liking her.

It came to her with devastating clarity that this was not enough. Not from Marcus. From him, she wanted love.

She settled in that thought for a moment, stewed in it until it sank in. Until she realized it was not quite true. Mere love was not enough either. If she were honest, she would admit that from Marcus, she wanted a love that came with an assurance. An assurance that his affections would never fail, or let her down, or hurt her, or cause her harm. If she had such certainty, perhaps she might be able to open her own heart to him.

But she knew this was not the way of love. It was the way of flesh and the demand of reason. The desire to keep oneself from ever being hurt again.

The way of Jesus worked in an opposite direction. It gave without asking for impossible assurances. It gave the way Jesus had, loving to death, knowing he might not be loved back.

She wanted what she could not have. Marcus on her terms, not God's.

SIXTY

Do not be anxious about anything, but in everything by prayer and supplication with thanksgiving let your requests be made known to God. And the peace of God, which surpasses all understanding, will guard your hearts and your minds in Christ Jesus.
PHILIPPIANS 4:6-7

Her second-floor apartment was full to bursting. Slaves and masters mingled, highborn and low eating at the same table. Lydia had never seen a gathering quite like it. Valerius's whole household had come, even his two-year-old son, and with him he had brought several friends, members of Caesar's household who were part of the imperial civil service.

Leonidas, drawn to Paul and Silas's frayed reputation in Philippi, had sauntered in, bringing a female actress of questionable reputation named Syntyche. She had been loud and coarse when she first arrived. Then Silas welcomed her with a warm smile, as if her thick face paint and fake blonde hair, marks of a prostitute to anyone with eyes, meant nothing. He treated her like a highborn lady, a dear sister, clean and upright. Lydia noticed the woman's loud speech growing quieter and eventually ceasing altogether.

Elianna and Ethan sat in a corner, speaking to Epaphroditus in somber tones. Rebekah had persuaded Viriato to help her bring up the heavier trays, though judging by his large grin, it had not required much persuasion.

The general had sent a note of regret, saying he could not leave his home. Lydia would have to take Marcus to meet him when he received his honorary plaque the next day. How she wished Aemilia could have met Paul. He would have been one of the few people to manage her strong temper without giving in to slavish obedience. And he would have shown her the way to God.

Lydia sat near Marcus, listening to Paul as he spoke to Timothy, encouraging him to grow in his faith. What a good father he was, though he had no children of his own.

The sound of footsteps on the stairs drew her attention. To her delight Agnodice walked in, followed by a dark-haired girl she did not recognize. She rose to greet her friend. "Agnodice! I never thought Luke would convince you to come."

"He didn't." Agnodice thumped the dark-haired girl on the back. "She did."

"Damalis!" Paul cried. Lydia realized it was true. She had not recognized the girl without her excessive face paint and the wild expression.

"I rejoice to see you," Paul said. "I am astounded your masters allowed you to join us."

Damalis's cheeks turned pink. "They don't know I am here. I told them I was going to visit Agnodice for a sleeping draft. Which I did. She told me about this gathering, and, well, I could not resist coming."

"Let your minds be at rest," Agnodice said, grabbing a chalice of watered wine from a silver tray. "If they hear about it, I will merely say it was a medical experiment to determine whether your powers were real or cheap trickery.

"I have tried to draw that thing out of her for twelve months with no success. Tell me how you did it. Before you, the poor child suffered from terrible nightmares and could not sleep. I gave her my strongest potions, and they afforded her an hour or two of peace. She had headaches that made her shriek in pain, and I was helpless to treat them. Now she sleeps through the night and has not suffered a single headache. This cure I would like to learn about."

Paul extended his hands in invitation. "I have no power to give you. No potion or balm. But I know of a man who has power over all things."

Paul addressed the whole gathering. "Brothers and sisters, allow me to ask a simple question. Do you live in peace, within and without? Is your heart contented?"

Leonidas shrugged. " 'Each of us bears his own hell,' " he said, quoting Virgil. "Peace is not a common companion for most."

"What if I told you it could be? What if I showed you a way out of that hell? You know Virgil. Let me introduce you to a greater philosopher, and a better man. For he is the Son of God, able to give you what Virgil never could."

With slow deliberation, Paul spoke, Silas jumping in with stories that supported Paul's teaching. Silas had a gift of speaking to the heart, as if knowing with razor-sharp accuracy what each one needed to hear. The hour had grown late when they finished, though no one seemed restless to leave.

"Remember," Paul said in the end. "Don't worry about anything; instead, pray about everything. Tell God what you need, and thank him for all he has done. Then you will experience God's peace, which exceeds anything we can understand. His peace will guard your hearts and minds as you live in Christ Jesus."

Syntyche rose to her feet. "I believe in what you say. I will follow this man. Come, Leonidas. Let us join these good people. Let us surrender our lives to this peace, which exceeds our understanding."

Leonidas scratched his jaw. "Now, dear Syntyche, do not jump into Paul's fiery invitation too hastily or you might find yourself burned.

Consider hard this decision. Paul is asking you to change your life, don't you see?"

Syntyche pulled up the neckline of her diaphanous tunic. "My life never made me happy, and that's the truth. So why should I cling to it?"

"And I will follow your Lord with my whole heart, Master Paul," Damalis cried.

Leonidas sipped from his cup. "Too much right living for me, my friends. I wish you well."

Lydia noticed that although Agnodice said nothing, she was in deep thought. Paul's words had touched her. She might not be ready to move beyond consideration. But with Agnodice, thought would always lead the way. Luke would know how to answer her many questions and counter her endless arguments. It might take years, but Luke seemed a patient man.

Elianna came to sit near Lydia. Chloris had fallen asleep, her head on Lydia's lap. Absently, Elianna stroked the silky hair. "Did I tell you why we arrived in Philippi so early? The captain of our ship decided to leave days before the initial plan, fearing storms if he left at the appointed time. I was beyond vexed, thinking of the inconvenience we would cause you, arriving a week too soon at your doorstep. But we were not early. We were in God's time.

"He brought us here just in time to hear Paul and Silas. A week later, and we would have missed them. How our hearts needed this encouragement and added strength. Needed our brothers' prayers. I want to thank you, dear Lydia, for opening your home to God. Because of your generous hospitality, we have been bolstered. Shored up, where we were starting to grow weak and despondent. The troubles of the world had wormed their way into our hearts. Now I feel fortified, ready to face this season of storms and challenges in Jerusalem."

Lydia waved a hand. "It has been my pleasure. Tell me, have you had any success finding a property that suits your needs here in Philippi?"

"We have not. We will stay a few more days. Then we are headed for Corinth. More opportunities abound there for people in our trade. We will be sad to say goodbye."

Lydia smoothed out a small wrinkle from her *chiton*. "Everyone is leaving me."

Marcus, who still sat on her other side, leaned over. "Not everyone."

Early the next morning, Paul and his companions took their leave. Paul kissed Luke and Marcus on both cheeks, and then turning to Epaphroditus, kissed him with equal warmth. Epaphroditus wept openly at this mark of favor and friendship.

The Pharisee turned to Rebekah. "Keep up with your studies, for you have the mind of a true pupil and the heart of a worshipper. Your father lost a great jewel when he cast you out of his home. But his loss has been our gain, sweet Rebekah." Now it was Rebekah's turn to weep.

"Lydia, our precious sister." Paul held her hands for a moment. "May God bless your home with his presence. Never forget your significance in his Kingdom. Fear nothing, for he will shelter you in any tempest you face. And open your heart to his plans for your future. They may not always match your expectations."

Rebekah handed Lydia two packages, which they had prepared beforehand. "We noticed you had lost your cloaks at the agora," Lydia explained. "And your tunics, though mended after your beating, are in poor shape. Here is a gift to remedy the problem."

Silas opened his package to discover a new cloak and tunic. He cheered. "The blessings of God upon you, dear lady. I have been freezing for days."

Paul wrapped his thick gray cloak about him and purred like a cat. They took their leave of the rest of the household, including the visitors from Jerusalem. Each one received a special word, a token of affection.

"My love to all of you in Christ Jesus," Paul said as he walked away. "May his grace remain with you, my dear brothers and sisters. I will remember you in my prayers always."

SIXTY-ONE

No weapon that is fashioned against you
shall succeed, and you shall refute every
tongue that rises against you in judgment.
This is the heritage of the servants of
the LORD and their vindication from me,
declares the LORD.
ISAIAH 54:17

Lydia's entire household came to cheer for the
general as he received his honorary plaque. It
looked like most of Philippi had done the same,
for the forum teemed with people. The general
had served many in his long life and was a
popular citizen of the city. Even Leonidas had
made a point of coming, since Varus was a
staunch supporter of the theater.

The general leaned on a delicately carved
cane with an ivory handle as he waited for
the ceremonies to begin. Lydia thought she
recognized the cane as one Aemilia had liked to
use years before. She noticed with a catch how
fragile Varus had grown in the past months.

Varus had asked that she, as his adopted
daughter, stand with him, while his nephew
and heir occupied the position of honor at his
right hand. Someone fetched a chair, she was

relieved to find, and Varus sat with a sigh.

The ceremonies began and were kept thankfully short in deference to Varus's age and health. Finally, they placed a crown of laurel leaves on his wrinkled brow and unveiled the plaque, which had been mounted on one of the public buildings, as everyone applauded.

After presenting the general with a small gift and a daughterly kiss, Lydia turned to find the rest of her household.

"Citizens of Philippi! Friends, Romans," a familiar voice cried out from the center of the forum. Lydia wondered what Antiochus was up to now and continued to walk, her back to him. "Let us not disperse yet. It is my sad responsibility to share with you tidings that would shock most of you. Tidings you have every right to hear, for they concern one of our own citizens."

Lydia came to a standstill. A chill went through her. She forced her feet to pivot, forced her body to remain where it was rather than run at the sight that greeted her: Antiochus and Jason, standing together at the center of the forum.

"My news concerns Lydia, the renowned seller of purple in our city. We have trusted her for years. Trusted her with our coin and our confidence. Trusted her to be an honest merchant."

Lydia closed her eyes. Her mouth became a grim line as she watched her life crumble before her eyes. Rebekah appeared at her side as she always did when there was trouble. Then Marcus arrived, followed by Elianna, Ethan, and Viriato. Even Epaphroditus was there.

At least she would not be alone when her world shattered. They stood about her like a wall of flesh, unmovable.

"This man is Jason of Thyatira," Antiochus continued. The crowd had come to a standstill. "He is a wealthy merchant from that city. It happens that he knew Lydia well when she was a young woman. Her father, a man by the name of Eumenes, was a Thyatiran dye master. Jason's mother, Dione, was for a short time in business with Eumenes. Short, because Eumenes was a thief."

"It is true," Jason said, his head bobbing up and down. "The man was charged for stealing from my mother and was flogged for his crime."

The throng gasped. A few jeered. Antiochus held up his hands, motioning for silence.

"Jason tells me that Lydia worked for her father when the theft was discovered. It's not likely that she would have been uninformed about his dishonesty. So here you are, people of Philippi. This supposedly honorable merchant is not only the daughter of a thief but has probably stolen herself. Who is to say that she has not been robbing us for all these years? Once a thief, always a thief. You judge among

414

yourselves what is to be done about this charge."

The noise grew louder than before, angry now. Paralyzed by fear, Lydia watched accusing fingers raised toward her.

You are the anchor of my soul, Lord. With the silent prayer reverberating in her mind, a steadiness poured into her. She took one step. *You are my hope.* She took another step. *My security.* Another step. *You ground me in all that is steady and solid and good.*

She now stood in the center of the crowd's view. In an instant, everyone hushed.

"It is true that my father, Eumenes, was charged with theft," she began. The crowd jeered. She held up a hand. "But the accusation was false. This man, Jason, and his mother, lied and cheated in order to rob us of our land and business. There *is* a thief standing in your midst. But it is not I. It is Jason of Thyatira. I cannot prove my claim. I can only ask you to judge me by what you know of me."

She pointed to one of the praetors. "You, Justus, wear a tunic you purchased from my store twenty years ago. It still looks vibrant. And you, Gaius—is that cloak not one of mine? Has it faded? Has it worn thin? Did you pay too much for it?"

Antiochus stepped forward. "Just because you have a few satisfied customers does not make you honest, Lydia."

Another grumble rose from the mob. Lydia dropped her head.

The sound of a crash interrupted the seething crowd. Silenced, everyone stretched their necks to discover the source of the unexpected noise. The general had taken a stance under his plaque. His cane was broken in two. His beautiful plaque, just installed, lay at his feet in tiny pieces. In his fury, he had shattered both.

"Are you speaking about my daughter, Antiochus?" the general said. "I have never known her to be less than trustworthy. Once she owed my mother a small debt, and she paid it in full before the debt came due. As to her father, I knew the man personally. He had better purple than you, and his prices were always fair. Not once did he cheat me or the friends I brought to him."

Lydia almost wept. Varus had never called her *daughter* before. Never defended her, even in private.

"She may have given a prompt accounting to your mother, Varus, but—" Antiochus began.

Leonidas interrupted, his actor's voice loud and compelling. "Whom shall we believe? This stranger from Thyatira, or our own Lydia? Many of us have tasted of her kindness. She helped me once, when she had nothing to gain by it. Lydia, a thief? Might as well call me a hater of wine."

He raised his silver chalice, sloshing over with purple juice. The crowd roared.

Demetrius stepped forward. "She helped me, also. In the years I have worked alongside her in the guild, not once have I glimpsed a shadow of dishonesty in her dealings. She has practiced nothing but integrity in our midst and is highly regarded by her colleagues."

Appollonia drew nearer to stand by her new manager. "She gave me assistance when my husband left me a widow. Others would have robbed me." She threw a glance in Antiochus's direction. "Lydia served me as a friend and asked for nothing in return."

Chloris's father, Belos, spoke next. "Mistress Lydia helped me as no other would. She took care of my little girl. You will never convince me that she is a thief."

Agnodice's voice rose. "People of Philippi, I wish I could give you a potion to heal you of your foolishness. Then again, I suppose I would be a lot wealthier if I could create such medicine, given the number of fools that populate this empire." The crowd chortled. "Consider what you know to be true of Lydia. The woman helps the poor, opens her home to strangers, gives you fair prices, assists a friend in need, and creates merchandise to make our city proud. What more evidence do you want? Stop this nonsense and go home."

"It is not nonsense, Agnodice," Antiochus said. "A charge has come against her, and we require a reckoning."

"I am Marcus Cornelius Marcius of Rome, a visitor to your fair city," Marcus said in his pure Latin. He charmed the crowd with his patrician manners. Philippians were easily impressed by these marks of the world's influence, and Marcus plied them with expertise. "Do you give me leave to speak in regard to these proceedings?"

The people cheered, and Marcus lifted his hand as a sign of his appreciation.

"You ask for a reckoning, Antiochus. But it seems to me that we have given you more than enough reckoning already. Any reasonable man here among us is convinced of Lydia's innocence. Evidence in her defense has been given from the highest to the lowest residents of this city. But you do not seem satisfied. Who is safe from such a tongue as yours, or from the depths of your suspicion? I suppose next you will accuse your own cousin Epaphroditus's father of being a thief."

"His father *is* a thief!" Antiochus yelled.

The crowd roared with laughter.

"Oh, come now, Antiochus. That is a good jest. What next? Shall you accuse our honored praetors of demanding the flogging of Roman citizens without a trial?"

The praetor, being reminded of the grave mistake he had made only days before—thanks in large part to Antiochus's prodding—stepped forward. "This has gone far enough. We believe Lydia. Jason of Thyatira, we command you to leave this city by morning. You have been here a brief time, and already disorder follows you. And, Antiochus, I expect you to cease this fondness for rabble-rousing. Another such public display, and you will answer to me."

SIXTY-TWO

And I am sure of this, that he who began
a good work in you will bring it to
completion at the day of Jesus Christ.
PHILIPPIANS 1:6

Secrets burrow in the ground of the heart like moles. They dig until the heart is pockmarked with their wounds. The holes they leave behind fester and overflow with all manner of poison, with fear and bitterness and dread.

For years Lydia had lived with secrets. Little by little, since Paul's arrival, she had pulled them out and brought them into the light, astonished to find that they lost their power once exposed. The poison drained, the holes filled. Her heart rested.

By forcing her greatest dread into the open, Antiochus had done her a favor. He had intended to cut her. Instead, his hand had ushered in the healing of God.

They were back at her home, she and her guests and the rest of her household. A feast seemed to have appeared of its own accord, and everyone was celebrating as if it were their personal victory. Even the general had ignored his aches and pains and joined them. He sat next to a flirting Syntyche, looking dazed and twirling his broken cane.

Agnodice wagged a finger at him. "Why did you smash that beautiful plaque, General?"

"I could not speak loud enough to gain everyone's attention. My age, you see."

The physician felt his arm muscles. "Not so old."

The general grinned, looking pleased with himself. "In truth, I did not like the plaque overmuch. It was rather small, didn't you think? So I promised the praetor that I would pay to replace it. I'll make certain the next one is a decent size."

A wasp had managed to find its way into the large chamber, and Leonidas chased it with determined glee, a shoe in one hand and a full cup in the other. "I have named it Antiochus," he yelled. "Their stings are on different ends. Other than that, they are very alike."

Agnodice hushed him and ordered him to behave. She would have had more success ordering the waves of the Mediterranean to conduct themselves more becomingly.

Lydia noticed Epaphroditus perching alone in a corner and joined him. "I wanted to tell you that you are welcome to stay here if you wish. You can continue to work for me. Your slate is clean as far as I am concerned."

His eyes widened. She gave his hand a

reassuring squeeze. "For what you did, I forgive you, Epaphroditus."

"Mistress, I am more ashamed than ever, now that I have learned of your history. Your father was accused, same as mine. Only he was innocent. And still, you remained upright and good. You lost everything you owned, and you did not allow fear to drive you into the wrong path."

"What you did is in the past, Epaphroditus. I, too, know the power of fear. It is hard to resist its crushing hold."

Agnodice interrupted, unaware of the nature of their conversation. "Lydia," she said, "will you tell us the full story of what happened in Thyatira?"

Lydia sat on a cushion and gathered her thoughts for a moment. "My ancestors lived in Thyatira for generations. Long before Rome became her master, our family made their home there. I thought I would spend all my days in the land of my forefathers and be buried with them in the soil of Thyatira. But God had other plans for me."

She told her story, glossing over her feelings for Jason. She told no lies. She chose merely to refrain from exposing certain details. This crowd was too big for such intimacies. Though she had learned to entrust her past with a few special companions, sharing personal details of her life with a large group of people was not something she considered wise.

"I always knew you were strong," Leonidas said. "But I did not realize what you had to overcome in order to achieve so much."

"I could not have done it alone." Lydia smiled, her eyes bright. "I had Rebekah, who has been better than a sister and wiser than a Greek lawyer. The general's mother, Aemilia, was like a grandmother and banker and manager rolled into one. If there is any victory in my life, it is because each one of you has played a role in it."

The hour had grown late when her guests drifted home. Lydia was wakeful, her body still caught in the upheaval of the day. She stepped outside into the moonless night, enjoying the stillness.

"May I join you?" a familiar voice asked. The darkness enveloped them so that she could only perceive the outline of his form.

"Of course."

Marcus remained silent, as if aware of her need for a few tranquil moments.

Abruptly, she chuckled, breaking the silence.

"What?" he asked.

"I am still astounded by how you managed to twist Antiochus's plan against him. How did you think of it? No one will ever believe his accusation against Epaphroditus's father now. It was utter genius. If your buildings are half as clever, you should be designing whole cities."

"It pleases me that he will not have to live with that threat hanging over him." He took a deep breath and held it. "Smells like rain."

"We need it. It has been a dry year."

"I hope Paul and Silas and Timothy have somewhere warm and dry to sleep tonight."

"You miss them?"

"I was with them for only a few weeks. But they felt like family by the time they left." He was silent for a moment. "I found the mason. The one who tampered with your marble lintel."

Lydia gasped. "You spoke to him?"

"He did not put up much of a fight. Loyalty, apparently, is not a virtue he holds in high esteem. He admitted Antiochus had paid him. Epaphroditus was with me, and Luke. We all three bear witness to his testimony."

"What next?"

"That is up to you. We can charge Antiochus publicly. It will be a scandal for him, though I am not sure he will end in prison. He will accuse you of bribing the mason. He will accuse the mason of lying. He might wriggle out of the charge entirely. He is a wealthy man and prone to giving fat bribes. He could emerge like a wounded bear, more dangerous than before."

"Or we could do nothing."

Marcus shrugged. "Also not an ideal solution."

"Once, when we were much younger, Rebekah

and I saw Antiochus behave with unimaginable cruelty." She told him about the rabbits. "I decided then that we should not speak up. I feared his anger and revenge." She pulled her mantle more closely about her. "I have regretted that decision a thousand times. Perhaps if we had gone to Rufus, he would have been able to intervene, to stop the twisted bent that had started to warp his son's character.

"I will not keep quiet out of fear this time. We will do what we can to preserve more people from being hurt by him. How many others will fill the shoes of Chloris and Epaphroditus and Demetrius and Appollonia if we do nothing? He will continue harming people. Even if we cannot manage to land him in a prison cell, at least the scandal might cause the people of Philippi to treat him with more caution."

In the dark, Marcus found her hand. "Would you let me help? Would you allow me to remain by your side as you fight this battle?"

SIXTY-THREE

I am my beloved's and my beloved is mine.
SONG OF SOLOMON 6:3

Lydia grew still. "You are generous, Marcus. I would appreciate your wisdom and prayers."

"You mistake me. My prayers you will have all the days of my life. As to wisdom, such as I have, I lay at your feet. But I am asking for more." His arms wrapped around her in the dark, and he drew her to him. "I am asking for a life together. I want you to be my wife."

Lydia grew rigid with shock. Marcus pulled her closer, as if the warmth of his body could melt the fear out of her.

"I have lived without a family for thirty years," he said, head bent against her cheek. "I liked living alone, without ties, free from complications. My parents' marriage was not happy. I never had a desire to repeat their lives. Then I met you. In the course of one week, my convictions shriveled to dust. I spent one day in your company and realized that being an unmarried man is tiresome. It is tedious and mundane and devoid of joy. You, Lydia of Thyatira, made me wish for marriage as I have never wished for anything.

"If your father lived, I would ask him first. Or, if Paul were still here, I would go to him as your spiritual father. I thought of approaching the general, but I was uncertain you would want that. Surely at our age it is acceptable for me to ask you directly. So I am asking, beloved Lydia, dear Lydia, excellent Lydia, will you be my wife?"

Lydia managed to pull herself out of his arms. Without a word, she ran inside.

"You told him no?" Rebekah asked.

"Not precisely."

"You told him yes?" Elianna prompted.

"Well, no."

"What exactly did you say?" Rebekah said.

"As I recall, nothing voluminous."

"By voluminous, you mean . . . ?" Elianna prompted.

Lydia chewed on a fingernail and examined the beads on her shoes.

Rebekah clapped her hands on her hips. "You mean to tell me that the man proposed marriage, and you did not say a single word?"

Lydia squirmed. "I might have gasped. Or perhaps it was a groan. I can't remember."

"Lydia, finally a man is valiant enough to ask you to be his wife, and you leave him without one word of encouragement?" Rebekah threw up her hands. "I despair of you."

"What do you mean valiant enough? I don't bite."

"Please. What man can measure up to you? You run a more successful trade than most of them. You are clever, resourceful, respected, beautiful. It's enough to make a man want to run in any direction but yours. I never thought a man would have the courage to overlook all that. He is going to have to live with you if he marries you, you know? Live with that long list every day and go to bed with it at night. It requires a strong man not to be overshadowed by all your accomplishments. Finally God has sent you a good man, a man your equal in strength and character and, most of all, in faith. And what do you do? You leave him standing like a broom plant in the dark."

Elianna giggled. Seeing Lydia's face, she covered her mouth.

"Lydia, do you care for the man?" Rebekah asked.

"That is a stupid question."

"Why is it stupid?" Rebekah looked mystified.

"Because the last time I cared for a man, as you so delicately phrase it, he turned out to be a swindling, defrauding, miserable toad and proceeded to destroy my father and me. If I do care for Marcus, then it is a sign of his unsuitability."

"You were young and inexperienced," Elianna said. "A lot of time has passed since then. You are not that girl. You have the Lord to guide your heart. You have years of godly counsel to shore up your mind."

Lydia pressed her hands against her belly. "I don't trust my own judgment."

Rebekah reached for her hand. "I do. I trust it implicitly. Trust it with my life." She patted Lydia's shoulder. "Now gather yourself together, and go and speak to that poor man who has had the temerity to fall in love with you."

"What am I to say to him?"

"You need not give him an answer one way or the other. What you have shared with Elianna and me belongs to his ears. He deserves to understand why you feel as you do. Your mistrust is not directed at him. It is directed at you. He should know that."

Marcus was, in fact, standing precisely where she had left him, leaning against the doorpost. She brought a lamp with her, remembering how dark it had grown.

"I am sorry, Marcus."

He gave a little smile. "No apology needed. I presumed too much." He shrugged. "You do not return my feelings. Forgive me. I did not mean to embarrass you."

"That is not true!" she cried.

"I did not embarrass you?"

He turned, and in the light of the lamp she saw

that he looked . . . broken. Her heart shrank at the thought that she had put that look on his face.

Lydia set the lamp down. She wiped her perspiring hands against her mantle. "It's not true that I do not return your feelings."

Marcus straightened and went to stand near her. He did not touch her this time. "But?"

"The only man I loved was Jason."

"You still love him?"

"God be merciful, I am not that foolish! No. It's only that . . . well, I think we established that I have better taste in fabrics than I do in men."

It took Marcus a few moments to grasp her meaning. "You are worried that you cannot trust your feelings?"

"I know you are nothing like Jason. Still, I cannot move beyond this terror. What if you are not all that you seem?"

Marcus smiled. "Truth will out, dear Lydia. No man can hide his true self forever. In the course of a month or a year, you will see the best and the worst in him. If you want, I will wait out your fears."

Lydia stepped forward until they were a breath apart. "You would do that for me?"

"I am tougher than fear, you will find, beloved. I will wait."

Lydia brought her suit against Antiochus to the courts at the start of winter. The mason, fed up with Antiochus's refusal to pay for several jobs, gave testimony not only on behalf of Lydia but also concerning two other cases where a competitor's building had been damaged.

To her amazement, once Lydia brought her complaint to the courts, others stepped forward, bringing their own cases. A father whose daughter he had violated. A man whose dogs he had tortured. Several customers who accused him of cheating them. None had felt prepared to face Antiochus's venom alone. Lydia's formal grievance, however, opened the door for others to gain enough courage to confront him. In the end, there were simply too many witnesses, too many accusations of impropriety for even Antiochus to deny.

It was a bitter trial that culminated in Antiochus's banishment. He left Philippi still a relatively wealthy man. But he left with his reputation in tatters.

Marcus stood by her like an immovable wall as she brought charges against Antiochus. He gave her strength when fear threatened to drown her resolve. If Antiochus sent anyone to try to harm her, his man could come nowhere near her, not with Marcus, Rebekah, Epaphroditus, General Varus, and Luke surrounding her like a shield wall.

Marcus was proven right. Within nine months, Lydia had learned to trust her own heart, because he had shown himself more trustworthy than any man she had known since her father's death.

Lydia wore purple for her wedding and, like all good wives, covered her hair with a mantle, as she would for the rest of her life when in public. Most of Philippi came to celebrate the event. The general insisted on paying for the wedding, though his nephew was none too pleased about it.

"Ignore his complaints," the general said. "He has no sense of family. Will that pretty Syntyche come?" he asked with twinkling eyes.

"She has changed her ways, General." Lydia narrowed her eyes at him. "Don't you go tempting her to change back."

Marcus sold his property in Ephesus and moved his faithful servants and belongings to Philippi. "We will need an addition," he said thoughtfully. "You are outgrowing your shop."

"Why do you think I am marrying you? This house is getting older and will soon need the attentions of an architect. I will save myself a lot of money if I wed you."

Marcus kissed her then as he kissed her on their wedding day, with an almost-dazed delight, both of them half-unbelieving that at their age, they had found lasting love.

Their home remained one of the central meeting places in Philippi where Christians gathered for decades. Marcus's addition to the house allowed the *ekklesia* to come together in comfort and security, setting deep roots in the Lord and growing both in number and in faith. Undergirding their community was always the love of Marcus and Lydia and the warm welcome of Rebekah. Through the years, they were encouraged by letters from Paul, who bore a special love for the church he had planted on one Sabbath morning by the banks of the river.

A NOTE FROM THE AUTHOR

Some lives seem to burn with a transcendent light, leaving an inexorable mark on history. Lydia's was such a life. The first convert in Europe, she succeeded in the realm of commerce where men dominated and ruled. Her home became the first church on the continent, one that yielded great influence in the spread of the gospel for centuries. The world changed, you might say, because of Lydia's intrepid generosity and leadership.

A few notes on this novel. The Bible is silent on the issue of Lydia's citizenship. However, while the ancient world was deeply impressed by Roman citizenship, biblical authors remained indifferent to it and only seemed to mention it when it became a relevant detail in a particular story of faith. We never hear about Paul's citizenship, for example, until he is unjustly beaten. I felt, therefore, that it was not unlikely for Lydia to have been a citizen of Rome, given her level of success.

A historical person named Antiochus, a seller of purple, really did live in Philippi around this time period. The city officials liked him so much that they dedicated a plaque in his honor. Beyond these facts, however, the whole story surrounding Antiochus is fictional.

My apologies to Epaphroditus (Philippians 2:25) and Syntyche (Philippians 4:2) for usurping their unknown stories and coloring them with my imaginary pen. One day in heaven I will have a lot of explaining to do.

Some additional explanations on locations are in order. The Agora in Philippi may not have been built by AD 50, though we have evidence of its completion not too long after this period.

The ruins of Thyatira lie under a modern Turkish city and have never been properly excavated. There is little written about the city, and the narrow information we possess comes to us courtesy of limited archaeological finds. However, there is some indication that a thriving Jewish community lived in Thyatira at this time.

The use of the terms *Lady, mistress, lord,* and *sir* are inaccurate, as the Latin language does not commonly use such terminology. But the titles of esteem used by Romans—such as *excellent* Antonios or *very strong* Silvanus—sound awkward to modern readers, so I chose to use more common honorifics that capture differences in station.

The first recorded mention of tree rings was in the third century BC, by a Greek botanist named Theophrastus. But not until Leonardo da Vinci's treatise in the fifteenth century do we come across written evidence of the significance of the rings. So Marcus's discourse on the matter may be anachronistic. Similarly, the legend of the patient stone, though a story I personally heard as a child, is most likely not as old as the first century.

As I always do, I have used a couple of quotes in the writing of this book, although this time I veered from my usual practice of using material from classical writers. In chapter 7, I quoted Theodore Roosevelt. His exact words were:

> The credit belongs to the man . . . who strives valiantly; who errs, who comes short again and again, because there is no effort without error and shortcoming; but who does actually strive to do the deeds; who knows great enthusiasms, the great devotions; who spends himself in a worthy cause; who at the best knows in the end the triumph of high achievement, and who at the worst, if he fails, at least fails while daring greatly.

Paul's words "There is nothing in the world so damaged that it cannot be repaired by the hand of Almighty God" in chapter 45 are a quote from "Appointment with Death," a television production based on Agatha Christie's Hercule Poirot as portrayed by David Suchet.

For Elianna's full story, please refer to my novel *Land of Silence*.

While the Bible provides profound inspiration for novels like this, the best way to study it is not through a work of fiction but simply by reading the original. This story can in no way replace the transformative power that the reader will encounter in the Scriptures. For Lydia's story, please read Acts 16.

ACKNOWLEDGMENTS

It's not easy being newly married and facing that toothsome dragon named Deadline, which makes me all the more thankful for my precious husband, John. His unwavering support, gracious patience, and constant strength made writing this book possible.

Every once in a while God brings someone across your path who changes your life for the better. My agent, Wendy Lawton, is such a person. I am grateful for her in more ways than I can express.

I remain profoundly thankful for my publishing home at Tyndale. The incredible fiction team, led by Karen Watson, has become like a beloved writing family. What a joy to work with Stephanie Broene and Kathy Olson, whose gracious counsel and direction transformed *Bread of Angels* into a much better story. It's a privilege to work with such wise editors. Maggie W. Rowe, Cheryl Kerwin, and Shaina Turner, how can I thank you for all your creative work in helping make these books available to more readers? I am indebted to Mark Norton from Tyndale's Bible team for taking the time to answer my convoluted historical questions. And not least, rich blessings to the sales team, which works so hard to get these stories into the right hands.

I am grateful for dear friends Lauren Yarger and Cindy McDowell who remain my writing partners and continue to help me with the thorny process involved in creating a new book. To Lauren I also owe the idea for one of my favorite lines in the book: *Apparently there was more than one way of making purple.* Her version of the line was much funnier. Molly Chase, thank you for your marvelous editing. You are a lovely gift. Deryk Richenburg, warm thanks for your sharp insight as a first reader and pastor.

I am indebted to my church in New England that is beautiful on the outside, while radiating the glory of Jesus within. For my boss and coworkers, without whose support I could not start a single book, let alone finish six, I am more appreciative than I can express.

Special thanks to every single one of my readers who keep buying these books. Simply, I write for your heart.

And finally, I am thankful for my beloved father, who went home to Glory as I was writing *Bread of Angels*. There is a little piece of him in this story.

ADDITIONAL COPYRIGHT INFORMATION

DISCUSSION QUESTIONS

1. Were you familiar with the story of Lydia from the book of Acts before reading this novel? If so, how well do you think the author incorporated the biblical account into her novel?

2. Lydia first encounters fear as a young child when she sees her mother die after a grisly accident. What are some of the ways this fear affects her? Are there experiences in your past that still affect you today? What role does Lydia's childhood experience play in her journey to faith in Jesus Christ—and yours?

3. Jason's betrayal left Lydia unwilling to trust her own heart. Can you describe a time when someone betrayed you or pulled you down? What was the effect in your life—tangibly and emotionally? How have you dealt with it since?

4. When Lydia flees Thyatira, she takes with her the stone with her grandfather's name, eventually using it as a cornerstone for her new shop. Do you have any tangible mementos from your past or family heritage? What are they? What is their significance to you?

5. Rebekah was mistreated and even disowned by her father, and yet she never lost her trust in God. Did this seem realistic to you? Do you know anyone who has gone through something incredibly difficult and still maintained a vibrant faith? What is it, do you suppose, that determines whether a tragedy makes a person "bitter" or "better"?

6. Should Lydia and Rebekah have taken action when they first learned of Antiochus's sadistic cruelty? When is it necessary to step forward and shed light on secret dangers? Has there been a time in your life when you acted too rashly in this regard? When you failed to act soon enough?

7. What made Lydia so ready to hear and believe the message of Jesus' salvation?

8. Lydia kept a part of her life secret because she felt she would be judged and even ruined if others found out about her past. What do you think is the effect of long-held secrets on a person's life?

9. Consider the examples of generosity in this book: Eumenes, Atreus, Lydia, Rufus, Aemelia, and others. What do they have in common? How are they different? How can you be generous with what you have?

10. Compare and discuss the following verses about wealth: Ecclesiastes 5:19, Matthew

19:23-26, 1 Timothy 6:17-19. How can money be a blessing? How can it be a danger? How should a follower of Jesus feel about profit and wealth?

ABOUT THE AUTHOR

Tessa Afshar is the award-winning author of *Land of Silence* and several other historical novels. She was voted "New Author of the Year" by the *FamilyFiction*-sponsored Readers Choice Awards in 2011 for *Pearl in the Sand*. Her book *Harvest of Rubies* was nominated for the 2013 ECPA Christian Book Award in the fiction category and chosen by *World* magazine as one of four notable books of the year. Her novel *Harvest of Gold* won the 2014 Christy Award for historical fiction. *In the Field of Grace*, based on the biblical story of Ruth, was nominated for the Grace Award.

Tessa was born in Iran to a nominally Muslim family and lived there for the first fourteen years of her life. She moved to England, where she survived boarding school for girls and fell in love with Jane Austen and Charlotte Brontë, before moving to the United States permanently. Her conversion to Christianity in her twenties changed the course of her life forever. Tessa holds an MDiv from Yale University, where she served as cochair of the Evangelical Fellowship at the divinity school. Tessa has spent the last eighteen years in full-time Christian work in New England and the last fifteen years on the staff of one of the oldest churches in America. Visit her online at www.tessaafshar.com.

Books are produced
in the United States
using U.S.-based
materials

Books are printed
using a revolutionary
new process called
THINKtech™ that
lowers energy usage
by 70% and increases
overall quality

Books are durable
and flexible because
of smythe-sewing

Paper is sourced
using environmentally
responsible foresting
methods and the
paper is acid-free

Center Point Large Print
600 Brooks Road / PO Box 1
Thorndike, ME 04986-0001 USA

(207) 568-3717

US & Canada:
1 800 929-9108
www.centerpointlargeprint.com

Hunter's Moon

Poems from Boyhood to Manhood

Books by
JOSEPH MEREDITH

Poetry

Hunter's Moon: Poems from Boyhood to Manhood

Hunter's Moon

Poems from Boyhood to Manhood

by Joseph Meredith

TIME BEING BOOKS
POETRY IN SIGHT AND SOUND
Saint Louis, Missouri

Time Being Books
10411 Clayton Road
Saint Louis, Missouri 63131

Time Being Books volumes are printed on acid-free paper, and binding materials are chosen for strength and durability.

ISBN 1-877770-83-3
ISBN 1-877770-84-1 (pbk.)
ISBN 1-877770-85-X (tape)

Library of Congress Cataloging-in-Publication Data

Meredith, Joseph, 1948-
    Hunter's moon : poems from boyhood to manhood / by Joseph Meredith. — 1st ed.
        p.   cm.
    ISBN 1-877770-83-3: $16.95 (acid-free paper). — ISBN 1-877770-84-1 (pbk.) : $9.95 (acid-free paper). — ISBN 1-877770-85-X (tape) : $9.95
    I. Title.
PS3563.E7364H86   1993   92-41085
811'.54 — dc20   CIP

Manufactured in the United States of America

First Edition, first printing (February 1993)

Acknowledgments

Grateful acknowledgment is made to the editors and publishers of the following periodicals in which these poems first appeared: ***Four Quarters*** ("The Operator," "The Tumbler," "Intimations of Closing on Opening Night," "For Andrew at Three Months," "The Voices," "Pumpkin Time," "The Handsome Young Poet and the Orange Eater," "Our Walks," "The Kid Poets," "The Seduction of Gravity," "Splitting Day," "Belfield: October, Early Morning," "Making Ends Meet," "Hunter's Moon," "The Glass Cutter," and "The Osprey"); ***ICON*** ("Guitars"); ***Kansas Quarterly*** ("Midnight, Walking the Wakeful Daughter," and "The Cold"); ***Painted Bride Quarterly*** ("Hippel's Wilderness," "How It's Done," "All-Star," and "Sunday Dusk"); ***Southwest Review*** ("The Old Man in the Garden" and "The Little Boy-Girl"); ***The American Scholar*** ("The Acid Test"); ***The Irish Edition*** ("Bodie Island, Before Dawn," "At the Wall," and "Working in the Dark"); and ***The Threepenny Review*** ("Teaching Goldfish How to Rollerskate").

for Walter and Anna

Contents

PART THREE: **Reaching Out in Darkness —
My Wife**

PART FOUR: **The Birth of Light and Air —
My Children**

PART FIVE: **Down to Earth —
Poems at Midlife**

Hunter's Moon

Poems from Boyhood
to Manhood

PART ONE: **Like Silk in Air —**
A Boy's Growing

* This symbol is used to indicate that a stanza has been divided because of pagination.

Teaching Goldfish

My father on his great haunches
leaned on one hand, working his way
down the splintery tongue and groove
of our front porch, packing the furrows
with putty, a ploughman in reverse,
a healer of dry rot and wear.

June of '55 was equatorial.
Oceans shimmered in the asphalt
up the street, all mirage.
Some teenage homilist fried an egg
on our neighbor's green Hudson,
slippery in the heat.
Massive, it seemed a rock
exposed by urban tide,
and the egg/anemone, spewed up,
bloomed on its weed-slick ledge.

My father, bright with sweat,
blew sharply up across
his drawn-in lip to percolate a cloud
at me. I could taste the salt.
His arms were flecked with dirt,
with bits of grey paint, wood fibers.
The stainless blade shed
bolts of bright acetylene
up my nose and made me sneeze.
"What are you doing, Pop?"

"Teaching goldfish," he said,
"how to roller-skate."

He didn't need to look at me.
At seven I was wise enough,
but only just, to see his point,
if not the fish. "Wise up,"
my brother spit sideways.
Pop was forty-seven, with energy enough
to kill a can of Red Devil
*

(We Cover the Earth!)
and stretch his weary knees.
To stop for nosy kids
would be the end of work.
And I was left to wise up
on my own.

Now, wiser than I ever meant to be,
I see him sometimes in my mind:
aswim in toil, hunkered down to wood,
putty knife flashing,
the grey fur of his chest bright,
the salt of him on my tongue,
keeping house and more together,
while all around him,
in pairs and alone,
golden, globular,
their tails like silk in air,
skate the splendid, smiling fish.

Thumper

I

The thumping started early.

"Hey, Freckles, you Cath'lic, ain't ya?"

The buck-toothed kid slobbers,
his heavy lips agleam with spit.
He has incorporated from the smell
of horse turds and ash cans on Ogden Street.
In 1918 you are ten and a loner;
he is twelve; his wrists are thick.
Down on one knee,
all you want to do is taste
the tatties you've been roasting
in the burning leaves,
leaves so thick you can build
a fire a day from All Souls to Christmas
till they soften under snow.
You don't turn around.

"Bet I know how you got them freckles."

Now your fear, the fluttering bird
inside your rectum, is curious.
You've wondered that yourself —
in all the clear-eyed faces
at home, not a fleck or a speckle —
not Lidie nor Charles nor the baby,
your mother nor your father.
It's as though some coal oil
in your Welsh blood was floating
in droplets on your milky skin.

The fire is red on your face,
and you feel the freckles
aglow and dancing.
His baggy plus-fours
brush your back. His hands are chapped.

"Bet some priest pissed on you
through the confessional screen."

Now I've seen pictures of you at ten:
the head of a wren, unfledged, grown huge
upon a wool-clad stick man.
But called to defend
your freckles and your faith,
you found what baling wire and beef
gristle bound up those sticks
just after the scalding potato —
charred skin, steaming white flesh —
crashed against his lips and teeth.

His screams stopped a horse car
dead in its tracks on Wyalusing Avenue.

II

The thumping continued.

"You wear the mask or you don't catch."

It is cold April in the park, 1924,
the wind off George's Hill so damp
you might as well be bare-chested.
Along the third base line the grass
is a bog from the morning rain.
As your cleats bite in, it speaks:
swing, swing, swing, swing.
A shag of cloud races toward the river.

All you want to do is play ball.
You can hit and you can peg
out to second from a crouch;
the way your wrist snaps
from behind your head, so fast,
the seams whisper past your ear.
Nobody you know is any better.

"I don't like the mask,
I can't see so good."

He's a senior, hotshot pitcher,
with hair the color of the clay
around the plate and a cowlick
like the ass end of a grouse.
He's testing your sophomore stones.
When he leans his face into yours,
the garlic and tobacco on his breath
make the thumping start,
the white edges of your vision
pulsing, crimping in like fielders
cheating on a bunt.

"You'll see my foot up your ass if . . ."
is all he gets to say before
you peg the ball, still clenched,
into his handsome brow.
The skin splits like casing
on a fat, dago sausage.

You never play ball again.

III

July of twenty-nine and just of age,
you are leaning against the deck rail
of the Camden ferry. I can see you,
through all these years, a snap brim
Panama in hand. In white summer cottons
and black oiled waves, you could be
Richard Arlen on holiday or Henry
Wilcoxin escorting Mr. De Mille's
newest starlet. Women sense this in you:
your hard teeth and easy laugh stir
them like pheromones on the night air
stir moths. There are places they want bitten.

The first star is already up,
leading you home to West Philly,
and the city glows red and black
*

where it rises from the river —
Dock Street and Water, and beyond
to Broad Street Station where you work.
Five years on the Pennsy have hobbled your temper.
Adrenalin is dead. Long live testosterone!
Anger and lust are both blood songs,
same rhythm, different tune.
Now Lilac Sachet on the river breeze
starts you humming.

Pop's Pranks

I used to wonder why you pulled so many pranks
and how you avoided all those years
getting the snot beat out of you.
Those were great stories, though, Pop.
Like the time you rubbed Limburger
into the old janitor's broom handle
in Suburban Station and then stuck around for the fun.
Or the time you squeezed ketchup into Murvine's
jelly doughnut, and how he threw it, bellowing,
out the window and hit the station master
smack in the breast pocket of his blue serge.
Or when Old Man Krause, dead to the world
in the caboose after a killing day in the yards,
mysteriously got his bald dome painted green;
didn't have a clue until he started for the streetcar.
But my all-time favorite was your hemorrhoid cure.
"Bring a jar tomorrow," you deadpanned,
"and take some of that grease from the journal box.
Make you right as rain. But you have to wear
a sanitary napkin to keep your shorts clean."
And then, days later, the poor slob
could hardly walk, he was so chafed from the Kotex.
That was a pisser, Pop. I spit potatoes and gravy
half across the table at that one.

Well, I used to wonder. I don't any more,
because there were other stories, too.
The falcon in the baggage car that sunk
its talons into the fat of your belly,
and to get it off you had to strangle
the damned thing till the tongue lolled out.
Or the horrendous thunder of the cars coupling
inches behind you on Delaware Avenue, pulling
the sweater you had slung over your shoulder
right out of your hand. Could have squeezed
you in half like Murvine's doughnut. And I remember
how you looked scared and dreamy for days
after Johnny Brower steamed full-tilt into Union Station
*

with a runaway packed with commuters and crashed
right through to the men's room. Living so close
to it every day, that was why, huh Pop?
Or did you know the big pranks wouldn't be yours?
Like the burning in your gut when you found out
the bastards had sold off all their stock
when they knew the Pennsy was going under.
Did you guess the cartilage in your knees
would turn to chalk after forty-four years in the cars?
Or does every railroader suspect the biggest prank
of all will be on him: a siding in the woods,
down a line you can't recall,
where the rails finally come together?

The Operator

for AMM at seventy-five

All those years ago, riding the streetcar —
New shoes, new gloves, Mary's hand-me-down hat,
Nervous the job might be too hard — you sat
Alone wondering, in your best dress, how far
Luck and a smile might take you. Who could know?
Once under the headset, though, you learned well:
Volumes to recite like the words of a spell.
Eventually you relaxed enough to let your smile show.
Smiling's what did him in, first caught his eye,
Until the blue eyes below the blue-black hair
Smiled back. Uncertain, strung upon the air,
All the future hung between you, like lines upon the sky.
Lightning swift, the raveled years now lay undone.
Little guessed the blue-eyed man he'd be the lucky one.

Working in the Dark

for Mary McKenna

"Why are you always working in the dark?"
My grandson wondered and flipped the switch.
The greyish globs I'd been slicing became tomatoes
again, scarlet and seedy, puddling the cutting board.
He didn't need an answer,
had already swooped upon an innocent jug
of milk like a hawk on a plump hen.
Now he chugged and sighed like a peasant.

It's a family trait, I suppose, this penchant
for shadowy kitchens, like thin lips
or flint eyes that spark with sadness.
Because my mother's kitchen faced a wall,
the area way on Ogden Street,
there never was much natural light,
only dim faces and bright talk,
the boozy spirits of bread baking,
or pot lids babbling their oniony breath
at every greenhorn cousin who needed a stake,
and more than one with English pounds on his head —
Earlys and Foys, poor Bridey McMenamin
shipped out to the States pregnant,
her small eyes like a beast's in a pit.
And not a pint of thanks in the peck of them.

One raw October when I was twelve,
I dodged the skin-abrading wind
to find my stepfather sobbing into his forearms
on the desperate, porcelain table. It was dusk,
but mother had not lit the gas.
"We're for it, Mary. They've closed me down.
The taproom's locked up like a tomb,
and eleven mouths to feed." I still see
his thick fingers fumbling at his throat,
the welt his collar made on the back of his neck,
*

and the brass button skiting, like a bullet into history,
for the darkness under the stove.
My mother's hand settled then on his oiled hair
with such a lightness, like a sacrament,
I stopped breathing for a bit,
the skin at the back of my arms tingling
as though bells rang in a darkened church.

Out of reverence, then, for the old dead:
Mother and Daddy McGillen,
Bridey and the fugitive cousins —
all gone now, gone to work,
as they had in life, in the dark places
we all come from and are bound for, even you,
boy, with your appetites and sad bright eyes,
though I would never say it aloud to you.

Youth and Age

Old man, what craftsman formed your hands?
The knuckles thick, the bones awry,
the veins show through in bands
like limbs against a dead, white sky.

The smith you seek in ignorance
wields a hammer hard as sin,
and when he makes his anvil dance,
he's a master artisan.

His shop is hung with sorrows,
his forge is hot as pain;
with years he pumps his bellows —
you'll not be young again.

I've a ball-peen of my own,
old man, can pound it all night long,
I'll coax some sparks from the gates of bone
until the dark is gone.

Nothing you can do, my boy,
when his hammer starts its song,
but recall the silken thighs with joy
and be glad he takes so long.

I Dream a Ballfield

I dream a ballfield for us in the Jersey woods.
No diamond, really, just a ragged space
Deprived of trees. We're full of piss and grace,
Rigged up in Boston flannels, duds,
Even as a rookie, Matthews wouldn't wear.
Anyway, we are light and free of pain.
Muscular again and quick, and Johnny Sain
Slaps fungoes, cussing, through the piney air.
We catch every ball he cracks our way
Easing from the springtime sky, then go
Laughing off to find some girls and know,
If only dreamed, these legs have had a day.
Veins relax and valves forget their art;
Each bit grows hard except the flyball heart.

Direction

for WJM

You gave direction.

"You're throwing it like a baseball.
Look, keep it down closer to your ear.
Let it roll off your fingertips.
And step up with your left foot."

At ten I was thin-armed and short;
for a week my wrist broke with every pass,
the big "Duke" sailing wildly —
no rotation, no trajectory.
You were out for freshman football;
Gallen and Gaughanie ran your patterns.
And as the days evaporated in the August sun,
you drilled pass after pass:
over the left shoulder, over the right;
buttonhooks and sidelines and curls;
and the swift, instinctive ball obeyed —
nuzzling onto their hands,
raging into their bellies.

Gaughanie already had the shadow of a beard
and such a slanting weight about his eyes,
it would take years before I recognized
the mortal sadness in that face.
Gallen was all bone and acne.
But they ran and they cut
till you called it quits.
And they endured me because you wanted them to.
You gave direction.

"Watch the receiver, not the ball."

You were Unitas in sneaks,
Van Brocklin on concrete.
And the ball knew.

"You HAVE to let it ROLL.
It's the rotation that keeps it true."

The day I got my school shoes
and we could almost smell the chalk dust,
I finally got it right.

"There y'go, pal, now that's trajectory."

The word arced and dropped upon me
like a spiral from the heavy air.

"Let's knock off," you said, "It's getting dark."

We couldn't know
how dark it would get as you moved
away from me into the shadows,
into high school, into the army.

I didn't see you again,
I mean really see you,
until your daughter climbed to your lap
one night and put her head on your chest.
You called her dear and stroked her hair.
And your man's hand, its thick veins throwing shadows,
the hand that gave the "Duke" its brain,
was the lightest thing that ever touched her.

For a moment I was breathless,
like catching one of your bullets in the gut.
She will spin as true, I thought,
as one of your arcing spirals because of you.
It is, of course, true also of me.
You gave trajectory,
and that, brother, is real direction.

No Pictures, Please

for Kay

I've never liked poems that begin
looking wistfully at a photo
(always from a box in the attic).
"See Papa scowl from this one," they say.
"Oh, it takes me back!" And before you can say
George Eastman, you're neck-deep in a thick
quicksand of significance that makes you wish
they'd found a loaded six-gun in the box instead,
or a doughboy's corroding dog tags,
or a charge-a-plate from Lits, anything
but Papa's dour old mug.

So when I found this poem dated 11/22/63,
I knew it was from your twenty-first birthday,
and I wasn't surprised to find no snapshots in it:
none of you smiling from behind a blazing cake;
none of that guy you dated, whose pompadour
sprouted spikes from his recent crewcut,
not peeking into your cleavage when the Brownie
didn't catch him; not even one of you flanked
by Mom and Dad before the bleak venetian blinds
in that stupid sack dress that looked
like you'd been stuffed into a taffeta Franklin stove.

All I found in it were a few JFK buttons,
a crumbling, black-bordered holy card,
and the memory of you at nine that night:
belly-down across the bed, one arm dangling limp,
as though you too had been shot, all cried out,
a plump cheek flattened against your nose,
breathing through your mouth, a shiny wire
of spittle holding down your head,
and your red-rimmed eyes open, open.

You, Summer, 1966

You, in white voile, tacking
on a bay of blue denim and bandana,
toward me through the crowded yard,
your palomino hair adrift in light,
and all the boys aflame
at the lines of you, the impudent sun
setting through your dress.

You, pressed standing against me
in the shadows, my hands full
of your hard flesh, the athlete
in you working for leverage
among the shut up morning glory,
the splintery trellis.

You, liquid whispers tickling
my neck, daring, but just,
to look up, and the procreative urge
so bright, I mistook it, in the pulsing
acre of lightning bugs, for love.

You, later, stiffening beside the box,
flag-draped, of your dead twin
who liquified in the Mekong summer,
the anger turning you paler and harder
all season till you seemed of stone.

You, your millstone teeth grinding
the hard words, hating me
for going to school, for not avenging him,
for not being dead.

Splitting Day

for JH

The truck dropped twenty tons of logs
in your driveway, and it took two months
to saw them into the eighteen-inch
segments now stacked neatly on the grass,
like a "Build a Forest" kit just waiting
for someone to say, "Match bark striations
A to B; avoid crimping cambium."
And today was splitting day for us city boys.

The sun poured in low over Donaghy's field,
lighting her up bright yellow like an instrument
of battle — a piston, a wedge, and a one-lunged
engine to drive her — the Lickety Splitter.
The rental agent had a chaw of Red Man
the size of a sparrow in his cheek
and a *Tutti per Muti* tee shirt
tied around his head and hanging
down his neck like a Legionnaire.
He said it true: "She'll take all you got, boys.
Un-fatigue-able. Work you to death
and chuckle when you take a blow (sspyyt).
Eighteen ton o'force she'll generate.
Split heartwood like cuttin' butter.
Why, if Saladin'd had a couple o'these
little ladies (sspyuut), we'd all be talkin' A-rab.
Ain't a castlegate nor sally port in Christendom
he couldn't o' cracked like he's crackin' walnuts.
That'll be seventy-nine-fifty."

The son of a bitch was right.
By the time the sun was high
and we'd done two cord, she was killing us.
Our lumbar muscles were singing
baritone-low and mournful, and we
were standing straight every five minutes
*

to see if we couldn't hush them.
With the stink of tannins, sour
and sickly, thick in our throats,
we shut her down for lunch.
Bird guns were cracking off toward
the willow grove, and we knew, somewhere,
the doves were dying.

By four o'clock
we were ready to change places with them.
Tremulous thoracic tenors had long since
swelled the choir of mourners.
Now we had a full-scale requiem going
and standing straight only struck new
chords of grief, the sinews in our arms
bleating like sackbuts and shawms.
She was taking all we had.
By sunset she'd done five cord,
splitting oak crotch and ironwood
like cutting a deck of cards. And no amount
of pleading, no entreaties of back
or shaking thigh, would halt
the inexorable cleaving of the wood.
Christendom was falling all around us.

In the floodlit blue haze of her exhaust,
she crackled and cooled, chuckling at us,
our hands so stiff we could barely close
them around the steering wheel to drive home.

A man knows one, maybe two women
in a lifetime who can do what she did:
split the heartwood and 'take all you got.'

Guitars

I heard her last night
for the first time in years,
my old Spanish Kay
with the soft nylon voice.
She was the first.
I had her re-bridged for steel
and my fingers learned to love the sting
of the heavy-gauge, copper-wound
strings pressed to the frets.
When I knew six chords,
I sold her for thirty bucks
and never looked back.
I bought a Harmony Sovereign.
She was Greta,
thick through the waist
like a burgher's wife.
I took her to the river bank,
and her bass rumbled out
like thunder over the light-loving water.
Keiko was next, a Yamaha twelve.
She was tiny in the body,
her action high and hard,
but she could do surprising,
bell-like, things to a man.
In six months, though,
all the bells had been rung.
I sold her
and took up with the Gibson
B-45 twelve with the blonde top
I'd fallen for in Zapf's window.
She was Martha:
big-bottomed, handsome, all-American.
She made a C-chord sound like sunshine,
A-minor ring like a church organ.
I took her to family gatherings:
brothers and sisters and brigades of kids.
We sang rousers to potato salad,
*

fried chicken, and cold cuts.
When the kids drifted down
to the quiet grass like seedlings,
she sang alone, feather soft,
to the kerosene lamps.
Since then, we have made some music.
But then, last night in bed
I heard, deep back between my ears,
like sighing, like the whisper of time
high up in the trees,
that soft nylon voice.

PART TWO: **The Young Grow Wise —
Teachers, Students, and Friends**

The Teacher

for RSM

Risking harm at class's end, your feet
Inching carefully to the floor, you gather
Text and folders, your tiny cane
Aiding your steps, and amble, smiling, out.

Small wonder, how does your child-sized body
Put up with the pain when the angry joints —
Ankle and knee, pelvis and spine —
Rasp against the crying ganglia,
Rebel in force against the slightest flexing?
Our petty aches must mightily bore you,
Who carry from the womb your brittle legacy.

Make us, through your courage, see the truth:
Awful pain can bring us wisdom if,
Like a child, we take delight in laughter;
Like a woman, we endure, endure, endure.

The Old Crusade

for CFK, Spring, 1990

So, the dark martyrdom ends.
The winds that burned the last
cosmos in their beds grow mild.
The day elongates slyly,
doves return, fiddleheads uncurl,
a thousand daffodils pour
from their horns earth's greening song:
the season of begetting begins.
What was still flows, what sleeping awakes
(and here the archangelic brass
and cymbals clash in tumult),
what was dead arises!

Forty springs and more you taught
us work's redemptive power.
And as our cold bones warm again,
the old paradox enthralls us still:
in loss is gain, in spending we renew.

You, who would have strode with Richard,
ever faithful, through the blazing gates of Acre
(or the fogs of Keenan's pipe) fill
our hearts with courage for the old crusade.

Through you the young grow wise,
and words become flesh in the world.
Your life engenders our vernal hope,
like sunlight rummaging the flower beds.
Resurrection's everywhere: the stirring ferns,
the daffodils, and, Christ, the doves!

Afternoon, After Eliot

for Jim and Kate

The autumn afternoon will come,
insinuating damp between bone and bone,
its light, fretted by the blinds,
slipping from russet to dun,
when you will enter this room
with a rustle of papers,
a collecting of plates,
and deliver your terms.

"I want to be in Strasbourg again,
to haunt the stalls along Rue de Cité ,
or genuflect in the half light of the crossing
and breathe the incensed air."

Capitulate, capitulate.
The coals but stub the darkness,
but warm the ashen grate.

And, if I, putting down the paper
and settling the glasses on my nose,
if I should gather you in,
if, like a wizened doryman
who has crossed himself to the Virgin
and thrashed the cold from his bones,
I make you my day's single catch,
would you be willing to settle
for less than no conditions?

"Let's be on the beach, instead,
Jamestown or Point Judith,
where the wind persuades the rocks to sand,
us two and a gypsy dog."

Capitulate, capitulate.
The coals but stub the darkness,
but warm the ashen grate.

The Kid Poets

for CFK

Ten years ago I sat cringing in a chair
across from you. Now you call me confrere.
You were fifty then. I was just a kid
who'd given you some poems. The thunder in the air

was partly your old railroad watch hid
in a storm of papers on your desk. I'd have fled
into the drizzling afternoon, given half a chance,
to calm my thundering heart. But then you did

the kindest thing: your hand danced a little dance
finding a rhythm you said was more than happenstance
in one of my "things." In the air between your face
and my face the thunder died. Only a quick glance

out the window convinced me you could not chase
the storm away, could not, by gesture, replace
cloud with sun, only turn a life around.
And all by a movement of pure masculine grace.

Now you are sixty; each rumble of the watch is more profound.
And my paternal stoop will in time pull me to the ground.
But still they come to you daily, the kid poets,
waiting outside your office, tight-lipped, without a sound.

The Handsome Young Poet and the Orange Eater

Propped against the podium
in the front of the room,
the handsome young poet laments winter,
longs for spring. He is weary, he says,
angst seeping into his shoes with the slush —
every bare branch a bone,
each house a tomb.
And all the while this kid behind me
is tearing small clouds of sunlight
from the rind of an Indian River navel
and slurping with peasant avidity
juice that smells like a celebration:
sharp and quick and wet.

Lament

(or Scaling Parnassus in Sneakers)

William B. Yeats
get off my case.
I can't write a line
but your reedy voice grates,
"Whoa, lad, that's mine."

How It's Done

Take the Cuban kid who calls you *coño*
that night just before high school begins,
the night you learn about adrenalin
and the powerful red drug of rage.
Watch carefully your knuckles disturb again
the symmetry of his beautiful lips.
Listen for the crunching of cartilage
in your right middle finger that ends the fight.
Note the finger's odd angle of attachment,
the instant of humor before the pain,
confirmed in brightness, settles in your teeth.

Recall Miss Kane, your third grade teacher.
Believe all brilliance, all beauty live in her eyes.
Step into that perfume she wears, trailing
behind her like a veil as she floats by your desk.
Lean your burning, shy face into it.
Tremble at the aura of her angora sweater
when she moves between you and the window light.
Feel the universe shudder and center itself
in the few millimeters of white strap
at the wide neckline of her dress.

When the soft fur of her sweater becomes
your aging father's beard, you are close.
Shave it again in the room you are certain
he will die in. Listen for the sound
the razor makes on his chin, fear
you will nick him in that soft valley
between his nose and cheek. Let
the mortal whiteness of his whiskers
whirling in vortex as you rinse the razor
appall you. Whimper at the crouching fear in his eyes.

When you hurl the world
   at the world of memory,
      prepare yourself for the collision.
         Catch all the debris you can
            at the point of your pen.

➙

An old man with beautiful lips lies dying.
He dreams he is a boy again, picking tobacco
with his father in the warm fields of Pinar del Río.
He feels the fine needles of sun on his hands and neck
until a woman steps between him and the window light. . . .

Poetica, My Ars

Five minutes before the bell, I saw
the doubt coming on, building in two or three
darkening faces, like a storm across a lake —
eyes narrowing a bit, lips compressing.
But Long Martha, with the Hemingway eyebrows
and the alpine cheekbones, said it first:
a premonitory clearing of the throat,
like the first nickel-sized drops, then boom!
"Why is this a poem? It doesn't rhyme
(Small lightning flashes in her eyes).
It doesn't have any special rhythm.
I mean, isn't this prose typed funny?"

Bishop's voice had let go the fish,
the foil-backed eye and weapon-like lip
were that impressive. But here it was
swimming back against a current of inexperience
and the rocks of old expectation.
Lovely Martha of the schoolmarm name
and the showgirl legs, though, was having none of it.

Which of the old answers would she have heard
in school between the bareback summers,
riding through the sweet mortal stink
of Maryland fields — the sun at once
lightening the wispy hairs at her temples
and darkening the long and growing longer legs?

'Best words in the best order . . .'?
     Too subjective.
'Powerful emotion recollected . . .'?
     Nothing there about technique.
'What oft was thought . . .'?
     Who forethought Bishop's fish?
'A poem should not mean/but be . . .'?
     An aging metaphysician's answer.
     She is nineteen and flamingly empiric.

Everything sounded like fiddle before it hit the air.

➜

"The poet asks us, in a semblance of the rhythms
of American speech," I began, braving the stormy eyes,
"to become empiricists of the imagination."
 Her lush eyebrows contracted,
 invisible threads sewing them together.
"The poem makes its truth, you see,
out of accurate and plentiful lies."
 Speed it up, you're losing her.
" '. . .the coarse white flesh/packed in like feathers'
may not be factual, but it is visibly, touchably true.

You measure this truth with your eyes and fingers
the way you measure the truth of a horse's mane.
You feel it scrape the soft hairs of your cheek;
 A lover's moustache on your neck.
you smell it dank in the crisp blood-filled gills.
 The tang of flesh long closed upon flesh.
And when the lies accumulate, denser and denser,
 Like the hairs of your velour eyebrows.
you have something you can then test
against your knowledge of the world.
Then they are as true as the magical smoothness
of rough horse hair brushed flat."
 Or the tension in your groin muscles
 as your knees embrace that massive, masculine back.

The bell rang then, and we left, both dissatisfied.

Grace

Permit me this.
Electricity moves not in the wire,
but around it and flows
in the direction of the current.
And though the wire does not change,
the world does: wheels spin,
computers reason,
light floods out upon the darkness.
This is, if you will,
the way of grace in the world,
not in you but around you
and moving where you move,
flowing out to change the lives you touch,
giving solace or salvation.

You have left the world
(you would add "finally")
of the blind and stupid boys
who could not see this.
Now you know, all unassuming as you were,
how strong the grace around you is,
the attraction it can generate —
touching one man then the next
with your stature, with your dimples
(ah, the dimples!),
and the beacon of your brilliant mind.

You doubt, I know, this force of yours.
Yet this I guarantee:
Somewhere in the dark tonight,
with the distances stretching toward sleep,
some man in bed, his eyelids closed,
will see your face.
And he will sigh, to no one, electrified
by the solace in your dimples,
the shock of your remembered kiss.

Coefficient of Return

for AS

From January frost and morning fog,
licked by thunderbolts of silver spandex,
there canters Drea Schwind in wide-soled
Nike trainers, headphones clinging tight,
putting in her early miles
despite the car-sick air, the jams
and traffic clots of Broad Street,
oblivious both to air and earth.

Just brushed by gravity,
her eyes like flicks of blue flame,
she bounds (think of fox terriers,
marionettes, skitterish colts
in Kentucky meadows) — a faun in winter.

The ground gives back her weight,
and more, with every springbok stride
(think of white-tailed deer
launched as if by thought
past thicket at the edge of woods).

The light at Broad and Somerville is long;
far down the block, in front of Holy Child,
she sublimates to mist, I think,
though it is really only truck exhaust,
a sliver of light dimming in the day.

Reason argues it takes lungs
like grain sacks and ligaments
tough as fan belts to move like that,
that the earth beneath her feet
will grow less generous year by year.

But the heart will not be reasoned with,
and the silver-legged girl
on hooves of polyurethane
disappearing down the street
has one grave heart in tow.

Run, Drea Schwind,
loosed from the tug of earth
that lugs the rest of us down;
Run, girl, to what panpipe tunes
you hear, on your quick-silver legs,
into all the frosty mornings of your life.

Ears

"I will never cut my hair," she says
and looks away, "and show my Dumbo ears."
Daughter of goldsmiths and saints,
she hates the ears that loom from her head
round as the loops of china cups,
despises, too, the nose on her face.
The ad boys have won the round.
She would rather ape a walking stick,
some Cheryl or Christie,
with dachshund snout and seal-slick skull.

How can I tell her those ears
(that men will surely nibble on
and pour their breathy love into like wine)
were shaped through ages listening in the dark,
that when Ireland bristled with oak
her ancient sisters cocked one ear
after the whimper of children under thatch
and the other after creak of Danish leather,
dip of Danish oars, slipping at dawn
up the mist-brimming Liffey streams,
greedy for the blood of Gaels?

How can I say her nose, spud-lovely
with its rounded bulb and small wings
(a nose she'll surely nuzzle babies with),
is blunt for being pressed so long
against the earthen smoke of turf,
the woolen mists of the man-drowning sea?

Or eyes that glint like sunlight
on a running brook have learned their squint
from faces on an empty beach, duffled against the spray,
that scanned the vacant ocean for a sign?

In all of Hollywood's homogenized honeys
is not more life nor the magnetizing knowledge
of pain than in this Gaelic face
with its vigilance, its nuzzlings,
and its glinting eyes that draw men
as if to smoke and soft drownings.

Scuba

for CM

Play ball again, they said,
and risk a lifetime in a wheelchair,
the great bones of your leg
grinding like apothecaries
behind the willful kneecap.
So you did what any athlete must —
sought another force
to test the spring
of your lively thighs. Water was the charm.
How different from the searing diamond,
a world all angular and loud.
So silent down below,
just bloodrush in your ears,
the rumble of your regulated breath
the painless flexing of your knees.
And there free to roam
the buoyant dark without a fair or foul.
How intimate the water's touch,
so bold, so all at once all over,
and the chest-thumping thrill
of knowing you would not be again,
ever, safe at home.
You got so good so fast,
we stopped fearing for you.
Had you ever failed?
That May Sunday at the quarry —
water cold as granite, granite sky —
when you did not crash
the slatey surface,
you took us by surprise.
And now our empty pledge
to roll you round a lifetime
to have you back
is all that grief allows.
That and this:
you surely mastered drowning, too.
One good sniff,
then the mothery bloodrush,
then the slate-sharp freedom of the dark.

Rise Again

for JH, badly hurt

You are not alone in this, tender child.
We all come brittle from the womb.
You sleep now in this sterile room,
broken, sobbing, dreaming frightful, wild

dreams full of headlights and rain,
the uncontrolled momentum of the car,
the irresistible medial guard,
and then the brilliant pain.

I cannot tell you how I grieve
the smiling, sun-filled child's face
hidden here. The stupid soul wastes
to silence at the rigid weave

of gauze and plaster on your legs —
a body more the girl you were
than the woman you will be. Terror,
the old fragility of flesh, drags

us down. But you will rise again,
stroll again, your face to the sun,
salt spray in your hair. Already it's begun —
the quiet, living mystery of mending bone.

Making Ends Meet

Dawn is a whisper that wakes me.
My wife sighs amid the crumpled
topography of the bed. I get up.
Outside, endless February howls into March
in a blow from the dark arctic that slides,
like a hurried lover, across the firm rump
of the Appalachians and batters this sleeping
house into a chorus of chatters and clangs
enough to raise the dead. It does.
I light a candle to dispel a ghost,
but it looms anyway from the shadows.

"I've sold my cello to make ends meet."

It is my tall student from years ago,
the pain in her eyes tuned to such a pitch
it could shatter glass. And me so brittle.
What will she do now, the sadness
of Mahler no more in her fingers,
Vivaldi's joy not in her wrist?
"It's okay, really, I'll get by."
She studied literature, instead, and finance,
and so she died before she died.

When they found her, thin as a bow,
hanging like an icon in the college chapel,
she was wearing her black concert dress.

Her body shrinks before my sight;
the rope becomes this blackened wick.
So small a flame is no defense.
What could I have done? Love is not enough?
Te voglio bene and here's a check?

Is it February does this,
or the clattering darkness of this house,
that makes aloneness so complete it settles,
a palpable chill, behind my kneecaps,
in my knuckles, in my neck?
Good practice, no doubt, for eternity
where all ends meet.

PART THREE:

Reaching Out in Darkness —

My Wife

Candles

a silly sonnet for my wife

Some men watching candles see only flame —
the old seductive dance of rapid oxidation —
and for a time their darkness has no name,
as they rejoice in bright intoxication.

Others in the room, their shaggy eyebrows knit,
are sad to watch the candles be consumed.
They only see the using up. They forfeit
hope, and all their passions lie entombed.

But we know, darling, darkness has its uses
for bridging gaps from spouse to spouse.
To the shaggy-browed I say, "You need some spruces
chopped and sawed to build a sturdy house."

Without the melting wax there is no burning.
We use each other up to stay the yearning.

The Glass Cutter

You stand with your back to me,
weight on your left leg, hip curving
desirably toward the couch,
laying out the pieces as you cut them.
I can't in reality see
what your strong hands are about.
But your back is always nice to watch,
and, framed by the window,
the mullions shifting reference as you move,
you become for a moment one of your creations —
shape and color and intersecting line.

Across the road, the crust of snow
in the ancient cemetery is purple
with last light. And down the long
southwestern slope, through the rank and file
headstones, waves of fine snow blow
smokelike through all that cold company.
I whisper, "It's warm over here, poor bastards."
Though the sun is gone, the sky remembers.
There and there, against the milk-glass sky,
rise the darkened cenotaphs that mark
the missing dead. You are mercifully alive.

I imagine the deftness of your hands
among the implements of what you do:
the copper foil, the flux and solder;
how they must guide the diamond-wheeled
cutter, exert just the right pressure,
follow exactly the curve you've drawn.
And at the rolling point of contact
the denser crystal wins: glass is scored.
"Scarred," I tease, "we crack more easily, too,
where we've been scarred." You say without turning,
"If you want omelettes. . . ." And I know
by the way your elbow raises from your side
that glass has cleft along a perfect curve
as though it had itself decided.

Out there a small cyclone of powder rises,
ghostlike, on the hillside, as if it overheard
and would warm itself by our stove.
My skin creeps faintly up my back.

How you shape and break these bits of glass,
how you reassemble them, bound in lead,
to resemble something of the world — what is it
this time, a purple hillside with headstones
against a milky sky? — leaves me dumb
at your quick, intelligent fingers,
at the guile in your hands.

Our lives, I think, are like this:
the fractured planes of dreams, broken bits
of what we'd planned, shaped and reassembled,
joined to one thing more than what two were,
a thing that teases out the colors from the sunlight.

"Stay out there," I say aloud.
"The warmth here's for the living."

Nags Head, August, '86

The body-lifting swell comes back
in bed, riding the spectral surf in silence
down the fine hairs of the inner ear.
Startled, my fingers grip the mattress.

All afternoon I braced my knees
against the thundering downwash,
played in the lulls between,
fought, with adroit toes in the soft bottom,
the noiseless, northward riptide,
like a sinister influence tempting
me out of my depth. Now in the dark,
like a ghost of motion, it is back.

You come like this, or the memory of you,
sometimes in the dark, so real,
so sudden I nearly yelp, toes curling:
in my guts, in my groin, I ride again
the buoyant swells of our loving.

Sunday Dusk

Sunday dusk in summer's fine preseason.
Honeysuckle and charcoal thicken the breeze.
An oil lamp burns a little island
in the darkening yard, and cold La Batt,
dulls, slug by slug, my sense of drought.

No one will die tonight.

I have had enough of death this year —
old teachers; young students; a one-time lover;
my great friend, so worn out at last
she could not keep her undies dry;
my father, his shins honed to sword blades
as he withered on the bed, afraid to sleep.
And with each death, a creeping dryness,
turning blood to sand.

But here's the world, poised like a diver
on the leaking brink of summer.
Three fat moths, winged cigar butts,
nudge the globe. A single bat
squeaks his angular, impossible flight,
faceting the sky above me. Nighthawks peel
the vertical air to its deep blue flesh.

Surviving droughts takes irrigation:
steady Gene Shay easing the airwaves;
rag-time rumbling from a steel-stringed Lo Prinzi;
Tom Rush's rare voice, like a hard gargle of gin;
you, on the fringe of lamplight, watering the yard.

Down to Earth

The Man

Against the garden wall, the pile
of last year's clippings, blackened
and sunk to a glistening mush,
bristles with maple seedlings —
their first leaves still wrinkled
like crumpled trousers by a heaving bed —
the urge to live so strong in them
they go down into most anything.

The wall itself, of local stone,
wears at each reticulation
out from the ever-greening moss,
a fine brown pelt of sporophytes,
as though it might shudder,
stretch, and bumble heavily away.
The patient moss clings
in every crevice, turning dust,
from a billion springs ago,
back slowly into dust.

The Woman

Oh, for crying out loud, cheer up!
The damned moss turns into more moss.
What do you think those sporo-things are for?
Why race for the grave?
You are not dead; I am not dead.
Why sit at that table,
in that cold circle of light,
writing your dead little thoughts,
while I sweat here under the covers
to feel the live firmness of your shoulders
and ache to be filled with you?

You have a lifetime yet.
The other will come soon enough.
We can make a lifetime of tonight
*

if you'll just put down that pencil
and let me hear your trousers
hit the floor. Cling to my crevices,
you big jerk. I'll be earth;
send your root down into me.

Summer of '88

This summer is god damned.
The dead thin brown
of it crunches underfoot
like excelsior
or stale tobacco.
Water rises from the earth
but does not fall
until I think I will drown.
Old people dry up and die.
The young jog anyway,
their Walkmans and their money
charms against the heat.
Misanthropy glistens on their skin.
No sweat dries.

Past midnight I am alone
in the kitchen, reading.
The air as taut as a fireman's net,
I could fall back and not fall.
My hams stick to the chair.
Liquid insects trickle
from behind both knees
down into my socks.
Around me, my defenses:
the harp of Derek Bell,
the cool notes falling,
falling on me,
falling softly;
Sociables by Nabisco
imbedded with poppy seeds;
cream cheese flecked with parsley,
celery, nuggets of carrot;
a golden Molson
in a green bottle spawning
tiny lenses of the summer night;
poor dead Wallace Stevens,
so married, so alone.

Then, barefoot, you appear,
solid and scalding beside me
in your panties
and a sleeveless undershirt
like my father used to wear,
sipping Boodles on ice,
too hot to touch.
The room assembles itself
around your horny feet.
Two crescent moons soak
below the breasts I love.
And if they are no longer
quite a matched set,
their altitude and azimuth
still chart my manhood.

"Ah, Meg Midwinter, isn't it?"
And you dance a few round
steps before the table
and slosh your gin,
and curse the heat.
Like souls in torment,
we cannot touch,
but let the spring-soft harp
rain down upon us and desire . . .
while poor dead Wallace Stevens
catches tigers in red weather.

Bodie Island, Before Dawn

Out from Wanchese harbor,
like monks to morning prayers, the lights of boats
process in silence down the southern edge
of sky, where one by one, without haste,
over the dark rim of the world, they drop.
The quiet, the solemn order of their going
shakes me, like coffins clicking shut,
or doors slamming in strange places.
With both hands raised, I offer coffee
like a chalice to the light-consuming dark.
It is a comic gesture more than not —
wide-eyed, pretending audience,
suggesting baggy pants and pratfalls.

An hour before, I lay awake filling
with water and desire, while you breathed clouds
of night into the room, regular as clockwork,
painting the space between us with indigo air
and the sibilant intervals of sleep.
How can flesh yearn more than this —
rising blind and reaching out in darkness,
parched for light and for your liquid places?

A day before, as wind clashed in buckthorn
and scrub pine, threshed mallow and sea oats
with rhythms metrical as surf, the sky
turned white before my eyes. At ten the sea
was silver, tarnished and clear in alternate bands
away to the sharp horizon, too piercing
to watch without tears.

And now as these obedient, tiny lights
wink off at the same edge, something
huge and black hovers here above us,
like a kingfisher poised to plunge,
while the children dream and you breathe
easy in your deep blue sleep. I feel it
*

more and more, spreading like mould along my bones.
We hold the thing at bay as best we can.
Coffee helps — and gratitude whispered to the dark:
for the lure of flesh,
    the thresh of wind,
        the silver-banded sea.

N.B. Bodie Island is pronounced by the residents as *body*, and in fact
appears in some eighteenth century maps as Body Island.

Belfield, October, Early Morning

If some morning you could share this sight
with me, could bear this earth-astounding light
that pours in low through air so clear
the sense reverts to trickery — I hear
Pastorius whistling for his son; Old Peale
assessing grapes, his terrier at heel —
if we could huddle on this bench sometime
beneath this daylight moon, a tissue-paper dime
so thin the sky shows through, or wonder how
against the rusting hardwoods, bole and bough,
the evergreens, still black, conserve the night —
or feel the sun's off-handed might
explode the billion perpendiculars of grass —
if . . . if every Eden did not pass,
and leave us to our otherness. Apart,
soul-blind, we grope in darkness for another's heart.
I want to give you something of this dawn,
these woods, this brilliant field, but you are gone.
So I will come again at noon, alone,
to mourn this sky-pierced, pale, discarnate moon.

Fair November, Last Light

for JMM

Four-fifteen and numb from talk,
my spirit drooping like impatiens in first frost,
I laid my weight against the heavy door
and pushed through into Autumn light
that gushed against my chest and face
with the force of open hydrants:
the hardwood ridge toward Germantown ablaze,
the campus radiant as a book of hours.
I could barely breathe.

All day a stiff wind had scrubbed the air
and built a bank of locust leaves
against the bricks where beds of mum
and scarlet sage levitate the edge of Olney Hall.
The lawn was strewn with hawthorn berries —
pale cream and red — and simmering with starlings.

Now the air was still, was fraught with far off smoke;
the crushed fruit of juniper betrayed a hint of gin
(Back in my throat a memory long dry
of candle-lit martinis in leather booths
and cleavage shadowed deep. My palms
remembered you — your warmths, your luscious weights).

In the bright outlining air, so much on fire!
the sage before the wall, the night-touched mums,
a cardinal like nervous blood
in the sumac's flaming top,
and tangled pyracantha burning Roland's Walk.
I put my bag down,
a turgor slowly rising,
and saw a dozen juncos rain like arrowheads
among the feeding starlings.

These spots of crystal sight, so rare!
The heart must gather all it can against the dark.
And night was coming on.
I had to go, but, damn, I knew,
*

through all these tingling frequencies of light,
I was alive, could hear again
in skin of palm and fingertip,
the urgent call of you.
I grabbed my bag and left,
grateful for the fiery light,
the constellated starlings in the grass,
and swilled the gin-sharp air.

Away From It All

My god, what a crowd at the cabin!
the men farting like Chaucer's pilgrims,
the women groaning and running for the air freshener —
and all of us, free for the weekend, laughing.
We ate stromboli at midnight
and drank beer at eight in the morning.
No voices pleaded, "Mommy, I'm hungry,"
or "Daddy, fix my bike."
What time we had was ours.
So many good people, so much living flesh,
the heart clicked its heels.

We left peanuts on the flat rock
by the wood pile and watched the chipmunk
stuff his cheeks and vanish into the angel pine.
We took turns in the canoe,
slipping off into the mist
that filled the bowl of the lake,
reappearing from the white stillness
like the ghosts of Algonquins.
We counted the leaves falling
into the lake all afternoon.
What time we had was ours.
And when the shadow of the mountain
crept up to the window,
we lit candles and grew still.

Maybe it was the flame — you know
what a sucker I am for candles —
or perhaps the wax
cooling into the voluptuous
swellings on the shaft,
but I thought of your strong legs
and the way your hips are carved
from carrying babies in one arm
and a voice said,
You are running out of time.
You will, someday, be away from it all.
And I could feel desire accumulating
like the slow, red snowfall
of the maple leaves into the lake.

The Voices

for JMM

I

What boy can know that he
will not be always five?
In that time of slow time
the house itself whispers
the adamant truth: "You will never be alone, never."
And so, tucked in, he clings
to the boy-sized Raggedy Ann
and nuzzles the red yarn hair.
His father, filling the door frame,
cuts a giant man-shape
from the doughy light in the hall,
and pulls closed the door. Then the house,
murmuring with the voices of his sisters
in the kitchen, shrugs its shoulders
just enough to swing the door ajar
and let in the honey-colored air
mother hums in the parlor.
"You will never be alone," the house says,
"Now wrap yourself in melody till morning."

II

No boy can bear to think
that he will always be sixteen.
Now with the door closed tight
and stopped with a man-sized shoe,
he listens for the house
to assure him: "You will not
always be alone, you will not."
Time touches his face
with the softness of angora,
and it smells so good he thinks
he will cry. He clings
to his truth, and the writhing,
*

fragrant darkness fills
    with the shapes of women.
They have breasts
the exact size of his hand
And buttocks intolerably smooth and firm.
Through teeth so white they light
the space behind his eyelids, they whisper,
"I will be yours, I will."
Tossing heads with manes of sunlight,
they fairly whinny at his touch,
and he rides them down the brilliant dark
into meadows of himself.

III

A man knows forty is an instant,
forty-one an eyeblink,
forty-two a heartbeat. . . .

In another bedroom, another door
is left ajar in case
some other boy of five
should cry out in the dark,
and a man listens for the house
to reassure him. But in the breath
that whistles in his nose,
other voices start to sing
from someplace out of time:
"You will be ours, you will."
And there is nothing
in the black to cling to
but you, my Raggedy Ann,
    my whinnying colt,
      my wife.

PART FOUR:

The Birth of Light and Air —
My Children

Intimations of Closing on Opening Night

The night you came, had I not sweated there,
biting my lip each time your mother winced,
primed for the gory climax of the scene
laboring nearer, I should never be convinced
such a thing had happened: the birth of light and air.

Almost. No witch's milk, no waxy scrim
to dim the glow, no slit-eyed tragic mask
to hint the thing is dust and must return.
But open-eyed you came and sighing, as much to ask,
"Am I awake?" or "Where have I been?"

And only this to mark you: emphatic in the light,
just behind the pulsing fontanel —
at the crown of your head — a simple smear of blood.
Then a denouement of cleansing and none could tell,
the play complete, what I took into the night.

For Andrew at Three Months

for JFN

My lumpiest dear, all florid globes of nose
and cheek and chin, lip and ear (but with eyes
that prick like a safety pin), a father tries
without success to see which way a child goes

before it's born. In a dark mood bred
of too little sleep or too much Cutty Sark
he thinks, wasting an afternoon in the park,
You'd bring a child to a world nearly dead?

I meant no harm. Still, though you'd never fastened
eyes on me, nor, smiling, ever bent
your fist around my finger, I would have sent
you, all hope, whirling on a fool's errand.

An hour most poorly spent within sight
of dogwoods drenched in sun, each petal tipped
in pink, each cruciform bloom equipped
with the promise of flowers awash in light.

We all inherit death, Andrew, but not death alone.
I give dogwoods in the sun to you, who cling like life to bone.

The Cold

I am given to the melodramatic.
So when the child has trouble breathing at midnight,
his lungs, small as pears, grow overripe with phlegm,
the coughing, like the bark of some insane dog, continues,
I think he will die before morning.
Then I think he won't.
There is little left to do but sit in the lighted kitchen,
in the dark house, drink coffee, and recall
the colds *I've* had and how *I* never died before morning,
or before nightfall, or before I told Mother I was sorry.

There is something insufferably cheerful
about a lighted kitchen in a dark house,
and though the child breathes in his sleep
like an aged wino, and the dog barks outside
like a sick child, here are the canisters —
jovial, plump, and mute.
The coffee tastes accusingly better than it ever has,
and, if it weren't so callous, I would toast a muffin,
or go into the yard and play with the barking wino,
because it is only a cold and I know he will breathe easy.
In the morning I will tell him I'm sorry.

Calligraphy of Snow

for Andrew, growing

Asleep, the child grows in the dark. The snow
beyond the window is etched with the prints of birds,
a random laying on of strokes that took
all day to make. Pretty writing? No
words, at any rate. Nor are there words

to show this other growing. Perhaps like spring:
into the arid cold one day come water
and sun. The world, so long a uniform
brown, is suddenly green; every living thing
again lives, then a month's surprise of color.

Though this is not precisely it — too slick
and easy to be quite the same. The earth
in spring performs a feat, sleight of hand
the heart applauds, one stupendous cosmic trick
designed to steal away the watcher's breath.

A boy's growing is more like those scratches
in the snow out there (and just as queer
to understand): a slow accumulation
of steps, taken while a father watches,
whose worth is whispered to the dark,
    though the meaning is unclear.

All-Star

for AMM in his tenth summer

During the anthem, cap covering your heart
in a gesture you have never shown,
you face the flag in center, taller than all
but one along the line from first to home,
and with a thickness through the shoulders
you've gained in just the last few minutes.
I am caught off base and out of time
by this sudden size and style.

At the ump's loud "Play ball," you settle
under your cap, tilting your head
back into it, like a big leaguer,
and the angle of your chin declares your intent:
"I can play this game. Let's do it."

By god, if you don't: creaming one to the gap
in right-center for a triple, scooping throws
from the dirt at first, as though you knew
the ball's mind and changed it.
With the game on the line,
they call you in to pitch.
How did you learn to stride
with self-possession in your step?

When you take the ball, kick back,
and sling it, without a hitch,
hard overhand for strikes,
I feel a major twinge
of something in my guts,
a giddy slippage as you mow them down:
strike three, strike three, strike three.

Here among strange mates, at this strange field,
I see you as I never have before: strong and fleet,
a boy, with gristle in his walk,
slicing away from me, heart covered more and more,
into the dark outfield of the next decade,
like a screaming liner I can never glove.

The Handsome Stranger

for Andrew

At midday mass, while you fetch the water,
the altar shimmers in pure clarity.
From the skylight overhead,
the mantle-blue heavens pour in.
Old Father Sean, with famine-shadowed skull,
turns in your direction for the cleansing,
his chasuble like molten emerald.
And you, a boy I used to know,
alb unearthly in this pond of glowing air,
come, cruet raised, to wash
an old man's hands.
        Who are you, boy?
Your soccer-wild hair,
blue-black as grackle wings,
subdued with cream, is combed;
azalea-pale, blood blossoms in your cheek;
so handsome in this flawless light,
a girl of twelve behind me sighs.
You have become a stranger,
a blurred page I can barely read,
all the pairings and the partings
of a lifetime still before you —
the thrilling whisper of your name
in the naked dark, the flint tears
freezing on December graves.

The noon sun makes this clear:
there's a man in you I will never know,
any more than I know the old priest —
the spatulate fingers thin as twigs,
the grey-jawed face,
the lupine hunger in his eyes.
And as you lift your elbow,
and the glass plays spectrums
on your neck and chin,
my heart bangs once hard,
like the closing of a heavy book.

At the Wall

Washington, D.C., January, 1990

The January sky was pale blue silk,
seagulls tearing strips of it in long arcs
from Lincoln's lap to the Capitol dome,
the day, somber as pilgrims,
we went to see for ourselves;
a day as fair as springtime despite
the piles of snow melting:
leaf buds swelling on all the trees,
lunchtime joggers looping around the Mall,
children with hot dogs everywhere.

Then it was there, the black wall with all the names.
Caught in history's loving embrace,
they were clutched to the mad bosom
of the world and drained dry.
Now they are chaff on the black granite,
all the many thousands of them.

Tommy Loughlin, altar boy and friend,
who shared his Latin homework
and got me through, was there
somewhere, in name, in the mirroring stone.
There and, of course, not there.
One morning in his twentieth year
he exploded into a coarse red rain
that fell on all the green earth
of a tiny trail outside Pleiku.
I wanted to say goodbye.

My son, who is tall and bright
and does his own Latin homework now,
moved off ahead into the crowd.
He stared, it seemed, at the darker him
trapped two feet into the wall,
and as he raised his hand
to touch a name,
the darker thing reached to clutch.

The Acid Test: Advice to My Son

If she touches you when she talks,
laying her hand lightly on your forearm,
do not assume she is the one.
For some women this is learned.
It is no more than tactile punctuation —
delightful in itself, so feel free to enjoy it —
but not the sign you crave.
For others it is much worse.
They think of it as *interpersonal contact*,
designed to add *positive reinforcement*.
Be wary. It means she wants something
you would not otherwise give.
Appraise the curve of her fingers on your arm;
some raptors sport exquisite plumage.
But if she leans into you when she laughs,
her shoulder touching your shoulder,
this is natural — a birch leaning toward the sun —
the free expression of her heart.
Slip your arm around her waist.

If you hear in her voice,
dark and warm as mulled wine,
viole da gamba play, and the region
from your belt to your knees
begins to deliquesce,
there may be strings attached.
Or if she says only things that please you,
you must conclude she is greasing the skids.
She is not the one you seek.
Remember, in talk as in music, some friction
is both necessary and desirable.
Strings do not sound so sweet
without the scraping bow.
And cloves are ground to powder
to mull the wine (I leave to you
the role of the hot poker).

In restaurants you may think you see
sparks of longing in her eyes.
I caution you: move the candle
before the wine arrives.
Between, the flame obscures,
but to the right or left, it gives easy access
to the kind of look that tells —
and darkens the dramatic dent
at the neckline of her dress.
And when you gaze deep into her eyes,
do not seek to see the movement of her soul.
It cannot be done.
When you look into a lake
you see no fish.
What you mostly see is your own face,
distorted, gazing back.
So with her eyes — and there diminished, too.
Treasure more the oddities you find:
the tiny flecks of gold and opalescent green
that make the sad grey iris dance.
In other words, should she "speak volumes"
with her eyes, do not think she is the one
before you find who owns the copyright
or check the date of publication.

The sure signs you seek are phantoms —
embers in the ash that seem to move.
You might, though, try this:
Imagine a dim room
down the long hallway of the future
(It helps to have candles here, too).
The shades are drawn. You are in the bed
and around the foot stand
several solemn young people looking
vaguely like the face you shave each day.
She prays in a chair beside you,
her fingers touching your forearm.
They are gnarled and pale as roots —
*

a hag's fingers.
What hair she has is white and brittle.
Her eyes have all but disappeared
into the flesh of her face.
Her voice grates on your ears
like a child's violin.
Now, if you find her
absolutely essential to the scene,
if the thought of her not being there
feels empty in your stomach
and full in your throat,
then, perhaps, she is the one.

The Little Boy-Girl

In the tub, all her roundnesses glistening
like oiled fruit, she informs with high seriousness,
"I'm washing my penis," and will not be persuaded
she has the other. She doesn't care who's listening;
she's nearly three: loving, swift, and fearless.

She's learned the name for what's between her legs
from her brother, who at five is tall and wise.
Her faith in him is perfect; she'll not be shaken.
All protests sink and swirl away with the dregs
of her bath. Her brother would not tell her lies.

He is her model in all things; they are kin
by more than accident of birth. The joy
she takes in running, thighs already hard
and sleek as a man's bicep, would be a sin
in times when speed afoot was all for boys.

Yet, when they fall together, breathless,
a turmoil of elbows and knees, she mugs him
with affection. She is a vessel, dispensing unwanted
kisses, strenuous hugs, in courtship deathless
as the family of man, no guile nor decorum.

In their fighting too, a kinship longer than she knows:
a thudding in the blood, by blood compelled
to stalk him from behind the loveseat and raise
the block to strike. The stunning vision grows —
the stealth, the bloodied rock, the brother felled.

The Tumbler

for Emily at four

What Olympiad do you point for, tumbling girl,
wearing your body like a skin-tight leotard,
as you cartwheel through the living room?
Since you turned three, I swear,
I've seen more of your bottom than your top,
head thrown down upon the sofa cushions,
feet waving precarious inches
from the woodcut of Undine on the wall.

How does your liquid soul
stay in, upside down like that?
I feel the sofa often
and peer into your ears,
certain you must someday spring a leak.

And what direction will you go
with your legs out east and west
and your torso north and south?
Your straddle split is so much like a cross
it gives a father pause, who bears
your handsprings in wonder all the more
for having seen you tumble into the world.

For now the world is your gymnasium.
Through it you flip with undulating arms,
your ligaments elastic, your spine a willow-whip,
taking this aging soul, all its elastic sagging,
along for the ride.

Somewhere Undine smiles,
and the gods nod their approval —
nine-eight, nine-nine, a perfect ten —
as they celebrate your liquid soul
and, oh, its snappy leotard.

The Age of Reason: For Emily at Seven

The maxi-pad stuffed down the bathroom sink
has been removed, the riot act duly read:
"In God's name, why? Will you pay the plumber?"
Vanquished, the tiny vandal slouches off to bed.
I go down to rest my knees and nurse a drink.
Two fingers wonder blindly where my hair has fled.

This respite in the evening — eyes shut tight
against the day, a tot of warm bourbon
red-balling through the blood (I swear I hear
the capillaries sigh and open wide) — by right
is mine, an hour's grace between disturbing
day and, lately, more disturbing night.

It has almost worked when her sobbing starts:
the slow exhale of pain, the halting search for breath.
Like music come through headphones, it seems within
my head, not heard, and tightens every tired part
of me, like someone in the dark has whispered, "Death,"
and Jack Daniels glorified, with all his art,

could not relax this knot. I climb the stairs.
Downcast, she steps along a road new-paved
in darkness and the ache of guilt. I feel the louse.
To dress a wound not long so cheaply salved,
I tickle, promise ice cream, stroke her hair.
Grown, my girl, the pains come doubled, solace halved.

Pumpkin Time

for Emily and Andrew

The driving home is filled with sky and farms.
The blue, electric dome elates the eye,
and stubbled fields — old corn, old hay — are suede
at fifty-five and trimmed in leather oak.
But interspersed, like wounds upon the hills,
some sumac, maple, bleeding upward, tempt
the heart to see a kind of death in this
reclining earth, a time when spirits walk.

Resist. The bounty stashed behind the seat
belies the thought, for we've bought crookneck,
acorn, butternut, and scallop squash;
and pumpkins big as orange boulders wait
transforming knives.
                  So burn the deadfall, burn
the leaves. Old mother snoozes down to sleep,
not die, with cinnamon and nutmeg breath.
And if some moon-gone night the drooling fiend
looks in, corruption oozing out his eyes
and evil sweating rotten from his pores,
we'll light the grinning jack o'lantern then
and scare him cold and empty-handed home.

Midnight, Walking the Wakeful Daughter

Late on a summer night maybe twenty years from now,
when these touches are lost as unnecessary covers,
you and a man nothing like me lie in bed,
through for the moment, though not asleep — lovers.

There is moonlight and the pulse of crickets.
His head, by your head. His arm, a weight
across your chest. All is shadow and the smell of sweat.
He breathes into your neck, "Baby, you are great."

Your fingers gauge the soft geometry where your belly ends.
The calm constriction in your throat is rising tears.
So much at peace, there is no reason to recall
the first man to hold you close, back all those years.

Father and lover, distinct. So it should be.
But if there is comfort in the weight of his arm near your heart;
if you feel the crickets as fingers tapping lightly on your back,
then remembered or not, these touches were the start.

PART FIVE: **Down to Earth —**
Poems at Midlife

Walt's Left Big Toe

It was crushed by a four-foot length
of cast iron pipe when he was nineteen.
During one of his layoffs from the railroad
he jobbed out as a steamfitter's helper.
That's when he dropped the pipe: "Christ,"
he said, "I thought I'd like to die."

So he hobbled around on his heel for a month
and the toe acquired a life of its own.
The nail thickened, turned spongy and blue,
the color of the veins in a ripe Stilton.

By the time he got to be my Pop,
he was forty and the toe had ruined
maybe three hundred socks, chewing
silk and cotton the same, poking through
like the head of an ugly snapper,
voracious and dumb. When I was a kid
I was afraid of it.

It was the color of a stone you'd find
by a stream bed, mottled and splotched
with brown mold and green. Hard as stone,
too. He cut pieces of callus from it
with shears the size of tin-snips.

As he got older, his left foot grew longer
than the right, as though that living toe
were dragging the rest of the bones inexorably along.

The last time he spoke to me, before they silenced
him with all their helpful tubes, was Monday night.
Visiting hours were over, and when I leaned down
to kiss his forehead, he whispered to no one in particular,
"Dear God, what's to become of me?" But he knew.
Then, "Joseph, uncover my feet." So I did.
His old shin bones were thin as reeds
but the toe was as ugly and dangerous and alive as ever.

I'm only telling you this because lately my left
big toe has been rubbing the front of my loafer.

The Old Man in the Garden

All of summer has turned brittle overnight:
the weightless shell of the wasp
I found this morning in a web;
the shucked husk of the mantis, riding light
as a shadow in the dry grass
that leans against the bricks, beyond hope or prayer;
and almost overnight, my father's fragile bones.

The yellow marigolds, robust yesterday —
so many small suns suspended in the green —
wilt and blacken, letting themselves down
like the heads of old men drooping off to sleep.
A hundred thousand maple wings spin
like gyros in the wind.
And the dogwood drips its scarlet berries on the ground
where light is sifted to the thinness of a scythe —
the green gloss of its leaves
spotted purple, spotted brown,
as though a dying man, thin fingers colder than ice,
had touched them in the night,
a touch as gentle as a father's, saddening and chill.

Each leaf will bear the fingerprints
and bleed to crimson in a week.
The sun ticks farther south each day,
and in a month, the white.

But the dogwood anchors memory:
the earth will lean to more congenial light.
What's weightless will have weight again —
a hundred thousand maples lodge beneath the snow,
and in the head of every marigold, father,
two hundred sons.

Perchance to Die?

Not for the first time, his father's face,
floating disembodied in the luminous dark,
has jolted him awake, his heart a claustrophobic
child kicking to repel the shrinking closet
of the rib cage. He tastes blood.
His diaphragm flutters at the edge of hysteria.

It is always the same: hale and smiling,
the head appears, assembling his father's face,
in the liquid geometry of the willful unconscious,
from features marshalled from another dream.
Though he never speaks, he hears his own voice:
"Daddy, I miss you so much, so much."
Then the primal graphics start:
the ripe plum of its brain dries,
the temples shrink away to dark hollows,
the lips recede beyond the teeth,
the wax-paper flesh turns to vapor,
and when the gap-jawed Jolly Roger speaks,
no sound but a tiny linen scroll drops out.
"You let me down," it reads. And he awakes
to the kick, kick, kicking in his chest,
the ancient rush of sea-sound in his ears,
and his gums trickling blood upon his tongue.

Last Laugh

The stroke left you damaged but alive.
Though more still worked than not,
a sinister leakage junked your symmetry;
the left half of your face already dead —
the lips and lid, the fleshy cheek
tugged, sunken, turned leaden;
your stricken tongue made into sludge;
all ugly and unwitting as a beast.

The right half was still my mother, though:
alive and smiling, its human eye
still full of fight; the skin cross-hatched
with diamond shapes by most of eighty years'
opposing motion — the earthward curve of hurt,
the tight upswing of joy — full yet
with light, with struggle and blood.

God knows why they propped you in that chair.
So much lead was in your face
you couldn't hold your head up.
The thin hair at the back of your skull,
five days uncombed, bent at crazy angles.
I couldn't see your face, just the hump
of your flannel nightgown, your hands,
blue-white as turkey skin, crossed in your lap.
We did not know yet this would kill you,
so when your second daughter made her joke
about our nag-faced aunt,
a small joke on the unequal numbers
of horses and horses' asses,
then the dull-witted monster drooled
against her will on to your hands,
but my mother's shoulders shook and shook.

Rewind

No voice can tell what life
you fled through, backward,
that last week in bed.
Each sunrise left you less
to do; the dark bloom
on your brain stem first
took away your tongue.
You loved us yet with your eyes,
till they went dark.
Nor could we crack the code
your right hand squeezed upon us.
Then all language ceased.

Still you panted onward,
faster and faster, sweating then
through all that you had been:
back through grandchildren and weddings,
past your five great labors,
to his first desperate
kneading of your thighs,
his tongue upon your breast.
Back to — what? Tell us, please.
The headlong rabbit dive
to the snug warren of the womb?

The faster you went,
the more you lost —
baby, fetus, zygote —
until finally, on the last day,
huffing like a marathoner,
you lost all conception of life.

April Fool

Everywhere around me things push up
through the darkness of the earth,
turn leisurely toward the sun
with a studied almost nonchalance,
as though to seem too eager
might have deadly consequence:
fiddleheads uncurl casually,
daffodils affect a bored awakening;
"Don't get caught," they seem
to say, "wanting life too badly."

I have known this same pretense in me:
the tiny hole they put Miss Hippel in
does not appall me;
the failing heartbeat of my father
does not buckle my knees;
the pulse of you,
so near in the darkness —
the urge so strong in me
I whimper with desire —
does not thrill me.

The Seduction of Gravity

The patching was done. I had bought two years,
at most, for the old roof, finding places
where the surface was black and bubbled
as leprotic skin, that, when I pressed them,
oozed the foul-smelling liquid too long
hidden from the sun. One rafter under the fascia
had turned spongy and fragile as mushrooms
in a dark forest. I had only bought some time.
The pack of shingles, weighty as a child,
on my shoulder, I carried back to the low
attic window I'd bellied through to get out;
and the can of cement, heavy as a vow,
pulled at my shoulder socket;
then the hammer and saw, trowel and shears,
gathered and arranged in the box
with scraps of lumber, I carted back to the window.
Everything was heavy, pulling me down.
And you were nowhere to be seen.
I felt weary and sore and grave.

I walked to the front edge and looked.
The skyline of the city five miles to the south
was so sharp in the clear air, I felt it
like a blade drawn lightly across my skin,
daring me. And the huge black rectangles
of Frankford's factories was a geometry
that sang under my spleen, calling.
Closer still, the green parabola of the sycamore's
dome was feminine, enticing as the great muscles
swelling the seat of your green corduroys.
I was growing hollow-boned, lighter.
Then, for an instant, I knew I could have you.
It's so easy, my heart said.
It's all yours, said my thighs.
My skin shivered, *Take it, have it.*
I found my arms spreading like wings.
Step out, soar, fly, be free.
*

I was trembling and convinced.
Then a voice between my ears called me an idiot.
You will die, fool, it said. *The earth
is possessive; her gravity monogamous.*
I turned and bolted, panting, back to the window,
pitching flat on my belly, scraping my cheek
in the filthy small stones, wanting you.
For a long few seconds I lay there, breathing,
feeling the marrow congeal in my bones,
knowing I would never fly — not to earth, not to you.

Her Cashmere Sleeve

Side by side, through Belfield's mottled lanes
they walk, not talking. " 'Farm Per-SEV-erance',
he whispers, "Old Peale, for all his pains,
could not make it work." Again silence
consumes the space between them, shy as children,
while his heart pounds out encyclicals of need.
Below her eyes the blue translucent skin —
a fragile weft of hurt and joy — feeds
his longing, as vapor feeds the morning frost
that vaults our shallow footprints with its lace.
Severed still his tongue from heart, still lost
the nerve to map with lips the contours of her face.
Then her cashmere sleeve, like ointment, thrills his hand:
his silence swells till he can hardly see — or stand.

Hippel's Wilderness

for EH

The canopy of buttonwood and elm
that kept the sun off Oakland Street is gone.
What must have looked like a tunnel to the future,
looking north to Arrott in nineteen nineteen,
full of shade and lovers, is thinned to few
old trees, standing here and there like awkward
strangers in a long, long hall.

The meadow where you played beside the stream
that trickled down to Frankford Creek, where wild
rose and blue-bell grew, is covered now
with homes and streets: Naples, Horrocks, Large.
And the rough mill boys who whistled their
embarrassed homage, who must have longed to stroke
your strong white legs and drown in hair
as curled and sweet as hardwood shavings,
but found no words, are mute as stones.

You have seen the faces fall away, like trees
along the street, and, grey, the soot from diesels
build up everywhere, traffic rattling
sashes up and down the block. But you
have saved a bit of city as it was.
In a yard smaller than a good-sized truck
Frankford as it used to be goes on.

From the white snow drops of March
to the garnet mums in latest fall,
you give us color, scent, and seed;
you give us names of things we never knew,
a textured rhythm to the seasons: crocus
pokes through pachysandra weeks before the daffodils;
seven colors of azalea and three
of columbine, cosmos like a low-born daisy;
garden phlox and street grass taller than my son,
white violets in the mulch pile,
dusty miller as softly furred as kittens' ears
with blossoms dark as blood.

So if the stream flows down in memory now,
and Oakland Street is open to the sky,
if the mill boys' silent praise whistles
only in the inner meadow of the ear,
the wilderness remains.

We pay you back in kind.
We teach our sons and daughters names of things.
For in the long cold turning of the year
we have the words if not the color,
the sound if not the scent.
And so we hope.

Harper

As from an ancient fire,
O'Carolan's air,
rising from this harp,
lofts a plume of embers,
that settle on us in the dark
with the force of touches
remembered in the flesh.
And in the open spaces
of my chest, in the dream
darkness behind my eyes,
something quickens: hills
upon hills fleeced with blooms,
the earthen smell of smoke
and rain, a deep indraught
of honey wine, inspirited
of clover and of heather,
weather in my face and hair,
and there, upon my teeth
and tongue, the salt
and tang of nuzzled skin.

But harp and air,
their power to engender dreams,
are smoke and shade
before the woman
who drives this instrument
with hands all sinew
bone and strength.
Her cunning fingers,
articulate and slim,
linger now, now fly,
linnet-swift, as though alive
themselves and free.
This woman, fairy-haired,
the spare moon flaring
in her eyes, who seems
all spark and mischief,
*

compound of New Grange
dark, stone and timber,
ignites the air around
like tinder.
Then all my skin feels bathed
in light and warmth
as though a shaft of flame
had pierced the solstice dawn.

Turlough O'Carolan was the last great itinerant harper of the 17th
century in Ireland, composer of tunes both beautiful and moving.

Onion Snow

All day a late March snow
pelted the flower beds
with its sodden cotton balls,
battered daffodils, bending
them like women bearing loads
of wash upon their heads,
and like some wrathful judgment,
burned the hyacinths to death.

They call it "onion snow" because
it stunts the quick flamboyant
green, thus bulbs grow fat and sweet,
swelling underground, out of sight.

Great grief does something like this:
freezing what the world sees of us,
burning lines into the flesh of faces,
stunting our blithe green growth.

Yet out of sight, a swelling;
deep inside something grows, profound
and good, toward final harvest.

Our Walks

for Claude, Spring, 1983

Clods of new-turned earth muddy our way again,
Lilac petals overlay the blacktopped drive,
All the bees, instinct humming through the hive
Under the hemlock's longest limb, send
Down a thread to let these worn hearts mend.
Even the light's the same as when (alive,

I felt, for the first time), our archive,
Stuttering, began. We walked here then.

For all its sameness, things change. Time
Rends the 'tattered coats' we're wearing thin.
In stitching words, we keep despair penned in,
Eager till our bones enrich the gardner's lime.
Now, at least, Easter for the word, now empty tombs.
Down by College Hall the single dogwood blooms.

Aengus in America

He was sitting, perfectly straight,
in the wing chair next to the lamp,
reading the *Evening Record*, arms extended,
belt loosened a notch, digesting the little trout
along with the murder of another Moslem
by another Christian group, when his wife,
a woman he loved dearly if he thought about it
(and he did), zipped the boy's trousers she'd been sewing.
It was as though a cold finger,
mortally well-aimed, had touched his prostate.
The edges of his vision darkened
till only a bright spot burned
dead ahead where the paper'd been.
He was parked again behind College Hall
on the ridge above the hazel wood.
He smelled the dusty plush upholstery of the Merc,
a million petals — lilac, azalea, mountain laurel —
trampled underfoot, and . . . passion.
Jennifer was unzipping her jeans.

That night he'd first seen her without a shirt.
He remembered gulping air and thinking
of the paleness and heft of her breasts,
". . . the silver apples of the moon."
He was an English major at the time
and could think entirely in other men's words,
if need be, and this night the need was great.
It would be years before a breast moved him so,
and then it was mostly obscured by the head,
round and furred like an animal,
of his infant daughter, nursing.
He'd been stiff with well-being.

He shook himself, still sitting in the umbrella of light,
still holding the paper at arms' length,
and when he touched thumb to mouth to turn the page,
his tongue sizzled with the coppery tang
of camphor and ammonia, and he was in the men's room
*

of the seedy bar in Bangkok, convincing himself
in the wee hours to marry the silken girl
laughing in the next room, the one
who smelled of Chanel and ginger and onions,
and fit against him like a wax impression.
Of course, he hadn't. He'd gone back to the Delta
where the smell of dope and buffalo dung
and his own fear festooned the thick air,
and since, at any moment, he could be dying,
that, by god, was living.

He saw himself, played with noisy desperation
by Alan Alda, stand and address his wife:
"I haven't much time. I must give you this letter
from your husband, which will explain everything, and be on my way
before they close the borders."
He wanted to yell, "CUT — DON'T PRINT THAT."
He tried to cross his legs, but his wingtips
were weighted with years, and a spot on the paper
that had once been chocolate icing from a cookie
pinned him to his chair. The film rolled on.
"It occurs to me, Doris," Alda was saying, "that someday
I will be dead, so despite the fact
you take my breath away, there are lips
still to be kissed, and 'golden apples of the sun'
still to be plucked. There was this girl,
you see, who used to be a trout,
and she called my name.
She called my name, Doris. You do understand?"

The screen went blank and the light came up,
like driving out of a tunnel.
His wife was expertly sewing closed a little
mouth-like tear in the knee of his son's trousers.
Everything was the same,
except, where he held the *Evening Record*,
all the blood had been squeezed from his fingernails.

Osprey, November, 1991

Three times this month
I've seen the grey sea eagle
as I crossed, coming or going,
the Walt Whitman Bridge.
First, harried by two crows,
it perched, implacable,
atop a hundred-foot pole
at the toxic embarrassment
that once was Publicker's.
If the osprey deigned to look
at them at all, it was,
in the soar and dive
of the tipsy crows,
as a king might regard
petulant daughters:
a granite nonchalance
amid inconsequent nags.
Then a second time,
with the morning sun behind it,
it cut across my line of sight
south toward Gloucester and,
like Naber in the clearest pool,
breasted the air and stroked, one two,
banking for the far shore.
Then today (good god, today!)
as I reached the highest curve
mid-span, with a vista ten
millenia of Delaware never dreamed —
not even the great-hearted,
bridge-naming, old man-lover ever
imagined the river on fire
like this in its westering bend
toward the airport;
and the air so clear
I could see steam plumes
of far Limerick like the ghost
of Mummer strutting the horizon,
*

and the vertical grandeur
of downtown aglow in light
no Dutchman ever caught on canvas —
the osprey hung beside me then,
eye level, for a second or two
on the water side of the cables.
And for one thrilling inhalation
we were kindred of the air,
before I breathed again
and started down the bridge,
back to the ground and the western bank,
arriving earthbound but fortunate
to pay my toll.

Hunter's Moon, Jiggs' Field, 1990

for JH

Five paces past the low wall,
around the point of the crumbling barn,
we step into the path of the moon,
like the headlight of onrushing night.
For a gasp quicker than a tail-flick,
it seems a runaway freight, throttle wide,
highballing a cosmic straight.
And we are frozen just for a second,
like prey whose brains must never comprehend
its crushing force.
Then it only hangs on a conjurer's thread,
as though risen from a pit at the world's rim.
And while the field we stalk rolls ever
into obsidian night, the moon floats
up and up, naming blackthorn, fingering ash,
calling trunk and limbs out of blank air.

Forty-two years old and I have never done this —
walk past nightfall a remnant field
arrayed in moonlight, all the stubble and mud
and deer prints whited with frozen dew.
The air kicks in my lungs like a thing alive.

Why do we walk here, Heron?
What do we hunt without guns,
hands sweating in pockets,
noses watering from the cold?
Before us looms the black
tree line of Lower State;
behind, your house. The only other light,
it is, from here, a plastic house
on the platform Pop built when I was eight.
The moon lays a silver path back to it,
and the bright windows shiver with six kids
laughing their way snug into winter,
with the two women we love to death.
*

We are killing them. They are killing us.
Day by day we love them and fail them,
and die a little more either way.

We walk on, the ground hardening underfoot,
spirits hanging on our every breath.
This is the field of Jiggs and Jim,
silent old men I've seen wave, passing
on the ancient John Deere that belches
and sheds clods of mud down Pickertown Road.
They live with their mother who feeds them.
One day the spell on them will break;
they will shudder and revert to oxen
to take their place in some Christmas tableau.
Or, for all I know, they might
have returned with Bran from Tir na nOg.
Should they slip from the tractor
and touch the earth, they will crumble to dust,
so long have they stayed in the Land of Women.

It was never supposed to be like this.
I learned to love too well from Mother.
She had a generous soul, a heart that broke
like crystal in the face of beauty or need,
and out flowed all you could ever want.
"There, there, Lambekins, it's *all* right."
Sometimes still her fingers stroke my hair.
From Pop I learned silence in the face of love.
"Isn't it enough I do things?"
"No, you must say it, and say it again."
But he could not, so he sang instead
"Beautiful Dreamer" while he peeled potatoes
and "You're My Everything" stirring slum-
gullion that steamed the panes above the stove.
He drew hearts on them and wrote LOVE.
Now he is dead whom it killed to speak,
*

and she is dead who was dying to hear.
They rest someplace darker than that tree line.
I will carve chess men from their finger bones
and set each against the other for eternity.
"Say it."   "I can not."
    Check.   Checkmate.

Heron, my old friend,
what do we search for in the dark?
The world wears us to nubs,
and the moon is a hole in the sky
pouring frigid air down our necks.
I want to follow the silver path back
to the kids and the women, to the Plasticville
house on the platform, but you push ahead,
down a slope where rain has dredged a gully,
and up a knoll on the other side.
There you stand, collar up, astride the hill
like a Druid elder awash in moonlight.

So this is what we have at forty-two:
nights to prowl a stubbled field,
days of drudgery and love;
words that stick in the throat,
and songs that do not.

In the glare of the moon,
teeth clicking like bones,
mud freezing to our boots,
I know both
what we hunt, what hunts us.

Joseph Meredith was born in Philadelphia in 1948 and educated at La Salle University and the University of Florida. His work has appeared widely in magazines such as *The Threepenny Review*, *Southwest Review*, and *Four Quarters* and anthologies, and among the prizes he has won is The Mary Elinore Smith Prize from *The American Scholar*. A former editor of *Four Quarters*, writing center director and poet-in-residence at La Salle University, Mr. Meredith lives with his wife, son, and daughter in the city of his birth. *Hunter's Moon: Poems from Boyhood to Manhood* is his first published book of poetry.

Also available from **Time Being Books**

LOUIS DANIEL BRODSKY
You Can't Go Back, Exactly
The Thorough Earth
Four and Twenty Blackbirds Soaring
Mississippi Vistas: Volume One of *A Mississippi Trilogy*
Forever, for Now: Poems for a Later Love
Mistress Mississippi: Volume Three of *A Mississippi Trilogy*
A Gleam in the Eye: Poems for a First Baby
Gestapo Crows: Holocaust Poems

ROBERT HAMBLIN
From the Ground Up: Poems of One Southerner's Passage to
Adulthood

WILLIAM HEYEN
Erika: Poems of the Holocaust
Pterodactyl Rose: Poems of Ecology
Ribbons: The Gulf War — A Poem

LOUIS DANIEL BRODSKY and **WILLIAM HEYEN**
Falling from Heaven: Holocaust Poems of a Jew and a Gentile

RODGER KAMENETZ
The Missing Jew: New and Selected Poems

Please call or write for a free catalog.

TIME BEING BOOKS
POETRY IN SIGHT AND SOUND
Saint Louis, Missouri

10411 Clayton Road • Suites 201-203
St. Louis, Missouri 63131
(314) 432-1771

TO ORDER TOLL-FREE
(800) 331-6605 Monday through Friday, 8 a.m. to 4 p.m. Central time
FAX: (314) 432-7939